THE
BIRD
OF THE
RIVER

BOOKS BY KAGE BAKER

The Anvil of the World
Dark Mondays
Mother Aegypt and Other Stories
The House of the Stag
The Empress of Mars
Not Less Than Gods
The Bird of the River

THE COMPANY SERIES

In the Garden of Iden
Sky Coyote
Mendoza in Hollywood
The Graveyard Game
Black Projects, White Knights: The Company Dossiers
The Life of the World to Come
The Children of the Company
The Machine's Child
Gods and Pawns
The Sons of Heaven

THE
BIRD
OF THE
RIVER

KAGE BAKER

A TOM DOHERTY ASSOCIATES BOOK
NEW YORK

THE BIRD OF THE RIVER

Copyright © 2010 by Kage Baker

A Tor Book
Published by Tom Doherty Associates, LLC
175 Fifth Avenue
New York, NY 10010

www.tor-forge.com

Tor® is a registered trademark of Tom Doherty Associates, LLC.

ISBN 978-0-7653-2296-8

First Edition: July 2010

Printed in the United States of America

0 9 8 7 6 5 4 3 2 1

Ἀρεσκέτω τοῦτο τῇ Ἀθήνῃ, Ἐργάτιδι.

May this please Athena, Workwoman.

THE
BIRD
OF THE
RIVER

THE SUN CAME UP. It warmed Eliss's back and felt good after the freezing night. From their camp up here on the hilltop she could look down into the river valley, where it was still dark. The river barges lay silent in the blue gloom, and only now a white transparent trail of smoke from a galley cookfire rose up through the shadows into sunlight, flaring into red and gold.

A thundering crash of disappointment followed, however.

Eliss found the pipe and pouch, right there beside their campfire. She crouched down and stared into her mother's face. It was a young face, but lined and exhausted, with shadows.

Eliss told herself that just because Falena had left out the pipe and the pouch didn't *have* to mean she'd been smoking the Yellow again; maybe she'd taken them out but resisted the urge. Maybe she'd realized how stupid it was to smoke Yellow the night before asking for a job, especially when times were so hard. Maybe, after struggling with herself, she'd realized how disappointed Eliss and Alder would be when they saw she'd broken her promise again. . . .

Falena sighed and shifted. Eliss looked back at her and watched as her mother opened her eyes. Eliss felt her heart sink. Falena's eyes were yellow again. After all she had said about starting a new life for them . . .

Eliss averted her eyes, too angry to speak. She watched sidelong as Falena sat up, yawned, and, noticing the pipe and empty pouch, swept them hastily under a corner of the blanket. Falena was in her early thirties. She had been plump and shapely most of her life, but in the last few years had grown thin, especially in her face; smoking Yellow took away the appetite. She used to say she did it so as to leave more food for Eliss and Alder, but then Eliss had discovered how much it cost.

And it cost more than the money they so seldom had. A thin diver found it hard to get jobs, for only plump women could survive the cold of the deep sea or the rivers. Worse: Falena did terrible, stupid things when she smoked Yellow. It was because Falena had done stupid things that they had wandered without a home the last four years, from camp to camp, from uncle to uncle.

Even the uncles were fewer and farther between now, as Falena's looks faded. Alder couldn't remember them all. Eliss could. The clearest in her memory was Uncle Ironbolt, who had had gang tattoos and a lot of money, and been a genial man when he wasn't drinking. He had actually provided them with a house for a couple of years, before a rival killed him. That had been back before Alder was born.

Eliss remembered Alder's father. Alder was now ten, small and stocky. He had used to be a placid child, calm in the worst crisis, but lately he had started to show a temper. He rolled over, on the far side of the ashes of their campfire, and sat up. "It's going to be hot today," he said.

"What are you, the Weather Cricket?" said Falena, giggling. He glared at her, seeing the yellow color in her eyes, and looked at Eliss. She looked back and made a hopeless gesture.

"Oh, what are the two of you so sour about? It's a bright sunshiny day! And maybe Mommy will get a nice sunshiny job today. Lissi, I'll pack everything up. You get dressed, baby. Lissi, why don't you take the baby and go down there, see if one of the stallmen will sell you something to eat?" Falena pointed down into the river valley.

Eliss rolled her eyes. She had no money to buy anything. Surely her mother knew that? But this was one of the lies to cope with it all: Falena was hoping the stallmen would have pity on two homeless waifs and give them something, a little fried fish or some boiled straj meal.

Alder pulled on a long shirt with a hood and stood up. "I'm dressed. Let's go."

"But people can still see your legs, baby."

"I don't care. It's hot." Alder was tired of hiding the color of his skin.

"Lissi, make him put some pants on."

"It's a long shirt," said Eliss. "Nobody'll see. It's hot, Mama."

"You kids," said Falena with a sad laugh, shaking her head. "It's so little I ask of you, you know? And all for your own good . . ." Eliss scrambled to her feet and took Alder's hand, leading him away down the hill to avoid another whining argument.

"What are we really going to get for breakfast?" asked Alder.

"Whatever we can find," said Eliss. Alder nodded and pointed into a green patch on the yellow hillside, a few feet off the trail.

"There's water under that. Got a stick?"

Eliss pulled a stick from a dead bush and gave it to him. Alder waded out through the yellow grass and dug with the stick, and in a few minutes came back with three big muddy tubers. Together he and Eliss found a spot just out of sight of the hilltop, where they settled on a fallen tree trunk and Eliss drew her little knife. She peeled the tubers and sliced them up. The tubers had crisp white flesh, juicy and cold, a little sweet. Eliss had no idea what they were but Alder always knew what sort of wild-grown things were good to eat.

They were still sitting there, crunching up the last of their breakfast, when Falena came wandering down the trail. Eliss stood up and waved and her mother came straggling over, lugging their bundles and the cookpot.

"What did you get?"

Eliss held out the third peeled tuber. "You want me to cut it up for you?"

"Thank you, Lissi baby, Mommy would like that."

Falena ate slowly, often stopping to remark on how nice the tuber slices tasted. Even when she had finished, she seemed disinclined to move from the fallen trunk.

"This is a nice spot, you know?" she said at last. "Beautiful view of the river. We should have made camp here last night, instead of up on the hilltop. Dumb thing to do. That cold old wind blew all night."

"Yes," said Eliss. "Well, why don't we go on down?"

"Oh, there's no hurry," said her mother, slowly rocking herself to and fro. "I mean, we're here now. At the river. Lots of barges down there. What do you say, kids? Why don't we just camp here a couple of days? Let me get my strength back from the long walk."

"No, I think we ought to go talk to the barge captains *now*," said Eliss. "We don't know how long they'll be there. Remember what happened at Port Blackrock?"

"And Green Hill," said Alder. "And Sendrion."

"All right, all right." Falena drooped. "You kids never forget anything, do you? Lissi, take the cookpot."

THEY WENT DOWN THE TRAIL, which was so steep they had to lean backward to keep from falling, and at the last descended through a gully cut in the crumbling mud of the bluff, backing down on hands and knees. Finally they stood on the plank platform of the river town. Eliss looked around with interest.

The place was beginning to awaken. A man, still munching his breakfast, walked up to one of the great warehouses and unlocked its doors. There were hammocks strung in the underbranches of a great tree that overhung the riverbank, and now people began to emerge from them, throwing out rope ladders and climbing down. They went to stand in line before a big tent on which was painted LOAD-ING OFFICE. People were waking up on the great barges and lighting cookfires, and so were the stallmen who sold fried fish and hotcakes.

A crippled man wheeled himself out over the planks to a sunny spot, put down a can for donations, and struck up a tune on a hurdy-gurdy.

Eliss was fascinated. She'd never seen such a place; all the other cities of the Children of the Sun were cut from stone, solid and permanent, sometimes without so much as a single tree to show the seasons changing. Here, though, everything endured by floating. The docks on which all the stalls and warehouses stood were made to ride and fall with the river's flow, like anchored barges. The stalls and warehouses themselves were lightweight and temporary, so many tents and board-and-batten shacks. And the Children of the Sun sleeping in *trees*? She had thought only the Yendri lived that way, in their brush villages back in the forests.

And here were some Yendri after all, wading out into the shallows off the far bank like so many herons, raising their hands to pray. No one was taking any notice of them except Alder, who stared. And no one had noticed what color Alder was at all. Eliss decided it was a good omen. If Falena failed to get a job, at least it wouldn't be because one of her children was of mixed race.

"Where's your certificate, Mama?" Eliss asked. Falena stopped and dug around in her bundle until she found the scroll, somewhat tattered and crumpled now, the certificate from the Salesh Divers' Motherhouse testifying that Falena was a trained diver able to hold her breath for as long as it took to recite the Prayer to Brimo.

"I guess I'll need it," said Falena.

"Of course you will!" Eliss felt the surge of anger and panic that came when she suspected Falena was going to sabotage herself again. "Are you crazy? You know that's the first thing they're going to want to see!"

"Don't upset me," said Falena, with an edge in her voice. "This is going to be hard enough." Alder tugged at Eliss's hand and shook his head silently. Eliss pursed her lips, but trudged doggedly toward the nearest barge, towing Alder after her, and Falena had to follow.

A deckhand was sweeping, sending puffs of straw chaff through the scuppers. "Excuse me," Eliss called from the foot of the gangplank.

"Sorry, I haven't been paid in a month," the deckhand replied, not looking up.

"We aren't beggars!" Eliss felt her face grow hot. "Does your captain need a diver?"

"What?" The deckhand raised his eyes. "Diver? No, we've got a diver. She's a good one too."

"Well, do you know of anybody around here who needs to hire a new diver?"

"Lissi—maybe we shouldn't—"

"Couldn't say." The deckhand studied them, looking puzzled. "You didn't check with the River Maintenance Office?"

"Should we?"

"Well, yes."

"Where is it?"

The deckhand pointed to a rambling shed on the next dock. "Thank you and may the gods bless you," said Eliss, and turned and made off for the shed, still pulling Alder along.

As they jumped the shifting space over the green water between docks, Falena said: "Lissi, I know we talked about this . . . but, you know, the truth is, I'm not so sure my lungs are up to it anymore, and—"

"All you need to do is stop smoking and they'll get better," said Eliss. "And if you have a job you can sleep someplace warm and there'll be enough food, so you won't catch so many colds. You'll be fine. Come on."

The River Maintenance Office hadn't opened for the day. There was a water clock behind the window-grille, with the pointer creeping up toward the hour.

"See, we can't talk to anyone yet," exclaimed Falena.

"It's only half an hour," said Eliss. "We'll wait." She dropped her bundle and sat, immovable, and Alder and Falena had to drop their bundles and sit too. The sun, which had been such a blessing after the bleak cold of the night, was soon unwelcome. It poured down sticky heat in the motionless air. The green trees all along the tops of the river gorge seemed to droop and melt as the day heated up; Eliss wouldn't have been surprised to see smears of green like candle wax running down the clay bluffs. The insects started in with a buzzing drone. The smell of the river, rank and weedy, became oppressive.

Just as Alder and Falena were getting mutinous, however, the pointer reached its grooved mark. There was a faint *plonk* and a little silver figure with a trumpet swung up from the rear of the clock. A shrill whistle sounded. At the same moment, a woman opened the door from within, kicking the sill where the door stuck.

"Good morning!" Eliss stood up, practically under her nose. "Are you the person we would ask about jobs for divers?"

The Rivermistress took a step backward. She wore a long necklace of green agate beads, her badge of office. "Are you looking for work?"

"She is." Eliss pointed at her mother. The Rivermistress looked doubtfully at Falena, who gave a feeble giggle. Her hair had gone limp in the heat and she looked tired and dispirited. The Rivermistress averted her eyes.

"Dear, you don't seem up to the weight," she said.

"She's been sick," said Eliss. "And she really needs a job."

"Where's her certification?"

"Right here." Eliss thrust the scroll at the Rivermistress, who took it and peered at it. "Of course she doesn't have the weight right now to dive in the sea, but the rivers are warmer than the sea, aren't they? And we thought, well, a river job would be perfect for her until she's stronger, just shallow warm dives. Please. I need my mother to get better."

The Rivermistress twisted up her face and retreated another step backward. "Of course you do. Come in. Have a seat. Let me see what I can do for you."

They filed in and sat on a long bench, with Falena fanning herself and making soft complaining noises. Alder sat with his fists clenched, staring out the doorway. Eliss kept her gaze riveted on the Rivermistress, who went to a great bound book on a lectern and turned through its pages. She looked older than Eliss's mother but strong, with no trace of gray in her hair. Eliss thought she looked kind. Eliss hoped she was.

"I could help her too," Eliss told the Rivermistress.

"Are you certified?" The Rivermistress looked up at Eliss.

"No-o, but I've been watching her dive my whole life."

The Rivermistress shook her head. "It's harder than you think, dear."

"That's what I always tell her," said Falena, shaking her head too. She rubbed her left arm. "Never listens. Everything's harder than you think, Lissi."

"You could try the *Bird of the River*," said the Rivermistress. "That's the big river maintenance barge. She's here now. They always need divers."

"What kind of work is it?" Falena asked.

"Clearing snags, mostly," the Rivermistress replied. "Salvaging wrecks, when they happen."

"That's not as hard as making hull repairs." Eliss looked at her mother. "You said so. How much does it pay?" she asked the Rivermistress.

"Food and lodging, provision for divers' children, and a copper crown piece for every snag cleared. With a doctor's care, if you get hurt. Bonuses for any wreck refloated and/or salvaged."

"That's not much," protested Falena.

"It's better than what we have now," said Eliss.

"It's the standard rate for shallow-water work." The Rivermistress closed the big book. "Take it or leave it. Your choice."

"She'll take it. Where do we go?"

The Rivermistress pointed. "Three warehouses down. The one on the end has a big kingfisher painted on it, right? And just beyond that are some pilings painted green, and that's where she's moored. You can't miss her. She's bigger than anything else. The *Bird of the River*. Her captain's Mr. Glass." She hesitated before adding,

"Though maybe you'll want to talk to Rattleman. Mr. Riveter, that is. That's the first mate."

THE *BIRD OF THE RIVER* was, yes, bigger than anything else, and that included the floating settlement itself. Eliss thought it was bigger than a few villages she'd been through, a whole separate town of huts and tents built on one barge. There was even a windmill, its vanes rotating lazily on a tower on the aft deck platform. The *Bird's* deck was broad and scarred, streaked with yellow mud. Women crouched around a central deckhouse where the galley fire had been lit; they waited to cook breakfasts or heat water, dandling babies as they gossiped. Men went back and forth in a line, loading on sacks and crates of supplies. Children dove from the rail into the river, or chased each other across the deck. At each corner was an immense capstan for hauling up chain and in the center a great mast was mounted, with a furled square sail and an observation platform above her crosstrees. Her figurehead was tiny by comparison, a sawn figure in her keel where it rose above the rails, the cutout shape of a little singing bird. Its flat wings were thrown out, its head arched back as though in joy.

"This must be where the gods will smile on us at last," said Eliss.

"Don't count on it," said Falena in a dull voice. But she followed her daughter to the edge of the dock.

"Excuse me." Eliss waved to get the attention of a small boy who sat on the nearest capstan, fishing. "Could we come on board and see Mr. Captain Glass?"

"Captain's drunk again," the boy informed them.

"See?" Falena said to her daughter.

"But you can talk to my daddy if you want."

"Well, is your daddy the—"

"Daddy! There's some ladies want to talk to somebody. Some ladies and a . . ." The child stared at Alder. "And they got a greenie with them!"

Alder ground his teeth. "Well, there it goes," said Falena, turning away. "I told you."

"Wolkin, what did I tell you about climbing up there?" A man strode toward them, a sack of meal on his shoulder, but he was glaring at the boy.

"Not to do it when we're hauling cable. But nobody is, Daddy. And anyway—" The boy pointed at Eliss and her family. "She needs to see you about something, and there's a greenie."

"Are you the first mate?" Eliss asked the man, grabbing at Falena's arm to keep her from skulking away. "Mr., er, Rattleman?"

"Rattleman Riveter."

"Right! That's who we were supposed to ask for. You need to hire a diver, right?"

Mr. Riveter looked them over uncertainly, shifting the sack to his other shoulder. He was a man of average height, lean and bearded and fearsomely tattooed, but his face was open and rather innocent.

"I suppose we do," he said. "Do you know one who's looking for a job?"

"She is," said Eliss, pulling Falena closer and waving her certificate at Mr. Riveter. "She's certified and trained and everything."

"Daddy, look at the greenie!"

"Wolkin, that's not a nice word!" Mr. Riveter peered at the scroll, slightly cross-eyed. "So, er, you're Miss . . . Mrs. Hammertin?"

"Don't call me that again," said Alder to the boy, quietly.

"You want to mess with me?" Wolkin threw down his fishing pole and jumped to his feet on the capstan. "You don't want to mess with me. I know Mount Flame assassin moves!" He balanced on one foot and struck an aggressive pose.

"And, er, it says here you're certified to deep dive. We don't pay deep divers' wages, though," said Mr. Riveter.

"That's all right. She doesn't mind taking a shallow-diver's pay," said Eliss.

"I'm a Yendri," said Alder to Wolkin. "You don't want to mess with me either."

"And, er, Mrs. Hammertin, do you have any, er, health problems of which I should be informed?" said Mr. Riveter.

"My chest hurts sometimes," said Falena.

"She's been a little sick," said Eliss. "But she's getting better fast."

"Oh. Well, that's nice to hear." Mr. Riveter eyed Falena, scratching his beard. "You're sure?"

"Yes!"

"Mount Flame assassins kill! You never even see them coming! Yaii!" screamed Wolkin, launching himself from the capstan at Alder. He judged his leap badly and missed the edge of the dock, vanishing in a fountain of green water.

"Wolkin!" A woman in a diver's harness ran to the edge of the barge and looked accusingly at Mr. Riveter. "He wasn't supposed to go in the water until his ear is better."

"I don't think he meant to fall in," said Mr. Riveter.

"He came in crying last night for the drops in his ear—" began the woman. She paused, waiting for Wolkin to surface, but the little trail of bubbles coming from below stopped. "Wolkin!"

Mr. Riveter dropped his sack, and Wolkin's mother began to scramble over the rail, but Falena had already slid out of her tunic and dived into the green water. Mrs. Riveter was poised on the edge of the dock, ready to leap in after her, when Falena resurfaced with Wolkin in her arms. The little boy's face was pale, he was coughing and gagging, and began to cry when his mother took him from Falena.

"He got caught under a cross-piling," said Falena.

"Please don't make me wash the dishes," Wolkin begged.

"We'll talk about it later," said Mrs. Riveter. She looked at Falena. "Thank you. Were you trying to get a diving job?"

"Yes, she was," said Eliss.

"You should hire her," Mrs. Riveter told Mr. Riveter, and carried Wolkin away up the gangplank. And that was how they joined the crew of the *Bird of the River*.

ELISS DID NOT SEE CAPTAIN GLASS until the next day, when they were making preparations to cast off. Mr. Riveter was the one who ran around shouting orders, making sure that the last of the supplies were stowed under hatches, that all the crew were present and accounted for, that all the children were firmly in the grips of their mothers when the cablemen cast off and the topmen swarmed up to let out the great sail.

Eliss was standing with Wolkin's family aft (Wolkin himself was in the family cabin, complaining from under four quilts) when she saw a big man emerge from the aft cabin and haul himself up the companionway. "Who's that?" she asked Tulu, Wolkin's twin sister.

"Him? That's the captain," the little girl replied.

The man was wide too, like a boulder dredged up from the depths. Eliss had expected someone with a name like *Glass* to be haughty and aristocratic, but Captain Glass looked nothing like the noblemen she'd seen, or even like a well-heeled gang lord. He wore only a pair of trousers, much strained at the seams. His beard was vast and untidy. Each of his arms was as big around as Eliss's whole body, yet for all his muscle he moved slowly. His eyes were dull, his features blunt.

He walked forward and stood watching the sail being set.

"There's not enough wind to get us upstream, Mr. Riveter," he said, in a bass black as mud.

"No, sir." Mr. Riveter saluted. "But we'll wet the sail and that'll help a little."

Captain Glass shook his head. He walked to the rail and stood there a moment, staring downriver. "The tidal bore's coming," he announced.

The men in the rigging turned to look; people ran to the rails and craned their necks to see. Some people cheered. Eliss, looking with the rest, saw a disturbance in the river far downstream. It was a wave, sweeping inexorably upward against the current, like white horses galloping up a green road. Marsh fowl rose flapping and squawking where it passed. It surged under the docks and lifted them until they nearly touched the underside of the trees hanging over the river gorge. Fishing boats rose and strained at the moorings. The *Bird of the River* pushed forward under its thrust, moving smoothly and steadily out upon the river, and began her long journey upstream.

"We're away, sir!" said Mr. Riveter, saluting again.

"Good," said Captain Glass, watching as the town at the river landing fell behind them. Eliss watched too until the town swung slowly out of sight around a bend in the river. She turned and saw that the way ahead was more of the same, white clay bluffs rising to either side and the green trees above leaning out, so that in places the *Bird of the River* nearly moved down a tunnel roofed over with branches. The air was hot, thick, wet, but at least was no longer motionless, now that they had gotten under way.

Some men went up on the aft deck with musical instruments— a pair of fiddlers, a man with a concertina, a boxhorn player, and a drummer. They sat down and lit up a pipe of pinkweed, passing it around. Eliss narrowed her eyes, watching them. Pinkweed wasn't as expensive or dangerous as Yellow, but it still made Falena forgetful. When the pipe had gone around, the musicians began to play, a creaking monotonous tune that was somehow comforting. Eliss was still watching them when she became aware that Captain Glass had settled his gaze on her. She turned to face him. "Who're you?" he asked.

"She came aboard with the new diver, sir," said Mr. Riveter. "Mrs. Hammertin has two children."

Captain Glass grunted in acknowledgment. "Where's the new diver?"

"Here, sir." Mr. Riveter waved Falena forward and she came obediently, with an uncertain smile.

"You can go," the captain told Mr. Riveter. "We'll talk."

He looked closely at Falena and spoke to her in a low voice. Eliss tried to edge near enough to overhear but couldn't seem to make out their conversation. Tulu ran up and pulled her into service in the relay-chain of children dipping buckets of water and passing them up to the topmen, who poured them down the great sail. Being wet made the slack sail catch a little more wind, but Eliss wondered if they'd have to do this the whole way upriver. By the time she turned back to the rail, Falena was stalking away from the captain, clutching her chest and looking furious.

"What's the matter?"

"He said I was a drug addict!"

Eliss's heart sank. "Well, you are."

"Not anymore! I stopped. Don't I get any credit for stopping?"

"Are we going to have to leave?"

"No. He told me he'd give me a chance, because of you kids. Nice of him!"

"Well, then, everything ought to be all right," said Eliss, desperate to be hopeful. "Shouldn't it?"

"It damn well ought to be," muttered Falena. "Because nobody on this stinking barge has any Yellow."

"You mean you've already asked?"

Falena just threw her a look and went stalking away to lie down in the little tent they'd been given.

ELISS STOOD ALONG THE RAIL for hours, watching the riverbank creep past. After a while she saw something red on the surface of the water, a long way upstream. Just as she was wondering what it might be, she heard a hoarse cry from the platform up on the mast.

"Red marker! Red marker at the bend!"

Mr. Riveter scrambled up into the shrouds to peer forward. "Strike sail!" he shouted. Instantly the topmen swarmed out along the yard and the great square sail rose like a window shade, and in no time was furled up tight. At once the *Bird of the River* lost her forward momentum, even beginning to drift backward on the current.

"What are they doing that for?" Eliss wondered aloud.

"Poles!" Mr. Riveter bawled, and then in a normal voice as he turned to her: "What?"

But Eliss was so fascinated by what happened next, it was a moment before she could reply. The musicians, back on the aft deck, struck up a brisk dance tune. Men ran from everywhere on the barge and, grabbing long poles from the port and starboard lockers, took up positions along the rail. They raised the poles all together, as though each man was poised to spear a fish.

"Strike *down*," ordered Captain Glass, and in one smooth wave-like movement the lines of men struck their poles down into the water, and leaned. The *Bird of the River* stopped her backward drift.

"What are we—" began Eliss.

"Ahead half *pace!*"

The polemen walked the barge forward against the current so that she seemed to crawl upstream on so many centipede legs. "It's because of the red buoy," explained Mr. Riveter, drawing Eliss away from the rail as the first of the polemen came running back to the end of the line. "Even the *Bird* would sink, if she ran on that snag at full speed."

"The buoy marks where a snag is?"

"Where a *bad* snag is. You've never been on this river before, then?"

Eliss shook her head. Mr. Riveter looked glum. "Your mother hasn't either?"

"She might have," said Eliss cautiously.

"See, this river—see all the trees? This river flows slow, and changes its course. Changes it all the time. This year there might be seventy bends between here and Karkateen; next year there might be fifty, or a hundred and fifty. And when the river moves like that, it cuts out the riverbank from underneath and the trees fall in. They become snags.

"River only flows one way, so all the snags point in the same direction. Downstream. Like hairs." Mr. Riveter stuck out his right arm and ran his left hand along it to demonstrate. Eliss was distracted by his tattoo, which showed a naked diver and the words MY BEAUTIFUL CLOWD MIST BELOVED.

"If you're traveling downstream, you just run over the snags, bump bump bump. They can't hurt you. But if you're coming *upstream*, then all the snags are pointing at you and it's like running against a phalanx of spears, see? And then you sink, and nobody upstream ever gets your cargo, and people go hungry, and then the owners fire you."

"And you'd know, eh?" said one of the polemen in passing. Mr. Riveter gave him a reproachful look.

"Which is why people going downriver are supposed to mark snags when they notice them," he continued. "So that the *Bird* can come along and remove the snag. See? Red buoy means a Class One snag, the worst, then a yellow buoy, which isn't so bad, then a white buoy, probably not so bad but worth collecting for the wood."

"Is the wood worth something?"

"Well, yes. I mean, it's about the only way to get free wood without pissing off the bloody Yendri—" Mr. Riveter halted and grimaced. "I'm sorry."

"It's all right," said Eliss. Most people weren't nearly as careful what they said.

"I mean—I mean I'm sure your brother's father was a, er, a fine— man—" Mr. Riveter looked fixedly at the buoy, which was slowly creeping nearer. "It's just that, you know, the rest of them get all angry with anybody cutting lumber in their forests. Which *we* never, ever do, because there are a lot of them along this river and we don't want to start any more wars, see? I guess I'd mind if they came into our cities and, er, dug up our pavements or something like that. But they don't mind if we take the snags. So we do.

"I mean, I get along fine with some of them. World isn't big enough to go getting into fights with everybody. . . ." Mr. Riveter's voice trailed off into an embarrassed muttering. He wandered away forward. Eliss looked back at Alder where he sat in the mouth of their tent, driven out when Falena had gone in to lie down. He was staring at the deck, looking unhappy. She went and sat down beside him.

"We have a place to sleep," she said, beginning the old game they had played since he had been little.

"We have a place to sleep *and a warm blanket*," he recited dully.

"We have a place to sleep, and a warm blanket, *and dinner tonight*."

"We have a place to sleep, and a warm blanket, and dinner tonight, *and breakfast tomorrow*."

"And who knows what, when summer comes?"

"And who knows what, when summer comes? *And summer is coming soon*. Eliss, I don't like it here. They called me a greenie."

"Just that one boy. That Wolkin."

"The other boys will want to fight me."

"Maybe not. People seem nice here."

"Sometimes I wish—" Alder began. He looked over his shoulder into the tent, and then shook his head.

The *Bird of the River* drew level with the buoy at last, and dropped anchor. "Divers!" cried Mr. Riveter.

"Mama, that's you!" Eliss turned to shake Falena awake. She came scrambling out between them, looking dazed. But the other divers had gone below to change and were now striding up on deck, big round confident women, fitting on their goggles as they came. "Mama, where's your goggles?"

Panicked, Falena rummaged in her bundle. "That's all right," said a rumbling voice from behind them. They craned their heads back and saw Captain Glass standing there. He didn't look angry or impatient; he had no particular expression at all. "You just watch, this time. This is a deep snag."

Wolkin's mother was one of the divers. She paused to kiss Mr. Riveter before she arched her body and dove from the rail, going so smoothly into the water there was hardly a splash. The other divers followed her. The men on deck began to recite the Prayer to Brimo, and around the time it ended Eliss saw the divers' sleek wet heads emerging from the water. They conferred briefly with the men and were passed the hooked end of cable from the nearest capstan. One diver was given a hacksaw. The divers went down again, the prayer was once more recited. A few small branches floated to the surface and drifted away downstream. Then, one by one, the divers bobbed up on the far side of the snag, and signaled.

Four men on deck grabbed up capstan bars and began to turn the capstan, round and round, hauling in the cable. It drew in, it grew taut; drops of water flew from it in all directions. There was a disturbance on the smooth green water and then, slowly, grudgingly, the snag broke the surface. It gleamed wet, pouring out liquid mud, a monstrous mass of snakelike roots and clumps of smaller roots like hair. Little eels dropped from it as it was winched inexorably toward the barge; little yellow crabs scrambled to keep hold, or ran to and fro and threatened vainly. Following the root ball was the long black trunk, like the neck of an animal, trailing the red buoy. It hit the edge of the deck with a *clunk* that resonated through the whole barge as the root ball was pulled level with the capstan.

Now the rest of the women and even the older children ran forward, everyone grabbing a root or a lower branch, and helped to pull the snag on board. It lay at its full length on the deck in a pool of still-flowing mud, a sodden massive thing, a defeated behemoth. Everyone cheered. The divers swam up to the barge and were helped back aboard, and an older woman came forward with hot drinks for them.

Tulu, dragging a pair of push brooms, approached Eliss. "Do you want to help?"

"What do I do?" Eliss took a broom.

"Squish away the mud and push the crabs and snakes back overboard," Tulu explained. Eliss followed her example cautiously, sweeping all sorts of nasty things into the water—besides the crabs and snakes there were snails, sharp-edged pebbles, and clumps of water weed. As the girls worked, other children were busy behind them, cutting away at the long roots with saws and clippers. In twenty minutes' time the snag had been stripped clean and set out on the deck to dry in the sun, and the *Bird of the River* had resumed her journey.

ELISS MADE HERSELF USEFUL. It wasn't hard; there were plenty of jobs to be done on the barge, and everyone except the littlest babies seemed to help out with them. Roots from snags needed collecting, to be woven into baskets or screens. Pots and pans from the galley needed to be scoured. Dinner needed catching, and while only the men went ashore to hunt, fishing from the deck was something anyone could do. When there wasn't work the little girls like Tulu played with their dolls or pretended to cook using mussel shells as pans. Little boys like Wolkin wrestled each other, or made bows and arrows that never managed to hit anything.

"DO YOU KNOW ANY YENDRI fighting moves?" Wolkin asked hopefully. Eliss and Alder, who were waiting in line for breakfast, looked at him in surprise.

"No," said Alder.

"My mother says I can't fight you because your mother saved me from drowning. Except I wasn't really drowning. It would take a lot more than an old pier piling to drown me. But anyway she says we have to be friends. So I was just wondering if you know any good Yendri moves."

"I don't."

"Your daddy didn't teach you any?"

"No," said Alder, and turned away.

"We haven't lived around the Yendri," said Eliss. "We've always lived around seaports. There aren't a lot of Yendri there."

"Oh," said Wolkin. "Want to see *my* moves?"

"All right," said Eliss, nudging Alder to turn around, but he ignored her. Wolkin proceeded to show her his moves, which mostly involved balancing on one foot while he uttered bloodcurdling screams, followed by a flurry of kicks and swooping gestures. When he finally wound down, Eliss said tactfully: "That's very nice."

"Thanks." Wolkin did a handstand. "You're pretty," he added, as an afterthought.

"Thank you." Eliss was astonished. Nobody had ever told her such a thing.

They collected their bowls of breakfast and carried them back to their tent. Wolkin followed after them, walking on his hands. He fell and rolled into a sitting position outside the tent as they went in.

"So, we're going to have a war," he announced. "I'm the larboard side general. You want to fight on my side? You can be my greenie—I mean, my Yendri forest commando."

"I don't want to," muttered Alder.

"Of course he'll play with you," said Falena, handing her bowl back to Eliss. "You eat it; I'm not hungry this morning. He'd like to make some friends his own age, wouldn't you, Alder?"

"No, I wouldn't."

"Of course he would. Alder, eat your breakfast and go play with your new friend."

Alder sighed. He emptied his bowl in a few spoonfuls and crawled out of the tent, and went off with Wolkin.

"I think he just wanted to sit and watch the water," said Eliss as she ate.

"He does that too much," said Falena crossly. "Just sits there and sulks. It's not right for a boy his age. They ought to be out doing things."

There was a lot of shrill screaming from the direction of the snag, and the pounding of running feet. "He's a little different, Mama," said Eliss hesitantly. "He's maybe not so much like one of us. Maybe he's more of a Yendri."

"They aren't that different from us," said Falena. "What he needs is a man around to be a father to him. The gods know I tried to find you kids a father!"

Eliss thought of Uncle Steelplate, who had used to beat Falena, and who had given her her first pipeful of Yellow. She fought back a wave of anger and said, "Did you ever try to find Alder's father again?"

Falena waved her hand. "How was I going to do that? We were miles away from that camp by the time I knew about Alder. And what would you have wanted us to do? Gone and lived in the forest in a bush? Not you. You were always complaining."

There was a bellowed order from Captain Glass. The screams on deck fell abruptly silent. Eliss was taking the empty bowls back to the galley when she encountered Wolkin leading Alder, who had a split lip and whose left eye was rapidly swelling shut.

"What happened?" She dropped to her knees and took Alder by the shoulders. Alder, mortified, said nothing.

"He just needs to learn some moves," Wolkin explained helpfully. "My daddy could show him. If you want. My daddy knows a lot of moves. He used to be a captain."

"Don't want to." Alder put up his hand to hide his eye.

"I got clubbed on the head, the last time we had a war, and there were buckets of blood," said Wolkin. "My mother fainted when she saw me. Really."

"You'll be all right." Eliss tried to give Alder a hug. He shrugged her off and walked away to sit by the rail.

"I was unconscious for three days and three nights," said Wolkin, but he was aware he had lost his audience. "I'm sorry. He got mad."

"Why do you play war, if people get hurt?" Eliss asked him.

"He asked that too," said Wolkin in surprise.

"Well, why?"

"Because it's fun—"

"White marker!" came a cry from the masthead. "White marker at the milepost!"

"Strike sail!"

Wolkin turned and ran. Eliss pulled Alder away from the rail and they went back to the tent. As they approached, Eliss saw Captain

Glass walking toward it from the opposite direction. He stopped beside their tent and looked down at Falena.

"White marker," he said. "That's an easy one. Are you feeling up to making a dive?"

"Yes, sir, of course," said Falena.

"Good. Why don't you get ready?" He walked on forward.

"Help me, Eliss!" Falena hissed at her, as soon as the captain was out of hearing range. Together they found Falena's goggles and got her undressed. When they walked forward to join the other divers, Eliss winced to see how painfully thin Falena looked beside them.

The white buoy was close in, and the snag was easy to spot, protruding up out of the shallows. There were even green leaves on some of the branches.

"This ought to be really easy," Eliss murmured in her mother's ear. Falena just nodded, drawing deep breaths.

"That's only a bush," said Mr. Riveter. "We don't need a whole crew for that. That won't even take the capstan. We can pull it out with some rope."

"I'll go down," said Falena, stepping forward. They passed her the end of a coil of rope. She took it and dove in, vanishing in the dark water.

They began to recite the Prayer to Brimo as the rope paid out. Midway through the prayer the rope stopped moving. *She must be tying it off to the trunk*, Eliss was thinking, when there came a sudden burst of air bubbles at the surface.

"Oh—" Eliss put her hands to her mouth. The Prayer to Brimo stopped. Mrs. Riveter vaulted the rail and plunged in after Falena. Raggedly the prayer was started up again, but most people had lined up along the rail to stare down into the water, unspeaking, uneasy. The musicians fell silent.

Two wet heads broke the water. Eliss exhaled in relief, before she realized that Falena's head was lolling on Mrs. Riveter's shoulder. Mrs. Riveter shouted for help. Two other divers plunged in and together they brought Falena up on the barge. She was limp, her eyes open and staring behind the goggles, her face contorted in an expression of horror.

"Mama!" screamed Eliss. She fell to her knees beside her mother. Another prayer was started up, this one asking for mercy from the gods, as Mr. Riveter pounded on her mother's chest. He crouched down to blow air into her mouth. Alder pushed his way through the crowd and stood there, staring. Captain Glass loomed behind him like a mountain. Mrs. Riveter pulled herself up on the barge and sat there, gasping for breath.

Falena didn't breathe, didn't move, didn't shut her eyes. The words of the prayer droned on. The river flowed on past them all and Eliss heard herself crying and wondered, in a dazed kind of way, how she could still sound so much like a little girl.

Mr. Riveter lifted his head and looked at her timidly. "She didn't drown," he said. "There's hardly any water in her lungs. Her heart just stopped." He slipped off the goggles and closed Falena's eyes.

"There's a dead man down there," said Mrs. Riveter, and coughed. "She was tangled up with him."

THE CRUELEST THING WAS THAT, however much Eliss tried to feel relief, however hard she tried to remember all the things Falena had done wrong in her life, the bad memories wouldn't come just then. Instead, the person Falena had become in the last few years faded away and all Eliss could see right now was Falena as she used to be, Falena young and smiling and brave. Her mother, who used to put on a funny hat and dance to make her laugh. Her mother, who had sung to her when she'd been scared and unable to sleep. That Falena, who hadn't been much older than Eliss was now . . .

That Falena had been lost for years, but now she was the only mother Eliss could remember. Now she had to mourn for her all over again.

THE OTHER DIVERS WENT DOWN and brought up the dead man. He was headless, naked except for a pair of leather bracers on his forearms and a big gold bracelet shaped like a coiling snake, that was sunk deeply into his bloated upper arm. There were tattoos on his gray skin. He had been young. Captain Glass, looking at the body, grunted.

"This is a nobleman," said Mr. Riveter.

I KILLED HER, THOUGHT ELISS as she lay in the tent with her face buried in Falena's blanket. *She said she didn't feel strong enough to dive and I made her do it anyway. I killed my mother.*

Alder, who had been sitting upright in silence with tears running down his face, said: "I never asked her about him."

Eliss wondered what he meant. There was a soft *pat-pat* sound, someone tapping the front flap of their tent before pushing it to one side. Mrs. Riveter crouched there, holding out a pair of bowls of boiled grain with ground-peas.

"You should eat," she told Alder. "They're fixing your mother up. She looks as beautiful as a queen. I gave them a new gown with embroidery for her. I'll let you know when you can come see her." She set the bowls on the floor of the tent. "Make your sister eat, now."

Alder nodded woodenly. Mrs. Riveter withdrew. "You should eat," he told Eliss. He picked up one of the bowls and stared into it. After a moment he said, "Do you remember my father?"

"A little," said Eliss. She sat up and blew her nose.

"What was he like?"

"He was just . . . we were traveling with a caravan," said Eliss. "I forget where we were going. Maybe it was Mount Flame City. I think it was. And the road went through the forests. Some Yendri tribesmen came out of the trees and talked to the caravan master. Everybody was scared because we didn't know what they'd do. I'd never seen a Yendri before. All they had on was flowers. It turned out they were only there to give us safe conduct until we got out of the forests.

"There was this one who walked beside our cart. He was good-looking and Mama kept smiling at him. And then . . . I woke up in the night and there was somebody under the blanket with her. They were all giggling and thrashing around and I was too little then to understand what they were doing. The next day the Yendri man made Mama a wreath of flowers. She blushed. She hid it away in her bag.

"The day after that we were out of the forests and the Yendri left us and went back to wherever it was they belonged. And a couple of months later Mama told me I was going to have a little brother or sister. That's all I remember," said Eliss, not adding how their neighbors had been so horrified when Alder had been born, and looked at her mother with such disgust after that, or how people had come and painted nasty words on the house wall until the landlord had asked Falena to leave and take her children with her.

"Did you ever know his name?"

"No," said Eliss. "Unless she called you Alder because that was his name. It's a Yendri name, not one of our names."

Alder nodded. He took up his spoon and began to eat. After a moment Eliss picked up her bowl and spoon and ate too, now and then pausing to wipe away tears. The grain and peas had been cooked in broth and tasted good.

"THERE'S A TEMPLE HERE," said Mr. Riveter. Eliss and Alder looked up at him from where they sat with Falena's body. Behind him they saw a real town, rising up from the riverbank in blocks of cut limestone. "It's Slate's Landing. I'm going to go up and talk to the priest, all right?"

"Thank you," said Eliss numbly. She watched him go ashore and climb the hill, walking between the green shadows of the trees and the bars of hot sunlight. Captain Glass had been sitting in silence on the other side of Falena's body, but now he shifted and spoke.

"You need to decide what you're going to do afterward."

"I don't know," said Eliss. The future in front of her was a terrifying void. She couldn't imagine life without Falena.

"You can go ashore and ask for help," said the captain. "The temple priest has to provide help for orphans. Or you can go back to Salesh, and ask for help at the Divers' Motherhouse; they're supposed to provide for any orphans of their girls."

"I guess I might," said Eliss, not wanting to explain in front of Alder that Falena had been expelled from the motherhouse when he had been born.

"The other thing you could do is stay on board," said the captain. "But you'd have to make yourselves useful."

"We could do that!" Eliss looked up at him. The barge was now the only link with the past, the last place Falena had tried to make a home for them. "I could do anything. Look after babies. Wash dishes. And Alder's strong. He could do anything too. Couldn't you?" Alder nodded. "And we could stay in the tent and not have to leave?"

"If that's what you want," said the captain.

MR. RIVETER CAME BACK DOWN the hill with the priest and his assistants, carrying wood for the bier and jars of perfumed oil. Falena's body was drenched in the sweet oil, scattered with flowers Wolkin and the other children had picked from the long grass on the riverbank. Mr. Riveter and the other men put the bier together and lifted Falena's body onto it. They went ashore in procession, the priest and the men carrying the bier, Mrs. Riveter walking with Eliss and Alder.

In the high temple courtyard the sunlight was blinding, reflecting off the white limestone walls. The hot stone underfoot burned their bare feet. The priest brought a torch from the altar fire; even the flame seemed transparent as water in the harsh light, throwing a waterlike shadow on the pavement. The priest looked uncertainly at Eliss and Alder before handing the torch to Mr. Riveter at last.

Mr. Riveter stepped forward and cleared his throat. "Er . . . to the Blacksmith our own Father. This is Falena Hammertin. She had a hard life and met her death trying to feed her children. Let that be remembered. And . . . carry her through the flame and may she sleep safe in Your arms."

He lit the stacked wood under the bier. When they were certain it had lit, Mrs. Riveter put her hands on Eliss's and Alder's shoulders.

"Now we turn our backs and wait," she told them. "The same way we would if she was getting undressed, because really she's slipping out of her old body."

Eliss, who remembered Uncle Ironbolt's funeral, nodded. Alder looked unwilling but obeyed. Behind them the flame roared up, uncomfortably hot on their backs.

Mama, I'm sorry your life was so hard. Eliss thought about that morning on the hill above the river landing, when Falena had wanted to camp, not to go down and ask for work. *If I hadn't made you get up and come with us, you'd still be alive. But, Mama . . .* A torrent of memory came back now and choked her prayer, of all the times Eliss had watched Falena making mistakes, simpering at the wrong men, men like Uncle Steelplate who beat her and stole from her and told her how worthless she was. *Why, Mama? Why did you only ever love men like that?*

Eliss pushed the memories away. Falena coming home glassy-eyed, with that funny fixed smile, and telling her something had happened to the rent money. Falena waking her in the night and telling her to dress quickly and quietly, because Uncle Bellows was very, very angry and they had to get out of the house before he came back. Falena lying beside her, wracked with sobs in the darkness in the abandoned shed where they were sheltering from the rain, weeping endlessly as the rain falling. *Why, Mama? You could have done anything else with your life.*

And the new life Falena had just begun was finished, and there would be no apologies and no promises to change, not this morning or any morning ever again. Falena's story was over. The anger swelled and swelled in Eliss until she felt she couldn't breathe.

She lifted her head and screamed. The anger shot out with the scream, leaving her empty and sick. Eliss sagged against Mrs. Riveter, who put an arm around her.

They walked back down to the river afterward. The men stayed to scatter the ashes.

THE CORPSE THEY HAD FOUND in the river was packed in salt and carried ashore, like a package. The priest took charge of it. Mr. Riveter had to make a report to the town's magistrate and Chief Warden, and came back looking pale and scared.

"They think the dead boy was one of the Diamondcuts," Eliss heard him murmuring to Mrs. Riveter. Mrs. Riveter made a shocked noise, and gestured to ward off evil. Eliss felt like doing the same. The Diamondcuts were one of the great families in Mount Flame, wealthy and powerful, far above the levels of the gangs.

"They won't come after *us*?" Mrs. Riveter said.

"They shouldn't," said Mr. Riveter, but his eyes widened in panic. "We just found the body! We treated it with respect. We took it to the proper authorities. Why would anybody start a vendetta against us?"

"'When a great house burns, the neighbors lose their huts too,'" Mrs. Riveter quoted the proverb. Captain Glass, who had appeared to be dozing on his feet by the mast, gave a mirthless laugh.

"If there's any blood debt, they owe us," he said quietly. "Their dead man killed one of our women."

By law they were required to remain at Slate's Landing until the dead boy's family came for his body, but the *Bird of the River* had a job to do; so the town magistrate granted them an exception, and the next day they set sail again.

"DON'T LOOK DOWN," ADVISED SALPIN. Eliss shook her head and took a firmer grip on the shrouds. She climbed steadily, proud of her steadiness. There was only one dizzying moment as she got past the crosstrees, when she had to let go and reach up through the hole in the mast platform, sliding her elbows above her head. Salpin caught her hands and guided them to the gripping bar, but she pulled herself upward and through without assistance.

"Well, you're obviously born to this," said Salpin, grinning. He was the concertina player among the musicians, a young man, black-bearded and handsome, just the sort around whom Falena would have giggled and nudged Eliss. Eliss was in no hurry for romance and, in any case, didn't approve of people who smoked pinkweed. She only smiled at him politely and accepted the safety line when he handed it to her. She fastened it on herself.

"Thank you," she said. She turned and looked out at the wide view, catching her breath. The whole world was spread out in an immense circle like a compass rose, and the *Bird of the River*'s mast was the pivot of the compass needle. Ahead of them the river valley stretched out to the east forever; to the north were the marshlands and the distant sea; to the south were forests, rising to the great black mountain where demons were supposed to live. "Oh, it's beautiful!"

"It's a good sign that you think so," said Salpin, sitting down and stretching out his legs. "Some people come up here just once. They look around, the way you're doing, and they make a funny little sound and their arms go around the mast, and they can't let go of it. Last time that happened it took three of us to get him down again."

"*Him?*" Eliss was gleeful. "It was a man?"

"It was a man. A big ex-soldier. Wasn't afraid of anything or anybody—and kept telling us so—but he got up here and he turned into a whimpering rag," said Salpin. "We had to rig up a rope chair and lower him down. He didn't stay on board long after that."

"That's funny," said Eliss. She sat at the edge of the platform, leaning on the rail to look down. The sight was heart-stopping, yes, the deck so far below and the people foreshortened and so small. Eliss spotted Alder sitting at the rail with Wolkin, who was gesturing as he talked. Automatically she began making plans for what she would ever do if she fell. *I could grab for that rope there—and if I missed it I could still try to throw myself* that *way and maybe hit those ropes. . . .*

Salpin pushed himself forward to the rail. "Well, let's begin. You know what to do if you see a buoy?"

"Shout out. And say what color, and where it is."

"That's right. But you use the Calling Voice. It's how you make yourself heard without getting hoarse. You sort of push your voice out of here—" Salpin reached for her waist to show her and, when Eliss drew back involuntarily at his touch, put his hands on his own diaphragm. "And you breathe like *this*. Watch."

He took a few deep breaths in a certain way. Eliss watched closely.

"And now I sound like this, but *now*—" said Salpin in a normal conversational voice, before booming out:

*"Then cried our noble duke, 'Who calls
From Lagin's bare and broken walls?' "*

His voice echoed from the riverbanks. Below on deck, faces turned upward to them. Someone catcalled, "It's me, noble duke! Your tailor! You still haven't paid me!"

"You try, now," said Salpin.

"But I don't know that poem."

"You can say anything."

"Er . . . *Hello! Can you hear me?*"

"That's good!" Mr. Riveter called up to them. Eliss was pleased.

"Old Sandgrind used to sing out so loud, they could hear him all up and down the river," said Salpin.

"Who was he?"

"Sandgrind? Sandgrind the fiddler. He had the best Calling Voice in the whole crew. Had the sharpest eyes too. He could spot a buoy from two miles away. He read the river like a book. He could tell you if a single twig lay on the bottom three fathoms down, just from the look of the water." Salpin shook his head. "But he was a gray old man. One fine morning I climbed up in the windmill tower to ask him what he'd have for breakfast and there he was, stiff in his blankets. We've still got his fiddle; nobody could bear to send it through the fire with him. I hope he doesn't mind."

"People sleep in the windmill?" Eliss turned her head to look down at its briskly turning vanes.

"*We* do," said Salpin. "It's our prerogative. You can't leave a fiddle or a boxhorn out in the damp, can you? So we need to be indoors. But we don't rate cabins of our own, so we get the tower. When nobody's using the mill," he added.

Eliss remembered a rainy night she and Alder and Falena had sheltered in a windmill. "How do you get any sleep? Windmills make noise all night long!"

"Best thing, for a musician," said Salpin. "The wheel goes around and the rhythm works itself into you. Makes you play better."

Eliss shrugged warily. She could never be sure when an adult was saying things to be silly, as opposed to truthfully speaking of something absurd. She looked down at the water.

"Tell me how to read the river."

"All right. See how smooth it is, all across here? The water's deep. But look ahead, look at that circling, surging patch there. There's a rock under that water, and if the *Bird* was just a boat, she'd bash her hull on it. She's too big to have to worry much about rocks, but you can bet that every freight captain has that place marked on his charts.

"And, speaking of charts! See that lady up in the bow?"

Eliss looked down. A sunshade had been pitched there, so she couldn't see much, but she had noticed the person under it before. The woman sat at a table with drawing pens and ink, and a pair of scrolls open before her, and she studied the river intently and now and then made notes. "Who is she?"

"That's Pentra Smith. She's our cartographer. She maps the changes in the river, and there are changes every trip. Every time we end a transit, she takes the changes in to the Bureau of Maps in Port Ward'b and they publish a new one. And all the freight captains buy them. If they didn't, they might find themselves stuck on a sandbar or even in the middle of the woods, next trip."

"What's that?" Eliss pointed to a curious pattern she had noticed in the water. It foamed and ran up the way the water did around the snag markers, but there was no buoy in sight.

"What?" said Salpin, and went pale when he noticed it too. He leaned forward and, in the loudest Calling Voice Eliss had heard so far, shouted: "Snag! Unmarked snag to larboard!" and in a normal voice to Eliss: "Excuse me. Stay there."

He scrambled out on the yard as orders were shouted on deck, and all the topmen hurried after him. Eliss had a good view as the sail was caught up and furled. The *Bird of the River* halted at once; the panorama of valley and trees seemed to march backward a moment, and then the polemen took over and the *Bird* inched forward once more. Salpin was sweating and breathless when he came back to the masthead.

"And that's why we're not supposed to sit up here in pairs, usually," he said. "Because if you start chattering away and not noticing things, then we could have a disaster. But you noticed. Good for you."

"I'm good at noticing," said Eliss. She had spent her whole life watching faces for the signs that meant a shift of mood, the signs of impatience or anger or other things. The river seemed easy by comparison. "Why wasn't that one marked with a buoy?"

"It might have just fallen in today," said Salpin, watching the divers as they went to the rail. "Or maybe the boat captains have been in a hurry and nobody stopped to mark it for us. They're supposed to, though."

The divers went in, with more caution these days than formerly. But nothing was found below, other than the snag itself, which was winched on board and stripped down with methodical speed. Salpin and Eliss watched in silence. Eliss felt a tightening around her heart, thinking of Falena. She looked down and saw Alder sitting alone on the aft deck, face turned resolutely away.

When the trunk had been stowed away and the sail let out once more, when the *Bird of the River* crept on her way upstream, Salpin cleared his throat.

"Let's go on. See those places there, where the water's a different color? Those are sandbars. Very important to know where those are. Even the *Bird* would be in trouble if she grounded on one of those."

"Should we call out?"

"We don't have to. The captain knows they're there," said Salpin. They looked down at him where he stood, a massive figure at the tiller, barely shifting his weight as he steered the barge. "They aren't like snags, which can fall in anytime and you'll never know where or when. Besides, he's got a feel for the water, has Captain Glass. He knows this river."

"He doesn't seem to do much," said Eliss. "Mr. Riveter gives most of the orders."

"Well, Rattleman's the first mate." Salpin waved vaguely.

"Does the captain get drunk a lot?"

Salpin looked at her obliquely. "Only when we moor at a town. He takes a barrel of wine and he rolls it into his cabin and he locks the door. Usually we don't see him again until we cast off. He never goes ashore."

"Never?"

"Never that I've seen, and I've worked the river ten years now."

"I wonder why?"

"There are a lot of stories," said Salpin, and shivered. "And there I go again, chattering away. Look, look ahead. There's an island, see? Look at the water and tell me: will we pass her to starboard, or larboard?"

Eliss decided she liked him, even if he did smoke pinkweed.

THE BOY CAME ABOARD at Chalkpit Landing.

Nobody saw him arrive. They were taking on supplies, with a

line of men proceeding up the gangplank bearing sacks of dried beans on their backs, and when they had all filed on the boy was standing there, patiently waiting to get Mr. Riveter's attention. Eliss spotted him as she was keeping the toddlers back from the gangplank. He was small and pale, nondescript, with sleepy-looking eyes.

"Are you Mr. Riveter?" he asked. His voice was like the rest of him.

"What?" Mr. Riveter looked around and noticed the boy.

"I'm Krelan Silvering, Mr. Riveter."

"Oh?"

"You, er, got Captain Crankbrass's letter about me?"

"Emon Crankbrass?" Mr. Riveter stepped closer, looking puzzled. "Retired? Used to captain the *Turtle*?"

"Yes, sir. That's right, sir. You got his letter?"

"No."

The boy drooped. "Oh. Oh, and I've come all this way . . . and I suppose it went astray somehow. You really never got it?"

"Well, no." Mr. Riveter scratched his beard, studying the boy. "What was the letter about?"

"It was about me, sir. It was a letter of recommendation. My father did him a favor once, and then . . ." Krelan shrugged, with a sheepish look. "My older brother got into some trouble and, er, my father thought it would be a good idea if he didn't have all his sons under one roof. You see, we live in Mount Flame and—"

"That's all right." Mr. Riveter held up his hands. "If it's something to do with gangs, then the less I know, the better."

"And, er, he wanted to get me out of the way awhile."

"Perfectly understandable."

"So he asked Captain Crankbrass if he knew any river captains, as opposed to sea captains, because I'm not very strong and he thought a river voyage would be better for my health, you know, and anyway my mother was afraid of my drowning at sea—and Captain Crankbrass said, 'I know just the place for him; I have a friend on a river barge.' They never sink, do they?"

"It's been known to happen," said Mr. Riveter, distracted as one of the bearers staggered and almost dropped his burden into the river. "Orepick! What's the matter with you? Watch where you're going!"

"So anyway Captain Crankbrass wrote you a letter and sent it by express runner. Maybe she went to the wrong landing?"

"It's always possible," said Mr. Riveter, grabbing the sack from Orepick and tossing it into the hold himself.

"On the other hand, if it's hard for even a runner to find out your exact location at any given time, then this must be a pretty safe place to be, wouldn't you think?" said the boy hopefully.

"I suppose so," said Mr. Riveter. "Look, son, what do you want?"

"Well, what the letter said was that Captain Crankbrass sent you greetings and asked after your wife and children, and then it said I was a fine upstanding person of a good old pureblooded family, and then it explained a little of the, er, the problem with the—you know—and then it asked whether you couldn't take me on and give me a job, until people's tempers cool down a bit or . . . or whatever happens."

"Like the Chainfires burn down your house and kill your brother and anyone else who happens to be nearby," said Captain Glass, swaying slightly as he loomed up behind Krelan. Mr. Riveter gaped in astonishment to see him on deck. The boy turned around hastily and craned his head back to look up at the captain.

"Well, er, that's putting it a little baldly, I must say, but—er—yes."

"Captain, sir!" Mr. Riveter saluted. "I was just about to explain how I'm only the first mate and all hiring decisions have to be finally approved by the captain. Sir."

"Good idea." The captain exhaled wine fumes. "And were you also going to ask him how likely it was the Chainfires would carry the vendetta all the way to tracking down this kid here and setting fire to the *Bird*?"

"Oh, I'm sure that wouldn't happen, sir," said Krelan. "I'm a no-body."

"Can you live like one?"

"I think so, sir. I'm the youngest of my family and they always pretty much treated me as one."

Captain Glass snorted. "Work out the details, Mr. Riveter," he said, and staggered back to his cabin.

"He doesn't get stupid when he drinks, does he?" said the boy, which surprised Eliss, because she had been thinking exactly the same thing at that moment. She grabbed up Mrs. Nailsmith's baby, who had been about to stagger out into the path of the bearers, and listened more closely.

"No, he doesn't get stupid," said Mr. Riveter. "Now, look, you'll have to work. This isn't like a navy ship with officers and commissions, see? And you'll have to drop your name, in case anyone should come asking after you. No Silverings on board."

"I could call myself Smith," offered the boy.

"No. Everybody calls themselves *Smith* when they're on the run," said Mr. Riveter, thinking hard.

"What about *Stone?*" said Eliss, dandling the baby, who wanted to get down. They both turned to stare at her.

"Stone is good," said Krelan. "Nice and undistinguished without sounding suspicious."

"Then you're Stone," said Mr. Riveter. "Do you know how to do anything useful?"

"I can cook, a little," said Krelan.

"Right, then! You can report to the steward." Mr. Riveter made a trumpet of his hands. "Mr. Pitspike! Here's an apprentice for you!"

The steward, a dour and red-eyed man, had been glaring down through a hatchway, supervising the storing of supplies. He looked up now; his scarlet gaze tracked until it settled on Krelan. He scowled and approached. Krelan smiled shyly.

"Seven hells, Riveter, what's that?" demanded Mr. Pitspike.

"You said you needed help," said Mr. Riveter.

"I said I needed another man. *That* looks as though it'd break in half if you sneezed at it."

"I'm not strong, sir, but I'm a hard worker," volunteered Krelan.

"Early riser, are you? Because you'll be getting up in the dark to light all the stoves, so the ladies can come in to cook. And you'll stir the porridge cauldron. And carry the oil cans. And peel the onions. And turn the spit. And wash the *pots!*" Pitspike spat out the last word so forcefully Krelan's limp hair was blown back from his forehead.

"Yes, sir." Krelan's voice trembled slightly. "Where should I put my bag, sir?"

"How the hell should I know?"

"I suppose in my cabin, then, sir?"

Mr. Riveter turned away hastily, busying himself with getting the gangplank pulled in. Eliss closed her eyes, waiting for the explosion. "Cabin?" cried Mr. Pitspike, mocking Krelan's enunciation. "This whey-faced little prat thinks he's entitled to a stateroom, does he? Lah-di-dah, isn't he just too precious for words? You'll sleep on the galley floor and like it, your lordship, and anyway the grease is good for the skin. Stow your bag somewhere and get yourself into the galley."

"Yes, sir," said Krelan faintly, saluting as Mr. Pitspike turned and stalked away.

"Only the captain and the first mate get cabins," Eliss explained, setting down Mrs. Nailsmith's baby, who toddled away chewing his fist. "And the cartographer. And the musicians. Sort of. Everybody else puts up tents or lean-tos. But you can put your bag in our tent for now."

"That's very kind of you," said Krelan. "Er—"

"Eliss."

"Eliss." He tried to say it with her accent. "A charming name. Short for Elista?"

"No. Just Eliss."

He followed her to the tent, where Alder was sitting in the doorway. "Mr. *Stone*, this is my brother, Alder," said Eliss, bracing herself for the shocked look. But Krelan merely smiled at him as he leaned past to put his bag inside.

"Pleased to meet you, Alder." Alder merely nodded, staring at him. "Well, I suppose I'd better find the galley if I don't want to be showered with more colorful invective. Good afternoon, Eliss."

When he had gone, Alder looked up at her. "Who's that? Is he sharing our tent? Or have you taken yourself a boyfriend already?" he asked sullenly.

"Don't be silly!" Eliss felt her face grow hot. "He hasn't got a place yet and I was just being polite. What's the matter with you?"

"Nothing," said Alder, looking down at the deck.

HE CONTINUED IN A SULLEN MOOD. In retaliation Eliss left him to himself and spent more and more of her time up on the mast platform, watching the river. Sometimes Salpin was on duty there; sometimes it was the boxhorn player Drogin, who was lean and taciturn and answered her questions impatiently.

So Eliss stopped asking questions, and watched the river instead. She learned how to tell a sandbar from the outflow of a stream, and the different shades of water where the riverbed was gravel, as opposed to mud. She watched where Captain Glass steered, and began to play a game of betting where he'd guide the barge next, based on what she could read of the river. She discovered that the boats that passed them, coming downriver with cargoes of quarried rock or grain or ore, left long trailing wakes that could be mistaken for snags.

There was the social life of the barge to watch too. Laundry Day, when the gears in the mill were connected to the great washtub, and afterward women quarreled over whose laundry was whose, and drying laundry fluttered from the rigging like bright banners. Corn-grinding day, when the gears were connected to the grindstone, and men went up and down into the hold with sacks of grain, or meal or flour. The mill drove the potter's wheel one day, the carpenter's saw the next, the blacksmith's bellows the day after, round and round the cycle of days.

Eliss watched and learned which groups of families were friends, who tended to eat and wash all together. The divers were the queens in the little society, deferred to by the wives of the artificers like the carpenter or the blacksmith or the potter, who were in turn deferred to by the wives of the bargemen; below them in rank were the wives and girlfriends of the musicians, except for those who were musicians themselves, who enjoyed a somewhat higher status. Pentra Smith seemed to occupy a place of her own, perhaps on a level with the divers, but she never seemed to socialize much. She came on deck every morning as soon as the anchor was raised, and kept to herself at her post until the anchor dropped again at night, when she went back to her cabin.

And there were things to be learned from the bits of conversation that drifted upward. Drogin was cross because he didn't have a girlfriend at the moment, which was because he insisted on keeping his boxhorn in his blankets with him at night, which he did because the horn's wood was sensitive to cold. Mr. Pitspike was cross because he suffered from a stomach ailment that prevented him from eating onions, which he loved, and he had to watch other people cooking them all day. Mr. Crucible had been too poor to buy Mrs. Crucible a wedding bangle, so he had tattooed one on her wrist instead, with great artistry, and she boasted that it couldn't be stolen, couldn't be lost, and never got in the way when she was washing clothes or cooking.

The *Bird of the River* drifted along bearing its little world through the breathless heat, as the musicians played and cicadas on the bank droned in counterpoint, and there were days when the country beyond the riverbanks seemed as distant and unreal as a landscape painted on a screen.

"I SUPPOSE YOU KNOW ENOUGH to keep watch for a couple of minutes," said Drogin, shifting where he sat. Eliss nodded. He swung himself around and climbed down along the shrouds. Eliss focused her attention on the river.

A small craft was coming downstream toward them, someone's private boat. There was a pleasure pavilion on deck, with what looked like a couple of noblemen and three or four ladies in it, laughing and waving at the *Bird of the River* as they passed. The *Bird's* musicians began to play the same tune the noblemen's musicians were playing, and the melodies echoed back and forth across the water. The boat's tillerman, shaking his head, gave them an ironic salute as the boat fell astern.

Eliss watched its wake, rippling away and fanning out . . . and there, just where it vanished ahead, was a spike of water running up. She drew in breath and used the Calling Voice.

"Unmarked snag to starboard!"

At once the shouting began below, and topmen came racing up toward her to take in sail. The *Bird of the River* slowed, reversed, stopped; but before the polemen could take her ahead, Mr. Riveter walked forward and peered out at the water off the starboard bow.

"Are you sure?" he called over his shoulder, and turned to look up at her. "I think that's just the wake of the boat."

"I'm sure," Eliss called down.

Mrs. Riveter, who had undressed and put on her goggles, came to stand beside him, looking out at the water. So did a few others of the crew. One or two shook their heads and looked up at Eliss doubtfully. Eliss clenched her fists on the rail.

"Captain, sir, it's just the wake of the boat," Mr. Riveter cried.

"Send in a diver," said Captain Glass, where he stood at the tiller. He didn't shout, but his voice carried.

"Send in a diver anyway?"

"That was what I said."

Mrs. Riveter said something to her husband and climbed down into the water. She swam out to the jetting water, examined it closely a moment, and then dove under. After a moment the jet disappeared. A moment later Mrs. Riveter surfaced, holding up a black branch.

"That was all it was," called Mr. Riveter. But Mrs. Riveter shook her head, swimming to the barge.

"This is just what was breaking the surface," she said, laying the branch on deck. "The rest of it goes down a fathom to a bigger snag. An ugly one. The next flood will shift it if we don't get it now."

"Seven hells." Mr. Riveter scratched his beard. "She was right, captain, sir."

Captain Glass only nodded.

"SO," SAID KRELAN AS HE RUMMAGED in his bag for clean clothes. "I understand you were quite the heroine today." Eliss, who was eating her dinner, lifted her head to stare at him.

"What?"

"He's talking about you seeing the snag nobody else thought was there," said Alder. It was so rare for Alder to say anything when Krelan was around that Eliss turned and stared at him too.

"What? Who said I was a heroine?"

"It's the talk of the galley," said Krelan. "I hear everything when I'm in there turning the spits. Mrs. Riveter says you're a natural spotter. Jeela Smith says you're another Sandgrind, though I haven't the faintest idea what that means. Mrs. Crucible says the gods send a good with every evil, and you're obviously the good that came with, er, something nasty I gather happened at Slate's Landing." He turned his back, pulled his tunic off over his head, and pulled on a clean one.

"Oh." Eliss felt the wave of sorrow for Falena coming. She braced herself, as she would with a real wave, and it broke and passed away. When she knew she could reply calmly, she said: "That was when our mother died. And we found the body of somebody who'd been murdered."

"Oh! I didn't know. I'm sorry." Krelan turned around, pulling his tunic down. "Was it somebody from Slate's Landing?"

"No, it wasn't," said Alder coldly. "It was some rich boy from a city."

Why are you so nasty to him? Eliss wondered, glaring at her brother. To Krelan she said: "I guess he might have drifted down from the landing, but the priest asked around and he didn't seem to belong to anybody. Besides, he was a nobleman."

"Really? How did they know?"

"Well . . ." Eliss thought about it. "He had on a big gold armband, shaped like a coiling snake. And some tattoos, not just gang tattoos but the kind some of the great houses wear. That was what I heard."

"It should have been easy to identify him, then," said Krelan, folding up his grease-stained tunic.

Eliss shrugged. "Maybe they did. I don't know."

"And he can't have been murdered by thieves, or they'd have taken that gold armband."

"Nobles kill each other all the time over nothing," said Alder. "You ought to know that. That's why you're hiding here, isn't it?"

"Alder! That's rude!"

"But too true," said Krelan, with a sad chuckle. "Er . . . I don't suppose I could put my dirty clothes with yours, to be laundered?"

THE MUSICIANS ALL MADE A POINT of bowing elaborately to Eliss the next day when she went aft to climb up to the mast platform, and struck up a tune she hadn't heard before. Salpin was already at the top, applauding her, when she climbed through. She ducked her head in embarrassment.

"Why are they playing that?"

"Why? That's *Sandgrind's Fancy*. They're playing it in your honor. Everybody's saying he must have been your grandfather, because you can read the river too."

"I don't think he was," said Eliss. She wasn't sure how she ought to feel. Nobody had ever done anything in her honor before. "On the other hand . . . you never know. At least, I don't."

"What was your family?"

"Poor people," said Eliss, looking down at the river. "They left Mama at the Divers' Motherhouse when she was five. She doesn't . . . she didn't remember much about them, except they couldn't feed everybody so they had to give their children away. And she always said my father was a sailor she met in port, but his ship sank and he drowned."

How threadbare and sad it sounded, the history of her family. Eliss had never told it to anyone before. She didn't think she'd tell anyone again.

"Oh. I'm sorry." Salpin's ebullience faded. He leaned on the rail, studying the water. After a while he said, "At least you know your mother is with your father now. She went under the water and met her true love there, maybe. Waiting to carry her away to a good place."

Eliss nodded. It was a nicer thing to imagine than what Falena had actually met under the water.

They sat in silence a long while, except when Salpin would point and say things, such as, "That's not a town, that's somebody's private boat landing," or "See that red color in the mud? That's where the stream comes down from the iron mine at Branka." Twice they spotted marker buoys—Eliss saw them first—and after the second one, while the *Bird* sat unmoving in the stream and the divers went in, Salpin scrambled down through the rigging and came back up with his concertina. When the *Bird* sailed on again, he sat with his back against the mast, a faraway look in his eyes. He played no proper song, but only little fragments of melodies that wandered like raindrops down a window, and now and then joined up to make a longer tune. Eliss watched the river all afternoon, while the music came together in bigger and bigger pieces. By the time the sun sank down behind them, throwing the mast's long shadow across the world, the song was complete. It was a bittersweet melody, sad but beautiful. The other musicians below left off playing and listened.

"WHY'S YOUR BROTHER MAD AT ME?"

Eliss looked up in surprise. She was alone on the mast platform, so intent on the river she hadn't noticed Wolkin's climb through the rigging. He sat down beside her now, looking mournful.

"Are you supposed to be up here?" Eliss asked him, looking to see if he wore any kind of safety line. She couldn't see one.

"It's safe," said Wolkin, putting his legs through the rail. "Anyway. He won't talk to me. Why is he mad?"

"He isn't mad at you," said Eliss, and then thought about what she'd said. "I mean . . . he isn't mad at any*body*. He's just mad. Probably because of what happened to Mama. He's only ten."

"I'm almost ten," said Wolkin. "I'd be mad if my mother died. But she won't, of course."

Eliss sighed, but decided to say nothing. Wolkin fidgeted.

"You think he might be mad because I said he was a greenie?"

"Maybe."

"I said I was sorry. I didn't mean it mean."

"I know."

"I mean, I get mad when people say my daddy was a bad captain. Tappy and Boley said it and I beat them up. You think if I beat up the other kids for him he'd stop being mad at me?"

"Are the other kids calling him a greenie?"

"Sometimes."

Eliss winced to herself. "No wonder he's unhappy. But I don't think he wants you to beat up anyone for him."

"I could. I could beat up anybody on this ship," said Wolkin. "That was my age, I mean. It wouldn't be any trouble." He edged a little closer to her.

"No. Thank you. Really."

"But I owe you a blood debt. Your mama saved my life. I have to kill anybody who hurts you. Or him."

Eliss bit her lip, trying not to smile. "It's very nice of you to offer, but I think you have to wait until you're grown up to pay blood debts. Besides, we aren't important enough for anybody to start a vendetta against us."

"You are so," said Wolkin. "And people will always go after Alder, won't they?"

"Maybe not."

"What's it like, being a Yendri?"

Eliss looked down at Alder far below. He sat, small and forlorn, by the aft rail, staring into the trees on the far shore. She felt a pang of guilt. "I don't know what it's like," she told Wolkin, and thought: *Alder doesn't know either, does he?*

"WOLKIN!"

Mrs. Riveter stood below, staring up from the deck with an expression of outrage. Eliss hadn't known the divers were taught the Carrying Voice too.

"Oh." Wolkin looked down. "Well, time to go."

Much to his embarrassment, he was lowered from the platform in a painter's seat, strapped in too tightly to move, and his mother dragged him below the moment his toes touched the deck.

"SO SOME OF THE KIDS here are calling you a greenie?" Eliss shook out her blanket. Alder, shaking out his own blanket, shrugged.

"Sometimes."

"Do you want me to talk to their mothers about it?"

"No!"

"But they shouldn't be calling you names like that."

"But they do. There's always going to be somebody calling me names, wherever I go. Haven't you figured that out by now?" Alder crawled inside the tent and wrapped himself up in the blanket. He punched irritably at Krelan's bag. "Hasn't your boyfriend got a place to put this yet? It takes up too much room!"

"He's not my boyfriend!" Eliss crawled in after him and smacked his arm. "Moron! People from great houses don't marry beggars like us!"

"Boyfriends don't always *marry* girls," said Alder, as though she were a half-wit to whom he was explaining something very basic. "Remember all the uncles? And anyway, we're not beggars! Mama was a diver!"

"We might as well have been, at the end," said Eliss. "And you might as well be a beggar now. I'm working to earn our place here and you just sit and look grumpy all day."

Alder's face crumpled up as though he was going to cry, but he kicked her instead. She kicked him back. They flailed at each other briefly.

"What's that?" Mr. Turnbolt, the night watchman, had just come on deck. Eliss and Alder froze, thinking he had heard their fight.

"That's the last of the sunset," said one of the musicians.

"Sunset? How much pinkweed have you been smoking? That's in the wrong place for sunset!"

"I don't know, then, maybe it's sunrise come early."

"Is something on fire?"

"The forest's on fire!"

"Get someone up the mast!"

Eliss scrambled out of the tent and ran for the rigging, as Mr. Riveter ran up the companionway.

"What's going on?"

"I'm finding out!" Eliss cried, conscious of a feeling of self-importance. Her hands and feet easily found the shrouds in the dark, and a moment later she had pulled herself up on the platform and looked away to the east. She caught her breath. A great column of opaque blue smoke stood in the sky, towering, underlit red by flames that leaped up from the forest below. The rising moon lit the upper reaches of the smoke with gold.

"It *is* a fire!"

"How far off?" Mr. Riveter shouted up to her. Captain Glass had come up on deck and stood beside him.

Eliss looked hard at the flames, trying to get an idea. "Three leagues," she answered. "It looks as though it comes right down to the riverbank!"

Mr. Riveter looked at Captain Glass. "That must be at Synpelene."

"Has to be."

"Should we put out and moor in midstream?"

Captain Glass shook his head. "Anybody comes downriver in the night, they'd be hard pressed not to hit us."

Eliss, who had been climbing back down, found the deck with her toes. "Are we going to be all right?"

"Of course we will," said Mr. Riveter. "Don't worry. We'll know in plenty of time if the fire comes this way."

"Do you want me to stay up there and keep an eye out?"

"No. That's what Turnbolt's for," said the captain. "You go on to bed."

"Yes, sir."

Eliss went back to the tent. Alder was sitting up inside, but as soon as he saw Eliss he lay back down and rolled up in his blanket. Eliss felt a pang of guilt, wondering if he'd been scared.

"Mr. Riveter says everything's all right," she said, and she pulled up her own blanket. Alder didn't reply. "It isn't very close. And anyway, how could it burn us up? We're on the river."

After a long silence from Alder, Eliss sighed and said: "We have a place to sleep."

Another long silence, until at last: "We have a place to sleep *and a warm blanket*," recited Alder.

"We have a place to sleep, and a warm blanket *each*, and *we had dinner tonight*."

"We have a place to sleep, and a warm blanket each, and we had dinner tonight, *and we'll have breakfast tomorrow*."

"And who knows what, when summer comes?"

"And who knows what, when summer comes? *And summer is coming soon*."

Nothing more was said for a while. Eliss assumed Alder had gone to sleep.

" 'Summer' just means something nice, right?" said Alder suddenly. "Because it's already summer, and it's just hot."

"That's right. 'Summer' means . . . it means better times are coming."

"I hope so," said Alder.

When she thought he was asleep at last, Eliss put her arm around him.

SHE WAS AWAKENED TWICE during the night by shouting as boats came down the river. One boat belonged to a Mr. Ingot, an itinerant barber. Eliss knew this because Mr. Turnbolt demanded he identify himself. She was about to go back to sleep when Mr. Ingot shouted that he was fleeing from Synpelene because it was under attack from bandits. Then there was a lot of muttered conversation, and Eliss's heart raced. She relaxed a little when she heard Captain Glass give the order to bring up weapons and arm all the men on the night watch; he sounded so calm she thought there must be no immediate danger. All the same, she could not fall asleep until she had worked out an escape plan. *If bandits attack, I'll wake up Alder and we'll grab a life preserver, and we'll slip overboard without making a sound, and float downriver until we come to a town. . . .*

The second time she woke it was just starting to get light. The wind had shifted and the smell of smoke was everywhere. Someone was yelling across the water. Eliss heard Mr. Turnbolt yelling back, "Did they beat them off?"

"Yes!" shouted the stranger from the passing boat. "Caught eight of them in the sewer tunnels under the forest gate! They'd just put the heads up on the gate when I left there. It's all mopped up now."

"Is the fire out?"

"No. Getting there, though. The greenies seem to be doing it."

"Good."

ELISS NEVER REALLY WENT BACK to sleep after that. She dozed fitfully and dreamed that bandits were running along the riverbank, and she was trying to explain to Alder about the life preserver, but he was afraid to go into the water because the headless bandits were in there. . . .

SYNPELENE WAS A WALLED CITY, closed up even on the side that fronted on the river, though there were docks outside the wall. This morning, under sunlight stained red by smoke, its river gate was wide open, but there were no boats moored on the copper-colored water. The *Bird of the River* came slowly up and anchored at the first dock.

Eliss, watching from the masthead, was very nearly on eye level with the armed women on the city wall. None of them went so far as to fit arrows to their bows, but they were red-eyed and grim as they contemplated her. From her high perch she could look into the city. There she saw stone towers smoking like chimneys, their roofs burned away, and far beyond the black expanse that had been forest scarring the green. It still smoldered along its distant margin, dark plumes rising up here and there. Like the smoke, the screaming of mourners rose from within Synpelene.

Eliss was climbing down when she heard other shrill voices raised. She looked down and saw Wolkin and Alder, confronted by a crowd of the other children. Just as Wolkin took a swing at someone, Mr. Riveter noticed and started across the deck for them. Eliss reached out, grabbed a rope, and slid the rest of the way down to reach them first. She hit the deck with a crash but managed to keep her feet. The children, startled, backed away in silence.

"That was *neat*," said Wolkin, round-eyed.

"Are they calling you names again?" Eliss spoke to Alder, rubbing her palms against her tunic.

"No."

"What's going on here?" demanded Mr. Riveter. The other children backed away.

"We were just going to go ashore and look at the bandit heads," said Wolkin.

"And that meant you had to fight someone?"

"No, but—" Wolkin avoided looking at Alder. "Alder didn't want to go, and Talmey asked him if he was scared, and Boley said he better not go because he might see his daddy's head up there. So I told Boley I'd punch his face."

"Stop doing that!" said Alder furiously. "And—and I'm *not* scared to go look at the heads. Let's go look at the heads!"

"Nobody's going anywhere until we get landing clearance," shouted Mr. Riveter. He waved his arms. "Seven hells! Both of you sit your butts down on that deck and stay there until I tell you you can get up! *All of you kids!* Line up on deck and sit down and *stay there* and the first one I catch fighting I'll drown with these two hands, do you understand?"

Grumbling, the children assembled and sat. Mr. Riveter stared around wild-eyed, looking as though he'd punch someone's face himself, until Captain Glass came slowly up the companionway. The captain surveyed the row of children without comment. He looked over the side at the scum of ash floating on the water, and sighed.

"Shall I organize a shore party, sir?" Mr. Riveter saluted. Captain Glass nodded.

"Get landing clearance. Find out what happened. Offer them the lumber from the snags. See if they can sell us any provisions. And, here—" He opened his wallet and passed a pair of gold pieces to Mr. Riveter. "Get me wine if they have it."

"This far up the river they're more likely to have whiskey, sir."

"Then get me as much whiskey as that'll buy. Double the watch and keep them armed."

"Yes, sir."

The captain turned and went below again, just as a door in the river gate opened and the landing master emerged. He was pale, with a bandaged head.

"*Bird's* master!" he called.

"Yes, sir." Mr. Riveter ran to the rail.

"Any trouble downriver?"

"None, sir. Permission to anchor and come ashore?"

The landing master eyed the logs stacked on the *Bird's* deck. "Granted. You have the liberty of the town."

"What happened?"

"Shellback," said the landing master, and spat. "He's got an army now! You never saw so many murdering bastards in your life. And half of them were demons. They just kept coming out of the trees. The only thing that drove them off was the fire."

"Demons! You don't think he's made friends with—you know—" Mr. Riveter jerked his thumb over his shoulder in the direction of the black mountain. The landing master gestured to ward off evil.

"Gods defend us, who knows?" His voice was hopeless.

THE HEADS WERE TOO FAR up on the gate to see much detail, and the women on the ramparts wouldn't let them come for a closer look. Eliss could tell that three of the heads were, indeed, the heads of demons, with protruding tusks, and their matted hair looked more like fur. Alder went very pale, staring up at them, but he did stare. Wolkin went pale too and after they had turned around to walk back across town he suddenly ran into an alleyway and threw up.

"Puke in your own street, why don't you?" shouted a man from a ladder, where he was pulling down burned thatching. Wolkin, emerging hastily from the alley, drew breath to say something rude, but Alder grabbed his shoulder and pulled him away.

"Let's not make anybody angrier," he said. "People have enough to be angry about."

Eliss nodded somberly. She saw, now, why Synpelene had built such a high wall around itself, and why the bandits had tried to take it anyway. It was a town of goldsmiths. Signs hung at ground level before each house, saying things like *A. Cutwire, Assayer* or *Smith & Sons' Filigree Specialists* or *Steelbrace's Fine Jewelery Designs—Step In, Prospective Buyer!* However welcoming the signs were, each house was like a miniature fortress, with narrow slits for windows and iron doors. Most of them were shut up tight today. Armed guards wearing different house liveries were on duty before them, leaning against the iron doors or pacing back and forth.

The town's inn, on the other hand, was a smoking ruin now. Though its windows had been barred with wrought iron, its front door had been wrenched away and was nowhere in sight. Three walls remained but the fourth was a tumbled mass of bricks in the courtyard of the house next door. The inn's sign hung drunkenly from a bracket, still informing the world that The House of the Golden Portal served fine food and drink. Under the sign bodies were laid out in a row, covered with an assortment of curtains, blankets, and one charred tapestry.

The owner of the premises sat on his front step, staring dully into space with one eye and occasionally fingering the bandage that covered the other eye. Eliss was surprised to see Krelan sitting beside the innkeeper, looking sympathetic. The innkeeper was speaking in a monotone:

"No, they didn't batter the door down. The bastards had a key. One of my keys. Can't think how they got one, but they had it. They wrenched it off its hinges afterward and took it with them. They must have thought it was made of gold, because of the gilding. What kind of idiot does something like that except a demon? It weighed a ton. That was a good door. I hope they carry it for miles before they realize it's gilded iron. I hope they all get hernias."

"I expect they went straight for your wine cellar," said Krelan. "Being demons."

"No, actually," said the innkeeper. "They went straight upstairs for my guests." He swiveled his eye at the bodies. "The first I knew of anything was hearing one of them scream. I was sound asleep in my own room. Come out on the landing and here's all these thieves throwing luggage about. Mr. Meltsilver had five cases of merchandise he'd bought for his shops in the cities, a fortune in jewelry, and the cases broke open falling downstairs, just raining gold bangles.

And Mr. Touchfire, he was a banker, he had a crate of gold ingots . . . and . . . Mr. Smelter was a gem dealer, he'd brought stock with him to sell . . ."

"What evil fortune," said Krelan. He reached into a pouch at his belt. "I hate to impose on you on this black day, but I wonder if you'd look at something and tell me if you recognize—"

"Come on," muttered Alder, tugging at Eliss's sleeve. "Wolkin is sick. Let's go back."

"I just ate some bad fish, that's all," said Wolkin as they walked on. But there were more bodies laid out in the town square, visiting prospectors who'd been robbed and had their throats cut, and Wolkin clutched Eliss's hand as they passed them. He was crying silently by the time they reached the river gate.

THAT NIGHT ELISS LAY AWAKE in the tent, trying to forget what she'd seen. Both the town and the river were quiet—the mourners had fallen silent at last—but the heat was stifling. Mr. Turnbolt and the town's night watchman were having a conversation in low voices, and the sound carried clearly enough for Eliss to hear every word.

"No, they got in through the sewer. No one can tell how they got the grate off. Came just before dawn. At first we thought it was only a handful, but they kept swarming, like beetles."

"Ugh! One comes out of a crack, you kill it, and three more run out?"

"Just exactly like that. Except we couldn't catch them. Not until the end. We fought them off all day. They kept setting fire to roofs. It was like a war in the streets, I can tell you. And there were more of them in the woods! All hiding in the trees, like Yendri."

"Were any of them Yendri?"

"No. Not that I saw. But they were in the trees. Not all demons, either. Some of them were *us*."

"Shellback's one of us."

"The bastard. He was the one gave the order to set fire to the trees. Cover their retreat."

"Now, I heard it was your people fired the trees, to drive them off."

"Who told you that?"

"Landing master."

"Doesn't know what he's talking about."

Eliss turned over and tried to pull her blanket over her ear, to shut out the conversation. Krelan's bag had slid forward, in danger of toppling on her face. She shoved at it. Something small fell out of the bag, landing with a clatter beside her.

Eliss picked it up and peered at it. It was a miniature portrait, done on an oval of ceramic. She couldn't make out any details in the darkness. Shrugging to herself, she thrust it back in Krelan's bag and pulled the drawstring tight.

THE NEXT DAY DAWNED BRIGHT; a wind had risen just before morning and swept out the smoke, freshening the air. Drogin emerged from the windmill and leaned against it, warming his long back on the sunwarmed planks. He raised the boxhorn to his mouth and played a sad, sinuous melody, trailing out across the sleepy water.

The *Bird of the River* was making ready to leave when Synpelene's gates opened. Two figures emerged and hurried across the docks. One was cloaked, in spite of the heat, carrying a heavy bag. The other was the town's mayor, in his yellow robes with a golden chain of office.

"*Bird of the River!*" he called. "I must speak to your captain."

Eliss, halfway up to the mast platform, stopped in the rigging to stare. Mr. Riveter, who had been shouting orders for setting the sail, turned.

"Er . . . captain's indisposed," he said. "I'm first mate. What do you want?"

"I want you to take on a passenger," said the mayor. "I'll pay his passage."

"But we're a diving barge, sir. We don't take passengers."

"Will you make an exception? Name your price," said the mayor. "He has only to go to the village of his people. He won't be with you more than a week or two." The man beside him dropped his hood, revealing himself as a Yendri in a white robe. Mr. Riveter made an involuntary noise of surprise.

"This is Mr. Llemlin Moss, he operated our bathhouse here, and I can personally attest that he is a good and trustworthy man," said the mayor quickly. Mr. Riveter scratched his beard.

"If he's good and trustworthy, why are you in such a hurry to get rid of him?"

The mayor glanced back at the gates. "Public feeling is running high in the wake of this catastrophe. Some of our citizens fail to distinguish between demons and Yendri, you see, and there have been— foolish and unfortunate words. Painted on the walls of Mr. Moss's establishment. So we thought it best to ensure Mr. Moss's safety before any further incidents could occur."

"He didn't have anything to do with the raid, though, did he?"

"Of course he didn't!" The mayor looked shocked. "He's a disciple of the Green Witch!"

The Yendri winced and, in a quiet voice, said, "The Unwearied Mother."

"Oh," said Mr. Riveter. "All right, then."

"Good!" The mayor drew out a small pouch weighted with something heavy and threw it across to Mr. Riveter, who caught it and peered into it. His eyebrows shot up his forehead.

"Right. Yes. Step aboard, Mr. Lichen."

"It's Moss." The Yendri picked up his bag and walked up the gangplank. Two of the polemen drew it inboard the moment he stepped on deck. The mayor of Synpelene raised his hands.

"Now-gods-witness-that-I-have-performed-the-duties-of-a-righteous-man-toward-the-stranger! Safe voyage, Moss!"

"But I wasn't a stranger," said Mr. Moss, but not as though he expected anyone to pay attention.

ELISS CLIMBED THE REST of the way up to the platform. As the anchor was lifted, as the tillerman edged the *Bird* out into midstream, she watched Mr. Riveter lead the Yendri to the locker where spare tents were kept. There was a lot of gesticulating and conversation she couldn't hear, for Mr. Moss had a low voice and Mr. Riveter seemed to lower his to keep him company.

She saw Alder crawl out of their tent and stand up, staring openmouthed at Mr. Moss. Mr. Riveter, noticing, turned to him and handed him a bundle of tent fabric. He gestured at Mr. Moss, said something, patted Alder on the shoulder, and hurried away from them.

ELISS DUTIFULLY WATCHED THE RIVER and caught two unmarked snags that day. While the *Bird* lay to and divers went down, she watched the deck. During the first stop Mr. Moss sat beside his tent and Alder sat near, talking earnestly to him. During the second stop Mr. Moss was not in evidence—perhaps in his tent—and Alder and Wolkin were sitting together on the aft deck, chattering like birds.

The fair wind continued. By nightfall they had made many miles upriver, leaving behind the shadow of desolation over Synpelene.

"HIS NAME IS LLEMLIN and he's a holy man," Alder said as Eliss ate her supper. He was so excited he had barely touched his. "I mean, sort of a holy man, but not like one of ours—I mean—yours. He's very quiet and he doesn't have visions or tell people what they ought to do. He just helps people. He had a bathhouse where people went to get poisons out of themselves and he had a medicine garden in pots. He says he's a—" Alder hesitated over the unfamiliar word. "A *disciple* of this holy lady. She lives up on the black mountain and she defeated the Master of the Mountain by just looking at him so he fell in love with her and had to stop being evil. And so did all his demons."

"But the demons are still killing people," said Eliss. "Eat your supper. It's getting cold."

"He says those are somebody else's demons, not the Master of the Mountain's. He let me help him put his tent up, did you see? And he says, the holy lady is like our mother. My mother, I mean."

"Your mother was Mama," said Eliss.

"I know," said Alder. "I meant the Yendri's mother. Because I'm a Yendri."

"You're a Yendri *too*," said Eliss. "You're still my brother."

"Only half," said Alder. "The Blacksmith isn't *my* father."

"Yes, he is." Now Eliss was shocked. "He's the father of all of us. You're a Child of the Sun, even if you don't look like one."

Alder shook his head stubbornly. "Nobody ever said that before. People always say, 'Look at the greenie!' Well, I am one. I don't like covering myself up to hide it. And—and I'm never going to do it again, either."

Eliss knew better than to argue with him when he was being obstinate. When he'd been little and hadn't wanted to go somewhere, he'd dig in his heels and stand as though rooted to the spot. More than once Falena had lost patience and said, "All right, I'm just going to leave you there," and walked away down the road. Eliss had trailed behind her, looking over her shoulder in growing panic, and in the end she would always have to go running back to get him. Even then, Alder would never move; Eliss had always had to pick him up and carry him, or drag him as he'd gotten older and heavier.

She shrugged now, pretending that what he'd said hadn't bothered her. "Suit yourself."

"Alder!" someone whispered hoarsely from outside their tent. "Alder, he's awake and practicing his moves! You have to come see!"

Wolkin stuck his head through the tent's doorway and widened his eyes for emphasis. Alder threw his bowl down and scrambled out on hands and knees.

"You have to finish your dinner first!" Eliss scrambled after him, but he ignored her. She looked out to see the two little boys standing side by side, staring at Mr. Moss, who had emerged from his own tent. He was standing in the light of the early moon, his arms raised, his palms together. Wolkin nudged Alder, who cleared his throat.

"Hello again," he said. Mr. Moss turned and regarded them.

"Good evening," he replied.

"This is my friend Wolkin," said Alder.

"Then good evening to you, Wolkin."

"Good evening," said Wolkin. "Er. Those look like pretty good fighting moves."

Mr. Moss blinked slowly. "Fighting moves? No; in fact I was praying."

"Oh."

"I *told* you," said Alder in an undertone.

"Well . . . do you know any fighting moves?"

Mr. Moss looked from one to the other. "I do not fight. We only learn defense."

"That's almost as good," said Wolkin eagerly. "My daddy taught me some defensive moves. Do you want to see?"

"I don't think he does," said Alder, but Wolkin had already struck an attitude, balanced on one foot while blocking furiously with his arms. He uttered a high-pitched shriek. Unfortunately that drew the attention of Mr. Riveter, who was consigning the watch to Mr. Turnbolt. He turned, scowling.

"You were supposed to be in bed by now!"

"But I'm *learning* something!"

"I know what you're going to learn next," said Mr. Riveter, starting toward him, and Wolkin gave it up and fled below. Alder was left staring up at Mr. Moss.

"Can you—would you please tell me—who are our gods?"

Mr. Moss smiled gently. "We have none."

"But you were praying."

"I pray to the Unwearied Mother."

"She isn't a goddess?"

Mr. Moss studied Alder a long moment. "Sit down. I will tell you about her."

"Excuse me," said Krelan. Eliss looked up at him, startled. He was standing by the tent, clutching a bowl of broth and a chunk of bread. "Would you mind a little company while I eat? There are four pole-men playing dice in my usual corner in the galley, and I wasn't quite brave enough to tell them to move."

"Go ahead and sit," Eliss told him. She looked at the broth and bread as he lowered himself to the deck beside her. "Is that all you're having?"

"It's all that was left. I don't get to eat until the rest of the crew dines," said Krelan. "I'm only the spitboy, after all."

"It must be quite a change from what you're used to."

"Yes, but it's better than being killed because someone has a con-tract out on my family." Krelan gave a dry little chuckle. "Besides, I don't eat much."

"You're too thin," said Eliss.

"I prefer to think of myself as fashionably slender." Krelan dipped his bread in the broth and slurped it. His shoulders were bowed with weariness, and his tunic stank of grease and soot. His bare feet were silvered with ashes, but they were narrow and shapely, with high arches. Eliss supposed that was because he was an aristocrat.

"So." Krelan swallowed another mouthful of bread. "How are you getting on?"

"All right." Eliss was surprised that he would ask.

"That was nasty, at Synpelene."

"Oh. Yes, it was." Eliss remembered him sitting by the innkeeper, encouraging him to talk. "That man you were talking to, was he a friend of yours?"

Krelan looked sideways at her. "A client of my family's. I didn't know him personally, but it was my duty to convey our condolences."

"Oh." Eliss thought how odd it must be to belong to a family so big and important you had *duties*. "I felt so sorry for all of them. How could that have happened?"

"From what I heard, someone unbolted the sewer grate from the inside," Krelan replied. He blew on his broth and sipped it. "That was how the bandits got in."

"Unbolted it from the inside? How could they have done that?"

"No one seemed to know."

"And somehow or other the bandits got a key to that man's front door." Eliss remembered the gaping hole where the door had been. "So . . . someone who lived there must have been working with the bandits. They went down and unfastened the sewer grating, and they stole a key from the innkeeper."

"Or had a copy made."

"That's right. There are people who can do that." Eliss remembered Uncle Ironbolt, whose friends had been thieves. "They push a key into soft wax, like a mold, and take it away and make a copy from the impression."

"So they do."

"But . . . nobody would let a demon live in a city like Synpelene," Eliss continued, frowning. "Full of gold like that. Which would mean it had to be one of *us*. But we wouldn't do a thing like that to our own people! So it had to have been somebody else."

"You think so? Well, so did the townfolk. And that's why Mr. Moss was escorted out of town, one step ahead of the mob with torches and swords." Krelan nodded toward the Yendri, who seemed to be telling Alder a story in a low voice. "Does he look like a conspirator to you?"

"No . . ."

"And why shouldn't one of us do such a thing to other Children of the Sun? What do you think Shellback is?"

"I don't know anything about Shellback. What is he?"

"One of us. A mercenary soldier turned bandit."

"But what kind of a name is *Shellback?*"

"Mercenaries like to give themselves demon names. It makes them sound scarier. And he's apparently recruited an army of other mercenaries, and some demons. They say the Master of the Mountain is keeping his army home these days, since he got married." Krelan glanced back at Mr. Moss. "Maybe Shellback thinks he can step in and become the new bandit lord."

Eliss shuddered. "What makes people do such horrible things?"

"They want the loot, my dear." Krelan tilted his bowl and drank the last of the broth. Eliss looked at him askance. No one had ever called her *my dear* before. He set the bowl aside. "May I trouble you for my bag?"

She pulled it out and handed it to him. He dug through it and pulled out a change of clothes. Once again he turned his back on her to pull his tunic off. The moonlight gleamed silver on his pale skin. Eliss remembered a fountain statue in a city she had lived in once, of a young fisherman holding up a fish that spouted water. The fisherman had been slender, shining-wet, and had the same narrow waist and triangular chest that Krelan had.

Krelan sniffed at himself dubiously. "I think it's more than time I had a bath," he said. "Please excuse me, won't you?"

"All right." Eliss watched him grab up his clean clothes and pick his way over to the *Bird's* larboard side. A moment later she heard him splashing in the river. All the men Eliss had ever known would just have stripped down right there in front of her without a word of apology, and laughed when Falena had protested. It was nice, Eliss thought, that Krelan had the manners of a nobleman, as well as the name.

NEXT MORNING, ALDER WAS AN UNCONSCIOUS bundle in his blanket beside her, only grunting a protest when she shook his shoulder and told him it was daylight. Eliss wondered how late he'd stayed up listening to Mr. Moss. She felt guilty for going on to sleep without making certain he'd got safely to bed at a reasonable hour.

She crawled out on deck and stood up. There was Mr. Moss, praying again, as though he hadn't moved all night. Hesitant, Eliss approached him.

"I'm sorry if my brother pestered you last night," she said. He lowered his hands and turned to her.

"You are his sister, Eliss? Yes, I can see. It was no trouble. It was my duty to answer his questions. But may I, in turn, ask you—how does it happen that he knows nothing of his father's people? Even in your coastal cities, we keep bathhouses. Your mother might have gone to any one of them and asked for help. We might have found his father for her. He would have gladly taken his child."

"Mama probably thought your people wouldn't care. And she wasn't very . . . organized," said Eliss uncomfortably. "But she would never have given him away. She couldn't have given up her own baby."

"With respect, it would have been easier for the child," said Mr. Moss. "Will you permit me to teach him, while I travel with you?"

"What are you going to teach him?"

"What he is. What we are. He has never heard the Long Songs, never even heard of the Unwearied Mother before last night. She holds out her hands to all children, but to lost children especially."

"But he's not lost," said Eliss. "He has me."

"To you also, she grants her grace."

"But I don't . . . Will it make him happier, to know what he is? Or will it just make him feel more like an outsider here?" Eliss gestured around her at the deck of the *Bird of the River.*

"It will make him whole," said Mr. Moss. "Who can live, being only half of what he should have been?"

Unwillingly, Eliss nodded. "All right, then. Just . . . just remember, he's my brother too."

Mr. Moss bowed. He looked like a tree bowing in the wind. "Of course," he said.

"Well. I'll . . . just let you go on with your praying now, all right? I have to go get my brother's breakfast," said Eliss, and hurried away.

LITTLE BRIGHT-EYED TULU RAN UP to her as she waited in line for breakfast. "Eliss, you know what? We'll be at the Lock and the Lake in two days! At Moonport! And you know what happens there? We have the Summer Party!"

"What's the Summer Party?" Eliss smiled at her, grateful to have something else to think about.

"It's where all the other musicians come off all the other boats and they all sit up there." Tulu waved a skinny arm at the aft deck. "And we fix up the deck all nice with lanterns and sweep it clean so people can dance. And they dance all night. And all the other people bring lots of food and drink. Especially cake. And jelly. Last year Wolkin ate so much jelly he got really really sick."

"I did not!" Wolkin, infuriated, shouted from his place in line.

"Yes, he did." Tulu leaned in close to whisper. "And he *cried*. Anyway, won't that be fun?"

"It sounds like it," Eliss agreed. They were by this time at the head of the line, where Krelan was ladling out porridge to all comers. He gave her an ironic salute with the porridge ladle.

"I look forward to widening my cultural horizons, don't you?" he said. "Two bowls, I assume?"

"Yes, please."

FOR A FEW DAYS NOW there had been bluffs rising on either bank of the river, and Eliss on the masthead was at eye level with the land as they sailed slowly past. This was open country, higher, not so much dense forest. Even dutifully watching the water, Eliss found herself observing details of the landscape: the distant scar of a quarry in a range of granite hills, or a flock of sheep grazing, or the red track of a caravan road. On the day they came to the Lock, she watched in amazement for hours as they passed field after field of vegetables and even trees, planted in neat rows, with Yendri tending them here and there. Now and again one would look up from his or her work and watch the *Bird of the River* as it glided past. All of them had silent thoughtful faces like Mr. Moss. Eliss couldn't remember ever having seen a Yendri woman before. They wore elaborate skirts made of scarves, dyed in all the colors of an opal, but wore nothing to cover their breasts. Both the women and the men sang as they worked. The songs were nothing like the cheerful dance tunes of the Children of the Sun. This was music like the mist blowing through the trees, or wind in the eaves; Eliss couldn't imagine anyone dancing to it.

By noon, when the Lock came in sight, Eliss could look at nothing else.

Ahead of them the river seemed to come to an abrupt end at a high cliff of stone like a wall. Eliss could make out stonework, something like a bridge and more walls, and on the starboard shore a few buildings. The water on the approach to it was smooth and deep-looking.

"Strike sail!" Mr. Riveter shouted, from below. "Ahoy the masthead! On deck!"

Eliss understood by this time that he meant she had to come down from her platform, and so she hurriedly swung herself down through the rigging, even as the topmen were racing up past her to take in the sail.

"What happens now?" she cried as soon as her feet touched the deck.

"Now? You just find a place to sit inboard," said Mr. Riveter. "We're almost there."

Eliss looked around for Alder and saw him sitting by one of the capstans, deep in conversation with Mr. Moss. A little irritated that he hadn't even looked up to see what was going on, she wandered over and sat by the companionway. Wolkin appeared out of nowhere and sat beside her.

"Don't be scared," he said. "I've done this hundreds of times. It's easy."

She hadn't been scared, but suddenly the water had become a good deal rougher. Eliss looked around and saw that the *Bird of the River*, now propelled forward by the polemen, was inexorably drawing nearer to the base of the tremendous wall. Water was roaring white from two great sluices to starboard and larboard in the wall, churning up the placid river and making it boil. Immediately ahead of them were two piers, extending to either side of a stone tower as big around as a city block and as high as the wall itself. On one of the piers stood a man, shouting something through cupped hands at Mr. Riveter. The thunder of the water drowned out his voice, but Mr. Riveter nodded and made signs to him. As the polemen guided the *Bird* forward between the piers, the man walked to one of two big levers and, jumping up and grabbing it, hauled on it with all his weight.

A mammoth door rose in the base of the tower, dripping riverweed as the *Bird* passed through the opening. When it was entirely inside the tower, the door dropped behind it with a thunderous crash. Eliss looked around. Wolkin huddled against her, not quite clinging. The *Bird of the River*, appearing small as a toy, sat at the bottom of a gigantic well whose upper end soared unimaginably far up into a little circle of sky. As she stared, horrified, Eliss heard another crash that echoed from the wet walls. The *Bird of the River* began to rise, like a float inside a water clock. Eliss found herself clutching Wolkin's hand.

"It's all right," he said, trying to sound nonchalant. "Now we go up the chimney! But nobody ever gets killed."

"I'm glad," she said shakily. The great well filled and they kept rising on its surface. The circle of sky at the top grew wider and wider. Eliss was sure they would emerge from the top and spill over, to fall thousands of feet to the river below. She mastered her terror and sat still, telling herself nothing bad would happen.

And nothing did. Some ten feet from the top, the well was open on one side, connecting to a waterway like the widest aqueduct in the world. There were even a pair of footbridges on either side. Quite calmly, the polemen stepped out onto them and began to push the *Bird of the River* along the aqueduct. And, after all, they hadn't far to go; for opening out beyond it was the great basin of a lake.

"Set sail!" cried Mr. Riveter. Eliss couldn't imagine how the top-men dared to scramble up so high, in such a precarious place, but they did. The sail opened out, was secured, and filled at once with a gentle breeze. The polemen jumped aboard hastily. The *Bird of the River* moved out upon the surface of the lake, serene and untroubled. Eliss heard a whistling whoosh beside her; Wolkin, who had been holding his breath, had just let it go.

"See?" he said. "We didn't fall off."

"SHOULD I GO ALOFT AGAIN, SIR?" Eliss asked Mr. Riveter as he paced along the starboard deck.

"No! No need here," he said. "This is the Lake! Strictly speaking, this is the Agatine House Memorial Lake Sacred to the Gracious Memory of Brandax Fifth of That Name."

Captain Glass, at the tiller, made a rude noise.

"We generally just call it the Lake," added Mr. Riveter. "But the Agatines did build the Lock, I'll say that for them. And the dam that made the Lake deeper. Used to be this was just a little lake spilling over in a waterfall. Used to be they had to haul the old *Bird* out on rollers and drag her up a portage road until they got above the falls. It must have been hell!"

"But the white water was beautiful," murmured Captain Glass. Mr. Riveter pursed his lips. Eliss, looking about, thought the Lake was beautiful now. It was a fathomless clear blue. Far off on one shore a town rose, all white arches and red roofs, like so many little castles on the green hills.

"Are we going there?" Eliss pointed at it.

"There? No! They don't want to see *us* there. That's Prayna-of-

the-Agatines. A private town. We're going to Moonport, over there."
Mr. Riveter pointed to the opposite shore. Eliss looked and saw big
stone warehouses and docks, with many boats and cargo barges
moored. It looked busy and crowded. People had already come out
on the decks to stare at the *Bird of the River*, and as she approached
some fetched out great curved brass horns and sounded greetings to
her. In return the *Bird*'s musicians assembled on the aft deck in their
full strength and played a ceremonial march.

The music made Eliss's heart dance. She looked around for Alder,
wanting to see if he was as happy as she was. He was sitting in the
bows with Mr. Moss, who was pointing to the town and, apparently,
telling him all about it. She sighed. Krelan emerged from the galley
deckhouse, staring around, as the lake breeze ruffled his hair. He
spotted Eliss.

"I've been given the afternoon off, would you believe it?" he announced to Eliss. To Mr. Riveter he said, "Good day, sir. I trust you're
well?"

"Yes, thank you," Mr. Riveter replied, a little nonplussed by his
formality. Krelan came to the rail by Eliss and leaned there, gazing
out.

"Gods below! Look at this blue water! You're not needed up the
mast either, I see," he said to Eliss.

Eliss shook her head. "No snags to spot," said Mr. Riveter. "Not
until we go out the other side and on upriver."

"How very nice," said Krelan. "May I use the tent, Eliss? I'd like to
change my clothes."

"Go ahead," said Eliss. Krelan walked forward to the tent and disappeared inside. Mr. Riveter leaned down to speak beside her ear.

"If he's, er, infringing on your privacy, I can always tell him to
keep his bag in our cabin," he said.

"Oh, no," said Eliss. "It's no trouble."

"As long as you're sure."

AS SOON AS the *Bird of the River* docked, it seemed the party began; not the big dance proper, but a certain air of holiday everywhere. The *Bird*'s crew were putting on their good clothes and going ashore, or crossing over to the other barges and greeting members of their crews like long-lost family. There were freighters loaded with coal, ore, quarried stone, or grain, but all of them were sprucing up their decks and hanging up strings of brightly colored pennants. Eliss, who at least had a clean change of clothes, went into the tent to put them on. As she was ready to emerge, Alder stuck his head in the tent.

"There you are! Mr. Moss is taking me ashore to meet some other Yendri but he told me to tell you I was going."

"Oh." Eliss scrambled out of the tent, hastily tying back her hair. "Where ashore? How long will you be gone?"

"I don't know!" said Alder. "I'm going now, all right?"

"All right! You don't have to be so impatient," snapped Eliss, but Alder was already gone. She watched him running to Mr. Moss, who spoke to him questioningly before they turned and went down the gangplank together. She stood there alone a moment as they walked away across the docks.

"Eliss?" Tulu tugged at her hand. "Mama wants to know: would you like to come shopping with us?"

Eliss turned and saw Mrs. Riveter watching her, beside Wolkin who was dancing with impatience, an outsized market basket in either hand. "Come on," said Tulu, and took her hand and led her to them.

"Come *on*!" said Wolkin. "All the good bargains will be gone!"

"You don't even know what a good bargain is," said Tulu.

"Yes I do! It's ten carrots for a copper bit!"

"You just want to buy jelly."

"No I don't!" Wolkin dropped both baskets and put his fists up.

"If you hit your sister you aren't going anywhere. Tulu, stop teasing him or you're not going anywhere either," said Mrs. Riveter calmly, drawing a shawl over her hair. Eliss picked up one of their baskets and they all went down the gangplank together.

THERE WERE NO GRAND HOUSES in Moonport; not even a central square with a fountain. There were rows of stone commodity warehouses, a guards' barracks, a forge, a restaurant, and a tavern. The tavern was called the Green Girl. Its painted sign depicted a Yendri woman, dressed like the ones Eliss had seen working in the orchards, but with a rather more welcoming expression and no gardening tools in her hands. This shocked Eliss a little. It was nothing to her surprise, however, when she came to the market.

Every city marketplace she had ever seen had been made up of shops selling out of the lower floors of stone houses, and an occasional handcart. In Moonport, the market was a row of stalls along the edge of a creek. The stalls were made of cut willow poles driven into the earth and lashed together. The older ones had taken root and sprouted green leaves. The shopkeepers were all Yendri men. The market might look like part of the wildwood, but it was thronged with folk of both races, buying and selling.

Eliss saw people from the river barges eagerly looking over wicker baskets full of fruit and vegetables. Some stalls were selling woven cloth, dyed in beautiful blues and purples and peacock greens. One Yendri was offering freshwater pearls for sale. Another was selling perfumes and essences in tiny cut-crystal vials. Several stalls sold honey and preserves, lined up to catch the light so they glowed red or gold. Eliss wondered where Yendri would get glass until she saw a glassblower of her own people trundling up crates of jars and bottles in a cart, and greeting a Yendri merchant cheerily before they got down to trading.

No one was staring, no one was muttering darkly. The Yendri were blank-faced and polite and the Children of the Sun were boisterous, but all of them were there to do business in good temper.

Eliss remembered cities where no Yendri would have been permitted to sell food, on the assumption that a Yendri would naturally try to poison people. Eliss remembered all the places her family had been asked to leave, once someone caught sight of the color of Alder's skin. And yet here—

And then *there* was Alder, standing with Mr. Moss before a booth festooned with beeswax candles. Alder was saying something in a breathless tone of voice to the Yendri man who kept the booth. The Yendri man smiled at him and leaned over the counter to shake his hand. He shook Mr. Moss's hand too and they laughed and spoke together. Someone said something funny and Mr. Moss's dark features creased in a grin. Eliss had never seen Yendri smiling before, except for Alder, when he'd been younger; recently he had become as stolidly blank-faced as an animal most of the time, and she had assumed it was because all Yendri were that way.

But they weren't, were they? They must only smile and laugh when they were around people with whom they felt comfortable. When had Alder stopped feeling comfortable around her?

Eliss dragged her gaze away from the candle booth, so angry she felt a lump in her throat. Wolkin and Tulu were deliberating before a stall that sold sweetmeats, including fantastic flowers of pulled sugar, and Tulu turned and caught her hand.

"Eliss, what should I get? Should I get a sugar rose or a sugar lily?"

"Don't get those! They just break into nothing in your mouth and then they're all gone," said Wolkin.

"Only if you crunch them up like a greedy pig," said Tulu.

"Get the cherry eggs. They're the best."

"No, because then you'll come and eat mine when yours are all gone."

"No I won't."

"Yes you will!"

"Stop fighting," said Mrs. Riveter, but distractedly, because she had spotted Mr. Riveter making his way through the marketplace with a great glass jar of something colorless in his arms. She leaned out and put a hand on his shoulder.

"Rattleman, that's *Yendri brandy!*"

"I know," said Mr. Riveter, looking a little desperate. "What am I supposed to do? Captain's orders. 'Get me as much plum brandy as this will buy,' he says to me, and gives me a fistful of gold. Nobody will ever say Rattleman Riveter didn't follow orders."

"But he'll kill himself if he drinks all that! You know he will."

"You haven't seen him drink the things I've seen him drink," said Mr. Riveter. "He'll weather it. Really. He went through a barrel of whiskey at Synpelene and his eyes didn't even turn red."

Mrs. Riveter just shook her head. Mr. Riveter hurried away through the crowd.

Tulu had by this time made up her mind to get a sugar lily. "What will you get?" she asked Eliss.

"Oh, I don't have any money," said Eliss.

"Mama, will you give Eliss some money so she can buy candy?"

"No!" Eliss was mortified. Mrs. Riveter, who had been watching Mr. Riveter struggle away, turned around.

"Tulu, mind your manners."

"It's only like a half of a copper bit," protested Tulu.

"Please, no," said Eliss.

"She'll have plenty of money of her own when we get paid," said Mrs. Riveter.

"Paid?" Today was just one shock after another.

"Didn't you know you'd be paid? You've been working every day," Mrs. Riveter said.

"I thought only the divers got paid!"

"*We* get paid for every snag we bring up, as contractors. You're earning a regular salary, though, as the masthead spotter. Nobody explained this to you? The crew gets paid at the end of every run, when we get back down to the coast."

"Oh." Eliss was dazzled.

"So you can *loan* her enough to buy candy, and she can pay you back with interest," persisted Tulu.

"Don't do it!" Wolkin said. "Tulu charges terrible interest."

"Don't borrow from me, then," said Tulu serenely.

In the end Mrs. Riveter loaned Eliss enough to buy a sugar rose, interest-free. Wolkin, on the other hand, borrowed from Tulu at an exorbitant rate and purchased a blue and green shawl woven of silk, which he gallantly presented to Eliss. "So you can look more beautiful at the dance party tomorrow night and maybe get a boyfriend who isn't so weasely looking," he told her in a hoarse whisper. Fortunately Mrs. Riveter, who was buying herbs from a Yendri apothecary, did not hear him.

THAT NIGHT, AS ELISS SAT UP waiting for Alder to come back, the musicians came stumbling aboard. Apparently one of the other things the Yendri grew was pinkweed.

"The absolute and total best," said Salpin, swaying slightly as he stood before her tent. "Green Valley Rose. You commune with your ancestors. I mean it. Old Threstin Cloud Fern is the only Yendri with a stone shop like ours. Want to know why? He used to keep his bundles of drying weed in one of their little shacks and then one night a lamp got tipped over or something and the whole place caught fire. People tried to put it out with buckets, but everybody who got too close just fell over and had lovely dreams. They say even the deer and the rabbits went wandering around in the woods walking into trees and giggling for days afterward. In fact, I'm going to fix up a pipeful right now, would you like to partake?"

"No, thank you," said Eliss.

"Oh, well, more for me. But there was something I was going to ask. You. I know there was. Think, Salpin! Oh! I have it now. You are coming to the dance tomorrow, right? I mean, I suppose you'll have to, because the whole deck gets cleared for dancing and all the tents get struck for the night. Hmm, where will you sleep? We can always fix up a place for you in the windmill." He waggled his eyebrows at her suggestively.

"No, but thank you," said Eliss.

"Don't mention it. Did I miss the point again? I think I must have. Please be sure to attend the dance tomorrow night, eh? At least to listen to the music. Promise me?"

"I promise," said Eliss.

"Thank you. Was that it? Yes, I think, no, I'm *certain* that was it. And off I go to commune. Good night, fair duchess." Salpin went weaving away across the deck. Eliss watched him go, smiling. When she turned back Alder was standing there, staring after Salpin.

"What did he want?"

"I think he wanted to be sure I'll be at the party tomorrow night," said Eliss. "And he offered to share his pinkweed with me."

"But you told him 'No thank you,' didn't you?"

"Of course I did." Eliss felt her smile fading away. "What did you think I'd say? And where's your Mr. Moss?"

"He's sitting up talking with Mr. Nightvine, but he told me I had to go home because you'd be worried if I didn't."

"Well, he was right! You're only ten! I'm supposed to look after you!"

"I'm safe with *my people*," said Alder. "I've never felt so safe in my life. They're all like me! Did you know Mama could have found my father any time?"

"I know now," said Eliss. "But I don't think Mama ever knew."

"She was probably too—"

"Don't! Don't you say that!" Eliss clenched her fists. "She never did that back then! She didn't even start drinking until you were three! If Uncle Steelplate hadn't—" Her voice choked off in her throat. Abashed, Alder shrugged and shuffled his feet. After a moment he sat down.

"It's just that it would have been a lot easier if I could have grown up with the Yendri. Don't you think? It would have been easier for you too. If it had been just you and Mama, you wouldn't have been thrown out of all those places we tried to live. A-and I'd know who my father was."

"But you and I would be strangers," said Eliss. Alder studied the deck and finally shrugged again.

"It was wonderful today," he said in a faraway voice. "Everybody talking to Yendri just as though they were people too. There's one old man, Mr. Yellow Broom, and he makes musical instruments— pipes and harps and even a fiddle. And the musicians from our boat were buying things from him. And they were telling each other how great he is, that he's just a master craftsman. Everybody up this end of the river knows about Mr. Yellow Broom, they said. And I got to meet him. He said I had good manners, considering I'd been raised by—by other people."

"Mama taught us good manners," said Eliss.

"The Yendri are *good*," said Alder. "They aren't sneaky, or poisoners, or, or anything. Do you know what I found out? They—we— used to live in this valley far away, a long time ago, and then some bad people came—but it wasn't the Children of the Sun—and conquered them, but Mr. Moss said then this holy man came, a *real* holy man who could do all this magic to help them. And then there was this other holy man who got turned into this bird? And he flew into the spirit world and brought back this magic child who made all the bad people let them escape? And it was only a little girl, and she was only a baby at the time!"

He was speaking rapidly, almost as if to himself, eyes wide.

"We have legends too," said Eliss.

"But these aren't just legends," said Alder. "They're *real*."

"Well, so are ours."

"If you say so," murmured Alder, not meeting her eyes.

EARLY NEXT MORNING HE WENT ashore again with Mr. Moss. Eliss, to show that she didn't care, threw herself into helping with the preparations for the Summer Party, and actually forgot about

Alder for a while. As the men moved the trimmed snags down into the hold, the women drew up buckets of water and sluiced down the broad expanse of the deck. The children—and Eliss—moved across with push brooms, scrubbing the bare planks until they were clean and smooth. Then a crate was brought up from belowdecks and opened, revealing dozens of blown glass oil lanterns, in all shapes and colors.

"Where's the blue fish?" fretted Tulu as Mr. Riveter dug through the box.

"There's mine!" Wolkin reached in and pulled out an amber demon-head. The other children crowded around, picking out green stars or fat red birds or purple seashells. The topmen strung lines out along the rail and hung up the lamps. As they were so engaged, the happy air was disturbed by Mr. Pitspike storming up the companion-way from below.

"Stone!" he roared, and glared around. "Where's the wretched boy? There's coal needs to be fetched up, and the baking ovens to be lit!"

To Eliss's mortification, everyone turned and stared at her. "I don't know where he is," she said. "The last time I saw him was yesterday. He changed his clothes in my tent."

"He went ashore," said Mr. Riveter, turning to Mr. Pitspike. "I saw him hiring a boatman to take him over to Prayna, across the lake. That was yesterday afternoon. He isn't back yet?"

"No, the slacker," said Mr. Pitspike. "So he's gone over to visit some of his lah-di-dah friends in their palaces, has he? When I only gave him the afternoon off? So much the worse for him! *Triple* potscrub duty when he gets back." Rubbing his hands together, he went into the deckhouse. Somehow the coal was fetched and the ovens were lit, and good smells came wafting from the galley as people baked goods for the party. Wolkin and Tulu stationed themselves on the roof above the galley skylight, watching avidly as the sweets were prepared.

Eliss carried the folded-up tent and her bundles below to the Riveters' cabin, where she had been invited to spend the night. She found herself wondering where Krelan was, and when he'd be back. She blushed, annoyed, when she realized what she was doing. She went back up on deck and looked across at Prayna-of-the-Agatines, with its palaces, its beautiful white walls and red roofs.

Places like that are as far away as the Moon, for people like me, thought Eliss. *And, really, they're pretty, but who'd want to live there? Always fighting to keep your place. Always looking over your shoulder to see who's coming after you with a dagger.* She thought about the dead boy tangled in the snag, and shuddered.

THE MUSICIANS DID NOT STIR until long after noon, when Salpin and a few of the others, red-eyed and shaky, came creeping out to beg strong hot tea in the galley. Krelan had still not returned and so Mr. Pitspike was in an even fouler mood, but some of the women had pity and made tea for them.

So they were all alive and tuning up on the aft deck when the guest musicians began to arrive from the other barges and the shore. There was a tattooed fiddler, a black-whiskered man with a hurdy-gurdy, and a stout man with a bass fiddle that he wheeled ahead of him on a little cart. There were four bright-haired girls with fiddles and flutes, and a pair of brothers with their boxhorns slung across their shoulders in velvet bags. And Yendri came too bearing drums and pipes, and one great harp that had to be carried by two young men while the old harpist followed, carrying his cushion under his arm. Eliss tried not to stare, since obviously everyone else was well accustomed to the Yendri visiting here.

Wolkin popped up at her elbow, chewing something. "See that old greenie with the harp? He's famous. His name is Yellow Broom. He talked to me, once."

"You shouldn't call them greenies," said Eliss automatically.

"I know. But these are *our* greenies. We see them all the time," said Wolkin.

"What did he say to you?"

"He told me to stop touching his harp," Wolkin replied proudly. "Did you see it up close? It's beautiful. Lots of curly carving and musselshell pictures on it."

"I haven't been close enough," said Eliss. "Why is it all right for them to sell us things and . . . come to our parties up here, when nobody would think of it downriver and along the coast?"

"I don't know," said Wolkin. "That's just the way it is. So, is Alder going to go live with them now? I wish I could."

"No, he isn't!" Eliss was startled at how angry the question made her. "He's just learning things about his—about his father's people, that's all. It's good for him."

Wolkin took a step back, startled too. He reached out and took her hand. "Don't be sad," he said. "You want to come have some cake? They're putting the food out now."

THE SUNLIGHT GLOWED IN THE WEST a while, making the lake a broad sheet of untroubled fire. As the glow faded, the lake reflected the first star, and then many stars, and finally the slow moon when it came shining over the eastern mountains. One by one, the colored lamps were lit aboard the *Bird of the River*. People milled about, helping themselves to food and greeting guests from the other barges. Plates of food and pitchers of beer were sent up to the musicians.

Finishing a long drink of beer, the tattooed fiddler took up his instrument, set it in the crook of his neck, and took a few experimental swipes with his bow. Satisfied that his fiddle was in good order, he began to play one of the wandering, circular dance tunes Eliss heard every day from the masthead. The bass fiddler set down the dish from which he had been eating plumcake, and began to plunk out an accompaniment. One of the boxhorns took up the melody line. Salpin joined him on the concertina. The old Yendri with the harp seated himself and moved his fingers over its strings, adding notes like a soft-voiced singer.

As though they had been waiting for him to go first, the other Yendri joined in, with drone-pipe and drums. People on the deck stopped talking, and began to sway with the music. Then the bright-haired girls joined in with their fiddles and flutes and it was as though smoldering coals had burst into flame: the music soared, couples reached for each other and swung out on the dance floor, moving round and round in the lamplight. The moon rose higher. Moonflies began to wake up in the trees, tiny winking lights like white stars among the oak leaves.

Eliss, swaying where she sat, looked up in surprise as Alder sat down next to her.

"Where's your Mr. Moss?" she asked, raising her voice over the music. Alder pointed to the rail, where Mr. Moss stood watching the musicians with evident enjoyment.

"He says I'm leaving you all by yourself too much," said Alder glumly. "He says you're my family too."

"Well, *thank* you, Mr. Moss," said Eliss, but the music and the night were so beautiful she didn't want to waste time being angry.

"You got here!" Wolkin sat down on the other side of Eliss and leaned around her to peer at Alder. "Has he been teaching you stuff?"

"All kinds of stuff," said Alder, grinning. "There *are* defense moves."

"Thank you, gods!" Wolkin threw up his arms. "You have to show me tomorrow!"

"And that's not all. Some of them fight, only Mr. Moss doesn't because he's a disciple of the Mother, but there are these men who . . ."

Eliss ignored them and watched the dancers. It was a slow dance, romantic. Mr. and Mrs. Riveter circled by, his hands on her hips, her hands on his shoulders. There too went Mr. and Mrs. Crucible, and Mr. and Mrs. Nailsmith, and some of the polemen and their wives—Eliss still hadn't learned all their names—and then, as Eliss watched, a Yendri man walked up to Pentra Smith where she idled at the table, and touched her shoulder. She turned, smiling, and they embraced. She led him out on the dance floor.

Eliss was too surprised to make a sound. Alder, however, grunted in astonishment. He pointed. "They're *dancing!*" Wolkin, who was busily eating from a dish of jelly, looked up briefly.

"Oh! Them. They're sweethearts or something. See, she does what she likes because she's the cartographer? And that's really important? So nobody says anything? And anyway they see each other twice every run. So everybody's used to it. And he's a nice gr— Yendri. And *anyway* they *have* to dance together because, well, do you see any Yendri ladies here? You don't. And the reason that is, is because their ladies go around with their—" Wolkin looked around to see where his parents were. He lowered his voice. "With their *boobies bare*. So they can't come around any of our men. Because our men would go crazy if they saw them."

"That's what Mr. Moss said too," said Alder, eyes wide. "Only he said it different."

"They couldn't help themselves." Wolkin nodded solemnly. "No man could. That's what I heard. And they have to protect their women."

Eliss, staring at the graceful couple, thought only: *All those years we were hounded from one place to another, all those people who spat on Mama for what she'd done . . . and up here no one even cares. How unfair.*

In time the slow music wound to its close. More beer was handed up to the musicians, and some of them lit pipes filled with pinkweed and passed them around. People milled about, ate and drank, and then a men's dance tune was struck up, quick-paced. The men formed lines, shuffled and stamped, flexed their muscles and strutted. Women catcalled from the sidelines. The drums thundered, the bass fiddle boomed, the whistles shrilled a raucous melody. Someone passed the men barge-poles and they struck the deck with them in unison, paired off in mock battles, wove in and out in figures, marched like a phalanx of spearmen.

Next a women's dance was played, sinuous fiddles with a throbbing bass line. The divers lined up and went through the movements of the Diver's Round, scarcely moving their feet. Their shoulders, their hips, their arms and graceful hands wove and described circles in the warm air. It was bawdy and at the same time delicate as water ferns, lewd and tender all together. On either side of Eliss, Alder and Wolkin fell silent, staring.

There were some songs after that, tunes everyone knew and could follow in the chorus. Salpin stood and demonstrated that he had a rich voice, as well as one that carried.

> *"Little girl among the nets, mending your father's nets,*
> *By the wall where the sea pinks bloom*
> *You have caught me in your nets, my heart among the nets*
> *By the wall where the sea pinks bloom.*

> *"But your father watches you, so sharp he watches you*
> *By the wall where the sea pinks bloom*
> *That I cannot speak to you, I cannot come to you*
> *By the wall where the sea pinks bloom.*

> *"Little lizard, go to her father, tell him his boat is on fire*
> *Little gull, fly to him, tell him his house is on fire*
> *Little crab, crawl to him, tell him the tavern's on fire*
> *Little girl, have pity on me! My heart is on fire*
> *By the wall where the sea pinks bloom."*

There was laughter and applause afterward. Salpin smiled and held up his hands.

"Thank you! Thank you. Now. It's become a tradition to present a new song every year. Last year my esteemed Yendri colleague Windwillow honored us with *The Lady and the Demon*. This year the silver plectrum has passed to me. Here is my offering. This is *The Ballad of Falena*."

He looked straight at Eliss and smiled. Then he seated himself, took up his concertina and began to play the melody he had composed, that day weeks ago on the mast platform. Eliss sat motionless, stunned. She looked at Alder, but he had been whispering with Wolkin and hadn't heard Salpin's introduction.

One by one the other musicians joined in, even the Yendri, who listened intently and began to improvise grace notes and harmonies. The music swelled, became something as exquisite as a tapestry. Down on deck people stopped chatting by the table full of treats and turned to listen, their mouths open.

Salpin began to sing. There was a beautiful girl named Falena, he told them, a child of the sea, and no mermaid was ever more beautiful. Her fair body cut through the green depths, bringing up pearls, bringing up rare shells and lost treasures, but no treasure was so fair as she herself was. He sang about a storm on the sea, that drove a ship onto the rocks while everyone on shore lamented and wrung their hands. But Falena had not feared the storm; she'd swum out to the wreck and seen a handsome sailor in the arms of the Sea Queen, struggling even as she drowned him.

In the next verse, as the melody shifted into major key, Salpin told how Falena had caught the sailor in her strong arms and pulled him up to the surface. She and the sailor had looked into each other's eyes and known they were true lovers in that moment, as they clung together. The Sea Queen sank down, but sent her curse after Falena: *All men are faithless, once I hold them in my arms! He will come down to me again.* But Falena and her lover had felt the sand under their feet, and came safe ashore.

The next verse followed a long run of harp notes, and then the story went on: Falena and her true love had lived together in a house on the shore, happy, and had soon had a little daughter. But the sailor felt the pull of the sea, explained Salpin, and so he signed on to a crew. He promised Falena to return with a silver comb for her hair; he promised that after this one voyage he would take her inland and settle down, in a place where the yellow wheat grew to the horizon. Six months went by, and Falena walked the white sea strand with her child in her arms, asking of every stranger whether he had seen her true love's ship.

Dark and ominous chords now, and back into minor key: a stranger in a boat-cloak told Falena she need not wear out her shoes anymore on the white sea strand. *His ship was wrecked, I saw your sailor sinking down; the Sea Queen took him to her bed, in her palace under the green water.* Falena wandered the world with her child then, from harbor town to harbor town, and in each place she'd dive down into the Sea Queen's country to search for her true love. But every time she came back up to the land, she left a little more of her soul under the green water, and a little more of her strength. The years went by and at last there was only a shadow of beautiful Falena walking in the world of the living.

Oh, how beautifully the music swelled now. Salpin lowered his voice, leaned forward to sing: Falena lost herself in the inland, in the places where the yellow wheat grew to the horizon, and begged there for her bread. She was far from the Sea Queen's curse, but the greenwood couldn't comfort her; the stones of the earth wore out her shoes. One day she came upon a river, and threw herself into the green water. At last, Salpin sang, at last the water was kind to her again, the Sea Queen relented of her cruelty and unsaid her curse; for Falena's true love met her there, and carried her away under the water. Their souls walked away together under arches of waving water-plants, into a garden of unfading lilies, and there they remain beyond the reach of all sorrow.

People were weeping when the music droned to its close. Eliss sat there, uncertain what she ought to feel. She looked over at Alder and saw him watching her, blank-faced. It was the most beautiful song she had ever heard and it was all in honor of her mother, but . . . *it wasn't true.* It left out all the bitter ugly parts of Falena's life. It was all about a brave and strong Falena, who had loved one man so deeply she had been faithful beyond death. Eliss's real mother had loved a dozen men.

But people were weeping. People were applauding. The other musicians were crowding around Salpin, asking him to write down the words, asking him to show them the chords. Even the Yendri were asking him. A strange excitement hung in the air, and Eliss somehow couldn't share it. All she felt was embarrassment.

"Are you all right, Eliss?"

She looked up and saw Mrs. Riveter kneeling down beside her. Eliss nodded and tried to say she was fine. To her horror, she burst into tears. Mrs. Riveter put her arms around her and held her as she wept. It was a relief, in a way, to let everyone think she was crying for the beauty of the song.

SALPIN WAS SO MOBBED by other musicians busily noting down chords that it was awhile before the music started again. The musicians played a courting dance, slow and passionate, and now the deck was crowded by couples embracing, circling around and around. Pentra Smith and her lover joined the throng. They held each other tenderly. Pentra's face was wet with tears. Eliss watched them in numb wonder, to think that Falena's hard life could inspire so much romance.

When the dance ended, the musicians struck up a quick merry tune. The young men on deck jumped forward, formed a line and stamped to the beat. People clapped in time. The boxhorns blared, the drums thundered. And then—

There came a happy roar from the companionway. All heads turned to watch as Captain Glass hauled himself up on deck. His stare was fixed and glittering. He stood there swaying, his jar of brandy under one arm. The other dancers backed away from him. Wolkin gave a whoop of laughter, quickly stifling it with both hands.

"Captain's *really* drunk now!" he said.

The music fell silent, in an uncertain discord. After a moment the captain noticed and turned his head to peer up at the afterdeck.

"What'd you stop for?" he bellowed. "I want my music! Play my music! G'wan!"

Drogin cleared his throat. "Which tune, Captain?"

"Give me a tune I can dance to!" The captain had a drink. "Like this!

Dah dah da-dada DAH!" He slammed the deck with his heel. The musicians looked at one another and struck up a tune, approximating as closely as they might what the captain's bawling had suggested. Drogin put his boxhorn up and began to improvise. The fiddlers joined in. It was a wild and reckless melody, ungraceful, but Captain Glass grinned wide.

"That's the way!" He began shifting his big body from foot to foot, and for a man of his size he was weirdly light on his feet. He kicked out and bounded forward. The deck boomed when he landed. Weaving from side to side, he held out his brandy jar and began to dance with it. He circled it, he tossed it in the air and caught it, he juggled it from hand to hand and balanced it on his head. He crouched, he twisted, he leaped back. The jar became prey he was stalking, a lover he was cajoling, a child he was rocking in his arms. He drank from it with relish, even as his feet pounded out rhythms underneath him, and never spilled a drop. Sweat gleamed on his body in the lamplight. So huge and savage was his merriment, Eliss didn't know whether to laugh or cower in terror. She rubbed her eyes and stared. Was the brandy jar levitating? Was it floating in the air, or was Captain Glass actually making it dance and hover by some trick of his fingertips, to partner him in his dance?

The Yendri began to drum for him. Captain Glass threw back his head and shouted in incoherent delight. He snapped his jaws. His muscles rippled, his gigantic legs blurred with movement. Eliss felt the *Bird of the River* trembling like a living thing. People had come to the shore of the lake, and out on the decks of the other barges, to stare.

The music reached a crescendo. Captain Glass threw the jar into the air. It rotated, too fast at first for anything to come out, but as it descended it seemed to hang in the air, bottom-up, and a stream of brandy rained down. Captain Glass managed to be in exactly the right spot to catch the brandy in his open mouth as the drums crashed. He batted the empty jar away like a leaf. It flew out over the rail and smashed on the prow of the next barge over.

The music stopped. Captain Glass's eyes rolled back in his head. He flung out his arms and staggered briefly before falling to the deck with a crash. He lay there on his back, motionless.

It seemed that everyone had been holding their breath until that moment, for the mass-exhaled gust fluttered in the captain's beard. Mr. Riveter ran out and waved his arms.

"Polemen! Make a stretcher! Captain goes down to his bunk!"

As he was shouting orders, Mr. Moss came up and knelt beside the captain. He felt for his pulse and frowned. He rose and spoke quietly to Mr. Riveter, but Eliss was sitting close enough to hear.

"I am afraid your captain has died."

"What?" Mr. Riveter turned and looked over one shoulder at him. "Oh. No, he's all right. He's done this before."

"But he has no pulse."

"No, he never seems to, when he gets this drunk. Don't worry! He'll sleep for a day and a night and then he'll be fine."

Mr. Moss drew back, profoundly dubious, and watched as Captain Glass was loaded onto a makeshift stretcher and hauled down the companionway by eight men. Meanwhile the musicians, who were a little unnerved, called for more beer and pinkweed, and spent several minutes restoring a state of calm before beginning another tune.

The moon traveled across the sky. After a while some of the women carried sleepy children belowdecks—Tulu was sound asleep with her head on Mrs. Riveter's shoulder as they vanished down the companionway, and beside Eliss, Wolkin kept nodding off and then sitting upright with a jerk. When Mrs. Riveter came to fetch him, he gave only a token protest before allowing himself to be led below. The musicians began to play slower, softer tunes, and the intervals between the dances grew longer as people smoked or went down to the table to eat. Alder began to yawn.

"Where are we sleeping tonight?"

"In the Riveters' cabin. They have room on the floor."

"Oh." Alder rubbed his eyes. "Mr. Moss says Yendri trevanion—that's, like, holy men and ladies—can sleep standing up if they want."

"So go sleep by the mast, then."

"*I* can't." Alder looked hurt. "You have to study for years and years before you can do that trick. I think. Why are you so angry?"

"I'm not angry," said Eliss. "Or maybe I am. I don't know. What did you think of that song about Mama?"

"It was pretty," Alder said cautiously.

"Yes, it was, but . . . why make her life like some kind of fairy tale?"

"It would have been nicer if it was. I think the song would have made her happy."

"But it was all made up. She never loved anybody that much. She was an addict. Why didn't he sing about the mean way people treated her, wherever we went?"

"Because she didn't have a Yendri baby, in the song. I was left out of the story," said Alder in a quiet voice. "Didn't you notice? And anyway, who wants to sing about things like that? The song is sad enough. Mama's dead. Let people think her song is true. It's a nicer way to remember her."

"But I *don't* remember her that way—" Eliss was saying, when someone standing at the rail said loudly:

"What's that in the water?"

"That's a rat, swimming," said someone else.

"No, it isn't! That's too big to be a rat!"

They turned to look, but couldn't see anything because everyone else was going to the rail to stare.

"Is that a man, swimming?"

"Who would be swimming across the lake in the middle of the night?"

"It's an animal, then."

"Well, it's swimming like a man!"

"You're crazy."

"You're blind!"

"Hello there," called a voice from out on the lake. "I trust I haven't missed the party entirely?"

Eliss scrambled to her feet and ran to the rail, pushing her way between Mr. Riveter and Mr. Nailsmith. "That's Krelan," she said.

"That's the little aristocrat," muttered Mr. Nailsmith to the man standing next to him. "Been to a party over at the Agatines', I'll bet. Just the sort of thing they do. Get a few bottles of fine wine in them and they'll start laying wagers about climbing civic buildings or stealing public statues or I don't know what all."

"Probably thought it would be funny to swim home."

"Lucky he hasn't drowned, the fool."

Everyone watched as Krelan swam up to the side of the *Bird*. He was pale in the moonlight, for his tunic was gone. He reached up to the rail and took hold, gasping.

"I don't suppose someone would help me aboard?" he inquired casually, but his hands were trembling, and then they saw the gash across his ribs.

TEN MINUTES LATER HE WAS WRAPPED in blankets and sitting huddled in the galley, as Mr. Pitspike mulled a saucepan of spiced wine. Eliss hurried in with his bag, which she had fetched from the Riveters' cabin, and Mr. Riveter followed her closely.

"Were you in a duel?" he blurted as he spotted Krelan. "And is anybody over there likely to know where you went? Would they follow you here?"

"It wasn't a duel," Krelan assured him, through chattering teeth. "I think it was a case of mistaken identity. And no, nobody will follow me here, I'm fairly certain. They think they killed me."

"How do you know?"

"I heard them."

"But what happened?" asked Eliss, opening his bag to find him dry clothes. He reached out, took the bag, and rummaged in it himself. It was a moment before he replied.

"It's quite strange, really. I went across to see an old family retainer. He used to attend upon my great-aunt, you see. She married one of the Agatines and I used to spend my summers here, when I was a child. He was very fond of me, and so I thought I'd pay him a call.

"I never managed to see him, as it happens. I stopped in at the tavern over there and had dinner first—it's so ill-bred to show up for a visit at mealtimes, especially since I didn't know whether he was living on limited means these days—and it was after dark when I left the place. I was walking up a rather narrow lane on the edge of a cliff when I noticed I was being followed. Two fellows in cloaks rushed me and one caught my arms while the other pulled out this fearfully long knife.

" 'This will teach you the worth of Lady Bellanilla's honor!' he shouted, just as though it were a play. Then he stabbed me! I felt it slide off my ribs but I certainly wasn't going to tell him he'd missed anything vital, so I threw myself backward and managed to wrench myself free from the other fellow's grasp. Unfortunately I went right over the wall on the edge of the path, which was a rather low one, and down I hurtled into the lake.

"Well! I'm not the brightest fellow under the sky-god's realm, but I knew better than to come up spluttering and calling for help."

"So you've some brains, at least," said Mr. Pitspike, handing him a mug of hot wine. "Drink that, you little idiot, and stop flapping your jaws so much."

"I want to be sure we're safe," said Mr. Riveter. "Go on."

"Thank you." Krelan sipped the wine cautiously. "Ahhh. Well. I swim rather well, as you must have noticed. I dove like a cormorant and came up some distance from where I'd landed. I swam into a thicket of reeds and hid there, trying to catch my breath. My two murderers, or would-be murderers, came along the shoreline looking for me. I heard them exclaim when they found my tunic. One of them said he thought I must have drowned, but the other said they had to be sure, or his lordship—didn't mention a name, simply called him *his lordship*—would have their ears off.

"I knew I needed a better place to hide, and I was frightfully afraid of leeches, so I dove back underwater and swam as far along the shoreline as I could, until I found an old boathouse. I climbed inside and crawled under a heap of sail, desperately hoping to get warm. I fell asleep. I slept through the night and waited all through today for a chance to swim back under cover of darkness. And that's all, really."

"And you're sure you don't know who this Lady Bellanilla was?" said Mr. Riveter. Krelan smiled mournfully.

"Do I look as though I could persuade any Lady Bellanilla to part with such a precious commodity as her honor?"

"The murderers thought so," said Eliss. "Or they wouldn't have attacked you."

"Mistaken identity," Krelan assured her. "I have a few cousins amongst the Agatines. Must be a family resemblance to some erring youth or other. I count myself lucky to have got away with no more than a sliced skin and a wretched night, but I'm quite sure no further assassination attempts will be made. They must have discovered by now that their real man is still alive, after all."

"I suppose." Mr. Riveter tugged at his beard. "All the same! You were supposed to be hiding out here, not paying social calls. From now on, you'll stay on board when we put into a town."

"I see your point, sir," said Krelan, drooping. "I suppose it wouldn't make a difference if I attempted to disguise my social status? What if I grew a mustache?"

Mr. Pitspike guffawed. "Hark at him! Boy's got a head looks like a peeled egg, and he thinks he can grow a mustache!"

Even Mr. Riveter smiled. "Well, you can always try—"

"Thank you, sir! I give you my word I won't set foot ashore until I have produced facial hair," said Krelan. He drank down the rest of his hot wine. "And now, with your permission, sirs, and yours, miss, I think I'll just crawl into the corner by the stove and sleep as one dead."

HE REVIVED THE NEXT MORNING, however. So, to everyone's surprise, did Captain Glass. The captain hauled himself up the companionway, bleary-eyed, and stared around at the light of day.

"Have we loaded up provisions?" he asked Mr. Riveter, who was packing away the party lanterns, helped by Eliss.

"Provisions loaded, sir," said Mr. Riveter.

"Good." Captain Glass squinted at the lakeshore. "Time to move on. Warp her out and set sail."

THEY GLIDED AWAY OUT of the Lake and upriver. Eliss climbed to her high place at the masthead and watched the grand mansions of the Agatines as they passed them by, the fair white walls, the lofty towers. Once, in Mount Flame, she had seen a white wolf at a street exhibition. It had just been fed and lay half-dozing, looking out disdainfully at the children who stared and poked their fingers through the bars of its cage. It couldn't be bothered to leap up and snap at them, but its teeth were long and sharp, its jaws like a steel trap all the same. With a shiver, Eliss turned her face away.

KRELAN, TRUE TO HIS WORD, grew a mustache. It was a tiny line on his upper lip. When he presented himself to Mr. Riveter for inspection Mr. Riveter peered at it suspiciously, and even applied a wet rag to it to see whether it would wash off. When it didn't, he threw up his hands and said he supposed Krelan would be safe enough going ashore if he wore a hood. Krelan bought an immense old hooded tunic from one of the musicians, which made him look even spindlier and more hapless, but he wore it, and the mustache, proudly.

HERE ABOVE THE LAKE the river kept its bed year in and year out, flowing between stony banks, between cliffs, through forests of immense ancient trees. The first time Eliss spotted a snag up here, she thought at first there was some sort of monster in the water. And yet, a flash of red festooned its looming bulk—

"Red marker! Red marker at the quarter mile!" cried Eliss, leaning down. She saw Mr. Riveter run forward to peer over the bow, and, to her astonishment, he performed a little dance before bawling out the orders to draw in sail and pole forward. They crawled nearer to the downed thing and Eliss saw that it was one of the giants from the clifftops, fallen with its wide spread of roots reaching out above it. A lot of rock had come down with it too.

There was so much other debris caught in the snag that they anchored there, and spent most of two days clearing out the hazards. The snag, when finally hauled on board, was even bigger than it had looked in the water, with a trunk so huge four men couldn't reach around it. Mr. Riveter rubbed his hands gleefully.

"Look at that," he told Eliss, who had come down to stare. "How much lumber do you imagine is in that thing? Saw it into planks and you could make a second *Bird of the River!*"

"And the Yendri don't mind?" Eliss glanced over at Mr. Moss, who was pointing up to the forests above the cliffs and saying something to Alder.

"Not so long as we didn't kill it ourselves," said Mr. Riveter. He gave a nervous glance at Mr. Moss. "We'll be at one of their settlements in a day or so . . . I hope he'll let everyone know the tree was dead when we got here."

ELISS WAS THE FIRST ONE to see the Yendri settlement, two days later. At eye level with the clifftops, she began to catch sight of dark masses in the branches of the trees, that she thought at first were the nests of great birds. Before long she saw that the masses were too squared off and uniform in shape to be nests. She was just registering that they were panels made of willow-twigs woven together when the *Bird* came abreast of one, just above the cliff.

Eliss found herself gazing into a room in the branches, where a Yendri girl sat on a platform, nursing a tiny baby. The walls were partly woven screens and partly silks. Here and there, dangling on cords from branches, were various household items: dippers and water gourds, a spinning distaff, a hand loom, baskets. For a moment the girl and Eliss were looking into each other's eyes. Then the *Bird* bore them past each other.

They live in trees, thought Eliss. *No wonder they don't like it when we cut down forests.* She fell to thinking about what her life would have been like if she'd been born among the Yendri, as Alder had been born among the Children of the Sun. She might be that bare-breasted girl, already a young mother, hiding up there in her airy nest. And Alder would be happy and outgoing, and Eliss would be the outsider, the one always living on sufferance. Would she resent her life? Would she feel a yearning for walls of solid stone, and a place in her own world?

Not that I ever had one really, she thought bitterly, *or any stone walls to call my own.*

But you have a place now, said another voice in her mind, like a more grown-up Eliss. She looked down at the river and had to admit to herself that it, at least, had accepted her.

She saw now a rickety-looking dock as the *Bird* came slowly around the next bend, and now beyond it the place where the forest floor opened up. There were fewer trees here, and taller, with bare trunks and high umbrella-canopies overhead. Sunlight slanted down through the green leaves and lit the . . . warehouses? They looked like warehouses, but made of palings driven into the earth, and roofed over with thatch rather than slate. Here in the open were more of the booths made of sprouting willow. Away through the tree trunks Eliss saw patchwork fields in different shades of green. The sound of singing came from the fields, droning unearthly voices floating across the space under the trees.

Captain Glass steered for the dock, and Mr. Riveter shouted commands for taking in sail and hoisting fenders over the rails. The *Bird of the River* drew up at the Yendri settlement, and only then did

Eliss see men emerging from the warehouse or climbing down from the platforms in the trees. They were all watching Mr. Moss, who had folded up his tent and was standing at the rail. As she watched, Alder came up and began to speak earnestly to him.

Eliss scrambled down to the deck. As she neared them, Alder turned to her.

"She wouldn't mind. Really. Would you, Eliss?"

"Mind what?" Eliss stopped, staring at him. He was clutching a bundle in his arms.

"If I just went to live with the Yendri for a while," said Alder.

"What?" Eliss felt a rush of panic. "*Live* with them? With people you don't even know?"

"No, these are *my* people," said Alder.

"You're only ten!" cried Eliss. "What are you thinking?"

"Alder, it wouldn't be right," said Mr. Moss. "She is your family and you are hers. Who should she have, if you left her? A man protects the women in his family."

"But she's with her people and she's fine," said Alder, growing desperate. "And I could be your apprentice and—and I want to go be a disciple and meet the Lady!"

"The Unwearied Mother herself would bid you stay here," said Mr. Moss.

"But *that's* where I belong!" Alder's voice rose to a wail as he pointed to the settlement under the trees. Mr. Riveter, who had come up to see what was going on, cleared his throat.

"Maybe—"

"No, no, no, no!" Eliss tried to grab the bundle from Alder's arms. He held on, stubborn, and after a brief tug-of-war the bag tore open. Alder's blanket fell to the ground with something else that rattled as it struck the deck: a doll made of wooden beads that had once been bright-painted. Alder snatched it up.

"I was keeping that because it's all I have from Mama," he said defensively.

"Mama didn't give you that," said Eliss, feeling a wrenching betrayal. "I did." She remembered the market fair when she was five years old, and the booth all hung with toys, so pretty in the morning sunlight, and how she'd offered the toymaker her copper piece she'd earned for minding Alder while Mama and Uncle Paver lurked in the alley across the street all day, selling pinkweed. The toymaker had told her it wasn't enough to buy a toy, but promised she could have one of the small dolls if she hawked for his booth.

So Eliss had stood in front of the booth all day, calling to people to come buy toys. She had danced and sung with tiny bundled-up Alder in her arms, and no one had noticed he was the wrong color, and many people had smiled and bought toys. Her legs were aching by the end of the day but the toymaker had kept his word and given her the doll. Alder had slept with it pressed against his cheek every night for years.

Now, to her dismay, Eliss felt her eyes filling with tears. Mr. Moss looked at her. He shook his head at Alder.

"You are too young to leave."

"Everybody else always left when they wanted to," said Alder. "Why can't I?"

"No Yendri would desert his family," said Mr. Moss sharply. "That is not our way. When you are a man, when your sister is no longer alone, then you may think about coming to serve the Lady. Not until then."

Alder looked down, abashed. "I'm sorry."

"I too." Mr. Moss softened his tone somewhat. He picked up his bag and his cloak. "The day will come sooner than you believe. Have patience until then."

Eliss took the torn bag from Alder. He let his hands drop to his sides. "I'll mend this for you," she told him. He said nothing in reply. Two of the cablemen wrestled the gangplank into place as Mr. Moss turned to Mr. Riveter and bowed.

"Thank you for your kindness. May the Lady bless you."

"You're welcome," said Mr. Riveter, watching in some concern as a Yendri man approached the gangplank. "Er. You might explain to your friend there about the big tree and how we absolutely did not cut it down."

Mr. Moss turned to look. The Yendri stood on the bank and called out something. Mr. Moss looked startled. He strode down the gangplank and the two men spoke together in low voices for a moment. Mr. Moss set down his bag and cloak and walked back aboard.

"He sends a warning to your people," he said to Mr. Riveter. "Brigands came through the mountains two nights ago. They were going upriver. Their leader was one of your men. The one who calls himself Shellback."

Mr. Riveter went pale. "They didn't plunder here, looks like."

"We hide ourselves too well." Mr. Moss smiled grimly. "Something we learned long ago. Why do you think we live in trees?"

He went ashore. The *Bird of the River* raised anchor and put out again. Eliss returned to her place in the masthead and Alder sat by the rail, staring at the Yendri settlement as it fell behind them.

We have a place to sleep, Eliss thought, looking down at him, but she knew he wouldn't respond if he could hear her.

THEY CAME TO BLUESTONE two days later and anchored at its dock.

"It doesn't look blue to me," said Alder, looking around.

"Looks gray," agreed Wolkin.

"It's just a figure of speech," said Eliss, studying the shopping list Mrs. Riveter had given her.

"I saw some one time down at Rivermouth," said Tulu, jumping from one paving stone to the next, carefully avoiding the cracks between. "It had really blue swirled through it. Like blue glass. It was beautiful."

"That's because it was the expensive stuff they export," said a new voice behind them. They all turned and saw Krelan.

"What are you doing here?" said Alder. "You were supposed to stay on board, weren't you?"

"Ah! But now I'm incognito," said Krelan, and pulled his hood forward to shade his face. "A man of mystery."

"You still smell like kitchen grease," said Alder. Eliss and Tulu frowned at him.

"Well, that too helps disguise my aristocratic origins," said Krelan lightly. He held up a pair of copper pans. "So do these. And now, if you'll excuse me, the lowly spitboy has an errand to run. I'm off to find a coppersmith to mend my master's pots."

"He's such a liar," said Alder, as they watched him walk away.

"Oh, he is not either," said Tulu.

"Why would you say such a thing?" said Eliss, picking up the market basket and looking around for a butcher's stall.

"I'll tell you why," said Alder as they walked. "You know what he keeps in that bag of his?"

"Clothes."

"And weapons."

"Alder, they all carry weapons. Rich people have swords."

"He has throwing knives."

"No!" Wolkin ran in front and walked backward, staring at Alder. "I wonder if he'd show us how? Mr. Smith-the-poleman can throw knives. I saw him hit every point on a target once."

"How do you know he has throwing knives in his bag?" Eliss demanded.

"I looked," said Alder.

"Shame on you, going through somebody else's things!"

"Well, he keeps leaving his old bag in *our* tent. And I don't trust him. I'm supposed to protect you, aren't I?"

Eliss almost smiled at that. Alder went on: "But that isn't all. He had a painting in there. A little roundy one. And you know who it was a picture of?"

"Who?" asked Wolkin.

"Some other rich boy. With a snake armlet made of gold. Just like the one on the dead boy who killed Mama."

Eliss stopped in her tracks, staring at him. *You shouldn't have told me here,* she thought, *not in front of the other children.*

"Gods below!" said Wolkin. "You know what he must be? He must be his brother! And he's traveling upriver to find out who killed him and avenge his murder! And those knives are what he's going to avenge the murder with!"

"You're not supposed to say 'Gods below,'" said Tulu.

"Well, you just said it too."

"We shouldn't talk about this," said Eliss.

"She's right," said Tulu. "We could all be killed."

"No, we couldn't," said Wolkin, going a little pale. "I'd like to see anybody try and kill me. I know secret moves."

"A lot of good they'd do you if somebody came and set fire to the *Bird,*" said Tulu, beginning to get tearful.

"That's enough!" Eliss glared at Alder. "It's probably something perfectly innocent and we're making a lot of fuss about nothing. There's a butcher. Come on!"

AFTER THEY HAD BOUGHT SOUP bones at the butcher's, they stopped at a sweets stall and bought sugar-sticks to cheer up Tulu, who had been crying quietly for ten minutes and convinced herself that they were all going to die that very night. The sight of Krelan placidly waiting outside the coppersmith's as Mr. Pitspike's pans were mended did nothing to ease her mind. Alder, consumed by guilt, gave her his sugar-stick when she dropped hers, though Wolkin deftly scooped up the broken pieces and rinsed them off in the marketplace fountain.

"Let's go up on the city wall," said Wolkin. "Maybe there'll be some heads on pikes."

"But you threw up last time," said Alder.

"No, I was just sick from some bad fish."

"All right," said Eliss with a sigh, hoisting the market basket over her arm. "But then we have to go buy tea and salt."

The city rampart was high and so wide there was room for little stalls along the inward side, selling things like inexpensive jewelry and smoking gear, or souvenirs carved from bluestone. There were no heads displayed anywhere, at which Wolkin professed loud disappointment.

"What's that?" said Alder with a frown, pointing out over the ramparts. They all went to the edge of the wall to look.

"That's the quarry, isn't it?" Eliss shaded her eyes. It was a gray-blue gouge in the flank of the hill that rose behind the town. The cart road and all the lower cuttings were gray with dust, but the upper walls had been washed clean by rains. Veins of rock blue as the sea ran through the wall, like a gigantic spray of paint.

"Yes indeed, miss, that's our quarry," said someone at Eliss's shoulder. She turned to see a member of the city guard standing beside her. "It turned a profit of fifteen thousand crowns last year. You can see the remarkable high-quality color in the strata we haven't even needed to dig out yet."

"That's nice," said Eliss, turning back to look at the quarry.

"What will you do when it's all gone?" said Alder. "There'll be nothing but a big ugly scar on the earth." His tone was accusatory, but the guardsman just smiled at Eliss.

"Oh, we're confident the high-quality brilliant blue rock will last a minimum of another two centuries. And profits are only expected to rise, with the demand for unique decorative finishing stone in rapidly expanding communities like Salesh and Ward'b."

"Are you a tour guide?" Wolkin asked him.

"Just a public servant, little boy. Are you visiting our city for long, miss?"

Eliss pulled her shawl a little closer around her head. "Not long, no."

"It's wrong to cut holes in the earth just because you're greedy," said Alder. Eliss looked at him in astonishment, but the guardsman ignored him.

"I'd be happy to give *you* a tour of the city, miss."

"Thank you, but I'm a little busy," said Eliss.

"That's right," said Wolkin, grabbing hold of her arm possessively. "We need to go buy some more stuff."

"That's right," echoed Alder. Eliss, who was trying to look anywhere but at the guardsman, stared out at the hills beyond the quarry. Out of habit she focused tight, noting details. There were harpwood trees, there was flamebush—flamebush only grew where the soil was scanty and rocky—there, she could see the bluestone outcroppings all around, and the summer grass was yellow and tired-looking, because it always died first where stone was close to the surface . . . and then something moved behind an outcropping. Then another something moved. There was a line of movement. Someone rose on his elbows and stared toward the city for a moment, then dropped down.

"There's men!" cried Eliss. "They're crawling through the bushes out there!"

"Where?" said both Wolkin and the guard.

"Right out there!" Eliss pointed. The guard stared.

"I don't see anyone, miss."

"They're right flat to the ground—see that line of rock sticking up through the grass? Look, look!" But the movement had stopped now. The crawling men had vanished into thicker bushes, where the land sloped down into a stand of trees.

"Perhaps it was your imagination, miss," said the guard. He looked coldly at Alder. "Though I suppose it might have been some Yendri."

"It wasn't," said Eliss. "I know what they look like! It might have been bandits."

The guard glanced out at the hills once more. "If you say so, miss."

"We're *going* now," announced Alder, and he walked away and Wolkin followed him, pulling Eliss by the arm. Tulu ran after them.

"Shouldn't we tell somebody about the bandits?" she said. "Somebody who isn't stupid, I mean?"

"They were really there," said Eliss, feeling dazed.

"It's probably the bunch *my* people saw and told *your* people about," said Alder. "Going somewhere to do something else evil. But it doesn't matter about this place. Who'd want to steal a bunch of blue rock? Except for greedy quarry owners."

"When did you become so self-righteous, anyway?" asked Eliss. Alder flushed and looked down angrily.

"There's Krelan again," said Tulu, edging closer to Eliss. Eliss looked up and saw him deep in conversation with someone outside a tavern. He was holding his hand up and displaying something small, saying something in a questioning tone of voice.

"Trying to find out who killed his brother," said Wolkin with relish.

"Don't start that again," said Eliss. "Come on. There's a spice booth."

As the lady who ran the booth measured out peppercorns for Eliss, she hummed a familiar tune. It was a moment before Eliss recognized *The Ballad of Falena*.

"Where did you learn that song?" she asked, a little crossly.

"What?" The lady funneled the peppercorns into a jar and closed up its lid before handing it to Eliss. "*The Ballad of Falena*? A man from one of the coal barges was playing it yesterday. We all asked him for the words. I think it's the loveliest thing I ever heard."

WHEN THEY WENT BACK DOWN to the docks, they found a lot of tumult and noise going on at the *Bird of the River*. A lumber dealer had spotted the immense snag and made Mr. Riveter an offer for it, and now had moved a crane into place to lift it from the barge's deck onto the pavement outside his warehouse. Mr. Riveter stood overseeing the process. Tulu ran up and tugged on his hand.

"Daddy, Eliss saw something—"

"Little queen, Daddy's busy right now. Wait until this is done.

We just made three thousand crowns!" He waved her away distract-edly.

"Tulu, it can wait," said Eliss.

"No, it can't," said Tulu. "Bandits could kill us all!" She looked around and, after a moment's hesitation, ran down the companion-way to Captain Glass's cabin.

"Tulu!" Eliss shoved the market basket into Alder's arms and ran after her. By the time she got down the companionway, Tulu was already hammering on the door of the aft cabin. "Tulu, maybe we should—"

There was a sound of vast movement beyond the cabin door, as though some immense center of gravity had shifted. *It's only the snag being lifted off the deck,* Eliss told herself. A moment later the door opened a crack. The captain's voice came through indistinctly.

"What?"

"Please, Captain sir, Eliss saw some men crawling through the bushes from the town ramparts and we think they're bandits but no-body will believe us but you know how good she sees," said Tulu.

There was a moment's silence. They could hear the captain breathing like a bellows on the other side of the door. After a long moment the sound grew a little quieter, and the captain's voice was more distinct when he spoke. "Eliss saw that?"

Eliss cleared her throat. "Yes, sir. They were crawling along, and we showed a guard, but he didn't see them."

There was a low rumble like a growl. "All right. Go up on deck, both of you."

"Yes, sir." Eliss grabbed Tulu's hand and they fled. No sooner had they set foot on deck than the captain's voice came roaring up the companionway after them, so loud it gusted dust and straw up the steps.

"MR. RIVETER!"

"Sir!" Mr. Riveter spun around. He ran to the companionway.

"Go ashore. Now. Go to the captain of the city guard and make a report. Tell them we heard rumors Shellback's operating near here. Tell them one of our crew spotted armed men outside their walls. And double tonight's deck watch. See the arms locker is in good order."

"Right away, sir!"

AFTER RECEIVING MR. RIVETER'S REPORT, the captain of the city guard himself came aboard, in his fancy armor, and interviewed Eliss. He did not speak like a tour guide. He listened gravely to her account of what she had seen and made notes on a tablet. Then he thanked her and left. She felt embarrassed and flustered.

ELISS WAS HAVING A NIGHTMARE. She was dreaming that Wolkin and Alder were swimming, but that the water began to vanish and was instead green leaves. Wolkin scrambled back aboard but Alder couldn't hear her screaming that he had to come back, and he began to go down and down into the swirling leaves, and she knew he'd sink right to the bottom and never come up again. Everyone came to the rail and shouted but Eliss couldn't get the words out, somehow, to warn him. She woke herself up making a guttural noise. Her arms and legs were stiff; she was covered in a cold sweat. She reached out for Alder and didn't find him.

"Alder!"

"Ssh!" He was crouched at the mouth of the tent, peering out. Now she heard the shouting from the docks. She threw aside her blanket and crawled to kneel beside him, drawing the door's flap a little further open to see out. The lumber merchant's big warehouse was on fire, with flames leaping from the door and white smoke curling from the high grated windows. Men were running frantically to the dockside water cannon, swiveling it round and dipping up buckets full of water to prime the pump. Some of the deck watch had run ashore and were helping them.

There was a thunder of feet and Mr. Riveter came running up on deck naked. He saw the flames.

"All hands on deck! All hands! Now!"

They heard men emerging from the other tents and the lean-tos. Shadows crossed back and forth on the tent wall.

"What's on fire?"

"Are we under attack?"

"Look, they can't get the water cannon working!"

"Fetch buckets! Go ashore and help!"

"Spears! Spears! Spears! Starboard watch, arm!"

"Daddy! Daddy, here!" Eliss recognized Wolkin's voice.

"YOU GET BELOW!"

"But—"

"*Wolkin!*" That was Mrs. Riveter's voice, thick with fury, from the companionway. Wolkin's little shadow went skittering back across the deck. Mr. Riveter's shadow bound on the shadow of a loincloth.

"The water cannon's been broken!"

"Bloody hell. It's like Synpelene."

"What?"

And now they heard the screams coming from behind the city wall. Torches bloomed along the ramparts, and Eliss heard a distant voice calling for archers. There was a dull concussion on the air followed by the muffled *boom* of an explosion. More screams from within the city.

"It's a trick! It's a trick, they're attacking inside!"

"Wait! You can't let my warehouse burn!"

"To hell with your warehouse, I've got family—"

"We'll save the warehouse!" Mr. Riveter called across the night. "Go!"

Someone came up to him and spoke quietly. Their two shadows merged into one. "You don't suppose it was the greenie boy, do you?"

Alder flinched.

"Don't be stupid," muttered Mr. Riveter. "He's one of us. He knows we didn't cut down the damned tree."

"I'm just saying, is all."

Furious, Eliss started to scramble out, but Alder grabbed her wrist. "Don't," he said. "Just don't."

"Are you all right in there?" That was Krelan's voice. He squatted down and peered in at them. He had clearly dressed in haste and was clutching a long kitchen spit.

"We're fine," said Alder.

"Good. All right, I'm going ashore to help fight the fire—"

"No, you aren't," they heard Mr. Riveter say before he turned to run down the gangplank. "You stay on deck, do you understand?"

"Yes, sir." Krelan stood up. Eliss crawled past Alder and stood beside him, staring across at the fire. It wasn't any bigger, which was a hopeful sign, and the *Bird's* crew had formed a double bucket line. They were beginning to be able to get close inside the warehouse entrance, and there was as much steam as smoke boiling from the windows now. On the other hand, the fighting inside the city was getting louder.

"Well, there goes my chance to be a hero," said Krelan. He made a few lunges and blocking moves with the kitchen spit. *I wonder why he has a set of throwing knives instead of a sword,* thought Eliss. Aloud she said: "This is just like Synpelene."

"You think so?" Krelan came close and spoke in a quieter voice.

"Don't you? Somebody knew the city. Somebody broke the water cannon and then started a fire. While everybody was trying to put out the fire, *they* attacked on the other side of the city. I'll bet they came through the sewers again."

"No," said Krelan. "I had a lot of time to kill, waiting for the coppersmith this afternoon. Just out of curiosity, I went and looked at the city drains system. The vaults come out right over there in the open." He pointed to a section of wall just beside the city gate. "Hadn't you wondered why the docks are a little, er, fragrant? I asked somebody, and he laughed and said this is a working city and they don't care about smelling like a lot of roses. But anybody trying to crawl into *this* city through its sewer would be spotted at once, you see.

"Not that I don't agree with you that somebody gave them advance intelligence of the city defenses," he added thoughtfully. They heard orders shouted within the city, and then abruptly the noise stopped.

"Doesn't seem to have done them much good," said Alder.

"Does sound like they've been squashed, whoever they were." Krelan looked at Eliss. "What was that I heard about you spotting bandits in the forest?"

Eliss blushed. She told him about what she had seen from the ramparts. He listened intently and applauded when she had finished.

"Sharp eyes," he said approvingly.

"We both have them," said Alder.

DAWN WAS BRIEFLY RED, as the sun fought to burn through the pall of smoke in the river bend and at last vanished into a cloud cover. The air was hot, breathless; thunder rumbled around the horizon.

The lumber warehouse had been saved. Within the town, however, there were now six heads on pikes on the ramparts. The *Bird's* crew, venturing ashore, learned that the raiders had broken through the city wall right into the quarry manager's office. Several of them had made off with the manager's strongbox, while others had streamed out the door. Some had gone straight for the town's arsenal, and had been in the act of affixing explosives to its doors when they had been caught and slaughtered by the city guard. Others had broken into a shop that sold bluestone souvenirs and taken a case full of gold-mounted jewelery, leaving a trail of dropped earrings all the way back to the quarry manager's office.

The city's officials came aboard and formally thanked the *Bird's* crew for their help in putting out the fire, but their faces were grim.

Eliss, having watched them go back ashore, turned to climb the shrouds to her place at the masthead. She ran into Captain Glass, standing behind her.

"Here." He opened his broad hand and held out something. She looked close. Glinting in his dark palm was a little charm on a silver chain. The charm looked as though it was made of crystal, cut and polished without facets into a smooth curving shape that suggested a ripple of water, or perhaps a coiled serpent, or even a wide eye. "Wear it. You've earned it."

Eliss stared at it, dumfounded. No one had ever given her jewelry before. The captain continued to stand there before her, immobile and solid as a brick wall. Eliss looked up at him but could read no expression on his face. She took the charm and slipped the chain over her head.

"Thank you, Captain sir."

"You're welcome." He turned away and went to his place at the tiller. Eliss looked down at the charm where it glinted on its chain. She tucked it carefully inside her tunic and climbed on up to the masthead.

The *Bird of the River* moved on.

"HELLO THERE."

Eliss looked down in surprise. Krelan was climbing the shrouds, smiling up at her. He hauled himself through the hole in the platform and sat, gasping for breath.

"Aren't you supposed to be scrubbing pots in the galley?"

"Mr. Pitspike is exceptionally cross today," said Krelan. "Mr. Pitspike threw a pot of soap grease at my head and told me that if he had to look at my asinine attempt at a mustache for one more minute today he was going to suffer a collapse and spray blood from his ears. Therefore I have the afternoon off."

"That's nice," said Eliss. "I think."

"I've observed that you do," Krelan replied. "Think, I mean. You also notice a great deal."

"It's my job," said Eliss warily.

"Do you listen as well as you watch?"

"Sometimes."

"I wonder if you have any idea why the flock of charming little girls who play with their dolls belowdecks are looking at me as though I had sprouted six-inch fangs this morning? I asked one of them if she wanted honey on her oatmeal and she burst into tears and ran howling to her mother."

"Oh." Eliss kept her eyes on the river. "One of them got the idea that you're the brother of the dead man we found below Slates Landing, and that you're out to get revenge. And that would frighten anyone who was poor and lowborn, you see, because whenever the princes fight among themselves, some of us always end up getting killed too. My mother, for one."

"I see." Krelan wrapped his arms around the railing and gazed down at the river too. "And they think I'm his brother because . . . ?"

"You're an aristocrat. And you came on board soon after we found the dead man. But mostly because . . . because somebody noticed you had throwing knives in your bag, and told the other children."

"I see." Krelan sighed. "But it wouldn't have been you, I don't think. You seem as though you keep secrets."

"It might have been me." Eliss's hands tightened on the rail.

"Or it might have been your little brother, who dislikes me. For several good reasons, I suspect, so I can't really take offense. Shall I be frank with you?"

"You can be whatever you want. You know that."

"Because I'm a nobleman? But that's just it, you see. I'm not. Actually."

"It's funny how you talk just like one of them, then."

"That's because I've been around them all my life. Please do me the favor of hearing me out, Eliss. You, of all people, deserve to know the truth."

"Why?"

"Because of what happened to your mother."

Eliss stared down at the surface of the river. There was a sandbar, but far enough to starboard to be no danger. There was the line of bubbles that meant some big river-otter was swimming past. There to larboard was the fresh undercutting of the bank that meant the river would collapse it in that place before much longer, and then there would be rockfall or even a snag to clear away . . .

"Go on, then."

"The body your people pulled out of the river belonged to Encilian Diamondcut. Have you heard of the Diamondcuts?"

"Everybody has. They had the big vendetta going with the Fireopal family."

"They did. All patched up now, at least if Denissa Fireopal and Thrason Diamondcut can bear each other's company long enough to have children. Thrason is the oldest brother, you see, the one who's to inherit the name. He had five younger brothers. Now he has four."

"Because somebody killed one of them and threw his body in the river?"

"But kept his head. That's a deadly insult. Almost worse than simply killing him. They took a *trophy*. The Diamondcuts want his murder avenged, of course, but they want Lord Encilian's head back too."

Eliss shuddered. "So what are you?"

"My family has worked for the Diamondcuts for twelve generations," said Krelan, with a sigh. "We do things for them. The sort of things that don't get written into the chronicles or embroidered on the tapestries. It's a very old and honorable profession, you see, we're quite rich as a consequence and we're almost a sort of shadow-nobility ourselves . . . only not really.

"Now I'm going to speak blasphemy, or at least my family would call it that. Encilian was a lesser son. He was weak, he was lazy, and he didn't care about his Family's honor or anything but enjoying himself. He lied. He stole things. He ran up debts. Nobody was all that sorry, or surprised either, to learn he'd been killed. *But he was a Diamondcut.*

"I'm a lesser son, myself. Not because of extravagant vices, I hasten to add! No. I'm my father's younger son by his second wife. My older brother inherited the name and half the property. He looks like a hawk, whereas I look like some sort of starved duck with mange. He's already taken a wife and produced twin baby boys, whereas I can barely get a girl to give me the time of day. He can lift a caravan cart on his back, whereas I . . . but you get the idea.

"When Encilian's body was found, old Lord Diamondcut summoned my brother. The matter was discussed. It was decided that I would be sent upriver to investigate Encilian's murder. I am to reclaim his head, if I can. I am to see to it that he is suitably avenged, once I know who killed him. If I can do that, I'll be avenging your mother too since whoever killed my master's son was indirectly responsible for her death. So we have a common cause, you see."

Eliss shook her head. "People like us aren't avenged when we die. We don't matter to anyone. You don't know much about the world."

"Not as much as I thought I did," said Krelan. "Not now I'm out in it. I'd be grateful for your help, Eliss."

Eliss gave an unbelieving snort. "What do you think *I* can do?"

"Keep my secrets," said Krelan. "It's hard to be discreet when you're scaring little girls. Maybe you could pass the word that I have those knives because my family thought I wasn't worth buying a sword for? Which is true, by the way."

"I can do that," said Eliss. She took her eyes from the river long enough to give him a considering glance. "So . . . if you're not actually a nobleman, what really happened at the Lake?"

"The Lake. I wish I knew." Krelan rubbed his side where the gash was a puckering scar. "I went over there to ask a few questions. Had anyone seen Lord Encilian in the last year? I asked after him by name, and I think that might have been a mistake. Generally I've been showing people his portrait, but I assumed that in Prayna there'd be no need. The Diamondcuts were well known to the Agatines.

"I went to the sorts of places he frequented—they exist even in Prayna—and asked whether he'd been seen there."

"You don't think that was a little stupid?"

Krelan looked reproachful. "I didn't just *ask*. There are certain signs one gives, making inquiries. Certain signals of the trade."

"What trade?"

"My family's trade."

"Oh."

"And my informant, whom I'd thought was trustworthy, arranged for me to meet someone after dark, who supposedly knew something about Encilian's murderer. I went to the place we'd agreed upon and walked straight into a trap. The rest of the story is essentially true as I told it."

"Essentially?"

"It means, true in essence."

"I know what the word means, thank you. What parts were different?"

Krelan raised his eyebrows. "Shrewd, aren't you? Well . . . I defended myself rather more effectively than I told Mr. Riveter."

"Did you kill somebody?"

". . . I might have."

"Because if you didn't, and whoever tried to kill you got away, they'll be looking for you. And once they get done looking for you in Prayna, they just might come across the lake and start asking questions at Moonport."

After a moment's thoughtful silence, Krelan said, "You know rather a lot about this sort of thing, don't you?"

"I had a few uncles who were in gangs," Eliss replied. She made a face. "Not that they were really my uncles. Anyway, what if someone from Moonport tells them you left to go upriver on the *Bird*?"

"That would present a problem," admitted Krelan. "But, no. Take my word for it that no one was capable of following me across the Lake, all right?"

"All right. But you still don't know why someone who knew your 'trade signals' set you up to be killed. Do you?"

"No," said Krelan unhappily. "No, I don't. What awkward

questions you do ask, young lady. Mind you, I'd rather be told a ven-
omous spider was crawling on my sleeve than have someone fail to
mention it out of a desire to spare my feelings."

"There you are, then." Eliss stared very hard at a pattern of ripples
and decided they did not signify a submerged unmarked snag.
"So . . . was your nasty lordship still alive as far as Bluestone?"

"It would appear he was," said Krelan.

"Hmmm." Eliss's gaze wandered to the deck below. She was a little startled to see Alder staring up at her, frowning.

"PEOPLE SHOULDN'T CLIMB UP THERE and bother you when
you're working," said Alder that night when they had rolled up in
their blankets.

"What, Krelan? He wasn't bothering me." Eliss turned over and
stared at the back of Alder's head.

"You were talking with him an awfully long time," Alder said, not
turning around.

"Look . . ." Eliss gazed up at the roof of the tent. She put up her
hand and traced the charm Captain Glass had given her, smooth and
cool on its silver chain. "Look. I'm growing up. Boys are going to be
talking to me. That's the way it is even with normal families who stay
in one place. Girls grow up and they start spending time with boys.
I'm going to. It doesn't mean I'm going to do stupid things. I'm not.
But I like Krelan. He's smart."

"He's dangerous."

Eliss nodded in the dark. "I think he is, yes. But we're just friends.
You don't remember Uncle Ironbolt. He was before you were born.
He was dangerous too, but he was nice. He was good to Mama. He
took care of us, until he got killed."

"Was he in a gang?"

"He ran a gang. I think. He had a lot of money."

"And Mama loved him," Alder stated, with an air of resignation.
"Stupid."

"Actually . . ." Eliss fell silent as a memory suddenly shuttled out of the dead past. Staring into the darkness with wide eyes, she saw Falena again—so young!—crouching beside her bed, whispering. *Of course I don't love him, I could never love anybody but your daddy. Half my heart died with Daddy. But Uncle Ironbolt has been very kind to us, Eliss. Don't you like this big house, all these toys? I can't protect you by myself but he can protect both of us.*

"Eliss, I have to protect you now," said Alder, sounding as though he was about to cry. "And if you're going to fall in love with people who aren't safe . . . and *nobody's* safe, I never saw that before but it's true, the Children of the Sun are just crazy, fighting and killing all the time! And what am I supposed to do?" His voice broke on a sob.

"That's Mr. Moss making you think that we're all evil!"

"It isn't! I always thought that. Not that you're evil, just . . . crazy. And I never understood why. And I always wondered why nobody else was like me. And then I found out *my* people are. So I'm trying to be one of them. And one of the things I have to do is keep you safe. Because the Yendri don't beat up *their* ladies."

"Nobody's going to beat me up," said Eliss grimly. "Nobody *ever*. And nobody has to protect me. I can protect myself. I always have." She turned on her side and put her arm around Alder. "Listen to me. You're only ten. You shouldn't have to worry about things like this yet."

"You did, when you were ten. And littler. I remember. You were always looking out for a place for me to sleep and carrying me when I was tired and telling me not to be scared. And if I let you get hurt now, what good am I?"

"I won't be hurt," said Eliss, hugging him. "I promise. And, and now we live on the river, you can see other Yendri a lot more and learn more about them, and everything will be fine. Come on. Things will be all right. *We have a place to sleep.*"

Alder was silent so long she thought he might have forgotten, but at last he answered. "We have a place to sleep *and a warm blanket each.*"

"We have a place to sleep, and a warm blanket each, *and we had dinner tonight.*"

"We have a place to sleep each, and a warm blanket each, and had dinner tonight, *and we'll have breakfast tomorrow.*"

"And who knows what, when summer comes?"

"And who knows what, when summer comes? *And summer is coming soon.*"

THE NEXT TOWN UP THE RIVER was Forge, and it was a holy place.

Eliss watched in awe as its crumbling towers became visible through the trees. She had never seen buildings so old. There on a ridge was the scar where the ore seam had been worked out, but green had softened the cut lines, and young trees and ferns screened the derelict workings. Below was the town, only a hostel for pilgrims and a tavern now, and the Forge itself.

The *Bird of the River* docked at the old stone quay. Eliss climbed down and looked around uncertainly. Families were clustering together on the deck, here and there, with children fidgeting in their best clothes and mothers fussing over them. She spotted the Riveters and struggled through the crowd to them. As she approached, she saw Mr. Riveter put something in Wolkin's hands.

"Now, hold on to it, and *be respectful,*" Mr. Riveter admonished. Wolkin nodded, his eyes wide. Eliss saw that he was holding a piece of tin cut from one flat sheet of metal, flat figures holding hands: a man, a woman, a boy, a girl. It was supposed to be iron, but any metal was acceptable from poor people. Eliss felt a pang: her family had finally come to the Forge, and she had no offering.

She looked around for Alder. He had retreated to the aft deck, keeping himself aloof from the crowd. Before she could start toward him, Wolkin ran weaving through the throng and shouted up to him: "Alder! Come on! We're going to the Forge!"

"I don't belong there," Alder said. Eliss clenched her fists.

Wolkin gaped at him a moment before yelling, "Well, but there's big *trees!* Come on! And there's a man who can juggle fireballs!"

That was enough to persuade Alder, who scrambled down and ran off with Wolkin. Eliss stood alone.

"Aren't you going ashore?" said someone at her elbow. She turned and saw Krelan.

"I don't have an offering."

"You can buy them there," said Krelan. "Look, will you go with me? If somebody's looking for me, they'll be looking for me alone. If we look like a couple, I'm sort of disguised."

"All right." Anything was better than staying behind, conspicuously alone. Krelan took her arm and steered her toward the gangplank, where people were crowded together, waiting to disembark. Eliss saw Mrs. Riveter looking around searchingly; her gaze settled at last on Eliss and Krelan.

"Eliss, have you got an offering?" she called.

"We're going to buy ours," said Krelan. Mrs. Riveter looked pleased. She nudged Mr. Riveter and murmured something in his ear.

Jostling Eliss were the musicians, each of whom had a cut-tin representation of an instrument in his hands. She remembered now hearing the commotion as shapes were cut from the metal sheet with hammers and chisels; if she'd thought to ask, somebody probably would have cut out an offering for her too. *But what would I have to offer?*

They stepped ashore at last. Most of the crew headed straight for the Forge, but Krelan tugged at her arm and they walked away in the direction of the tavern. Eliss looked around. It wasn't at all what she had expected. Moss grew on the slate roofs of the buildings, and trailed from the branches of gnarled trees. Almost it seemed more like a Yendri place, except for the smell of the Forge and the distant ringing on its anvil. And a certain quality in the air . . . there was a heaviness, the way things felt just before a thunderstorm. The tiny hairs along Eliss's arms, and on the back of her neck, rose. In under the trees, the light seemed filtered and dim, almost like dusk, and the firepit in the yard of the tavern glowed out bright.

"So many trees," she murmured, half to herself. Krelan turned to look at her, bright-eyed.

"You've never been here before?"

"No."

"Come on. I'll show you something." He led her to a great tree that overhung the tavern yard. Firelight flickered on its trunk, gleaming on the places where the boles had been rubbed smooth by the passage of people entering the yard. Grinning, Krelan took a knife from inside his boot. He tapped on the trunk with his blade, producing a metallic *ting-ting*.

"Oh!" Eliss stared at the trunk. She tilted her head back to stare up into the branches, seeing now that all the fantastic gnarling, the stiff dense leaves, were in fact cast and welded metal, gray-green with age.

"Then up from the raw earth he summoned,
Quickspringing, the veins of copper and malachite
And five leagues round forged the forest,
His own grove, sacrosanct, unfading—Don't you remember?"

"I thought it was just a story," said Eliss, turning, gazing up at the forest canopy. The big trees were all around, stretching back into the forest as far as she could see, with only here and there a thin live tree stretching up toward the light between the verdigris leaves. The same moss draped both the wild and the made trees. "Just, you know, scripture."

"I suppose it might have been," said Krelan. "Originally. But maybe the priests made this place so it would be real. It's here *now*, and nobody knows how old it is."

Eliss shivered. Was this how the gods were supposed to make you feel? She thought of the centuries these trees had seen, never changed by the seasons, never plundered by crows, never affected by disease or fire. Unfading.

"Let's have something to drink," said Krelan. The whole crew had been paid from the proceeds of the big snag, and everyone had a little money to spend. They took a seat at one of the tables in the yard. After a moment a server came out and bowed to them.

"Welcome, pilgrims. Some wine?"

"Tea, please, and could we see a menu?" asked Krelan.

Eliss looked down at the tabletop. It was bronze, cast to look like rough-hewn wood. She had never in her life sat at a table and ordered from a menu. Krelan's voice had been casual, ordering as though he'd done it a thousand times. The server came back with a chalkboard and held it up for their inspection. Krelan looked at it critically.

"Bring us a new loaf, hot, please, and the honey assortment. With jam."

The server bowed again and retreated. Eliss felt her mouth watering. She reached an unobtrusive hand to the canvas pouch she wore sewn into the sleeve of her tunic, and reassured herself that she had money there.

"This is nice," she half-whispered.

"Hm? Yes, it's nice. You've really never been? I came with my family when I was eight."

"We never came up the river until this year."

"Everybody's supposed to come at least once. Or so the priests tell us. You'll be making up for it now, I imagine, living on the *Bird*. Twice a year."

"Probably." Eliss looked out at the pilgrims lining up before the Forge. There were Alder and Wolkin in line, whispering together. She looked back at Krelan. He leaned back in his seat, watching the tavern's door. For all his ridiculous mustache and shabby hood he seemed somehow poised and elegant, not at all the hapless galley drudge he played on the *Bird of the River*.

The server came back and set out their tea. "I wonder if you could answer a question for me," said Krelan.

"What would you like to know, sir?"

"Is there a way to find out whether a particular person made a particular offering on a certain date?"

"The priests' clerk keeps a record," said the server, gesturing off toward the Forge.

"Thank you. I only ask because my wife's brother—" Krelan glared at Eliss "—has been bragging for the last six months that he came here and made an expensive offering in honor of our wedding, which is why I oughtn't ask him to pay back certain sums of money he borrowed."

Eliss blinked. After a scrambling moment of confusion she thought fast. "Are you going to start in on that *again*, husband? Gods below, can't you ever let it go?"

Laughter glinted in Krelan's eyes, but his face remained cold. "Money's money, Balicia." He looked up at the server. "Married six months, and thorns in my pillow already."

The server gave a tiny smile and shrugged. "One silver bit, sir."

Krelan sighed and tossed a silver piece on the table. The server scooped it up and departed. Eliss fumbled in her sleeve for her purse. "I think I've got change for my half."

"No, no. My treat. You did marry me on a moment's notice, after all." Krelan poured their tea. Eliss watched, feeling a strange combination of exhilaration and terror.

"So we're going to the clerk to see if your lord made an offering here?" she asked, trying to sound casual. Krelan nodded.

"The question is, how far up the river did he get? At least, that's the first question. Once I know that, I'll have an entirely new set of questions to ask. My compliments on your quick wit, by the way."

Eliss shrugged, blushing. "So . . . has it changed much, since you were here before?"

"Well, everything is somehow smaller, of course." Krelan sipped his tea carefully. "Ah. Just ready to drink. Don't wait; it tastes best hot. Other than shrinking, nothing has changed, really. Same souvenir shop. Same tavern. Same hostel. Same office and priest's house. And the Forge, of course. A few more bushes growing up there where the iron workings used to be. The ruins down at the end a bit more crumbled and overgrown."

"What did they used to be?"

"Hm? Something to do with the iron workings, I suppose. Must have seemed like the end of the world when those played out, mustn't it? In fact, I remember being a child and reading somewhere that it was taken as a horrible omen, and there promptly followed a series of wars and plagues that left half the cities devastated, because of course the gods wouldn't want us to waste an omen like that, would they? It wasn't the end of the world, though. Life went on. It always does."

"It does," Eliss agreed, sipping her tea. Krelan had been right; it was almost too hot, but delicious. "Did you have a lot of books to read, growing up?"

"Books of fables. Volumes and volumes of the glorious history of the Diamondcuts. No stories about *my* family, of course, because we were the Diamondcuts' shadows. My grandfather always said it with a capital S. *Shadows.* It was something to be proud of, being invisible. I thought it was rather unfair, in those days; now I see how useful invisibility can be. But what about you? What do people read when they don't have to steep themselves in the bygone glories of their masters?"

"We never had books." Eliss gazed into her teacup. It reflected branches and sky. "When Alder was a baby we lived for a while in a building with a lot of other people. There was an old man there, he'd been a scholar, and he still had some books. He taught me to read. So I can read signs and public notices and things. I started a novel once, but we had to move before I could finish it."

"What novel?"

"It was called *The Silvergilts of Delairia*. It was about this family who had been rich, but now they were poor, and they lived in this old falling-down house."

"Sounds like the Diamondcuts." Krelan chuckled.

"But they were *nice.* They were nice to each other and they figured out ways to get by, you know, the father built a little boat and caught fish for dinner, and dug clams, and the little girl of the family painted pictures on clamshells and sold them, and that brought in money. The mother would make big pots of soup out of whatever they had, and they'd all share." Eliss remembered vividly her longing to slip into the book and be part of that family.

"And you never finished it?"

Eliss pressed her lips together, shaking her head. She didn't want to remember that night, when Falena had pulled her out of bed and told her not to make a sound, and wrapped her in a blanket and carried her outside to the back of a cart. Eliss had waited, clutching Alder in her arms, as Falena and Uncle Paver ran back and forth in the dark loading bundles on the cart. She had finally fallen asleep on the long jolting ride through darkness that followed. She had long ago forgotten the reason they had had to run away, but her grief at losing *The Silvergilts* was still a vivid ache.

"Well, perhaps you'll find another copy, someday. Ah! Here's our order." Krelan moved the tea things to one side as the server brought their tray.

THE HOT BREAD WITH HONEY was so delicious Eliss had to restrain herself from eating it all. She managed to keep back a slice for Alder, wrapped in the greased paper that had lined the tray and slipped into her pocket. Krelan observed but did not comment.

"Now," said Krelan as they left, "what's next? Shall we look for an offering?"

"Yes, please."

He led her next door to a low-ceilinged shop whose sign reading SOUVENIRS AND OFFERINGS READY-MADE was half obscured by lichen. Inside were racks and racks of offerings, both in iron and tin, shaped like everything imaginable. Eliss lingered by the rack of family groupings, sorting through them. All had a father and mother figure, and every possible number and combination of children, but there were none featuring children alone.

"May I help you, miss?" An old woman appeared out of the shadows behind the counter.

"Don't you have a boy and a girl?"

"Over there." The woman pointed behind Eliss and went to pull out a pair of figures, slightly smaller than the father and mother figures.

"Oh." Eliss examined it. "I need one where the boy is smaller than the girl."

The proprietress glanced over at Krelan, who was lingering at a display of offerings shaped like weapons. She stepped closer and spoke in an undertone. "He's not *that* short, dear."

"No, it's for me and my little brother," said Eliss, feeling her face grow hot.

"Oh." The proprietress raised her eyebrows. "I can put one together. Just a moment."

She retreated behind the counter and Eliss heard subdued metallic noises. A moment later the proprietress returned with a pair of single figures hooked together with little metal rings, a girl and a smaller boy. "There you are, dear. Anything else today?"

"Just these," said Krelan, setting down a sheet-iron dagger on the counter. "We're together."

"Two silver bits, then, sir."

They took their offerings and walked out, but there was still a long line of people waiting to get to the Forge. Krelan glanced at them, and then at the clerk's office.

"Let's go ask, first."

The clerk's office was a long low building back under the copper trees; its doorposts were cast to look like trees too, reaching bas-relief branches up into the roofline. A young man was just emerging. He wore a leather apron and had a pair of steel pens thrust through the topknot in his hair.

"You would be the clerk," said Krelan, in the same confident and slightly bullying voice he'd used with the tavern server.

"The Assistant Clerk, sir, actually." The boy wrung his hands and bowed. "My master's at the Forge. If you'd like to wait—"

"No, no; you'll do. I require information." Krelan slapped his coin pouch. Eliss wondered how long it would be before the Assistant Clerk noticed Krelan was small and shabby and had a ridiculous mustache.

"What information, sir?" The Assistant Clerk was still bowing and averting his gaze.

"I'm resolving the affairs of Encilian Diamondcut. He journeyed upriver some half-year since. His lord father wishes to know what he spent on an offering, the precise date and amount, if you please."

"Oh! I remember him. Yes, sir." The Assistant Clerk hurried back inside the office. Krelan strode after him. Eliss followed, marveling at what a mere tone of voice could accomplish. The Assistant Clerk ran his finger along the spines of a shelf full of ledgers. He pulled one down and carried it to the desk.

"Here, sir. It was at Winter Solstice. Very crowded then, but of course you remember something like one of the Diamondcuts visiting. Here it is." He turned the ledger around for Krelan's inspection and ran his finger down one of the columns, stopping at an entry in red ink. "Just there."

"Hmmmm." Krelan frowned magisterially. "What's this? A miserable ten copper bits spent?" The Assistant Clerk seemed to shrink.

"I'm sorry, sir, one must record the truth. He bought one of the tin offerings from the shop. A male figure."

"His father will not be pleased."

"I wish I had better to report of the young gentleman, sir. I would have thought, with that pleasure-boat and all, he'd have offered something more fitting his illustrious name, but—"

"A pleasure-boat?"

"Well, sir, yes, sir, he had his little pleasure-craft, not one of the big party boats, you know, more of the sort the gentry race in. The *Fire-Swift*, it was called. Very fine."

"I see. And was he with a party of revelers?"

"No, sir, he was alone. But he had a manservant, of course."

"Lord Diamondcut expresses his gratitude," said Krelan, tossing a gold crown piece onto the ledger. "He would, however, prefer that this disgrace of parsimony went unrecorded. Can the entry be blotted out?"

The Assistant Clerk looked up beseechingly. "Oh, sir, we can't—it has to be the absolute truth, the gods are so near here after all and—well—"

"That will grieve Lord Diamondcut. Consider it carefully, Assistant Clerk. Ask yourself whether a bit of spilled ink to obscure a line constitutes a falsehood." Krelan turned and stalked out, leaving the Assistant Clerk stammering apologies. He took Eliss's arm and hummed a jubilant little tune.

"Now, *that* was gold well spent," he muttered to Eliss.

"Was it?"

"I just found out a great deal. No one told me he'd taken the *Fire-Swift*. Or that he had a servant with him. And he got this far!"

"So . . . do you think the servant killed him and took the boat?"

"Anything's possible," Krelan said, in a lowered voice as they walked down toward the Forge. "A damned stupid servant, if he did. It'll certainly make my job easier."

Eliss thought about what Krelan's job would entail, and shuddered. It didn't seem right to dwell on such things here. They took their place in line and waited. Most of the *Bird*'s crew seemed to have made their offerings and gone back to the barge; Eliss saw no one she knew in line. At the doorway stood the priest's clerk, with a tablet and stylus. As each pilgrim stepped up to the door he took down their name and offering.

The woman with an iron loom went in and emerged shortly afterward. The man with an iron caravan-cart went next. After him went the family, a mother and father and three adolescent boys, the youngest carrying their cutout sheet iron representation. Waiting, Eliss watched the firelight from inside playing on the stone posts of the doorway. She clutched her offering self-consciously, wishing Alder had come with her.

The family emerged, talking quietly among themselves. "You can go next, if you like," said Krelan.

"Name, please?" inquired the clerk.

"Eliss Hammertin."

"And you have brought?"

Eliss held up her offering, not sure what to say. The clerk nodded and scored characters quickly into the tablet. He waved her inside. She walked in through the doorposts.

The Forge was a wide room, low-ceilinged and opening at the back under the very biggest tree. Leaning against its trunk was a boy wearing only a loincloth, his hair slicked up with oil so it looked like flames dancing on his head. His palms were gilded with paint. His face was as serene as though he dreamed. He was effortlessly juggling flaming coals, keeping a circle of them in the air.

To one side was the Forge itself. It looked like any blacksmith's forge in any city anywhere, but for the fact that it was much bigger. The priest, heating a bit of iron in the fire, seemed likewise twice as big as any man Eliss had ever seen. She felt like a child as she approached the anvil.

The priest turned to her. He was as dark with soot as the juggling boy was fair, but his light eyes burned in his face. Something about him reminded Eliss of Captain Glass. He looked at her searchingly.

"What have you made with your life, Child of the Sun?" His voice was hoarse.

"This, Father." Eliss laid the tin figures on the altar. "There's just me and my little brother now. Our mother died. I'm taking care of him as much as I can. It's all I have, so far."

He looked down at the two little figures. "That is what you're making of the end of your mother's life, child. What will you make of your own?"

Eliss thought about it. "I'm working on the *Bird of the River*," she said. "I watch out for dangers. Snags and things. It's a good job. I'd like to stay."

The priest grunted. He took the pair of cutouts and, reaching up, hung them in the lowest branches of the great tree. Looking up, Eliss saw that it was festooned with offerings.

"Good. Work hard, Child of the Sun."

"I will, Father."

"Come and be kissed by True Fire."

Eliss stepped close to the Forge. The priest took her hand and passed it through the dancing flames. "Receive the blessing and go in peace."

SHE WAITED AFTERWARD while Krelan went in. They walked back down toward the quay together in silence, both thoughtful.

Several more boats had drawn up to the quay and souvenir vendors were now walking back and forth, hawking charms from trays of amulets and medallions; tiny copper trees, tiny anvils, even carefully packaged lumps of slag. Pilgrims were waiting to get off boats or get back aboard boats. Krelan suddenly unlinked his arm from Eliss's.

"That's the landing master's office, isn't it?" he said, nodding in the direction of a booth on the quay. "Would you mind very much waiting here? I'm going to see whether the *Fire-Swift* posted a destination."

"Go ahead." Eliss watched him stride away through the crowd. She turned and looked down on the *Bird of the River*. There were all the people she knew, returning to their places after receiving their blessings: Salpin lighting up a pipe on the afterdeck, concertina in his lap. Mr. Riveter carrying a keg of something on his shoulder, heading down the companionway. Mrs. Crucible hanging up wet laundry on the rail. Pentra Smith taking her seat under her sunshade, cutting a fresh point on a reed pen. Wolkin and Alder sitting together at the rail, talking earnestly.

Eliss had an eerie sense of disconnectedness from them, as though they were characters in a play she was watching. *This was the end of Mama's life,* she thought. *What do I want to do with my own?* Not that the poor ever had much of a choice; you took what you could get in life, and were grateful if you got anything. All the same—

"Saw you going in," said someone at her shoulder. Eliss turned and saw the oldest of the adolescent boys in the family who had gone into the Forge before her.

"That's right," she said, and turned her gaze back to the *Bird of the River.*

"So . . . are you a widow or something?"

Startled, she looked back at him. "No. Why are you asking, anyway?"

"Because I saw you didn't have a husband on your offering. Just you and a little boy. So I wondered if you needed money."

"I have money, thank you." Eliss turned away from him, pulling her shawl close.

"I mean, I wondered if you ever did things for money." The boy sidled around into her field of vision.

"No." She was more startled than offended. He was trying to proposition a girl *here,* of all places? She started to walk away from him, but he followed and grabbed her arm.

"Sure? Because you could make two gold crowns. We could go over to the ruins, nobody'd see us. Look." He held out the coins in his palm.

"No. Really." Eliss tried to pull her arm loose. He wouldn't let go. "Take your hand off me. I mean it."

He looked scared but mastered himself enough to grin at her. "O-or what? What'll you do, beggar girl?"

"This." Eliss showed him what Uncle Ironbolt had taught her to do if she was ever grabbed. His face went a nasty color and he doubled up, clutching himself.

"How dare you insult my wife!" shouted Krelan, appearing suddenly beside her.

"What have you done to my son?" screamed the boy's mother, racing toward them with the rest of his family close behind.

"He propositioned me," said Eliss. "At the Forge!"

"She's lying, I didn't—" the boy said, gasping.

"He'd never do such a thing!" The mother leaned in threateningly. Eliss leaned away.

"How dare you call my wife a liar!" said Krelan, in tones of out-rage.

"He offered me two gold crowns," said Eliss, miserably aware that everyone on the *Bird of the River*'s deck could see the farce being played out.

"What a filthy lie! Where would a boy his age *get* two gold crowns?" the mother shrieked.

"They're in his hand right now," said Eliss.

"They had better not be." The boy's father stepped forward sud-denly. He crouched and prized his son's hand open. The coins were still there, glued to the boy's palm with sweat. "Where did you get these?" he said, thunder in his voice. The boy stared up at him in ap-palled silence. The father raised his hand to clout him. The mother grabbed the father's arm.

"Don't hit him! If you weren't such a brute he wouldn't *do* these things!"

"Let's go," said Krelan in an undertone, putting his arm around Eliss. They slunk away through the crowd that was beginning to gather, and walked on down to the quay. Half the deck watch of the *Bird* were lined up and applauded Krelan and Eliss as they came up the gangplank. To Eliss's horror, Alder and Wolkin stood there too, staring. Alder had gone very pale.

"You should have beat him up," Wolkin told Krelan accusingly.

"No," said Alder in a choked voice. "I should have—" He turned and stalked away.

ELISS DIDN'T NOTICE ALDER wasn't on board until the evening of the next day, when they had left Forge far behind them.

The *Bird* had just anchored for the night. Eliss climbed down from the masthead and, not seeing Alder anywhere on deck, went and crouched down to peer into the tent, where he had been sulking that morning before they left Forge. The tent was empty.

He's playing somewhere with Wolkin, she thought, but just to be certain she went and looked in the areas on the aft deck where Alder sometimes hid himself when he was in a bad mood. He wasn't hiding. With an impatient shrug she collected their bowls from the tent and went to stand in the dinner queue outside the deckhouse.

Dinner that night was fish stew. Krelan saluted her with the ladle as he gave her her portions. Carefully carrying two full bowls, she started back toward her tent and saw Mrs. Riveter waiting in line with Wolkin and Tulu.

"Wolkin, where's Alder? Can you go tell him he needs to come eat his dinner?"

Wolkin stared at her a long moment, his eyes perfectly round. Then he burst into tears and ran away.

"What in the world?" Mrs. Riveter turned to look after him. "Wolkin!"

"What's he done now?" Mr. Riveter said, coming up the companionway.

"She just asked him to go find Alder—"

"Wolkin! Come here!" Mr. Riveter sprinted across the deck after Wolkin, who was hiding behind one of the capstans. Eliss, standing perfectly still with two bowls of hot stew in her hands, heard her heart pounding in her ears. She set the two bowls down on a bench beside the deckhouse. She told herself that nothing was wrong.

"What's the matter with you?" Mr. Riveter demanded, dragging Wolkin back by one hand. Wolkin was crying, wiping away tears with the other hand and leaving dirt-trails across his face.

"Wolkin, where's Alder?" Eliss asked, keeping the panic out of her voice.

Wolkin only sobbed. Mrs. Riveter came and knelt beside him. "Wolkin, why are you crying?"

"They were talking last night," said Tulu.

"Shut up!" Wolkin howled, stamping his feet. "He went back to the Yendri. He said he wanted to find his daddy. I wanted to go too but he wouldn't let me. He sneaked ashore this morning before we left."

"You knew about this?" Mrs. Riveter grabbed Wolkin by the shoulders. Eliss found herself observing everything in close focus: the folds of the scarf with which Mrs. Riveter had bound up her hair, the snail-smear tracks of tears on Wolkin's bare chest, the pink and green beads in Tulu's necklace. She put out a hand and braced herself against the side of the deckhouse.

"We have to go back," she said, as calmly as she could. "We have to turn around and go back."

There was a silence, punctuated only by Wolkin's sniffling.

"Er," said Mr. Riveter. "Well. To be honest. We can't go back. The *Bird* doesn't turn around. Except at a lake. I, er, I think it might be best—I mean, he wanted to go live with his people, and he's at the age where a boy needs his father, or somebody like a father anyway, and—and—"

Eliss turned and ran back to the tent. She crawled in, looking frantically for Alder's bag. It was gone, along with his blanket. She backed out of the tent to find that Mr. and Mrs. Riveter had followed her. So had Wolkin, who was rubbing his eyes.

"What did he tell you?" she demanded of Wolkin.

"He said—he said you weren't alone anymore. Not now you had a boyfriend. So he was free to go. Because he couldn't protect you from anything. And he didn't like living with us. Not the people on the *Bird* but—" Wolkin made a wide gesture. "Children of the Sun."

"But he's only ten." Eliss felt her voice breaking. "He's never been by himself. I'm supposed to look after him."

"You can't look after him your whole life, dear," said Mrs. Riveter, taking her by the hands and lifting her to her feet. "Maybe it really is for the best. Think how happy he was, when we stopped at Moonport."

It was true. The shock of change made her reel, but Eliss could see Alder so clearly in her mind's eye, sure and confident, following the river back to the Yendri settlement. He had always known how to find food. He would be all right. And he wouldn't think twice about her, left alone here.

Krelan came running across the deck to them. "Eliss! I'll go after him for you. Let me get my bag and I'll swim ashore."

"No," she told him, swallowing back the hard knot of anger and grief. "They're right. He wasn't ever happy except with the Yendri. If you brought him back he'd only run away again."

"If you're sure." He took her hand and looked into her eyes. "I'm sorry, though."

ELISS WAS GRATEFUL, the next day, to be able to escape up the mast. She sat alone on her high platform and focused all her attention on the wide expanse of green water. Twice she caught unmarked snags, with no more warning than a shadow under the water in the first instance and a trailing branch in the second. One of the pole-men saluted her and yelled, "Sandgrind's grandkid, that's you!"

When evening came they moored at an island in the river. Mr. Riveter and two others among the fathers went ashore briefly and made certain it was safe; then the children ran ashore and picked berries and ran wild until their mothers called them back at supper-time. Eliss stayed aloft until the first stars appeared, when it began to get chilly. As she came down, a small shadow stepped out from the aft deck. It was Wolkin, looking melancholy.

"Mama would like to talk to you," he said.

"Why aren't you in having supper?"

"I won't eat until you do. That's my punishment. I'm punishing myself for not telling you about Alder."

Eliss reached out and took his hand. "You couldn't have stopped him. Nobody could ever make him do something he didn't want to do. Don't feel bad."

"I *tried*," Wolkin said. "He was just so mad."

"Let's not talk about it anymore," said Eliss, feeling the knot of unhappiness coming back. She squeezed his hand and they walked over to the deckhouse. Mrs. Riveter and Pentra Smith were sitting together in the dusk.

"Are you going to eat something now?" Mrs. Riveter asked Wolkin.

"I guess so." He heaved a theatrical sigh and then looked up at Eliss. "You want me to go fetch your dinner? I could do that! I'll go fetch your dinner."

He ran off. Mrs. Riveter patted the bench beside her. "Sit down, Eliss."

Eliss obeyed, feeling an eerie thankfulness at being told what to do. Mrs. Riveter and Pentra looked at each other and Mrs. Riveter cleared her throat. "I hope you won't mind a personal question, dear."

Eliss shook her head. "What is it?"

"Are you and the—the spitboy—planning to pair up?"

"No." Eliss felt her mouth go dry. "We're just good friends."

"That's good. It's nice that you're walking together, but, you know—"

"Oh, I know. I mean, he's an aristocrat and when he finishes— I mean, when whatever it is blows over, he'll go back to his family."

"So he will," said Mrs. Riveter, sounding relieved. "In the meantime . . . since you *haven't* paired up with anyone, it's not really right for you to sleep in that tent all alone, Eliss. Not as young as you are."

"I can look out for myself."

"Yes, we all saw that. All the same . . ."

"There are two bunks in my cabin," said Pentra Smith. "I've been stacking rolls of paper on one of them. The paper can go in a locker now, if you'd like to sleep in the bunk."

Eliss sat wordless a moment, stunned. "But I don't rate a cabin," she stammered.

"Oh, I think you do," said Pentra. "With the crew calling you Sandgrind's kin? You're as good a lookout as he was, and you're young. You may become even better."

"Here's your supper," yelled Wolkin through a full mouth, running with a bowl and spoon. He held it out to Eliss. "It's peas and rice and things. It's good."

"Thank you." Eliss took the bowl. Last night the tent had been full of ghosts. It was the last link with Falena, the last place they'd all been together. That hadn't stopped Alder from leaving, though. She'd lain awake a long while wondering where he was, whether he was scared, whether he was hungry. But Alder was becoming a man now, and men never wondered the same way as women about the people they left behind, did they?

Eliss thought about *The Silvergilts of Delairia*, about how often she'd longed to escape her family and be part of someone else's. It had happened now, hadn't it? Except for the fact that *she* hadn't run away anywhere; her family had escaped her.

Wolkin sat down and leaned against her. "Do you like it?"

She spooned up a mouthful and nodded. "It's good."

"Now you can do something else for her," said Mrs. Riveter. Wolkin jumped up and saluted. "Go get her bag out of the tent and take it to Pentra's cabin."

"Aye aye!" Wolkin ran halfway to the tent and then came sprinting back. "What about the *boyfriend's* bag?"

"Oh! That comes too. Please," said Eliss.

Wolkin made a face, but he turned and ran to obey.

"YOU CAN HAVE THE DRAWERS on that side," Pentra told her, rearranging folded clothing. Eliss stared around at the cabin. It was tiny, but as neatly fitted together as the inside of a sewing box, with a bunk against either wall and a dresser built into the wall opposite the door.

"I don't think I'll need all of them," said Eliss, feeling awkward. "More like only one. I don't have much of anything."

"Ah, but you will have," said Pentra. "When we get back to the coast and everyone gets paid, you'll want to buy yourself a good wardrobe, won't you?"

"I guess I will." Slowly Eliss went through her bag and placed its contents, one by one, on the bed. Her spare tunic, her spare pair of long stockings, the pretty shawl Wolkin had given her, the tangled mass of Falena's clothing that she hadn't been able to bring herself to think about. An old metal comb. A little box containing the oddments she'd saved from childhood: a broken string of beads, a little figure of a man Uncle Ironbolt had carved for her, a seashell, a piece of glass colored an impossible deep blue.

Eliss put the clothes in a drawer and set the comb and the little box on her side of the dresser top, since Pentra had thoughtfully swept her belongings to one side. Eliss looked at them self-consciously. How glamorous Pentra's things were, compared to her own: a pair of cut-crystal perfume vials, a comb and brush set inlaid with silver, a matching jar holding several long hair pins of silver, of jade, of mother-of-pearl. A jewel case upholstered in brocade.

And Pentra was like her things, elegant and poised as she rearranged her side of the cabin. She spoke with just a trace of the accent of the western islands, well-bred and educated. Her clothing was sober and practical, but Eliss had glimpsed some beautiful silks and brocades as Pentra had emptied the other side of the dresser for her.

"This is very kind of you," said Eliss.

"Not at all," Pentra replied, briskly gathering up rolls up paper. "I've felt a bit guilty having the whole place to myself, to tell you the truth." She opened a locker under the bunk and slid them in. "And if I have too much room my belongings tend to rather sprawl outward into every available corner. This is the best solution to both our difficulties."

"I'm glad." Eliss tried the locker under her own bunk. It opened smoothly. She put in Krelan's bag. "Er . . . you should know that I'm keeping Krelan's things for him, because he doesn't have any place for them in the galley. So he might come knocking sometimes."

"Krelan." Pentra sounded amused. "The little spitboy. He seems like a nice enough young man."

"He is." Eliss remembered him offering to go after Alder. She wanted to ask Pentra about her Yendri lover, how they'd met and whether she'd had the same troubles Falena had had. Instead, she asked: "How did you become a cartographer?"

"I like certainty." Pentra took out a nightgown of white lawn. Turning her back, she slipped out of her clothing and pulled on the gown. "I mean, I suppose that was at the root of it. My grandfather had a big library, and when we used to go to his estate for the summer I loved to look at the collection of atlases. There was one in particular that was just beautiful, with pictures in the margins in colored ink. Dragons and mermaids and all sorts of creatures. And a compass rose so lovely . . . I'll show you how lovely it was."

Turning back, she displayed her bare shoulder. Eliss saw an intricate compass rose tattooed there, beautifully worked in scarlet and blue, black, and gold. "I loved it so much I sneaked out of our compound and had it copied onto my own skin," said Pentra. "My father and mother were aghast, of course. *Girls* mustn't have themselves tattooed! It was perhaps their first inkling that I wasn't the daughter they had planned on having. However, I think it's brought me good luck. I always know exactly where I am, in a manner of speaking."

She slipped into bed. "A map gives you that too. You can look down on the world just as the gods must, and see everything that exists all laid out before you, with everything showing its proper relationship to everything else. You can travel, in a sense, without ever leaving your library. When I got a little older I drew maps of my own, made-up places. I had a tutor who encouraged me, and then I discovered that there were people who actually drew maps for a living!"

"And you studied and got certified as a cartographer?" Eliss climbed into her own bunk, uncomfortably aware that she had nothing more than her tunic to sleep in. Pentra raised an eyebrow, but did not comment upon it.

"Not just then." She leaned up on her elbow and blew out the lamp. Her voice in the darkness sounded wry. "My tutor encouraged me until my family discovered he was spending his time persuading me to scholarly pursuits, at which point they discharged him.

"What I was *supposed* to be gaining from my education, you see, was a light gloss of intellectual sophistication, such as familiarity with the better-born poets, overlaying a solid foundation of dancing, music, painting, and household management. Just what I would need to shine as the lady wife of some politician or courtier or—better still—as a duchess or countess.

"I suppose I knew all this from the time I was a baby, really, but you can know something for a long time without being really aware of what it means. I was rather shocked on the day I was called before my family's council and informed that I had been engaged to marry a man I had never met."

"And you were in love with somebody else?" Eliss was fascinated.

"Oh, no; I wasn't in any position to meet anyone else, you see, I'd been sequestered in the family compound from the moment I'd entered puberty. Possibly because of my little mistake with the tattoo, so I suppose I'd brought it on myself."

"Were you angry?"

"No. I simply thought, 'Oh, now I'll have a husband and I can finally see something of the world.' But when it was arranged for us to meet each other, I saw that he wouldn't do at all."

"Why not?"

"He was ignorant, and proud of it. His family had made a great deal of money in a very short time, which didn't bother me (though my mother was mortified), but he was at some pains to tell me they'd done it without ever opening a book. When I informed him I would want a library, he laughed a great deal and then advised me he would break me of the habit of reading. Nor would I travel in his company. He wanted a wife to stay home and weave his shirts, while *he* was out seeing the world."

"What did you do?"

"Went back to my apartments after the interview was concluded, and wrote a letter to my family explaining that I had no intention of marrying my chosen husband. Then I packed a bag, taking care to include all the ugly jewelry I'd been given over the years. I stole from my brother's clothespress and dressed myself as a boy, and made a rope out of my bedsheets tied together. I left my family compound by a window and never looked back once my feet touched the pavement."

"And . . . and you sold the jewelry for money?"

"I did. I traveled all the way to Port Blackrock and resumed my proper identity as a lady (though I was careful to change my name) and took a room in a hotel. I hired a cartographer to teach me the arts of surveying and representation, and when I knew as much as he could teach me I applied for a certification. I worked for a surveying company for some years and then I became cartographer on the *Bird*."

"It sounds so easy." Eliss marveled at the pictures in her imagination.

"It wasn't. It required a good deal of study, and then a lot of hard work and living in conditions I'd only ever encountered in the most lurid of novels. But I didn't mind. I was free to do what I wanted to do."

"Didn't your family try to get you back?"

"They did. By the time they located me I was legally free in any case, though that wouldn't necessarily have stopped them. But we came to an understanding. Since I wasn't the spineless compliant child they would have preferred for a daughter, they agreed to let me go to ruin in my own way, as long as I never used my family's name or came begging to them for money. I kept my end of the bargain and they have kept theirs. All in all a satisfactory arrangement." Pentra yawned.

"And you've never needed to ask them for money?"

"No. I have a trade, after all! And a talent for it, I flatter myself. Just as you have a talent."

Eliss wondered what she meant for a moment. "Being able to read the river?"

"Of course. Ideal situation, really. Earning your own way doing something you like, when you're actually good at it . . . we're lucky ladies." Pentra sounded drowsy. "Good night, Eliss."

"Good night."

Eliss curled up under her blanket, trying to imagine a life lived like Pentra's. She decided that the first thing she'd buy herself, when they were paid, was a good nightgown.

When she slept her dreams retold Pentra's story like an adventure out of a book, with brightly colored pictures drawn in the margins. Only, the story went on and green vines were drawn stretching across the page, and a handsome Yendri man with flowers in his hair danced with the heroine of the story . . . and then it wasn't a Yendri man but someone else, and the heroine was someone else too. . . .

ELISS HAD JUST COUNTED OFF the third sandbar of the morning when she saw the demon.

She assumed he was a demon, anyway, since his skin was spotted like an animal's fur and his hair grew halfway down his spine. More than that she couldn't tell, because he was floating facedown in the water, drifting toward the *Bird of the River* as she made her way upstream. Eliss was so startled all she could manage to shout was "Body!"

Everyone on deck looked up at her, just as startled. She managed to point and add, "Off starboard bow!"

Now the musicians saw it too and began shouting and pointing. Krelan, who had come up from the depths of the galley to dump a pail of grease into the slush-barrel, ran to the edge and pointed too. Mr. Crucible got the gaffhook and pulled the body up on deck. He turned it over. Yes, a demon; it had tusks. There was an arrowbolt embedded in one eye. Eliss, staring down from her platform, saw the eye fill with black blood, just as the demon struck out feebly with one clawed hand.

There was a concerted scream and near-stampede as all the women on deck grabbed for all the children who had run to see the demon. Mr. Crucible backed away quickly. In a blur of motion, Krelan grabbed a root-cutting machete from the tool rack, and then the demon's head was spinning free of its body and had rolled into the scuppers.

All this happened at once, within a few seconds. The screams from the women on deck died away. Yet someone was still screaming. . . . Eliss, distracted, looked up. The *Bird of the River* was just rounding a bend in the river. The headland and screening trees drew back like a curtain to reveal a pleasure-boat with gaily striped sails, with little fishing skiffs clustered around her.

But it wasn't a landing. Men had thrown lines from the fishing skiffs onto the deck of the pleasure-boat, and swarmed upon her deck. There was the woman, screaming under her pink sunshade as she wrestled with a demon who was attempting to rape her. There were the pleasure-boat's crew, fighting for their lives. Two other bodies floated in the water.

"PIRATES!" roared Mr. Riveter. Captain Glass steered the *Bird* straight for the pleasure-boat. The women on deck collected the children and fled below. Some of them returned, minus the children but clutching bows and pulling on quivers full of arrows as they came. The polemen swarmed for the arms locker and by the time the *Bird* came within range she was bristling with defenders. The captain dragged the tiller back at the last minute and the *Bird* swung around ponderously, presenting her broadside to the pleasure-boat and crushing some of the fishing skiffs between their hulls.

It was over quickly. Some of the pirates ran across the pleasure-boat's deck and dove into the river on the other side. Eliss spotted them swimming for shore. Some reached the shore and ran off into the woods; others took arrows fired from the *Bird* and flailed, splashing, before rolling over in the water and drifting motionless. Most of the pirates who fled were Children of the Sun. Only the demons remained on the pleasure-boat's deck, fighting even when they must know they were doomed. Men from the *Bird* boarded the pleasure-boat—Eliss could see now that her name was the *Dancing Girl*—leaping over the skiff debris being ground to yet smaller pieces.

Eliss saw Krelan, still clutching the machete, beheading another demon as he made what looked like an impossible leap into the air. She saw one of the *Dancing Girl*'s crew, a well-dressed man who looked like a lord, taking the opportunity to bind a scarf around his wounded arm before driving his sword through the heart of a demon who had fallen to the deck wounded. The woman under the pink sunshade had killed her attacker with a tiny golden-hilted dagger and crouched above the body now, weeping as she plunged her dagger into its throat repeatedly. There was blood all over the *Dancing Girl*'s deck.

Captain Glass bellowed the order to strike sail and lower anchors. As the topmen climbed all around her to obey, Eliss looked down to see whether Alder was all right, caught herself, and clenched her fists. She climbed down while the *Bird of the River* moored beside the *Dancing Girl*.

"The gods bless you for your timely aid," the lord was saying to Mr. Riveter, as Eliss approached the rail.

"What happened?"

"I should have thought that was obvious," said the lord, scowling. "We were attacked by river pirates." Mr. Riveter blushed.

"Yes, my lord, I only meant—in a general way. Are you all right? Have you lost anyone?"

"One or two of my household, I think," said the lord, looking around. He pointed to one of the bodies floating in the water. "There. Damn. That's one of mine. Retrieve his body, please."

"Yes, my lord." Mr. Riveter saluted, and ran for the gaffhook. The lord walked aft to speak with the woman in a low voice. The surviving servants and those who had come over from the *Bird* busied themselves with dragging the bodies of the pirates from the deck and pitching them into the river. On the *Bird*, the children came swarming on deck again, to stare at the bodies in the water. Wolkin ran to the rail by Eliss.

"Did you see him chop the head off that demon?" he exclaimed, pointing at Krelan, who was helping a servant mop blood from the *Dancing Girl*'s deck. "He has *moves!* Eeee-yah whack!"

"He did it again, to that one." Eliss pointed at a headless body floating in the water. Wolkin peered down at it and went a little pale.

"Well. Well, maybe he isn't so weasely after all. Do you think he'd teach me how to do that?"

"I don't think it's something you can teach in a day," said Eliss, watching as Krelan expertly swilled bloody water into the *Dancing Girl's* scuppers. He set about picking up the contents of a tray that had been scattered on the deck during the attack: pieces of fruit, a decanter, a pair of goblets. Eliss saw him halt, staring at one of the goblets a moment. He placed it back on the tray and carried it aft to the area under the pink sunshade, and presented it to the lady with a bow. She, still weeping as she spoke with her lord, impatiently waved at a table. Krelan set the tray down and turned to go. The lord turned and spoke to him, clapping him on the shoulder. Krelan smiled deferentially and replied. The conversation went on for some time, as order was restored to their respective craft. The woman wiped her face on her veil, shouted angrily for a maidservant, and went stalking into the *Dancing Girl's* great cabin.

"She looked mean," Wolkin observed.

"You should have seen her killing one of the pirates," said Eliss. "She looked *really* mean then."

"I wish I could have seen the fight." Wolkin sighed. "I could have climbed up to the masthead and seen everything from there and still been safe. Next time we see pirates, can I just climb up there with you and you not tell Mama? Because we couldn't get shot at up there. It's too far up in the air."

"How often do we run into pirates?" Eliss looked down at him, startled.

"Oh . . . once in a while. Last time Tulu and I were only one and a half, so I don't remember. Anyway, can I go aloft and watch from there?"

"I don't think your mama and daddy would like that," said Eliss, gazing out again at the *Dancing Girl*. Krelan and the lord were still deep in conversation. Two polemen from the *Bird* carried over the body of the lord's servant that had been pulled from the river. The lord looked aside long enough to give a terse order. Three of the surviving servants took charge of the body and, weeping, wrapped it in canvas.

"Besides," Eliss continued, "if it's been eight years since the other pirate attack, it might be eight years until the next one. You'd be seventeen then, all grown up. Probably you'd be expected to fight, by that time."

"That would be great," said Wolkin fervently.

"And anyway, what if the pirates had fire-arrows? They could reach the platform, you know."

"Oh, well, if I was fighting I wouldn't be up there." Wolkin climbed up and stood on the rail. "Anyway, pirates don't fight with arrows, they have swords and tridents."

"Really?"

"Because they don't want to burn a boat until after they loot it and kill everybody."

"Oh."

The door of the *Dancing Girl*'s great cabin flew open and the woman leaned out. "Magoron," she shouted. "*Please* take a moment to come see whether I'm alive."

The lord broke off his conversation with Krelan and turned and strode to the cabin. He slammed the door after him and the muffled sound of a furious argument came from the cabin. Krelan, meanwhile, walked forward and spoke in a low voice with the servants as he helped them wrap the body of the other dead man.

"I didn't think rich people had fights," said Wolkin.

"Of course they do. All those vendettas."

"No, that's just sort of war. I mean yelling at each other about things. Like, 'You spent all your pay on wine! How am I supposed to buy food? You leave your clothes lying around!'" Wolkin spoke in a shrill falsetto. He stretched out his arms and walked along the rail, carefully placing one foot in front of the other.

"Maybe they're more like us than we think." Eliss watched Krelan take something small from inside his hood and show it to the servants. Was it the portrait of Encilian Diamondcut? They stared intently and then began to speak all at once. Krelan held up his hands. Looking over his shoulder at the great cabin, he leaned in closer to them. One of them began to speak, rapidly, with gestures, and from time to time the other two would interrupt him or nod in agreement.

THAT NIGHT AS ELISS WAITED near the end of the dinner line, Krelan caught her eye. He mouthed, *Meet me in the bow afterward?* She nodded and, after receiving her bowl of dinner, waited around until everyone else had been served. Krelan loaded up his own bowl and they walked forward together to the *Bird*'s bow.

"Did you find out something?" Eliss inquired as they sat down by the rail.

"You were watching us. Tell me first what you saw, and what you think it meant. This is a test." Krelan looked quietly gleeful.

"All right . . . You picked up a bunch of things that had been knocked off the table. And one of them interested you. It was a goblet. There was something about the goblet that . . . did it have something to do with Lord Encilian?"

"It did." Krelan blew on his soup. He tilted his bowl and sipped.

"So it must have belonged to him. They looked like fancy goblets. Did it have his personal crest or his house sign or something on it? It must have."

"It did."

"So somehow or other one of his goblets got on that boat. So . . . at one time or another, *he* must have been on that boat. The goblet might have got there a couple of other ways, but that's the easiest explanation."

"So it is. And he was, as it happens."

"And you know this because you got Lord—what's his name?"

"Lord Chrysoprase."

"All right, you got Lord Chrysoprase to tell you. He was very friendly with you. I'll bet he saw you cut off that other demon's head during the fighting. You talked for a long time. I'll bet . . . he offered you a job as one of his bodyguards, since two of his were killed."

Krelan gave her a sharp look. "You must have heard us."

"No. It just makes sense. The lord's on a cruise, he's just lost two of his people, he doesn't want to hire just anybody, and here's this boy who's shown how good he is at killing enemies. And you're good at sounding like anybody you want to be, and you must have talked to him as someone who's worked for nobles." Eliss felt a little smug, looking at Krelan's expression, until it occurred to her that Krelan might have accepted the job offer.

"You *are* good." Krelan nodded slowly.

"So . . . he told you something about your lord being on the boat. Or maybe he didn't. Because his lady called him away. So you went and talked to the servants. You showed them your little portrait of your lord." Eliss realized she'd miss Krelan if he left. And he might just pick up and go over to the *Dancing Girl*, mightn't he? If that was what it took to find out more about how Encilian had died.

"I did show them the portrait. That much must have been obvious."

"And . . . they told you a lot. Because you talked to them a long time. And there must have been something, well, not quite *right* about what they told you, because they looked so scared and shut up so quickly when Lord Chrysoprase came out again."

"Gods below." Krelan drank more of his soup. "If you can tell me any more, I'm going to propose real marriage. You're better than a temple oracle."

"It's just watching and paying attention," said Eliss, drinking some soup. "Same as with the river."

"But most people don't pay attention." Krelan glanced over at the lights of the *Dancing Girl*, where Captain Glass and Mr. Riveter were dining with Lord Chrysoprase. "And they don't think about what they see. Can you tell me any more?"

Eliss thought about it. "Lady Chrysoprase doesn't seem very

happy with her lord. She feels neglected. So . . . maybe Lord Encilian slept with her, behind her husband's back? Maybe their boats were at the same landing for a few days. And that would maybe explain why the servants looked so scared, and how one of Lord Encilian's goblets got on board their boat. And maybe *that* means Lord Chrysoprase found out and murdered him!"

"I thought so too." Krelan took his spoon and dredged up rice from the bottom of the soup bowl. "But he didn't. Yes, Encilian moored beside them at a place up the river called Silver Trout Landing. Yes, they visited back and forth on each other's boats for a few days. Yes, he romanced Lady Chrysoprase and may even have done the wicked deed. And yes, somehow or other one of his goblets got on the wrong boat, either because Lady Chrysoprase wanted it as a keepsake or because Encilian's personal crest looks a bit like Chrysoprase's and someone got them mixed up clearing the table. *But* Lord Chrysoprase didn't kill Encilian."

"And you know this because . . . ?"

"Because he was still alive when he left Silver Trout Landing."

"Lord Chrysoprase might have sent an assassin after him."

"He might have, but he didn't."

"How can you be sure?"

"Because he never found out about Encilian and Lady Chrysoprase."

"He might have, but hidden it from the servants."

"People like that don't hide anything from servants," said Krelan, and snickered. "We might as well be animals. Scandals, infidelities, digestive afflictions—nothing's too personal for the servants to see. Take my word for it. And he doesn't have Encilian's head. Which he would have kept as a trophy, if he'd had Encilian killed for adulterizing. And believe me, the servants would have noticed if some assassin had brought it back for him. Imagine having to dust something like that!"

Eliss shuddered. "Did they say whether he still had his servant with him?"

"What? No. I mean, they didn't mention it."

"So . . . in the end, all you've learned was that your lord was alive as far up the river as Silver Trout Landing."

"That's about it. That, and that he was still behaving like Encilian."

"Then . . . I don't suppose you'll be accepting the lord's job offer."

"No."

Eliss was surprised at the wave of relief that washed over her. Sternly she told herself not to be an idiot. *He'll go anyway, once the job's done.*

The deck watch cried a challenge, and then the gangplank creaked and groaned as Captain Glass and Mr. Riveter came back aboard. To Eliss's surprise, Captain Glass looked around, spotted them, and came forward. He was dressed in his best clothing, a striped tunic big enough to have served as a tent and a jade chain of office. Mr. Riveter was likewise wearing more clothes than Eliss had ever seen on him. He looked stiff and uncomfortable, but Captain Glass was grinning.

"Spitboy," he said. "His lordship was impressed by you. Just spent most of an hour trying to buy your services from me." He looked over his shoulder at Mr. Riveter. "Why don't you go below, Mr. Riveter? You look like an eel wrapped up in a paper parcel."

"Aye, sir." Gratefully, Mr. Riveter wandered off to the companionway.

"Yes, his lordship wanted to know all about you, spitboy. I had to be tactful."

"Oh, dear." Krelan seemed to shrink.

"Told him you weren't mine to sell. Told him you were under an obligation to the gods. Told him you were working as a galley slavey as penance for something you did."

"Oh. Well, that's as good a reason as any. Thank you, sir."

"You're welcome." The captain loomed over them both, gigantic against the stars. "That was some neat work you did with the machete, spitboy. Not quite as feeble as you look, are you?"

" *'Terror lends strength to even a paper man,'* " Krelan quoted.

"And paper's stronger than most people think," said the captain. "Writs of execution, for example. Or contracts for vendetta killings. I wouldn't want to think somebody might carry out one of those on my boat. But then, I guess if someone had anything against one of *my* crew, he'd have taken care of business already. So we don't have anything to worry about, do we, spitboy?"

"I shouldn't think so, sir."

"Good." Captain Glass turned his enigmatic grin on Eliss. "How are you, Miss Vigilance? The brother is all right, you know. Doing what boys have to do. And you're doing what you have to do. The world rolls on. You've dried all your tears, right?"

"Yes, sir."

"Good." Captain Glass put his head up and sniffed the night air. "Rain coming tomorrow," he added, before abruptly turning and walking aft.

RAIN DID COME, after a long breathless night. Eliss woke once in the cabin, gasping for air, and found that she'd kicked off her blanket. After a while Pentra woke and climbed from her bunk, and opened a bladed vent in the cabin's rear wall. It admitted no light, but abruptly the smell of the river filled the room and the air was a little cooler. Pentra went back to bed. Eliss lay wakeful a long while, listening to the river noises, the night noises, and eventually the grumble of distant thunder. She slept and dreamed of green leviathans coiling in the water, and cloud-gods dropping fire from heaven. Later she dreamed of armies marching across the deck overhead.

NEXT MORNING RAIN WAS POURING DOWN, though the summer heat still lay heavy over everything. Eliss had no rain gear; she came timidly on deck and saw everyone working stripped down to near nudity, the men in loincloths, the women in loincloths too with single lengths of cotton cloth bound over their breasts. Making a note to buy herself some cloth when she was paid, Eliss splashed out on deck and was soaked to the skin in seconds. The rain was warm as bathwater.

A tarpaulin had been stretched over the galley queue, and a couple of planks leaned up on end by the deckhouse to keep rainwater outside from spattering into the porridge cauldron. Krelan, with his thin hair plastered flat on his head as a painted doll's, stood in a puddle of water as he ladled out porridge into bowls. People huddled together under the tarpaulin, wolfing down their breakfasts, watching the rain. Eliss finished her breakfast quickly and ran for the rigging, clinging tight to the slippery ropes.

It was terrifying being up on her platform, but exhilarating too. Rain beat down all around her; the sky sat low on the river valley, hiding the mountaintops under a level line of cloud. Eliss leaned back her head and gulped in air. The rain washed her face. She remembered Alder running gleefully through the rain and jumping in puddles, scandalizing anyone who saw him.

So many times we had to tell him to stop doing things he loved to do. At least now . . . now he can enjoy the rain.

She pushed back her wet hair and looked down at the deck. Krelan was working hard with a bellows, trying to keep the galley fire from going out. Pentra came up the companionway with a pair of wax tablets under her arm, instead of her usual paper and ink, and dumped the collected rainwater from her sun canopy before taking her place at her drafting station. The musicians had come out of the windmill and conferred briefly before going back inside; now they emerged with tin whistles and struck up a shrill dancing tune.

Eliss saw children dancing to the music, naked on deck in the rain, screaming with excitement. The women came up with buckets and pails to catch water for hair-washing. Captain Glass came up on deck, nearly naked himself. He stood at the tiller, laughing quietly as rain sluiced down over his face and broad chest and dripped from his beard.

Mr. Riveter, in nothing but his customary loincloth, walked backward on deck staring up at the vanes of the windmill. They were nearly motionless in the steady rain, until a breeze came up the valley. The vanes began to rotate, flinging out water in all directions. "Topmen!" Mr. Riveter roared. "Set sail! Cablemen, stand by to raise anchor!"

One of the drummers found a tin pail and began to beat out a staccato rhythm on its bottom, accompanying the whistles. Men raced up along the shrouds and ratlines and loosed the great sail. It fell in heavy rustling folds, dry at first but darkening with the rain, and snapping out taut as the wind caught it. Over on the *Dancing Girl*, Lord and Lady Chrysoprase's servants, sweating in oilcloth rain gear, were preparing to cast off. Lord Chrysoprase emerged from the great cabin and took the tiller, as one of his servants hurried to hold an umbrella over him. He nodded curtly at Mr. Riveter and shouted the order to raise anchor. Mr. Riveter's order echoed back.

The *Dancing Girl* slipped out into the current and away downstream. The *Bird of the River* moved off upstream, as her children danced and the river boiled white with rain.

THE RAIN CONTINUED STEADILY for three days. Now and again thunder would rumble around the four quarters of the sky, and Eliss learned to catch a rope then and slide down to deck as fast as she could, because of the hazard of lightning. On one occasion the topmen were aloft too when the thunder started, and one of them grabbed her around the waist and slid down a rope with her.

"Sorry," he said as soon as their feet touched the deck. He was young, and while not handsome he wore a gold ring set with a fire opal in one ear. "The lightning was coming fast, is all. And I've always wanted to rescue a princess from a tower," he added, grinning foolishly.

"I'm no princess," said Eliss, pulling her tunic down.

"Sure you are. You're the daughter of Beautiful Falena, after all," he said, and then ran for cover as the lightning flashed blue-white over their heads. Eliss barely noticed it, staring after him. She thought, *Am I the only one who really remembers my mother?*

The Ballad of Falena was everywhere now. They anchored for a night at Red House Landing, and an elderly beggar with a concertina was playing the song in the inn courtyard.

"CARE TO GO ASHORE WITH ME for dinner?" Krelan gave her a meaningful look as she approached the galley queue that night.

"What, to the Red House?"

"Why not? Just wait until I'm done serving everybody and we'll go over together."

"All right." Eliss took her bowl back to the cabin and put on her clean tunic. After a moment's hesitation she took out the shawl Wolkin had bought her and wrapped it around her shoulders. The girl who looked back at her in the polished copper mirror looked very grown-up, very much a girl who was going out to dinner with a boyfriend. And Alder would have scowled and sulked at being left behind, and Eliss would have felt guilty for leaving him.

But I have to grow up sometime, Eliss thought. *It wasn't fair that I had to be somebody's mother and stay a little girl too.* She was wondering whether she ought to comb her hair when Krelan came hurrying down the companionway.

"Oh, good, you haven't locked the door. Just let me slip inside and change." He stopped and stared at her before slipping inside the cabin. "You *do* look nice. But then, you generally do," he added from inside, a little muffled.

"It's just the shawl," said Eliss, glad he couldn't see her blushing. "It was expensive."

"Ha! No, my dear; money couldn't buy your looks."

"You're just flattering. I'm nothing special."

"No, indeed." Krelan's voice was serious. "I mean, I *would* flatter you, if I needed something, because don't all men? But in your case there's no need to make anything up. That's the big difference. That and the fact that you've got brains." He emerged from the cabin, pulling on his hood. "There! Do I look like some harmless little twit?"

"I'm afraid so."

"Good!" Krelan took her arm and they walked back up the companionway.

ALL THE OTHER RED HOUSES Eliss had ever been in had been on caravan routes, crowded with travelers bedding down for the night on the floor. This one was nearly deserted, and eerily silent. The old man with his concertina had spread out his blanket in a far corner of the hall and his snores were already echoing from the high rafters, but other than that no one seemed to be spending the night there. There weren't even many diners, other than a couple of parties who had come up from the boat landing.

"I've never had a seat by the firepit before," said Eliss, looking around. She adjusted a fold of her shawl self-consciously. Her family had always been over there in the shadows, making up beds on the floor with people like the old musician, and young Eliss had looked over in awe at the well-dressed diners at the best tables.

"No caravan parties filling the place up," said Krelan. "This high up the river, they're only going to get barge crews or pleasure-boats, and if you can afford a pleasure-boat, why would you bother eating at a Red House?"

"What's wrong with Red Houses?" To Eliss they had always seemed elegant places, warm havens at the end of a long cold day of travel, a luxury only to be indulged in when whoever Falena had been currently with could afford it. Krelan arched an eyebrow.

"The food's a little basic," he said.

But their dinners, when brought, were well prepared. "Damn," remarked Krelan in surprise, and said nothing further until his plate was empty.

"See?" Feeling gleefully adult and sophisticated, Eliss speared the last fried dumpling on the end of her knife.

"I suppose if you depend on the barge crews for your custom, you'd better serve good food." Krelan pushed his dish away and leaned back in his chair. He gazed around the room. "And, to be honest, I'd never eaten in one of these before. Well, well. *That's* the house security, unless I miss my guess."

Eliss followed his gaze. Sitting alone in the far corner of the room was a big man, soberly dressed and not noteworthy in any respect. He had a tablet open in front of him and seemed absorbed in making notes, but as Eliss stared at him he looked up and met her eyes. She looked away, abashed. Krelan got to his feet.

"I think I know you, don't I?" he said lightly, advancing on the big man's table, so Eliss got up and followed. "I think I met you at my uncle's house."

"I think you did," the man replied. Eliss saw now that the tablet contained a word puzzle, half-completed. Krelan sat down and placed his hands on the table in a curious way: both index fingers out straight, the other fingers folded under. He only kept them that way a moment, but the man noticed, and made the same gesture back. He looked inquiringly at Eliss.

"A secure friend," said Krelan.

"Very well, then. You're a little young."

"Born into the work, I'm afraid. Took the oath when I was eight."

"Ah." The man looked at Krelan more closely. "Yes. I might know your name. What can I do for you, brother?"

"You can tell me how long you've worked here."

"Five years."

"Good. And you're the only house man?"

"I am."

Krelan reached into his hood and brought out the little portrait of Lord Encilian. He slid it across the tabletop toward the other man. "Seen him? It would have been a little after the Winter Solstice."

"Hm!" The man tapped the portrait with his fingertip, just over the serpent armlet. "Well, I know who he is. Or was. But he never came in this place, brother. Not really the sort of stop his sort would make, is it?"

"You're sure?"

"I'm sure. Anyway, I heard he died." The man surveyed Krelan. "You don't mean they sent a kid like *you* to do anything about it?"

"They did, in fact."

The man shrugged. "No offense. But no, as far as I know he never even moored at the landing. Red Houses are too, what's the word? Déclassé, I suppose, for one of them, and there's nothing else here."

"No night life, eh?"

The man chuckled and jerked his thumb at the concertina player. "Old Leadbrick's just about it. Nothing much happens here except a fight now and then when barge crews come in to drink."

"No bandits attacking?" Eliss asked. The man looked at her in surprise.

"No. What would they steal? The souvenir shop's full of junk. The Housekeeper barely breaks even. It's been bad this summer, though, hasn't it, downriver?" He began to look thoughtful. "Bluestone, last I heard. And, what's the gold place? Synpelene."

Krelan nodded. "Asking you as a brother, then: anything you can say that might give me a clue?"

"What, about who did it?" The man rubbed his chin, studying the portrait. "Not really. I'd say the chances are good it happened up in Karkateen. Plenty of ways a boy like that might run into trouble, up there."

"That's what I've been afraid of."

"Don't envy you your job, brother."

"Well. For your trouble." Krelan produced a gold crown from

nowhere and slid it across the table to the man, reclaiming the portrait in the process. The man nodded and deftly made the coin vanish.

"Anytime."

AS THEY WALKED BACK DOWN to the landing, Eliss asked: "Why is Karkateen a dangerous place?"

"You've never been?"

"No. No jobs for a diver there. We almost went once. A man we were living with was offered a job there, but he left Mama and went by himself in the end." At that moment it came home to Eliss: that would never happen again. No more desertions. She had lost everyone, but at least she was free. She didn't have to become the sort of woman who clung desperately to someone else for salvation. *Alder was free too. . . .* No wonder he had wanted to run away. "What's it like in Karkateen?"

"It's a wild city. It's where the river ends. Or begins, I suppose. There's a lot of what my grandfather used to call *lottery rich* up there, and you should have heard the disdain with which he pronounced those words! Believe me, servants know who deserves money and who doesn't. In this case it comes from emerald mines. So there are a lot of mansions owned by people who were clever enough to know what to do with the money they made from emeralds, and a lot of, er, retail establishments frequented by people who *aren't* clever enough to know what to do with the money they made from emeralds. And then there are the people who don't find any emeralds."

"And we're going there?"

"Of course we are. That's where the *Bird* makes her turn and goes back downriver toward the coast. Would you mind very much if I ask you something, Eliss?"

"No."

"Why did you ask our friend whether there'd been any attacks by bandits?"

"Well . . ." Eliss shrugged. "There have been a lot of them, haven't there?"

"There have been, yes." Krelan fell silent.

NEXT MORNING THEY DISCOVERED Mr. Pitspike had gone ashore to visit his son, who happened to be the cook at the Red House, and he had yet to return by the appointed time of sailing, though the Housekeeper thoughtfully sent a message to say he was merely dead drunk and not dead. As a consequence Captain Glass postponed their departure a day, and so the crew seized the opportunity to do laundry. The *Bird of the River* was festooned with drying clothes in short order. Eliss was sitting by the rail, trying to begin a novel Pentra had loaned her, when she looked up through shirts fluttering in the breeze and saw the group of Yendri making their way along the riverbank.

There were three of them. One was shorter than the other two. Eliss set the book down and stood, feeling her heart pound.

Three Yendri, and she knew them all. The handsome one, and wasn't it odd how she now could tell them apart enough to see distinctions like that, the handsome one had danced with Pentra. The one in the white robe was Mr. Moss. Alder was walking between them, still clutching his bag. He had been crying and looked sullen.

But he was all right. He was alive and all right. He hadn't drowned or been killed by demons or gotten lost. All her bitter anger dropped away and Eliss felt light enough to fly.

She heard a cry of surprise from behind her on the deck, and running feet. A second later Pentra was beside her at the rail, waving frantically.

"Denuseth!"

They were coming down on the landing now. The handsome one looked up and grinned. Yes, he *was* handsome, wasn't he? He waved back at her and they kept coming. Alder looked up, saw Eliss, and his face screwed up as though he was going to start crying again.

Now other people on deck had noticed and come to the rail to stare. Eliss turned and ran down the gangplank. She threw her arms around Alder and hugged him tight, blind with tears. Alder drew a deep breath.

"I'm sorry I ran away without telling you," he said. "I apologize."

Eliss only clung to him, her throat too tight to get any words out. She heard Pentra saying to—to Denuseth, that must be his name—"It was so kind of you to bring him back."

"No, it was selfish. An excuse to see you again."

"Are you all right?" Eliss managed to say at last. Alder nodded, but she couldn't remember ever seeing him look so unhappy.

"And I bring news from Caiwyr." That was Denuseth again. "A letter, and a bag of apple tea."

"How is he?"

"Well. He'll tell you the rest."

It had been easier to be angry at Alder than to imagine him dying alone somewhere. Eliss thought of all the ways in which she had been comparing Alder to the uncles who had come and gone, when he was only a little boy after all, and miserable at having to live in the wrong world.

Eliss swallowed hard. She looked up at Mr. Moss, who was watching them, without any expression she recognized. "Thank you," she said. "Mr. Moss, would it be all right—would you take my brother as an apprentice?"

Mr. Moss nodded slowly. Alder pulled away from her and looked up into her face. "Please," he whispered.

"Is it truly what you wish?" said Mr. Moss.

"Yes," said Eliss. "It is. As long as I know he's safe, it's all right."

"He will be safe with us."

"Eliss, I'll be so careful, I'll learn things and—and I can send you medicines if you ever get sick," Alder babbled.

"It's not as though you won't see each other again," said Pentra, holding out a handkerchief to Eliss. "Twice a year, the *Bird* stops at Moonport."

Eliss nodded and wiped her eyes. "I'm sorry you had to come so far for nothing," she told Mr. Moss. He shook his head.

"Without this, both your lives would be poisoned," he said. "Now that weed is pulled."

"Have you got your blanket?" Eliss looked down at Alder.

"I have my blanket. And a place to sleep." His slow smile brightened to radiant happiness. "And summer is coming *soon*. It is, Eliss. It finally really is."

NEXT DAY the *Bird of the River* set sail and continued on her journey, Mr. Pitspike having been carried aboard semiconscious the previous night. With Denuseth and Mr. Moss, Alder stood on the landing and waved good-bye to Eliss, who watched him from the mast platform as long as she dared. He seemed taller already.

She felt an odd sensation, like a tug on her attention. She looked down at the deck. Captain Glass stood at the tiller, his broad expressionless face turned up to her.

"You did good, Vigilance," he called.

THAT NIGHT AS ELISS WAS GETTING ready for bed, Pentra came in with a little pot of hot water.

"I'm going to make some tea," she said. "Would you like any?"

"Yes, please. Thank you." Eliss sat up. She watched curiously as Pentra opened a locker and got out a canister and a small pottery jar with a spigot. She set them on the dresser, shook some of the canister's contents into the jar, and added the hot water. "Er . . . all I have to drink out of is my bowl, but you don't have to fill it all the way."

"Wait." Pentra set the pan aside and took something else from the locker. She turned around and opened a wooden box to reveal a set of celadon cups nested in velvet. "These will do. We can use a pair of these, don't you think?"

"If you don't mind—they're awfully nice."

"Well, they're meant to be used." Pentra set out two cups on the dresser. She checked the jar, swirling its contents a little. A pungent sweetness filled the cabin, a smell like orchard leaves in autumn. "Mm. Ready soon."

"What kind of tea is it?"

"I don't know its real name. I've always called it apple tea, because of its scent. It isn't made from apples, though. It's an herb. My son grows it for me."

"You have a son?" Eliss was shocked. She hadn't thought Pentra was that old. Pentra nodded.

"Caiwyr. He's just about your age. Studying at a Yendri, well, we'd call it a temple, but *they* wouldn't. He's a disciple of the Green Witch, which is what *we'd* call her, but the Yendri certainly wouldn't. They call her the Unwearied Mother."

"She's supposed to be like a goddess." Eliss remembered Alder describing what he'd heard. "Except they haven't got any."

"She works miracles all the same, or so I am given to understand." Pentra checked the tea again and carefully set one of the cups under the spigot. She filled the cup and presented it to Eliss. "And anyone can become a disciple. Even children of double heritage, like my son, or your brother."

"Is . . . is your son's father Denuseth?"

"Yes." Pentra filled her own cup and leaned against her bunk, inhaling the tea's fragrance.

"You . . . how did you manage? Because Mama—" Eliss stopped, abashed.

Pentra sipped her tea. "How did I manage . . . the fact is that I was still rather angry about my family, during my first few years as a free adult. I wasn't nearly as free nor as adult as I thought I was, in fact. I think on some level I wanted to shock them still further, and the best way to do that would be to take a Yendri lover. Possibly the worst reason in the world for beginning a romance with someone.

"I was part of a mapping expedition at the time. We camped near a Yendri place and some of them came over to find out what we were doing, because we were more or less on their land, though of course they don't have the same conception of property that we do. One of them was this big devastatingly handsome savage and I thought, well! That's for me. So I behaved like a little wanton idiot and we got to know each other rather better.

"And of course I discovered he wasn't a savage at all, but in fact a much more civilized person than I was. Made me thoroughly ashamed of myself. Worse still, I fell desperately in love with him."

"Why was that bad?"

"Because he wasn't about to come live in our cities, and I wasn't about to come live in the forest. We quarreled and I left with the expedition, crying my heart out. I cried a lot harder a month or two later, I can tell you, when I discovered the baby was on the way."

"What did you do?"

"Sublet my nice rooms and took a caravan back to the Greenlands. Got out at a watering stop and took the expedition's trail back into the forest. The other passengers thought I was insane. But I found Denuseth again, and lived with his family until the baby was born."

"You lived with the *Yendri?*"

"Had to, dear. You know yourself what our people would have thought about it if I'd stayed in one of our cities."

Eliss nodded, remembering the day Alder had been born. Kindly neighbors had suddenly become cold, or hostile outright. "But . . . what was it like?"

"Awful. At first. I thought so, anyway. Everyone was very kind, and being with Denuseth was wonderful, but . . . one sleeps outdoors. I had never done that except on an expedition, when at least one had a tent, and one knew one was coming back to four walls and a roof and hot bathwater. And the Yendri bathe a great deal, they're cleaner than we are in that respect really, but they only bathe in cold water, so that was a shock. They don't use fire very much, in fact they only really cook food for invalids. So you can imagine I spent the entire time cold and hungry and picking twigs out of my hair.

"And so bored . . . Yendri tell long stories in their own language, beautiful to listen to as music, but I didn't understand them unless Den translated. They hold wonderful dances, but as time went on I wasn't really up to dancing much. Den's mother taught me how to spin cotton and weave on a loom, and I loved doing that. Wove a great many blankets for the baby. But I knew I could never stay there."

"Couldn't he have come with you and opened a bathhouse or something?" Eliss inquired. "Yendri live in cities. I've seen them."

"Yes, but Den wasn't a white-robe. And trust me, dear, he'd have been as wretched in a city as I was in the forest. Love may conquer all, but it has a hard time keeping its temper when it's always uncomfortable and never gets a full night's sleep. We talked about our situation a great deal.

"And then the baby was born and I saw at once I could never take him away with me. He was as much a Yendri as your brother is.

"I left him with Denuseth and I went back home. It was the hardest thing I'd ever done. I ate in my favorite restaurants. I went to the theater. I bathed in copious amounts of hot water and curled up in my own bed in my cozy room and I was absolutely miserable for months. I missed my baby. I missed Denuseth. I couldn't be happy in either world, and I'd done it to myself.

"But it worked out. Eventually."

"What did you do?" Eliss remembered her tea and tasted it. It had a sweet haunting flavor.

"I was working in the city archivists' office when a friend told me that the *Bird of the River* needed a cartographer. I presented myself and Captain Glass signed me on. The first time we stopped at Moonport, Denuseth was there with Caiwyr. Somehow, he'd known I was coming. One of those mystic Yendri things, I suppose. I'd been praying we'd meet again, I had this box full of toys I'd bought for my child, and I felt so foolish but he was delighted with them when he finally saw them . . . I'm sure they made a bigger impression on him than I did." Pentra's gaze was far away.

"What happened then?"

"What?" She looked down at Eliss and smiled. "We had a lovely visit and when the *Bird* sailed on, I sailed with her. And since then I see Denuseth twice each transit, at Moonport. Caiwyr used to come with him until he went to train for a disciple, but he sends me letters now. He wants to open a bathhouse and herbalist's establishment at Moonport, when he's fulfilled his novitiate. We're very proud of him, Den and I.

"Now, I wouldn't in any way counsel you to follow my example in romance. I was selfish, and foolish, and have paid for it with a great deal of heartache. But you can see, can't you, that your brother *will* be all right? He's in the proper world at last. It's bound to improve his temper." Pentra drained her cup. "There's a little tea left. Would you like a bit more?"

THE SUMMER DAYS MELTED one into another, an endless journey past yellow meadows, past open savannahs scattered with oak trees, under a hot blue sky. Sometimes where they moored for the night there were thickets of blackberries, and people would go ashore and fill pails full of them, and for days the staining juice got everywhere. Mr. Pitspike made blackberry wine, storing it in stone jars belowdecks, and one night a couple of the jars exploded and woke everyone.

When the weather was too hot, everyone slept on deck; when it became oppressive enough, people gave up on sleeping and the musicians simply stayed up all night, playing quietly as the stars drifted across the vault of the sky. Sometimes stories were told, folktales and hero-epics in the early evening, darker stories after the children had finally nodded off. Drogin had a bloodcurdling series of anecdotes about the Old Wars and the dead who were supposed to haunt the battlefields forever after. Kettrick the fiddler had once lived in a haunted house in Mount Flame, where each full moon at midnight a ghostly fight took place on the front stairs, and one night a city warden had gone to break it up and seen only skeletal figures clutch-ing clubs and knives, and he had gone raving mad.

Salpin swore he had once been benighted on a mountain road and walked side by side with the Master of the Mountain himself, whom he had seen, quite clearly and distinctly, every time the moon had come out from behind the clouds; until, in a flare of lightning and a clap of thunder, the demon-lord had transported him to a for-est clearing on a mountaintop. There a great assemblage of demons in fine clothes awaited, and Salpin had been forced to play his con-certina for their amusement until daybreak, when he had been given a drink that knocked him unconscious, and woke hours later by the side of the road with a pocket full of gold.

After a couple of hours of this sort of story most listeners felt an agreeable chill, enabling them to doze until the sky lightened and the stars winked out, and another day on the river began.

"MR. PITSPIKE SAYS WE'LL BE AT SILVER Trout Landing to-morrow." Krelan put his head through the mast platform entrance. Eliss, who had been trying to decide whether a particular ripple was a submerged rock or an otter, jumped in surprise. "Do you want to come ashore with me?"

"I'd like that," said Eliss. "Wasn't that where your lord is supposed to have stopped?"

"So I was informed." Krelan pulled himself up and through.

"Do you want me to pretend to be your wife again?" Eliss gave him an arch look.

"I just want you to listen as I talk to people," said Krelan. "We won't get a chance to do much more. It isn't that kind of place."

"What do you need me for, then?"

"You notice things," said Krelan. "And I'm beginning to think you're smarter than I am."

BY LAW the *Bird of the River* was entitled to supplies at every town on the river, as part of the tithing arrangement for clearing out navigation hazards. The inhabitants of Silver Trout Landing found contact with the barge distasteful, however, since they considered themselves more of a destination resort or enclave than a mere town, and so they had built their cargo dock and warehouse a few hundred yards down the waterfront from their main moorings.

The *Bird* drew up at the warehouse dock and anchored. Eliss climbed down on deck and found Krelan emptying a bucket of grease as he stared across at the pleasure-boat moorings.

"How are we ever going to get over there?" he said in an undertone, looking panicked.

"There's a road." Eliss pointed at the stone promenade that led from the cargo dock to the moorings. It was wide, with a graceful balustrade and marble busts at regular intervals along the walkway.

"I know, but we're *poor!*" said Krelan. "If we attempt to wander out on that walkway we'll be stopped by one of their security men before we've gone ten paces. And I lost my Young Nobleman costume in Prayna."

"What do you want to do over there, anyway?" Eliss shaded her eyes with her hand, peering through the sunlight at the moorings.

"Talk to the Harbormaster, and anyone else I can find to interview, if I can just get to him. I can tell him I'm working undercover, which is the truth anyway. Look at the boats to see whether any of them are the *Fire-Swift*, maybe with a new name. But I certainly can't get you over there."

"Maybe you can." Eliss was struck by an idea. "Go put on your clean clothes. Captain, sir?" She turned and hurried to intercept Captain Glass, who was just going down the companionway to his cabin. "How long are we staying here?"

He squinted at her. "Just as long as it takes to load on provisions. They don't want us here any longer than that. We smell."

"A couple of hours?"

"Three or four." He looked at her thoughtfully. "Make it quick, Vigilance."

"Yes, sir." Eliss ran across the deck to Pentra, who was rolling out a fresh sheet of map paper over her drafting table.

"Pentra, may I borrow something?"

FIFTEEN MINUTES LATER MR. RIVETER, busily overseeing the loading-on of jars of cooking oil, was distracted by Eliss and Krelan walking down the gangplank. Krelan was neat if undistinguished in his clean tunic, but Eliss wore an actual gown of reed-green silk with a veil and sun hat. Mr. Riveter scratched his beard, trying to find words to express his astonishment, but Krelan clapped him on the shoulder before he could speak.

"We're just going ashore. I'm playing a little joke on an elderly uncle of mine. Won't be but an hour or so."

Eliss meanwhile had ventured to the promenade. As she approached, a guard in a white tunic bearing the embroidered words SILVER TROUT LANDING MOORING OWNERS' ASSOCIATION stepped out from between a pair of busts of former Mooring Owners' Association presidents and said, firmly but politely, "May I help you, miss?"

"Lady Sirilyne has an engagement with one of the parties moored at the Landing," said Krelan, who had run to catch up with her. The guard raised an eyebrow.

"Does Lady Sirilyne usually travel by barge?"

"She does when she has met with an unforeseen mishap whilst traveling and had to accept transport on the first available vessel that could carry her to a more civilized spot," said Krelan.

"Sir, if you please," Eliss said, imitating Pentra's accent as closely as she could. "This is a private matter."

"And she would appreciate, and moreover her father and uncles *and* brothers would appreciate, no additional complications to her already distressing situation," said Krelan meaningfully. The guard gulped, looked over his shoulder, and stepped aside.

"Gods grant you greater felicity, madam," he said.

"Thank you," said Eliss. Krelan took her arm and walked her swiftly past.

"Just for future reference," he said quietly, "you wouldn't say *thank you*. Not to a guard. You're a great lady. He hasn't done you a favor; in fact, he's overstepped his authority by questioning you. Right now you're probably thinking of having a couple of your servants come back here and beat him within an inch of his life. And he knows it, and he's sweating about it."

"So I should be haughtier?" Eliss gazed about her in enjoyment, trailing her hand along the marble balustrade.

"Moderately. Too haughty is wrong too, though. A really refined lady doesn't deign to react to anything much. She lets her servants do it for her."

"What if I stub my toe? Do you swear for me?"

"Yes, actually." Krelan snickered. "I run around in circles exclaiming over the *shocking* condition the walkway is kept in, and I fall to my knees and examine your foot, and if I'm a *very* privileged servant I remove your dainty sandal and inspect your foot for injury and massage it. And then I scream abuse at whoever's responsible."

"Nobody's responsible for a stubbed toe!"

"Somebody's always responsible. Someone can always be blamed. You, as a real lady, are going to gaze into the middle distance as all this is going on and pretend you haven't noticed. And if I do collar some luckless gardener or groundskeeper and drag them before you, with kicks and threats, you will look down from your unimaginably high distance and say 'That's enough, Mr. Stone. I am sure he has learned his lesson,'" Krelan added in a genteel falsetto.

"That's not what some of the rich people I've seen would do," said Eliss. "They'd yell and kick the servant, and probably the gardener too."

"Ah, but those aren't *nobles*. They are merely rich. Even my family is rich. The aristocracy have a whole other code of nice behavior. The ladies, anyway. You would never dream of shrieking at an underling.

The very idea! And when you'd gently pardoned him for his offense, he'd cringe and say, 'Oh, thank you, gods bless you, your ladyship!' And he'd mean it too."

"How silly."

"My dear young lady, this is the very foundation of Society," said Krelan in a pompous voice. "You mustn't question it. Right, here we are; now I'll have to stop talking and laughing with you, or all these people will assume you've given me undue privilege."

Eliss looked around. It was a world of white marble. White columns held up the arching sign that read SILVER TROUT LANDING, with a trout of real silver curved above the letters. White marble lined the canal that led back inland a quarter mile from the landing, to a distant circular pool out of which a white fountain jetted crystal water at the sky. The walkway along either side of the canal was paved with marble, edged with more balustrade, and the quaint buildings visible off above the pool seemed to be marble as well. Before her, the dozen or so pleasure-boats drawn up into slips were white too, fresh spotless paint without so much as a trace of mud. Only their canvas awnings were blue or green or red. They all had names like *River Princess*, *Idle Days*, *Vulpina*, or *Goldpin's Folly*.

Krelan was staring intently at the boats. "Do you see the *Fire-Swift*?" Eliss asked him.

"No. I need to look more closely, though. Now, we need to play out a little scene for the benefit of the Harbormaster, who is watching us. Can you gesture inland and seem to be telling me to stay here while you go, er, admire the famous fountain?"

"You mean like this?" Eliss made a graceful gesture. "Now, you stay here, you terribly ordinary person, and don't get into any trouble, because I'm going to go admire the famous fountain. How long should I be gone?"

"Can you find something to do for twenty minutes?" Krelan bowed and rubbed his hands together, the picture of servileness.

"Ladies don't *do* anything," said Eliss airily. "They just look down

THE BIRD OF THE RIVER

from on high." She turned and sauntered away along one side of the canal, feeling pleased with herself.

Before she had gone very far she was uncomfortably aware that Pentra's jeweled sandals, while pretty, were thin-soled, and the white-paved walkway was hot; all her green silk draperies were hot too. Still, Eliss managed to proceed in a dignified way past more busts of old balding men and thin-nosed women, each one with a little golden plate underneath giving the name of a former president of the Mooring Owner's Association and the dates they had served in office. Further down the canal walkway these gave out and instead gilded bronze statues of the gods looked across the canal at each other.

Now and again a pleasure-boat emerged from the pool at the other end, making its way along the canal out to the river, and Eliss stared frostily at the wealthy people on deck. *I'm too refined and highborn to do something like wave,* she told herself. However, when a lady reclining on pillows under a sea-blue sunshade nodded to her, Eliss unbent so far as to nod back.

She reached the pool. At its far edges a few boats were moored, each in its own slip above which white marble steps led up to an arcade, which ran in nearly a complete circle around the pool. The fountain still jetted away in the very center, a series of concentric bowls rising one out of another. In the lowest, and widest, a clever device set a pair of mechanical swans flapping round and round, endlessly pursued by a mechanical swimming fox. Even the swans and fox were enameled white.

Eliss walked around the pool slowly, looking up from under the brim of her sun hat at the shops within the arcade. No screaming banners or hawkers here; gold lettering above each doorway, silently informing her that this was a bank, and *this* was a ladies' salon, and the place next door sold fine wines and spirits. Next to that was a Provisioner's—nothing so ordinary as a market. Oh, and here was a fine hotel, taking up all the rest of the circle. On the terrace under its arcade languid women sat on tiny wrought-iron chairs and had iced drinks brought to them by obsequious waiters.

But there aren't any walls, thought Eliss in wonder. *All this money, and anyone could walk in here by a trick, like I did, and steal things. . . .* Well, perhaps not as easily as that. She noticed now that other men in white tunics stood silently here and there, unobtrusively keeping watch from between statues. *All the same, someday a fox is going to catch these swans.*

Eliss dawdled in front of each of the boats, long enough to determine that none of them was the *Fire-Swift,* nor did any of them look as though their names had been recently painted over with something different. When she judged twenty minutes had gone by, she wandered back along the other side of the canal.

Krelan stood by the Harbormaster's booth, speaking with him in a low voice. The Harbormaster glanced over, let out the crank that lowered a tiny ornamental bridge, and Eliss picked her way across.

"I'm bored, and nobody I wanted to talk to was there," she announced in a petulant voice. Krelan turned and bowed.

"I am disconsolate to hear it, my lady. Shall I not fetch your trunks from the barge after all?"

"No. I think I want to go on to a real city."

"It is my pleasure to obey." Krelan took her arm. Nodding at the Harbormaster, he escorted her back along the walkway to the loading dock.

"Did you find anything out?"

Krelan nodded. "Encilian was here, all right, and he spent a lot of time on the *Dancing Girl,* but Lady Chrysoprase spent a lot of time on board the *Fire-Swift* while Lord Chrysoprase was drinking up at the hotel, and everyone thought it was an outrageous scandal but no one mentioned it to Lord Chrysoprase."

"Were any of those boats the *Fire-Swift?*"

"No. Encilian only spent about a month here before going on upriver. He filed a destination of Karkateen with the Harbormaster.

Lord and Lady Chrysoprase sailed about a month later, and they've been back twice since. They live in Prayna. But Encilian hasn't been back."

"Well, he couldn't be. He's dead, isn't he?"

"And didn't die here."

"What about his manservant? Was he here too?"

"Yes."

"Have you thought about trying to find the servant? If he wasn't the murderer, and he wasn't killed at the same time, he might know who murdered his master."

"Oh, he'd have been killed," said Krelan confidently.

"How do you know?"

"He'd have died protecting Encilian. Any sworn man would."

Eliss turned to stare at him. "You mean you would have too?"

Krelan nodded. "And, yes, I know, he was a disgrace to the Diamondcut name. But he *was* one of the Family, so I'd have protected him. You don't understand loyalty oaths."

"I really don't," admitted Eliss. "It seems crazy to me. *Was* the servant a sworn man like you?"

"I . . . I assume he was. I don't know." Krelan frowned. "You know, I don't know where the servant came from."

"Because, you see, if he was just an ordinary person, he might have run for his life when whatever it was happened to your lord," said Eliss, trying not to sound sarcastic. "I may not understand loyalty oaths, but I understand ordinary people."

Krelan thought about that as they walked along. "So," he said, trying to regain his composure, "what did you think of the famous fountain?"

"It was pretty," said Eliss. They came to the *Bird of the River*, and the polemen hauling on sacks of rice paused in their work to let them aboard. Somebody in the line hummed *Duke Rakut's Processional*. Eliss turned and stiffly waved her hand at them all, like a noblewoman, and everyone laughed.

As she stepped down on the *Bird*'s deck, Wolkin came running to her. "Eliss! Look what happened to me—" He stopped short, with his mouth open. "You look like a goddess!"

"How very kind," Eliss drawled. Then she saw the purple mess in his hair and the purple dye all over his face and chest. "What *did* happen to you?"

"Another jar of blackberry wine exploded, and I was *right there* and saw everything," said Wolkin proudly. "It was amazing."

WHETHER OR NOT SHE LOOKED like a goddess, it felt wonderful to pull on her own clothes again and scramble up to the mast platform. Eliss swung her bare feet in the cool air and watched from her high vantage point as the *Bird* moved upriver past Silver Trout Landing.

The *Bird*'s gigantic wake made the boats at the outer moorings bob up and down like so many toys. Water splashed over the stern rail of the nearest and slopped on a spread carpet. Instantly a servant appeared from nowhere and sponged it off, pausing only to shake his fist and shout abuse at the *Bird of the River*.

"DID THE DRESS FIT?" Pentra asked, that night after the lamp had been blown out.

"Yes, it did. Thank you."

"I suppose I oughtn't ask why you needed to go ashore there."

"We just . . . wanted to see the fountain. It's a famous fountain."

"I know."

"And of course I couldn't go dressed as I was."

"No, I imagine not. Was the fountain worth the visit?"

"Oh, yes. But the Landing was a bit, you know . . . snooty."

"It is, yes." Pentra was silent for a little while before asking: "Do you like young master Krelan?"

"We're just friends. He's nice."

"He seems very nice. Very funny."

"He is. He makes me laugh."

"It looked as though he spent a while talking to the Harbormaster."

Eliss twisted a lock of her hair, wondering what she ought to say. "He chatted with him, yes, I think. But then he'd seen the fountain before."

"I expect he had. You know, of course, that sometimes young gentlemen of his station have certain matters to which they are obliged to attend?"

"You mean vendettas? Yes, I know."

"Good. Then I'm sure you have the good sense to be careful, in the event those matters press for his attention."

"I know. I lived in Mount Flame once. Rich people kill each other in the streets all the time."

"They certainly do." Pentra sighed. "I must say, that was one thing I didn't miss while living among the Yendri."

A WEEK LATER ELISS WAS READING the river when she saw something peculiar. There was the running rill that suggested a little snag, one perhaps a fathom down, nothing unusual. Just forward of it, however, was a funny welling pattern in the water she'd never seen before, and there the water seemed a lighter color. She drew a deep breath.

"Unmarked snag at the mile marker!"

As Mr. Riveter shouted orders and the topmen came hurrying up to take in sail, Eliss swung herself down through the shrouds and ran forward. While they anchored just below the snag, she found Mrs. Riveter pulling on her goggles for the dive.

"It doesn't look very big, but there's something funny about it," Eliss told her. "Be careful."

Mrs. Riveter nodded. She dove in, as the other divers got ready, and everyone recited the Prayer to Brimo. Long before they got to the end, however, Mrs. Riveter came back up and swam to the *Bird*'s deck.

"It's a wreck," she said.

"Oh!" Mr. Riveter's face was a study in mixed emotions. "Fetch out the salvage buoys!" He went running aft and met Captain Glass, who was coming forward.

"We've found a wreck, sir!"

"Vigilance found it, did she?"

"Yes, sir, and my missus just dove on it."

"I had a feeling. Had a feeling for weeks now. Where is it?" The captain addressed this last remark to Mrs. Riveter, who was still treading water as the other divers jumped in.

"Two fathoms down, sir. It looks as though it burned."

Mr. Riveter's shoulders drooped a little. "Badly?"

"No, dear. It's mostly intact."

"Maybe it can be repaired!" Mr. Riveter grabbed one of the salvage buoys as they were brought up and passed it to her.

"Why does that matter, sir?" Eliss asked Captain Glass. He shrugged.

"Wreck's mostly intact, she can be refloated and she's ours to sell. Wreck's mostly *not* intact, we can still haul her out of there and break her down for the lumber. But if she's just a lot of charred wood, she's no use to anybody, and we've still got to dig her out of the hole she's in."

The *Bird of the River* anchored there. The crew worked quickly to set out salvage buoys, big floating markers striped in red and black. Every diver on board donned her goggles and went down to help survey the wreck, for the law required full documentation on a wreck's precise situation before salvage was permitted. Pentra rolled up her map and rolled out fresh paper. She began a drawing of the wreck based on the details the divers brought back.

The *Bird of the River* took on a holiday atmosphere. Children ran ashore and played. Mr. Pitspike shouldered an ancient crossbow and went ashore to hunt, and returned near nightfall with a deer and four ducks. Special hot drinks were brewed up in the galley and taken out for the divers. Eliss babysat, walking up and down the deck with Mrs. Crucible's fat toddler clinging to one hand and Mrs. Firedrake's fat toddler clinging to the other, as their respective mothers worked in the green swirling water.

As evening drew on she saw a low spreading pall like smoke to the southwest, a distant stain on the sky, and wondered uneasily what it might be.

WHEN IT GREW TOO DARK to work, the divers came aboard and were robed in thick quilted gowns, and brought hot food while a fire-basket was lit on deck for them. Wolkin and Tulu came and snuggled themselves close against Mrs. Riveter to warm her, one under either arm. The musicians played for them.

Salpin told a story about a legendary shipwreck that had been loaded with a duke's ransom, and made the crew who had found it so rich, they had all retired to Salesh-by-the-Sea. He told another about a haunted wreck. He told another about a ship that had been transporting a bride to her wedding when it sank, and how years had passed before the wreck was found and raised; but when the cabin had been opened they found the bride still there, dressed in her wedding finery, as beautiful as the day she had set out; yet as soon as the air came into the cabin she'd melted away like mist, leaving only her braided hair and her rings and bangles.

Late in the evening, after the children had been put to bed, Mrs. Crucible asked Salpin to play *The Ballad of Falena*. Eliss sighed and stared into the fire as the musicians played. Her mother had become a beautiful melody, a sentimental story, and Falena would have been pleased by that. Alder had been right. It was just the sort of thing she would have enjoyed listening to herself.

So why does it still make me angry? Eliss wondered. *It's not just because it isn't true. It's because it feels as though she got away with living her life the way she did. All the stupid mistakes she made, all the lies and broken promises, and she gets to become a pretty legend in the end.*

Mrs. Crucible, noticing her expression, nudged her gently. "I hope the song doesn't make you sad," she said.

"No. It's all right."

"It's just that it's so beautiful. And it's our song, after all. Nobody ever wrote a song about divers before."

"Really?"

"He's got it right. We do run the risk of leaving our souls down there, every time we go into the water," said Mrs. Firedrake. The other divers nodded. Eliss looked uncertainly from face to face. It hadn't occurred to her that the song was about more than her mother.

And the adult Eliss voice in her mind murmured, *Maybe Mama's life was about more than Mama too.*

AS SOON AS THE SUN was high enough to light the water next day, the divers went back in. Eliss collected sacks of rice and peas from belowdecks and stacked them like sandbags to make a sort of pen. She laid down blankets on the deck inside, filled it with, as many toys as she could find, and climbed in with all the toddlers and not-yet-crawling members of the crew.

The babies thought this was novel and diverting. Eliss rolled balls back and forth with the toddlers, changed diapers, offered teething toys, and watched with one eye as the divers came aboard and gave descriptions of what they were finding to Pentra. Captain Glass walked by at one point, looked into the pen, and snorted.

Around noon Krelan came out of the galley and wandered over to Pentra's drafting table. Eliss watched as he looked over Pentra's shoulder at the drawing in progress. He was frowning. He spoke briefly with Pentra. He turned, looking around, shading his eyes with his hand, and at last spotted Eliss. He strode across the deck to her.

"What ho! You've built a baby bunker?"

"It works," said Eliss. "Do something for me?"

"Your servant, my dear. What?"

"Rig up a sunshade for us? Just a tarpaulin or something."

"At once, madam." Krelan busied himself with a tarpaulin and bits of rope, and shortly had a serviceable awning in place. He leaned on the piled sacks and stared absently at Mrs. Tinware's baby, who was reducing a biscuit to a mass of crumbs and drool.

"It would appear that the wreck is somebody's pleasure-boat," he said.

"Really?" Eliss turned around to peer at him. "And it's been burned. Maybe it was the river pirates."

"Perhaps."

"How badly is it burned? Are we going to be able to salvage it?"

"Oddly enough, it's *not* very badly burned. So, yes, they're going to attempt to float it as soon as the documentation is finished." Krelan waved a hand at the windmill, where the cablemen and some of the musicians were busy hooking up its gears to a device like a large pair of bellows.

"I hope they don't find bodies inside." Eliss picked up Mrs. Ironlatch's baby, who was determinedly crawling over his sleeping brother. "You'd think the pirates would have burned it completely."

"Well, it's a funny thing: once you've set fire to a boat and jumped off it, you really don't have a lot of control over what it does next," said Krelan. "Especially if it decides to sink fast."

Eliss nodded. Mrs. Ironlatch's baby fretted and dug his fist into his eye. She rocked him in her arms a long moment, until he abruptly fell asleep with his head on her shoulder. She turned her head as far as she dared to look at Krelan, who was watching her, and quietly said: "Do you think it might be the *Fire-Swift?*"

"I don't know what to think," said Krelan.

THE DIVERS WORKED IN SHIFTS. While some of them stretched out in the sunlight and drank hot broth, others worked on the wreck, closing up all the holes they could find and attaching cables. When that had been accomplished, a long air pipe of wax-soaked canvas was attached to one end of the bellows. The divers took the other end below and directed it into a tight aperture they had fitted through one of the wreck's portholes.

Mrs. Crucible surfaced and waved, and a cableman stationed at the windmill threw a lever. The gears engaged, the bellows began to pump, and the flat canvas serpent filled with air.

"It'll come up soon now," said Krelan. His voice was taut. The river began to churn above where the divers had been working. Carefully, Eliss put Mrs. Ironlatch's baby down beside his brother and rose to her feet.

She watched the water doming out, surging and curling, with here and there a few massed air bubbles belching to the surface. The divers were scrambling back aboard. Men waited tensely at the capstans, bars in place. More air broke the surface and then Eliss saw the blackened stump of a mast rolling upward, the thing that had drawn her attention to the wreck in the first place.

"Capstans!" roared Mr. Riveter. The men went round and round, the cables drew taut and dragged the wreck farther out of the water. Now she bobbed for a moment on the surface, a white-hulled pleasure-craft, fouled with mud and weeds that clouded and waved around her. All her spars and rigging were gone, and the roof of her cabin had been eaten away by fire, but the rest of her was intact. Air gushed from a hole in the side of her hull that had lain mud-downward, missed by the divers, and she sank down again until the cables pulled her hard against the *Bird of the River*.

Now the polemen ran forward with grappling hooks and hauled on her, as the capstans kept going round, and slowly the wreck inched upward and onto the *Bird*'s deck. Black mud poured from her wound, as she groaned like a dying thing. She lay at last with her stern to the *Bird*'s bow, trailing weeds, and crabs dropped from her and scuttled madly for the water.

Rigid with tension, Krelan made his way across to the wreck. Eliss watched as he walked about it, stepping around the men who were unfastening the cables. He disappeared behind it for a moment, and Eliss knew he must be looking at the name carved on the wreck's stern.

When he reappeared his face was pale. He walked rapidly back to Eliss. She saw that he was trembling.

"It's the *Fire-Swift*," he whispered.

Mrs. Ironlatch's baby woke and began to wail.

FOR A LONG WHILE the wreck just sat there on the deck, as the divers waited for the mud stirred up by her raising to settle, so they could see whether anything remained on the bottom. The cablemen got busy disconnecting the bellows from the gears and hooking up a pump instead. Krelan sat in the baby pen beside Eliss, staring at the wreck.

"Are you all right?"

Krelan nodded. "It appears I was not quite ready for this," he said, with a weak-sounding laugh.

"But you knew your lord was dead," said Eliss, offering a wooden doll to Mrs. Ironlatch's baby.

"I know. I didn't like Encilian. I wasn't surprised to hear he'd been murdered. But the *Fire-Swift* . . . it wasn't even his boat, you know. It belonged to the Family. He must have 'borrowed' it, the way he 'borrowed' so many other things, and just took off on a pleasure sail. Everyone thought he'd vanished just to evade certain responsibilities he had. And months went by and nobody heard from him, and then his body came home in its box of salt . . . and you'd have thought the world had ended. Nobody missed *him*, but what an insult to the Family!" Krelan flexed his hands nervously as he spoke.

"But you're not a Diamondcut," said Eliss. "Why do you care?"

"Because . . . you don't understand. Seeing something of *theirs* wrecked like this"—Krelan pointed to the *Fire-Swift*—"it just doesn't feel possible. All my life I've lived at the edge of the power and the grandeur of the Diamondcuts. They might as well be gods to us. It's one thing to kill *a* Diamondcut, but that someone would dare to do this . . ."

Eliss shrugged. "But they aren't gods. And somebody did dare. Probably river pirates. They wouldn't care if your lord was a Diamondcut or a nobody, as long as he had something they could steal."

"You're right." Krelan knotted his hands together. "Well, they'll care now. The Diamondcuts will come after them. The earth will shake. The river will run with blood."

"Good luck. Getting rid of pirates is like trying to kill cockroaches," said Eliss, not unkindly. "I wonder if your lord's head is in that cabin? Or maybe the servant's body?"

"The head wouldn't be." Krelan sat up, making an effort to throw off his shock. "The head would have been a trophy, probably. Maybe one of the Family's enemies commissioned the pirates to take it. Oh, oh, and if that's the case it will start the old clan wars again. Gods below, I hope it wasn't one of the Fireopals. Please, gods, no. Anyway. Maybe the servant's in there. I'll have to look."

"Anyway, you finally know what happened." Eliss wondered if he would leave the *Bird* now.

"Maybe. I know *where* it happened, anyway. I'll have to get a message back to my brother." Krelan rubbed his face with both hands.

There came a hail from the far side of the river. A fishing boat was making her way upstream, under every scrap of sail she had. At least . . . Eliss squinted at her. She looked and smelled like a fishing boat, but armed men stood on her deck. One came to the rail and called again.

"*Bird of the River!* What's the wreck? Who did it?"

"Looks like pirates," Mr. Riveter called back. He went to the wreck's stern and peered at the name. "She's the *Fire*-something. A rich man's boat."

Someone on the fishing boat swore.

"What's it to you?" asked Mr. Riveter.

"How long since you passed Silver Trout Landing?"

"Not a week. What's happened?"

"The place has been sacked," the fisherman cried. "Boats looted and sunk. Hotel burned, bank robbed, all kinds of gentry killed or taken for ransom."

Mr. Riveter stared, openmouthed. Eliss felt chilled, as though a shadow had passed over the sun.

"They didn't do this." Captain Glass's voice boomed out over the water. "This wreck is months old."

"Was it pirates?" Mr. Riveter found his voice again.

"Shellback," called the fisherman, walking aft to shout over the stern as his vessel passed the *Bird*. "Renegades and demons. They came from the woods. Maybe working with some pirates too. The hostages were taken off inland though. You want to be careful! Arm your deck watch!"

"The fox caught the swans after all," murmured Eliss.

NOTHING ELSE WAS FOUND where the wreck had lain, and so the divers came back aboard. The water pump was attached to the canvas hose and sucked up water, which one of the cablemen played over the *Fire-Swift*, sluicing off mud. He aimed the water into the boat next. Water, and more mud, began to run from the hole near her keel. Krelan, biting his knuckles, climbed out of the baby pen and stood as close to the wreck as he could, watching the water gush forth.

Mrs. Ironlatch, wrapping her hair in a towel, came aft and peered into the baby pen. "There's my big boys! Did you miss Mama? This is a good idea," she added, nodding at the pen as she scooped up first one and then the other baby.

"I used to make pillow forts when my brother was little." Eliss glanced at Krelan.

"We ought to make some pillows and build a permanent one. I'll ask my man."

"That would work," said Eliss, just as a shout came from the direction of the *Fire-Swift*. A mass of something had blocked the hole. Krelan ran forward.

"I'll climb aboard and see what it is, shall I?" he cried.

"There could be something nasty in there," said Mr. Riveter.

"Let him," Captain Glass said. "He's nimble as a rat. Aren't you, Stone?"

"Yes, sir, thank you, sir!"

Mr. Riveter shrugged. He bent and made a stirrup of his hands for Krelan, who vaulted up and over the *Fire-Swift*'s rail. Eliss heard him skidding on her tilted deck, and thumping and splashing as he moved around inside.

"Are you all right in there?" called Mr. Riveter.

"Fine, thanks." Krelan's voice echoed hollowly. "I see the blockage. It's a cushion." A moment later the rotted mass vanished back inside the hull, and muddy water streamed out.

"Any, er, bones?"

"Not that I can find, sir."

Mr. Riveter grinned, and a couple of the cablemen raised their fists in triumphant gestures. Dead men were bad luck, and worse: they tended to complicate salvage rights.

"What *is* in there?"

"Nothing much. Bedding. Looks like some clothes. She was scuttled." Krelan's voice was thoughtful. "You can see the chisel marks all around the hole. Here's the chisel, in fact."

"So they looted her, scuttled her, and set fire to her," said Mr. Riveter. "It was pirates, all right." He patted the side of the *Fire-Swift*. "*Stupid* pirates. Look at all that fancy brightwork! That'll bring a good price."

"I suppose. I'm coming out," said Krelan shortly.

Eliss heard more skidding and staggering, and then Krelan reappeared above the *Fire-Swift*'s rail. He tossed out a sodden mass of stuff, which hit the deck with a slap, and climbed down.

"You may resume hosing her out," he said, and stalked aft to Eliss.

"Oh, I may, may I?" grumbled Mr. Riveter, but he waved his hand and gave the order.

Krelan sat down on the deck and watched the river while Eliss handed off their babies to Mrs. Crucible and Mrs. Firedrake, both of whom complimented Eliss on the baby pen. When they had gone, and Eliss was taking down the sunshade, he got up to help her.

"It wasn't pirates," he said.

"How do you know?"

"They left too much." Krelan was still pale, but with anger now. "Anything valuable and loose seems to have been taken, but real pirates would have taken everything. All the ornamental brass and the stained glass window. The bedding was fine stuff before it rotted. They left a chair that belonged to old Lord Diamondcut, a beautifully carved antique. Ruined now, of course, but the rest of the salvage is going to make the *Bird* a handsome profit, I can tell you."

"So somebody wanted to make it look as though pirates had done it," said Eliss. "But they didn't do a very good job. They just wanted to get rid of the *Fire-Swift*."

"I think so, yes."

"Maybe your lord wasn't even killed here. Maybe it happened upriver and they sank the boat here." Eliss looked upriver and down as she folded up the tarpaulin. "We're nowhere near a town. Nobody would have seen."

"That's a possibility."

"And the dead servant wasn't on board, was he?"

"He wasn't."

"Have you thought that it really might have been the servant who killed your lord, after all?"

Krelan was silent a moment, stacking the sacks of rice. "I suppose I'll have to entertain that possibility," he said at last. "Give me a hand getting these back below?"

DESPITE THE FACT that Mr. Riveter was itching to take the *Fire-Swift* apart, they had to wait for submitting a formal report, and she had to be inspected by an officer of the law. So she sat on the *Bird*'s deck for two days, while the *Bird* fought her way upriver to the next town.

They pulled into Latacari at nightfall on the second day. Latacari was a mining town, with a huge open pit beyond the city walls. Her smelters glowed red through the night, with patient lines of priests working the bellows, and iron ingots were piled before the city's temple for anyone to help himself to the holy metal.

"STAND STILL," MRS. RIVETER SCOLDED. "It's caught on your ear." She adjusted Mr. Riveter's chain of office. He stood before her in his best clothes, wringing his hands.

"I should comb my beard."

"You don't need to comb your beard. It looks fine. Eliss, may I have the sash?"

Eliss handed it to her, as Mr. Riveter fretted.

"Mr. Crucible! Organize a loading detail. They've got wheat for us on the dock. After that's loaded on we need iron. Two barrows' worth."

"Working on it, Mr. Riveter!"

"And I've still got to get the captain's drink," Mr. Riveter murmured, half to himself, as Mrs. Riveter tied his sash.

"Send someone else to do that," she told him, standing back to survey the overall effect of his official splendor.

"I suppose I could. You! Mr. Stone!" Krelan, who had been trudging aft with the grease bucket, turned.

"Sir?"

"Here's money." Mr. Riveter fumbled in his pouch. "Go ashore and get a keg of the best whiskey that'll buy, and bring it back for Captain Glass."

"Yes, sir." Krelan slipped the coins in his own pouch and looked inquiringly at Eliss. She nodded, eager to go ashore.

Mr. Riveter was seen off for his visit to the Temple of the Law, clutching Pentra's finished drawing of the wreck of the *Fire-Swift*. The wreck still sat, securely lashed down, on the *Bird*'s deck, though two of the polemen had had to be posted on more or less permanent guard to prevent children from climbing on it.

"I've got the afternoon off," Krelan told Eliss as he hurried up the companionway. "And a lot to do. Do you mind if we take care of a few things first?"

"No." Eliss threw her shawl around her shoulders. "I thought we might go to the temple too."

"Why not?" Krelan took her arm. "Come along then, Mrs. Stone."

Eliss smiled as they went down the gangplank together. "Who's Mrs. Stone?"

"Mrs. Stone is the beautiful young wife of the miserable kitchen lackey Mr. Stone," said Krelan. "Or, as his master Pitspike is forever correcting him, *galley* lackey. Mr. Stone is a wretched feeble thing with absolutely no wealthy connections whatsoever, and completely unlikely to draw the hostile attentions of anybody intent on carrying out a vendetta."

"How did he get a beautiful wife, then?"

"He has no idea, but is desperately grateful." Krelan looked around through the pink smoky light. "Where's a map board?"

They found the location of the nearest runners' house and went into the Sending office. Eliss waited patiently while Krelan wrote a letter and slipped it into a tablet case. He carried it to the window, where a bored-looking clerk inspected the label.

"You need it sealed?"

"Please." Krelan fished a signet ring from the depths of his hood while the clerk melted wax for him. She poured it into the lock and he sealed the tablet. Eliss, watching, saw that the signet emblem was a dagger.

I shouldn't be surprised, she thought. *I shouldn't forget what his family does for a living.*

"Special rate for speed and she needs to wait for a reply. Reply to be forwarded to Karkateen," said Krelan as the clerk rang for a runner. She looked at the address label and raised her eyebrows.

"Two gold crowns, then," the clerk said.

Krelan paid without so much as a wince and they walked out together. "There we are," he said. "I've reported about the *Fire-Swift* and you'll be pleased to know that I've asked about the manservant."

"I just think it's important," said Eliss. "Have you got any more money?"

Now Krelan winced. "A lady never asks *that*, you know."

"I'll never be a lady. I was going to say that if you do have more money, you ought to buy yourself some nicer clothes. I mean, here we are in a city."

Krelan looked around in distaste at the sooty shop fronts. "Here? I don't think I can find any tailor-made custom-dye-lot rough silk ensembles such as I'm accustomed to wearing."

"Buy something off the shelf, then! It's bound to be better than what you've got on." Eliss looked down at Krelan's tunic, which was showing its age and also a great deal of kitchen grease he had been unable to scrub out. He sighed.

"Undeniably true."

They found a shop that sold perfectly serviceable formal wear, even if it wasn't anything the wealthy lords of Mount Flame would care to be seen in, and Krelan managed to find something in his size. As he was paying the shop owner, he asked casually: "Could you tell me the name of the best hotel in town?"

"That would be the Garnet," said the shop owner, counting out his change. "Next to the temple. Expensive, though."

"I'll risk it," said Krelan stiffly.

They walked on down the street. "You're going to ask whether your lord stayed there?" Eliss inquired.

"That was the plan." Krelan's footsteps slowed as they came to Garnet House. He looked up at its porphyry columns, looked down at his shabby tunic. "Hmmm. I ought to have changed in the clothier's."

"Do you want me to do it? I'm dressed a little better." Eliss gestured at her shawl. Krelan looked startled at the idea, but intrigued.

"Let's see how you do," he said, and passed her the little portrait of Encilian. She looked at it closely for the first time. *This is the man who killed Mama*, she thought, and then scolded herself for being morbid. Still, Encilian looked like the sort of person who wouldn't have cared if his death had brought about the accidental death of someone else. Handsome, but the portrait's painter had caught the nasty expression in his eyes. He wore sky-blue silk, with the gold serpent armlet of the Diamondcuts bunching up the silk on his upper arm.

Eliss took a deep breath. "Let's go." Adjusting her scarf, she walked in through the big double doors of the Garnet. Krelan skulked after her.

She saw at once that, however splendid its porphyry columns were on the outside, inside the Garnet was nothing like the white hotel at Silver Trout Landing. The lobby was full of prosperous families who had come on pilgrimage and business travelers, just a little shabby at the edges. Somewhat less intimidated, Eliss made her way to the front desk and smiled at the clerk.

"I'm wondering if you can help me, sir," she said, trying to speak with Pentra's precise diction. The clerk raised his eyebrows in inquiry, and Eliss held up the little portrait. "This is Lord Encilian Diamondcut. My brother's his manservant and I'm trying to find him. I think his lordship stayed here, a few months ago. Would it be possible for you to look in your books and tell me when?"

"Oh! We did have one of the Diamondcuts here, I remember." The clerk dove under the counter and brought up a ledger. "Yes. Just a moment . . . here. Two weeks before Spring Equinox. Yes. Here's the entry. 'Lord Encilian and manservant.' He only stayed one night, as I recall. Not happy with our accommodations."

"And this is such a nice hotel!" Eliss exclaimed. "But then, my brother told me his lordship was," she lowered her voice, "a bit difficult to please."

The clerk rolled his eyes in agreement. " '*The higher the birth, the thicker the mattress he requires,*' " he quoted softly.

"Actually my brother wasn't sure whether he'd remain with his lordship or not. I wonder if the man with him was my brother after all. Does your book give the servant's name?"

"Oh, no, miss. Just says 'manservant.' "

"Oh, dear."

"I remember the man, though. Handsome. Looked a bit like his master."

"Yes, that sounds like my brother. My brother's handsome."

"I thought to myself, 'Hmmm, his family must have worked for his master's family a long time,' if you know what I mean."

"So he was still with him here. Thank you so much, sir. My mother was a bit worried," said Eliss, aware that beside her Krelan had stiffened. As they went out to the pavement again she saw that he looked angry.

"What's the matter?"

"That insolent bastard!"

"But he was nice!"

"He insulted the Family."

"What, just by saying your lord was picky? You've said worse about him."

"It's different when I say it. I have privilege. Who in the nine hells is *he*, a miserable desk clerk, to imply things about the Family?"

"'Imply things'?"

"Specifically all that about the servant's family having worked for the Diamondcuts a long time, nudge nudge, *if you know what I mean*," said Krelan, still fuming.

"No, I don't know what you mean."

"He was suggesting the servant was a Diamondcut bastard. Which was why he looked like Encilian."

Eliss looked askance at Krelan. "So . . . you're saying rich men never go to bed with their servant girls and get them in trouble."

"No." Krelan kicked at a pebble. "Just that a common clerk has no business talking about the affairs of his betters."

"They do, though. All the time. And now *you* know that your lord was here and so was the servant, and you even know what the servant looked like. Which you didn't know this morning. So there's no point being so angry." Eliss looked up at the temple. "Here! Let's go in. You can pray for help."

Grumbling, Krelan let her drag him inside. "You were very good in there, by the way," he added in a whisper, as they stood in the gloom letting their eyes adjust. Eliss made a sarcastic half-curtsy and, spotting the Father Smith's chapel, made her way in and found a seat. Krelan sidled in after her.

Eliss closed her eyes and breathed in deep, letting her irritation evaporate. *Father, this is your child Eliss. I know I told you I was trying to take care of my brother, Alder, but things have changed and . . . he's gone. I tried hard, but he needed to go with the Yendri. Even so, he's one of your children too, whether he thinks he is or not, so please watch over him and keep him safe, because I can't anymore.*

And please let Mama sleep all right in the Fire Garden. Or . . . wherever she went, like maybe off with my father under the sea. Like in Salpin's song.

And . . . I can't ask you to help my friend Krelan with what he's doing, because he has to kill somebody, and I know you don't like things like that. But can you please keep him safe too? Except for what his family does, he's nice. And funny. And smart. And handsomer than he thinks he is. Except that mustache looks really awful on him.

And . . . that just leaves me, Father. But I'm all right. I don't need anything. I'm working hard.

She opened her eyes and looked up at the painted wall, where the Father Smith was depicted as he most commonly appeared: in the long coat and wide hat of an itinerant blacksmith, a looming figure the color of a storm cloud, features indistinct except for the eyes. The eyes were set with glass and had a light behind them, and the forge in front of the Father's figure was a real forge, an anvil beside a dish of coals glowing dim under a gray fur of ash, with a dish of blessing tokens next to it. As Eliss watched, a priest shuffled into the chapel and leaned down to blow on the coals. They flared bright a moment, underlighting his face. He stood patiently by the forge until Krelan and Eliss got to their feet. They went to him and bowed their heads for his blessing.

"The gift of iron," he said, touching an iron token to the coals and presenting it to Eliss. "The gift of iron," he repeated, giving a token to Krelan.

"We thank you for iron," they chorused, and went out. As they crossed together under the great dome, Eliss saw a new chapel going in at one side. The painter was climbing down from his scaffold. Looking past him Eliss could see on the wall the unfinished image of a Yendri woman, draped in white but with one breast bare, standing among white lilies. Krelan, curious, ducked his head to look in.

"The Green Witch," he whispered. "In our pantheon, now. Talk about changing times!"

As THEY EMERGED FROM THE TEMPLE, Eliss saw the street vendors' carts lined up along the lane in front of the market quarter. She could smell grilling sausages and spiced dumplings. Her mouth watered as she remembered all the times in her childhood in which she had been dragged hurriedly past carts like these, because there was no money to buy anything. Gleefully she realized she had money *now*.

She touched Krelan's arm. "Let's not go to a restaurant. Let's eat from the carts. Doesn't that smell good?"

"If you like," said Krelan in surprise. They wandered along the carts a long while, sampling the sausages grilled with onions and peppers, the little dumplings filled with minced meat and spices, the freshwater prawns fried in batter. Everything was delicious. Krelan stuck a couple of shrimp tails on his fingertips and did a bizarre little dance for her with his fingers, making Eliss laugh until she had to wipe away tears. Full and happy, they walked back down the hill to the harbor arm in arm.

"Whoops," said Krelan, as he spotted the *Bird of the River*. "I was supposed to buy a keg of whiskey."

"There's a shop." Eliss pointed.

"The very thing."

A few moments later they resumed their walk, with Krelan carrying the keg of whiskey on his shoulder. As they came to the gangplank, so did Mr. Riveter, accompanied by a city official. Mr. Riveter's eyes widened as he saw them.

"Excuse me, your honor," he said, bowing to the official, and darted close and grabbed Krelan's arm. "You're only bringing his whiskey *now*? Get it in to him, quick!" he muttered.

"Aye, sir." Krelan hurried aboard after them. Eliss followed, noticing that such of the crew as was on deck had retreated to the far larboard side and were gazing toward the companionway with worried expressions. Mr. Riveter led the official to the *Fire-Swift*, and Krelan and Eliss went down the companionway with the keg.

Eliss felt an impact within her ears the moment her foot touched the deck, pressure like a silent explosion. The air was hot and dense, breathless. The captain's door was visibly vibrating, rattling on its hinges as they watched. Something very big, somewhere, was growling.

Krelan's eyes were perfectly round. He cleared his throat and tapped on the door. "Captain Glass, sir?"

Something struck the other side of the door, hard. Something spoke in a thick roar. "*WHERSSSS IT?*"

"Er. I've brought your drink, sir."

Now Eliss could hear breathing like a bellows laboring. When the voice spoke again it was a little clearer, though its fury was still palpable.

"*LEAVE IT AND GO! NOW!*"

"Aye, sir!" Krelan set the keg down in front of the door and turned. Together he and Eliss ran up the companionway. Looking back, she saw the door open and something greenish—not a tentacle, surely! Surely only a hand looking strange in the funny twilight!—snaking out to pull the keg inside. Mr. Riveter, wringing his hands as the official walked around the *Fire-Swift* making notes on a tablet, glanced over at Eliss and Krelan as they emerged on deck and wiped sweat from his brow.

THEIR SALVAGE CLAIM WAS ACCEPTED, after the official climbed into the wreck and went through all the *Fire-Swift*'s lockers. He gave Mr. Riveter a receipt, told him he'd file the notification, and had the wreck removed with a crane to one of the warehouses on the waterfront.

"What happens now?" Krelan asked, watching the dark bulk of the wreck swinging in its cables against the sunset light.

"They store it for us," said Eliss, leaning on the rail beside him. "If it works the same way it works with sea wrecks, they notify the registered owners and ask them if they want to buy it back from us. Either they do or they tell us we can keep it. Either way, we get some money."

"Distasteful." Krelan turned away.

"Would you rather we held a funeral for it? Dress it up nice, hire an orator to say 'This was a fine boat, and pleased the gods'?"

Krelan smiled. They were both a little uneasy, though, as they walked past the companionway. It was quiet down there now.

THEY BEGAN TAKING THEIR MEALS together even when there wasn't anything to discuss, sitting companionably side by side of an evening as they ate rice and peas or noodles or stew. Mr. Pitspike only prepared about four different dishes for the general crew, and they made a running joke of coming up with fancy names for them, a new one each time the same dish came round in its monotonous cycle.

"Ah! And tonight it's . . ." Krelan inhaled the steam rising from his bowl of little rubbery dumplings in broth. "Hmmm. Semolina Delights in the Saleshian Style, with a dense sauce of Imitation Sea-Dragon."

"How do you make Imitation Sea-Dragon sauce?" Eliss wanted to know.

"Duck broth with extra salt and a fish head thrown in and a lot of chopped parsley to make it green." Krelan slurped the broth. "Mmm. Wouldn't hurt to add some wine."

Eliss found herself admiring the way his slender fingers cupped the bowl. She looked aside and tilted her own bowl to drink. *You just miss having someone to take care of,* she told herself. *You're not really falling in love. You looked after Alder and Mama all those years, and Krelan looks so pathetic sometimes you want to take care of him too, and you can't get used to being alone, that's all.* But she liked the way he sat with her as they shared their meals, not too close, not too far away.

"Can I eat with you?" They looked up and saw Wolkin, glowering as he clutched his bowl.

"Have a seat, hero." Krelan patted the deck. Wolkin folded up in a sitting position beside them, his lower lip still stuck out.

"What happened?" asked Eliss.

"Nothing. Except I was just playing a little with this monster I made with a piece of Mama's bread and I just pretended it was climbing on Tulu and she yelled and hit me so I hit her back. But she hit me first. But Daddy made me eat someplace else anyway."

"Can't hit girls, hero." Krelan shook his head.

"But she hit me first."

"But you're stronger than she is. Aren't you?"

"Not when we were babies," said Wolkin. "She used to be bigger than me. Then I got bigger."

"My point exactly. Now you're bigger, and you'll stay that way. Heroes don't hit their sisters, even if their sisters hit them first. And the same for any other girls."

Tell that to Uncle Steelplate, Eliss thought bitterly, *except that Mama never hit him at all.* Then she chided herself, wondering why she was still thinking about Uncle Steelplate after all these years. "What exactly did the monster do when it was climbing on Tulu, Wolkin?"

"It bit her." Wolkin looked sheepish. "Then it jumped in her bowl and splashed her."

"Would you have liked it if somebody had done that to you?"

"I guess not."

"There you are, then."

"So, hero . . ." Krelan looked sidelong at Wolkin. "Why doesn't Captain Glass ever go ashore when we put in at a town?"

"Because he gets drunk." Wolkin picked out a dumpling, ate it, and licked his fingers. His eyes widened. "Oh! And you went and forgot to bring his booze the other night, and he got mad! And everybody could hear him snarling in there, and there was green stuff coming through the walls!"

"There was *what?*"

"It's like . . ." Wolkin waved his hand and ate another dumpling. "See, he's been a river captain for so long, he's got river water in his blood? And drinks a lot of Yendri brandy too. And maybe the river water in his blood makes river-weeds in there. And when he has to go without his booze for too long, maybe all the . . . the green stuff sweats out of his blood. I was sick once and sweated yellow stuff. It was sort of yellow anyhow."

"*There was green stuff coming through the walls?*"

Wolkin nodded. He slurped his soup and picked out another dumpling with his fingers. "Where's your spoon?" Eliss asked him, but he just shrugged. Krelan set his bowl down and leaned forward.

"Why does the captain get drunk when we put in at a town?"

"Well, there's a lot of stories," said Wolkin thoughtfully. "Like he was in love with this girl, and they had a baby, only she left him? So he made a vow never to set foot on land again until someday when she comes back to him? Or, like, she died and he swore never to set foot on land because she died on land? But *some* people say he's under this curse. That if he ever sets foot on shore again, because he's doomed to sail the river forever until he, I forget what, something happens, anyway if he ever sets foot on shore he'll turn to dust. Because he's hundreds and hundreds of years old really."

"Really?"

"Well, he's really old. I heard my daddy tell Mama that he was sailing the *Bird* when he was a boy, my daddy I mean. Was a boy. And Captain Glass was on the river even back then. And he *never looks a day older.*" Krelan lowered his voice dramatically. "And *some* people say he offended the holy gods and—oh, wait, that's why he's doomed to sail the river forever."

"Doesn't explain why green stuff came through the walls," said

Krelan, raising one eyebrow. Wolkin made a noncommittal noise as he stuffed dumplings in his mouth.

"Maybe he's just a demon," said Eliss. "They shift shape sometimes."

"And it would certainly explain the drinking."

"Demons drink booze all the time," agreed Wolkin through a full mouth. "My daddy was saying to somebody about the bandits, the Shellback ones, that every place they've attacked, it's always their demons who get killed? And that's because they go straight for the booze or, erm, other things and don't pay enough attention to fighting. And that's why there's so many demon heads on the walls."

"That's undoubtedly true." Krelan rubbed his chin. "But I think that means Captain Glass can't possibly be a demon, then, can he? He'd be drunk *all the time*. A demon wouldn't be able to pay attention to anything long enough to be a ship's captain."

"They aren't all like that," said Eliss. "We lived in a town for a while where there was a sorcerer who had a demon servant. It lived in his house and even wore some clothes. It loved numbers. Maths problems, you know? It kept all the accounts for all the shopkeepers in town. It calculated the Duke's portion taxes at the end of the year too."

"I've heard some of them are like that," Krelan said. "They get obsessed with things."

"It could talk too. Sometimes people would call it a Yendri and it would get mad. *He* would get mad. It was a man demon. He said anyone who was too stupid to know the difference between him and the Yendri deserved to be eaten." Eliss shook her head, remembering the demon. His skin had been yellow as flowers, and his eyes like a pair of faceted emeralds.

"What happened to him?" asked Wolkin, fascinated.

"Nothing happened. He just lived there, and made more money for the sorcerer keeping people's accounts than the sorcerer made selling protections and things."

"And there's the Master of the Mountain, who has a whole demon army that does what he tells it," said Krelan. "So I suppose it's not beyond credibility that our captain is a demon."

"But not the kind who eats children," said Wolkin, looking from Eliss's face to Krelan's to see if they were joking. "Right?"

"Obviously not," said Krelan. "Have any kids ever gone missing on the *Bird?*"

"No."

"There you are, then."

Wolkin gave a sigh of relief. Eliss thought: *Most other men would have told him some made-up story to scare him, because they'd have thought it was funny to frighten a little boy. But not Krelan . . .*

GILDER'S LANDING, Bisonder, Trastarine: the *Bird of the River* crept up on each one, passed its docks or stone wharves with glacial slowness, and finally left it in her wake. At each little town, Eliss went with Krelan to show Lord Encilian's picture at the better shops, at the better inns, discreetly asking questions. Everywhere they went, people were worried about Shellback's band of thieves, or about river pirates, and Gilder's Landing even had masons hard at work building extensions to the city walls and new fortifications on the waterfront. Consequently it was a little hard to pull their attentions to the question of whether or not a handsome young lord and his servant had passed that way, all those months back.

But Krelan was patient, and Eliss was good at finding the right people to ask. So they learned that at Gilder's Landing Encilian had still been alive, because he had ordered the best meal the tavern keeper had, thrown it across the room after tasting it, and laughed when the tavern keeper had presented the bill. They learned he had still been alive at Bisonder, because he had tried to buy a gold chain in the marketplace, but Bisonder was a poor town and had no such merchandise to offer him; so he had left in disgust. They learned that people remembered him at Trastarine because he had taken the Patron's mooring slip, and refused to apologize or move his boat. Later he had gone to view the Patron's fossil excavations, and had been heard to declare, and loudly, that it was a wretched place that had no entertainment to offer but a lot of rockbound curiosities.

Everyone remembered the servant too. He had seemed embarrassed by his master's behavior.

"But why would your lord stop at any of these places at all?" Eliss asked. "They don't seem like the kinds of places he'd want to visit."

"Well, he didn't stay long anywhere, did he?" Krelan said. "Just put in, went ashore, made a nuisance of himself, and left next morning."

"Was he maybe looking for something?"

"Why would he need to do that?"

"WHAT'S THIS PLACE?" KRELAN ASKED as they came in sight of the first of the docks. He had come up to draw water to wash the breakfast pans. Eliss had come down from her perch, since the river's face glinted in the morning sunlight untroubled.

"Krolerett," said Mr. Riveter, who stood in the bows with a rag-ball fender, ready to kick it over the side as they came to the dock. "Big market town."

"How long will we stay, sir?"

"A few days, maybe. We need fresh food."

"The captain will want extra whiskey, then?"

Mr. Riveter gave him a sharp look. "Two barrels. And I'll fetch them aboard myself, thank you very much."

"SO I SUPPOSE CAPTAIN GLASS was annoyed by having to wait for his tipple," said Krelan as they climbed the broad stone staircase leading up from the wharf.

"If he was, he didn't say anything to you." Eliss shaded her eyes with her hand, studying Krolerett as they came to the top of the stairs.

"No. Just exuded green supernatural slime," said Krelan. "Through the cabin walls, no less. Which clearly made an impression on Mr. Riveter."

"Well, their cabins are next to each other."

"But it doesn't bother you?"

"Weird things happen sometimes," said Eliss. "So Captain Glass has a curse on him. He's still a good captain. Maybe it's the will of the gods. Who knows? Sometimes things just happen for no reason."

"It's not the will of the gods part I object to," said Krelan. "It's the things happening for no reason."

"Why?"

"I suppose I like my universe to be an ordered place where everything makes sense," said Krelan. "The gods running everything, and under that the Diamondcuts, and under that my family serving the Diamondcuts, and sort of alongside us all the Dukes and Tyrants and Patrons and other Noble Families, and under that the merchants, and . . . everybody else under them. Everybody following their own foreordained track. Reason prevailing. Nothing going out of balance."

"But there isn't any balance. That's just made up. A Diamondcut can end up dead in the river mud, and a demon can fall in love with a goddess. Things just happen," repeated Eliss, shifting Mrs. Riveter's market basket to her other arm. "Sometimes they're even *good* things. Come on. Let's explore."

Krolerett was only a pair of wide streets, crossing each other in an open square, but they were thickly lined with shops built of limestone blocks. Here and there too, were the wicker booths of Yendri merchants who sold baskets of carrots and fresh herbs. Eliss spotted a Yendri bathhouse, draped with green poppy-silk banners, and was amazed to feel something like affection as she walked past and glimpsed a white-robed Yendri standing at the counter inside. *Maybe someday that will be Alder. . . .*

The streets were crowded with people: grain dealers just arrived from the inlands by caravan, miners looking to buy equipment, hunters bringing in kills, boat crews from the river. There were inns and eating houses and even, in one vacant lot where a building had fallen down, a hastily built stage on trestles and a players' cart. At the intersection there was a beggar on every corner, whining for alms without much success; all but one of them looked muscular and strong, under the rags and filth. There were plenty of curbside vendors here too, offering foods cooked over braziers or deep-fried in kettles of oil. There was commotion and shouting to clear the street, as a team of men led by a one-eyed showman pushed a great wheeled cage along. Within it, four demons snarled and spat at the crowd.

"This is tedious," remarked Krelan, after being jostled from the high curb for the third time in two minutes. "Let's seek a respite from the crowd somewhere, shall we?"

"Where?" Eliss settled a string of onions in her basket, and accepted change from a Yendri grocer.

"What about there?" Krelan pointed at a building across the street. It had big windows and lamps mounted along its wall. GOLDEN HOSPITALITY was painted above the door, with a mosaic depicting a smiling man offering a golden goblet to make the point for anyone who couldn't read.

"It looks expensive."

"I'm buying. I think that last jostler broke my foot."

"Really?"

"No, but it was a near thing. He was wearing hobnailed boots." Krelan took her arm and tugged Eliss with him across the flow of traffic. She glanced down at his feet.

"You should probably think of getting yourself some boots next. Sandals are comfortable, but they don't protect you much."

"I have a plethora of elegant boots at home," said Krelan as they stepped up on the curb. "My family prides itself on being well-shod. Also in walking quietly. But there I was, planning to infiltrate a barge crew and I thought, 'Sandals! That's just the sort of low-profile footwear the lower classes inhabit, isn't it? I'll wear sandals.'"

"Except that we mostly go barefoot on board," said Eliss. "And the really poor don't even have sandals."

"Well, now I know." Krelan opened the door for Eliss and she slipped inside. He followed and they both stood blinking in the comparative dim silence, which was pleasant after the glare and bustle of the street. "Oh. It's an inn."

Eliss glanced at the front desk, and at the dining room entrance opposite. "We can still get some tea or something."

"Splendid." Krelan led her inside and they found a table by the windows. They ordered tea and biscuits. Eliss settled the market basket on the floor between her feet, and sat back on the bench to gaze out the window.

Just across the street, a man in nondescript clothing leaned against the wall next to the grocer's booth. He wore a wide-brimmed hat, shading his features. Something about him tugged at Eliss's memory. She thought back over the morning and placed him: he had been leaning against a shed on the docks when they had come ashore from the *Bird of the River*. When everyone had had to scramble for the curb as the cage full of demons went past, he had been sampling sweetmeats from a vendor's cart just across the street. Now he lounged in a slanted square of shade, calmly eating sugared almonds from a pastry cone.

"Your tea, sir and madam," said a waitress, setting her tray at the edge of their table. As she set out the tea things, Krelan drew money from his pouch. Encilian's portrait came with it, tangled in the strings. It fell with a clatter on the table.

"Oh!" The waitress tilted her head to look at it. "Isn't that—" Her eyes filled with tears and she looked away.

"Who did you think it was?" Hastily, Krelan stuffed the portrait back into his pouch.

"He stayed here," said the waitress. "Months ago. Please, do you know him? Can you send him a message?"

"Who did you think it was?" repeated Krelan, leaning forward to speak to her in a low voice.

"Lord Encilian," said the waitress, blotting her tears on the hem of her apron. "He had some fancy last name. Diamond something."

"Diamondcut."

"That was it. Are you his friend?"

"I know him," said Krelan, studying her face. "I can certainly get a message to his family, if it's important."

"Oh, he wouldn't want his family to know! I'm sure. He didn't care for his family, he told me. He was going to come back here and settle down. He said he liked it here."

"Did he?"

"And he's going to build a fine big house on the hill up there. He said so. But I thought he'd have come back by this time, you see, and . . ."

Eliss eyed the girl's waistline. *Poor stupid thing*, she thought. Krelan drew out the portrait again and slowly laid it on the table.

"You're quite sure this was the man?"

"Of course I am." The waitress touched the painted serpent armlet. "I remember that. It was heavy gold. He let me hold it . . ."

Krelan's face was stern. "How long did he stay here?"

"A week, sir. He had our nicest room. There wasn't room for his servant and he stayed on the boat. I didn't care for the servant. Cheap piece of goods. But his lordship was . . . he was so kind. Told me that this place had quite taken his heart. Asked me all sorts of questions about it, because he wanted to buy that hill up there and build a palace on it. He was just going up to Karkateen to see to some business first, and then he was coming back. Only, now . . ." The waitress twisted her apron in her hands, close to tears again.

"Only now he's never come back," said Krelan. "My dear, I think perhaps you misunderstood him. I know the man. This isn't the sort of place he'd choose to live."

"You may think so, but I know what he told me!" said the waitress fiercely. "He said he'd wandered the world and only wanted to settle down somewhere quiet. A-and raise a family . . ." Her mouth spasmed down at the corners. She struggled to calm herself a moment before adding, "He went and opened a bank account. Why would his lord-ship do that, hmm, if he wasn't planning on coming back here? You tell me!"

Eliss glanced out the window, embarrassed. The man in the wide-brimmed hat was no longer standing there against the wall.

"Well, a bank account is something, I'll admit," said Krelan. "Which bank, may I ask?"

"There's only the one. The Merchant's Bank. I've been so afraid that something might have happened to him in Karkateen, you see, because that's so big and there are thieves there—"

Krelan held up his hand. "As it happens, I'm one of his family's agents. I'll see what may be done for you." He opened his pouch and took out five gold crowns. "This is for you, in the interval."

The waitress stared at the gold, astonished. "Gods bless you, sir! Gods bless you for your kindness!"

"It isn't kindness," said Krelan stiffly. "It's duty. I can't tell you to hope for happiness, do you understand that?"

"I suppose so." The waitress swept the coins into her hand and fingered them all together, listening for the heavy clink of gold. She sighed. "I'm not such a fool as you think, young sir. But if there's any chance—" Her voice broke and she walked away quickly, before turning and coming back to snatch up her empty tray.

"It sounds as though your lord was being himself again," said Eliss, when the waitress had gone at last. Scowling, Krelan poured out their tea.

"Too damned true. The old lord will have to be told about this, though. The Family looks after its own, even the by-blows. And now I really have to buy myself a pair of boots."

"What for?"

"If I'm going to say I'm one of the Family's agents, I'd better look like one." Krelan took up a biscuit and bit into it ferociously, scatter-ing crumbs.

"She didn't even look at your sandals."

"I meant that now I'll have to go to the bank and present myself, so I can see what Encilian was doing opening a bank account."

THERE WAS A DEALER in ready-made leather goods at the near corner, with a store of boots. Krelan fussed at the clerk and tried on one pair after another, while Eliss stood in the doorway and watched the street.

The showman with his cage of demons had set up in front of the players' stage, and the leader of the players and the showman were presently having a screaming argument about who had a right to be there. The leader of the players was an older man and the showman was big and young, tattooed in several colors, with a bellowing voice that carried; but in the end he was the one who backed down, and gave the order for his men to move the wheeled cage.

Eliss stood back against the wall as the cage moved slowly up the street. The men grunted and sweated, for the sun was now high overhead. The demons inside the cage, shaded by its roof, lounged in elaborate enjoyment.

"Push harder, red boys," said one, whose speech was unimpeded by tusks or excessively long fangs. "We'd like to get to the top of the street before nightfall. Hey, pretty girl!" Seeing Eliss, he got up on his knees and waved part of his anatomy at her. "Bet you'd love to know what it's like to take a ride on *this*, eh? You can, you know. I'm very tame. Just you pay my master five crowns and he'll be more than happy to arrange the whole thing."

"How much would he charge me to geld you?" said Krelan, stepping forth from the shop and taking Eliss's arm.

"By the Blue Pit, look! It's a talking shrimp!" the demon retorted.

"Just ignore him," said Eliss as the wagon passed. "Did you find nice boots?"

Krelan did a little dance step by way of answer, sticking out his left foot at the end and waggling it. "Very nice. They aren't Jasper's of Salesh by any means, but they'll do for this town. Come on. Let's go to the Merchant's Bank."

"Where are your sandals?"

Krelan held them up. Eliss took them and tucked them in her basket. "All right, let's go."

The bank lay at one far end of the cross-street, a big building of limestone carved with bas-reliefs of the gods bringing wealth to Krolerett. As they rounded the corner, one of the beggars cried, "Alms for a poor blind man!" Krelan fished out a copper and tossed it into his bowl.

"You shouldn't have given him anything," said Eliss as they walked on toward the bank.

"My dear! I'm appalled at your heartlessness."

"He wasn't really blind. Didn't you see how thin the gauze over his eyes was? He could see you perfectly well. It's an old trick. And didn't you see how big and strong-looking he was? He'd never get away with that in the cities."

"Where there are a better class of beggars?"

"Where there are really disabled people. They police the streets themselves. If they caught someone like that faking, he'd be beaten black and blue with crutches in no time."

"How diverting! Tell me, how does a lame man beat someone with a crutch, if he isn't a faker too?"

"He sits down and hands his crutch to a simpleton, and tells *him* to hit the bad man really hard," said Eliss. "I've known a lot of beggars. Believe me, they have a whole system of rules and regulations worked out."

"One learns something new every day. In fact, there's a whole world I never knew existed, isn't there?" They came to the bank and Krelan disengaged his arm from Eliss's. He tugged at his clothes to smoothe them, cleared his throat, and seemed to stand a good inch or two taller.

"Right. Do you mind very much sort of lurking in the background? As though you were my servant? I need to be a bit more impressive than I was at Forge."

"Fine," said Eliss. They went in. A pair of guards stationed near the door eyed them briefly, then clashed the butts of their spears on the floor. Eliss supposed they did it to remind people that the premises were guarded.

"Wait over there, please." Krelan waved his hand at a wooden bench against the far wall. Eliss took a seat. She had never been inside a bank before, and looked around curiously. Three clerks stood behind a high counting table, waiting on merchants who seemed to be depositing profits. The floor was a mosaic depicting the gods presenting the different coin denominations to a body of mortals in old-fashioned clothes. Lamps, extinguished now at midday, hung from the vaulted ceiling. To one side were closed shutters in the wall, as though someone's private office lay beyond. The air was still and quiet and cold, which seemed odd when Eliss thought of all the anger and desperation that money generated.

Krelan had approached a fourth clerk and spoken to him. The clerk hurried through a door behind the counting table and a moment later returned with a portly bank official wearing a chain of office.

"Now, what is this? Who are you?" demanded the official.

Krelan spoke to him in a voice that was also still and quiet and cold, very different from the weak voice he'd used when first he'd come aboard the *Bird of the River*. "This is my authority," he said, and drew a tablet from his pouch. He presented it to the bank official, who opened it and peered down at it a moment.

"Oh," said the bank official, in a much lower voice. He seemed to shrink a bit within his robes. He handed the tablet back and looked up at Krelan with nervous eyes. "How may we assist the noble Family?"

The merchants glanced over at them and abruptly decided the bank was not a good place to be. They grabbed their receipts from the bank clerks and hurried out. Krelan waited until they had departed and said: "Lord Encilian Diamondcut opened an account here in the spring."

"He may have, sir. We pride ourselves on our confidentiality," said the bank official.

"Lord Encilian is deceased. Regard his death attestation," said Krelan, drawing out another document and opening it before the official's eyes. The official read closely.

"Oh, dear. My condolences to the noble Family. Such a young man too! Dear, dear. You've come to close out his account, then, sir."

"Precisely," said Krelan, allowing a faint shade of graciousness into his voice. Eliss tried not to smile. She looked out the window and saw, to her surprise, that the blind beggar had moved from his corner and was tapping his way along the street toward the bank, waving a stick before him.

"The Merchant's Bank of Krolerett is happy to comply with the noble Family. Brasspunch! Fetch the vault key."

"Immediately, sir." One of the clerks fled. The bank official leaned close to Krelan and lowered his voice still further.

"I must advise the noble Family that the circumstances were somewhat irregular."

"Were they? In what way?" Krelan inquired. Eliss watched as the beggar reached the end of the street and sat down on the curb, right in front of the bank. Did he think merchants on bank errands would feel particularly compassionate?

"His lordship opened a joint account."

"With whom?"

"With his manservant, sir."

"Manservant!"

"And ordinarily with a joint account we would require authorization from representatives of both parties, you see, sir, or at least attestation that the other party was also deceased—"

"He opened an account in his name *and* the manservant's?"

"Quite so, most irregular, and I made very sure to point out to the young lord that such an arrangement might present difficulties at some future date. He was not disposed to be advised in this matter, however."

A merchant came in with a courier's sealed pouch strapped to his chest. He had not even looked at the beggar. He shrugged off the pouch and one of the bank clerks unsealed it and began to count out the contents.

"The most noble Diamondcuts require the name of the manservant," said Krelan.

"Of course, sir, and may I just assure the noble Family that under the circumstances, which are indeed peculiar, the Merchant's Bank of Krolerett will of course waive all requirements relating to the second party? The servant was—er—"

The clerk Brasspunch hurried up, presenting the key with a bow.

"Thank you," said Krelan, taking it.

"Mr. Brasspunch, be so good as to fetch the file for Lord Diamondcut," said the bank official. As the clerk hurried away obediently, the official added, "I very much regret that I cannot recall the servant's name without referencing the documents. We'll have them for the noble Family in just a moment, sir."

Krelan tapped the key against his chin thoughtfully. "Now, why in seven hells would his lordship want to open a joint account with a servant?"

"He said it was for convenience's sake, sir. In case he should need to send his servant to make a withdrawal for him. I tried to convey to him the possible danger in trusting a servant, but . . ." The bank official looked at his shoes and coughed. "His lordship was most emphatic that his orders were to be carried out in every respect."

"Of course."

Eliss frowned, watching as beyond the window two more beggars ventured down the street toward the bank. One limped, a crutch under his arm; one, twisted by palsy, staggered along leaning on the walls of the shops as he came. Why were they deserting the intersection for this quiet dead end of the street?

"The file, sir." Brasspunch emerged from a back office and presented a tablet with pendant seals. The bank official took it and opened it.

"Here we are! The servant's name is Stryon Waxcast." He turned the tablet so Krelan could see it. Krelan took the tablet, scowling.

"Waxcast? Not a common name."

"With respect, sir, not in these parts, but I have heard of several Waxcasts down toward Synpelene," said the bank official.

"This seems to be in order. . . ." Krelan studied the tablet a moment longer before closing it with a snap. "Well. The deposit, please."

"This way, sir."

They walked back into the depths of the bank and vanished through a doorway. Eliss watched as the beggars reached the end of the street. These were fakers too, she realized; the one with crutches had well-muscled legs, and while the palsied one held his arm twisted up under his shoulder, the arm was not withered. They sat down, one on either side of the beggar who was feigning blindness. This was *wrong*. . . .

She saw the showman with his wagonload of demons come around the corner up at the intersection. To her surprise, he too started down the street toward the bank.

"Just show you to our private room in here, and you can open the box and assure yourself that all is as it ought to be." The bank official's voice came again as he returned through the door with Krelan.

"Very good. Thank you."

The street sloped downhill, so the wheeled cage was proceeding at a much quicker pace now. Eliss felt a tightening in her throat. Too many odd things happening at once . . .

"Of course, I will need to be present when the box is opened— and the law requires that we have one additional witness, for form's sake, you understand, sir, to assure that all is as it should be. I can call in one of my clerks, however—"

"No need. I have a maidservant. Mrs. Stone?" Krelan looked into the main room. "I require you a moment."

"At once, your lordship," Eliss said, making a face at him as she got to her feet. She found her gaze drawn again to the window as she walked forward. The wheeled cage lurched to a stop just in front of the three beggars. The blind beggar ripped away the gauze bandage over his eyes. The one-eyed showman flung open the cage's door and the demons leaped out, just as the beggars scrambled to their feet. All the pieces came together in a moment of revelation.

"They're thieves!" screamed Eliss. "They're going to rob the bank!"

The merchant, who had just collected his receipt and was in the act of pushing the door open, looked up and said "What?" His legs were quicker than his brain, however. He fled through the door and was away up the street before the first of the demons came charging in, brandishing a club. The guards had their spears up and warding him back, but the windows snapped out as the other demons leaped through, followed by the beggars and the men who had been pushing the cage. By that time Eliss herself had vanished around the corner, pulled by Krelan past the bank official into the shuttered room.

Krelan put his finger to her lips. She heard the bank official, out in the corridor, shout once and say, "Thieves! Call the—" before there was a dull thud. There were a couple of nasty cries. Eliss recognized the sound of a man trying to yell with a cut throat. She put her hands over her ears, fighting back an unpleasant memory.

"Oh, look, he's got a gold chain," said a new voice, one neither cold nor quiet. "Thank you, dead man."

"Please! No!"

"He's got a key too. Here! Clerk. Answer quick and you don't die. Is this the key to the main vault?"

"N-no, that's the key to the private accounts vault."

"Where's the key to the main vault?"

"In Mr. Coppersheet's office!"

"Him? Feriolekk, take this one in and get the vault key. Do as you're told, clerk, and you live."

Eliss lowered her hands, struggling against terror. She looked around the private room, in which there was nothing but a table and a pair of chairs. *No vaults in here. Nothing anyone would want. Maybe they won't come in.* Krelan had taken up a position behind the door. He had a dagger in his hand—briefly she wondered where he had gotten it—and his face was completely blank.

"People in the street, Shellback!"

"Raker, Shirrigal, go grin out the windows at them. Shoot anybody who gets close. *Where's that fucking key?*"

Not seeing what was going on was almost as painful as the terror. Eliss moved to the shutters. She found a tiny chink where one metal slat was just far enough out of alignment with the others to provide a view into the front room. She peered through. The two guards lay dead on the floor and so did the bank official, in a spreading pool of blood. His chain of office currently swung from the fist of the one-eyed showman, who had thrust aside his eyepatch and was glaring around the room with two good eyes. Several men and another demon stood guard on three clerks, who were flattened up against the wall behind the counting table. A pair of demons armed with crossbows stood at either window. As Eliss watched, one of them took aim and shot at someone in the street beyond. There was a scream and a rising babble of voices up the street.

"Here!" A demon strode into view—the one who had called Krelan a shrimp—pushing the terrified Mr. Brasspunch ahead of him. Mr. Brasspunch held out a key.

"Finally." The showman—*So this is Shellback,* Eliss registered—grabbed the key. "Shadow, Tooth, take this. You, clerk, show them where the vault is. Crow and Knacker, put the clerks on the floor."

"Down on your faces!" roared the demon, and the terrified clerks dropped.

"They're all staying back, lord," said one of the demons at the window.

"Good." Shellback handed the other key to one of his lieutenants. "You, go see what you can get out of the private vault. You, go with him. Everything in the bags. Follow the plan."

"Right."

Krelan tensed at the door, but no one came in. Eliss heard footfalls in the hallway and busy noises. Somewhere in the depths of the bank, coin was being shoveled into bags. Somewhere else it sounded as though boxes were being opened and either tossed aside or emptied, with rattling and clinking, into other bags. One of the clerks was weeping and praying. Another might have been praying silently: Eliss could see his lips moving as he lay on the floor, his face turned toward her. Shellback slipped the gold chain over his head, admiring it. He was a young man, unshaven, good-looking as far as Eliss could tell. The pool of blood on the floor grew larger.

Now there was more noise from the street. There were shouted orders and the sound of tramping boots.

"Lord," said one of the demons at the windows, "there's soldiers coming."

"What!" Shellback ran to the window. One of the men guarding the clerks leaned over to see too.

"They've called the militia," he said.

"They don't *have* a fucking militia! He *said* they didn't have any militia!" said Shellback.

"Looks like one to me," said one of the demons, speaking carefully around his tusks.

"I'll fucking kill him," said Shellback. "I will. Get the clerks up where they can see them! *We've got hostages!*" He bawled the last sentence out the window, just as a bolt came zipping through. It missed him by inches and plunked into the wall behind the counting table. The clerks were dragged to their feet and held up to the windows, grasped close, each with a blade at his throat.

Eliss looked away and met Krelan's eyes. He gestured toward the floor. *Get down,* he mouthed silently. Eliss thought of lying terrified on the floor, unable to see, unable to tell what was happening, unable to do anything but lie there being afraid. She shook her head. He scowled at her. She shrugged and put her eye to the shutter again.

The demons had backed away from the window and the clerks were being held there in a line, sweating, and the thieves holding them there were sweating too. Shellback paced behind them. The demons watched him.

"Are we dead?" asked one of them.

"No. No, everything goes with the plan. A few changes, that's all. We have *them.*" Shellback jerked his thumb at the clerks.

"Somebody's coming," said one of the men holding the clerks.

"You in the bank," called a voice from outside. Eliss saw the officer of the militia walking out to the end of the street, visible in glimpses between the bodies of the hostages. "Let's talk."

"As long as you like," Shellback shouted. He turned and stared down the corridor, presumably at his men who were filling bags with money, and made hurry-up gestures.

"You're Shellback, aren't you?"

"My fame precedes me!" Shellback held up his hands like an orator. The demons grinned and stamped their feet.

"This is a new tactic for you, isn't it?"

"Never do to become predictable!"

"Didn't work very well, did it? I mean, there you are, and here we are. Where's Mr. Coppersheet?"

"Now, who would that be?"

"The man in charge. Him with the gold chain."

"Then I must be the man in charge now, because I'm wearing the chain!"

"So you killed him?"

"Him and the guards too. Stupid to keep just two spears in here, wasn't it?"

"Well, see, but we knew we'd just established a civil guard for the whole town. We didn't think anybody'd be stupid enough to get themselves in the fix you're in. See, now you're trapped."

"Looks that way, doesn't it?" Shellback winked at the demons. His men came up from the corridor, dragging the filled sacks. He shook his head and signed that they should go back, and pointed down the corridor and mouthed *Back wall.*

"So what it comes down to is, you're going to die in there. I know this. Your men can see the troop I've got lined up across the street. They know they're outnumbered. The demons probably don't care, but the others know you've killed them. Unless we can cut a deal, Shellback."

"What kind of deal?" Eliss watched Shellback making gestures at one of the demons, who stared in blank incomprehension. Grimacing, Shellback crossed the room in two strides and picked up a wooden case one of them had carried in. He thrust it into the demon's arms and whispered, *"Back wall, remember?"*

"You let the hostages go. Do that and surrender, and your men will live. You'll die. The demons will die. But, and I swear this by all the gods, your men will live."

Shellback laughed loudly. The demon smiled around his tusks, slapped his forehead with one hand, and ran off down the corridor with the wooden box.

"Laugh if you like, but I'll bet your men aren't laughing. I think they're thinking about turning on you," said the officer of the militia.

"I think you don't know them very well!"

"Listen to me, Shellback's men! The first one of you comes out the door with his head, that man gets a full pardon and a reward."

"They're not listening!" Shellback paced back and forth, watching something going on down the corridor.

"They can't help but hear me. The Krolerett Merchant's Council will pay a thousand crowns to any one of you who turns on Shellback. Two men turn, two thousand crowns. Three men, three thousand. Gold crowns. The more of you turn, the more you'll be paid. You outnumber the demons, don't you? You can earn more than you would have made sharing out the loot. Think about it. Think about being true sons of the Father Smith."

All the while the other was speaking, Eliss watched Shellback watching what was going on down the corridor. He gnawed his lip. When the other finished, there was a long moment of silence. Shellback stepped close behind one of the men holding hostages and muttered, "Ask him to swear by the gods you won't go to prison."

"Can you swear by the holy gods we won't go to prison?" the man shouted obediently.

"I swear by all the holy gods you won't go to prison!"

The two demons, Feriolekk and the one who had carried the wooden box, came running back. "It's set!" Feriolekk told Shellback, who grinned.

"Don't trust him! You have to be *alive* to spend cash, my friends," cried Shellback. He dropped his voice. "Right. Tradeoff. Demons take the hostages. You four run with me to the back. Just as we planned, eh? Feriolekk, the minute it goes, kill 'em. Then fight for your lives."

The minute what *goes?* Eliss wondered, as the demons traded places with the men holding the hostages, who had begun to whimper and scream.

"You were a good lord," said Feriolekk, as a sudden dull *boom* came from the rear of the building, but Shellback had already turned and bolted with the other men in the direction of the explosion. Eliss looked away from the shutter at last, but not soon enough to miss the sight of the demons killing the hostages. Someone grabbed her wrist.

"*Now* will you get down?" Krelan murmured in her ear. She let him pull her to the floor with him as he sank down, and braced his body against the bottom of the door. Eliss lay on the floor, staring at Mrs. Riveter's market basket with its string of onions poking out of the top, while bolts snapped and thumped through the windows. There were horrible high-pitched screams. A bolt came through the shutters and buried itself in the wall opposite, not near enough to have killed Eliss if she had still been on her feet but too near, all the same. Eliss shut her eyes and prayed.

"He's still moving! Kill him!" someone shouted. There was a thump and a snarl that faded into a gurgling noise. Eliss heard the heavy tread of boots walking on broken glass.

"They blew out the back wall!"

"Smith, take your men and go after them. Maybe they'll drop the loot."

"Did they kill them all?"

There was a pause. "Gods below, they killed everybody."

"Not us," yelled Krelan. "We hid in here!" He rolled away from the door just as it was kicked open. Eliss looked up into the eyes of a grim-looking guardsman with a cocked crossbow. She burst into tears.

It was, as Krelan afterward told her, the best thing she could have done.

THEY WERE MARCHED to the Krolerett Civic Hall, which was doing double duty as a temporary barracks, and questioned at some length by the officer who had stood out in the street and attempted to bargain with Shellback. Once Krelan had presented his tablets, the questioning was done in a quieter tone of voice, but was no less intensive.

"You stated the thief identified as Shellback said, quote, 'They don't *have* a, er, militia. He said they didn't have any militia. I'll, er, kill him,' unquote," said the officer, reading off the tablet whereupon he had been taking notes.

"That's what he said," agreed Krelan wearily. Eliss sat staring into Mrs. Riveter's market basket. Onions, radishes, herbs, a bag of cough and cold tea, a jar of sweet syrup, Krelan's old sandals. And, buried under them all, the box he had been about to open when the thieves had attacked.

"Who do you suppose *he* is?" The officer lowered the tablet and looked at Krelan.

"You're asking me? I would think it was their informant. Whoever it was told them you had a bank and no walls around your town." Krelan rubbed his eyes.

"So you think we have a traitor in our midst?"

"No," said Eliss. Both men turned to look at her. "If it was somebody who lived here, he'd know you have a militia now."

"That's true," said Krelan. "Wouldn't it be more likely it was someone who passed through here a few months ago, before all the trouble started? You *don't* have walls. The town *is* wide open."

"Krolerett has always been an open town, young sir," said the officer, with a faint edge to his voice. "It facilitates trade."

There were shouts from the hallway outside. The officer looked up. "Excuse me a moment," he said, and got up and left the room.

"You should probably not say anything else unless you're asked," said Krelan. "But you made a good point."

"Thanks so much," said Eliss crossly. "It ought to be obvious that somebody—"

She halted, as more puzzle pieces came together, and couldn't believe how blind she'd been. "This whole summer," she said in a faint voice. "Oh, gods below, every place we've been—think about Synpelene! We—"

The door opened and the officer came back in, trying not to grin.

"Did you catch them?" Krelan inquired, with a warning look at Eliss.

"No." The officer dropped into his chair and leaned back. "But we got the loot. They'd dropped it into a hole and covered it with branches, and kept going. Deep hole, had to have been dug beforehand. Same with the cut branches. So they planned all along to leave it and come back. Because, who'd try to run three leagues weighed down with gold?"

"Congratulations," said Krelan. The officer shrugged.

"We still lost five good citizens."

"May we go now?" asked Eliss.

"Soon," said the officer. "The merchants of Krolerett thank you for your assistance in this matter. We appreciate your public spirit. We would just like to verify that you did in fact arrive on the *Bird of the River*. As soon as we hear from her captain, you will be free to go. Would you like any tea?"

"Yes, please," said Eliss.

"You, sir?"

"Thank you, yes."

The officer left the room again. Krelan grabbed Eliss's hand. "What about Synpelene?"

"What if your lord hired his servant when he was in Synpelene?" said Eliss. "If a lot of people named *Waxcast* live there? What if the servant's been working with Shellback the whole time? Think about it. Every place we've been that's been attacked, your lord and his servant had been there. What if he was using your lord to get inside the rich places, so he could find out where the expensive stuff was and where the weak places were? And then he passed the information on to Shellback!"

"But . . ." Krelan's voice trailed off as the implications hit him.

"Think about it! Think what happened at Synpelene! Somebody who knew the town made it easy for the thieves. The sewer grate was unfastened *from the inside*. That hotel where all those poor men died, didn't the innkeeper say the thieves had gotten hold of a key somehow?"

"And Encilian stayed there," said Krelan slowly. "The innkeeper remembered him. And the man would have carried his master's key while they stayed. He might have made a copy."

"He must have! And everywhere else they went ashore, he would have been prying into each town's secrets. He knew where the safe was at Bluestone, and the armory and even the jewelry shop. He knew about the water cannon on the docks. He knew a *lot* about Silver Trout Landing, because they stayed there a month, and he must even have told Shellback about that lord and his boat, what was his name, Lord Chrysoprase? He knew how many servants they had and I'll bet he knew where all the valuables were kept," said Eliss.

"And the little towns with nothing much of value haven't been attacked," said Krelan. "And there's nothing worth much at Latacari except iron, and nobody steals that."

"But we know they stayed *here*. They opened an account at the bank together. The servant must have talked him into it somehow. And while they were in there he had a good chance to look around. But that was months ago, before the town bought a militia. Which they probably did because of all the other attacks. Which was why Shellback said what he did, what was it? *'He said they didn't have a militia.'* He was talking about Waxcast."

"Maybe he was." Krelan narrowed his eyes.

"And when Waxcast had learned as much as he could . . . then he must have thought he didn't need your lord anymore. So he killed him and threw his body in the river. And he sank the boat to make it look like river pirates had done it."

"But he took his head," said Krelan. "Why do that?"

Eliss thought about it. "Maybe to make it look like a vendetta killing? Maybe to keep the body from being identified, if it washed up somewhere? But then he'd have taken the snake armlet too . . . I haven't figured out all that part yet."

"But you may be right," said Krelan. "And if you are, it makes my job easier. All I have to do is find Stryon Waxcast, and exact retribution."

His face was like a stranger's as he said it, cold and remote-looking. Eliss shivered.

"Do you think he might be in Karkateen?"

"He might be. I'll certainly have to look for him there," said Krelan, turning as the door opened. The officer came in, closely followed by Mr. Riveter, who had thrown a tunic on in his haste but forgotten to put on shoes.

"You're free to go," said the officer. "All vouched for."

"Thank you, sir," said Krelan, and when they were outside on the pavement he added, "That was fast. We never got our tea."

"Captain said to go into town and find you," said Mr. Riveter, his eyes wide. "Captain said you'd got into trouble. Actually *opened his door* and put his head out to tell me. Then I came up the hill and there were all these guards standing around putting demon heads on poles in the center square. I asked one what was happening and he said to go ask at this office. I went in and asked and the one in charge says, 'Who did you say you were?' I thought I was going to be arrested!"

"I suppose they're all edgy because of the robbery," said Krelan. The streets were still so crowded, what with people standing about watching the demons' heads going up on poles, that the three of them fell into single file as they made their way along the pavement going downhill to the river.

"I don't ever remember a summer this bad for thieves," Mr. Riveter said, half over his shoulder as he walked in front. "I heard the Master of the Mountain got married, thought to myself, 'At least that'll keep *him* home nights,' and lo and behold here's this new one Shellback pops up, and to make things worse he's working the river."

Krelan said something in agreement. Eliss didn't hear what, exactly, because her attention was captured by the man in the wide-brimmed hat, who darted out of an alley as they passed it. He had a knife in his hand. He lunged toward Krelan from behind.

Eliss screamed and threw herself at him. Krelan turned just as the blade entered his side, rather than his lower back. Eliss shoved the attacker, driving his head into a wall. From somewhere within the folds of his clothing a pastry cone flew out and hit the wall too, and the sugared almonds cracked like crossbow bolts as they scattered on the bricks. Krelan, having spun around with the blade still in his side, ran his own knife up under the man's ribs.

"DO YOU WISH TO FILE a claim of vendetta?" intoned the officer. Krelan, grunting as Mr. Riveter bound up his side, shook his head.

"Was this killing the result or continuation of a vendetta?"

"I suppose it might be. He was a professional. Carried no identification."

"All right. Under Krolerett Civic Ordinance Number 302, Subsection 5, you have the legal right to claim trophies including but not limited to the assailant's weapon, clothing, footgear, ears, head, organs of generation, fingers and or hand, or hands. Do you wish to petition for any or all of the above?"

"I do not."

"Under Subsection 6, you then have the right to make recommendations with respect to the disposition of the assailant's corpse."

"I waive that right."

"Very good. We're all through here, then, sir, except for you just signing this tablet releasing the Krolerett Civic Body from any responsibility in regard to the matter of your assault." Flipping open a tablet, the officer held it out to Krelan while retrieving a stylus from his belt and offering it with the other hand. Krelan took them both, signed, and gave them back. Smoothly the pair of temple deacons moved in with their stretcher and removed the huddled body of the assassin, covering his face with his hat. He had been an ordinary-looking man. Eliss, staring at the broken pastry cone and candies on the pavement, thought: *he never got to finish them.*

Her sympathy evaporated, however, as Krelan got effortfully to his feet and went pale. He nearly fell. Eliss and Mr. Riveter both grabbed for him.

"I think I'd like to go lie down for a while," said Krelan in a faint voice.

"Come on." Mr. Riveter crouched and got his arm around Krelan's legs, and swung him up in his arms like a bundle of twigs. "Seven hells! You can't weigh any more than Wolkin. I'll just carry you."

"Well, this is embarrassing," observed Krelan as they proceeded down the street.

"You can't walk. You'll have to come back to my room," said Eliss. "I can sleep on the floor. Krelan, that's the second time someone has tried to kill you!"

"You aren't going ashore again without a whole false beard on," said Mr. Riveter. "Told you that mustache wouldn't disguise a damn thing! Next town we're at, you write to your father and ask him how much longer this vendetta is likely to drag on, eh?"

"Yes, sir," said Krelan.

"But—" said Eliss. He caught her eye and, almost imperceptibly, shook his head.

THEY WEREN'T ABLE TO SPEAK privately until Krelan was stretched out on Eliss's bed in the cabin and had been visited by Mr. Pitspike, who insulted Krelan extensively before forcing him to swallow a pint of chicken broth laced with bull's blood and treacle and departing with a sarcastic remark concerning Krelan's new boots.

"This is a comfortable bed," said Krelan thoughtfully, when they were alone.

"Why would somebody try to kill you?" said Eliss. "For no reason at all!"

"Oh, there's always a reason," said Krelan. His voice was light and careless, but he was still pale, and seemed shrunken somehow. Eliss suddenly saw what he would look like as an elderly man. *If he lives that long.* It wrung her heart.

"But what reason? Who knew you were going to be in Krolerett, besides me?"

"Ah. That's the question, isn't it?" Krelan shifted on the pillow. "Nobody on the *Bird* knew we were going ashore until we decided to go. It's no one on the *Bird*, I'm fairly certain."

"But who would want you dead in the first place?"

"My brother, for one."

Eliss looked at him, astounded. "Why?"

"Business," said Krelan. "Family business, I mean. I inherited a lot of money, considering I'm a younger son who doesn't amount to much. My brother got to be head of the family, but his inheritance doesn't quite meet his needs. If I die, he gets it all."

"That's horrible!"

"Well, I can see his point. He has two children. He's always assumed I could never find anyone to marry me, so the implication there is that I'll fritter my fortune away on jolly pastimes. Also I'm smarter than he is, and he's never trusted me . . . and he has two little boys to protect."

"You mean he thinks you'd kill them?"

Krelan shrugged. "It's happened before, in our family. Among the Diamondcuts too. There's a reason we're called their shadows. And there's an awful lot of inheritance involved, you see."

"But . . ." Eliss sagged into a sitting position on Pentra's bunk. "You'd never do such a thing."

"I wouldn't, no. I like my nephews. I'd cheerfully leave my inheritance to them, if I could do it on my deathbed at a respectable age. But my brother can't be expected to take my word for that." Krelan gave a wan smile. "It all makes sense. That's why I was nearly killed in Prayna, even though I'd given all the right passwords. He must have arranged for someone in the business to be watching for me. In fact, that must be why he saw to it that I was stuck with this job in the first place. Send me off to the back of beyond on a miserably difficult quest. Get me out of the way so I can be killed on the quiet. And here I thought he was just testing my skills."

Eliss thought bleakly of her own family. *Maybe we weren't so terrible after all. At least we loved one another.* "You wrote to your brother at Latacari," she said. "So he knew you were still alive there."

Krelan nodded. "I wonder if Mr. Sugared Almonds has been following me on the way, waiting?"

"Can't you go to the Diamondcuts for protection?"

"Oh, gods, no. Something like this is far beneath their notice. All the Family wants to hear from me is whether I've done the job I was sent out to do. Hmmm . . . and they'll want to know about that poor waitress. If she's carrying Encilian's bastard, they'll make provision for it."

"Who *cares?*" Eliss cried. "Krelan, your brother's trying to have you murdered! What are you going to do?"

"My job, if I can," said Krelan wearily. "What else can I do? That's the only part I don't understand. He could have had me poisoned at home, if he wanted to get rid of me. Waiting until I'm on a job for the Family to murder me puts the job itself at risk. That's disloyal. My grandfather would have disowned him for it. I can't tell you how many times we had it drummed into our heads, that the Family came first . . . we're nothing without them."

"That's stupid," said Eliss vehemently. "They're nothing but a lot of rich people who quarrel all the time."

But Krelan shook his head. "I remember when I was . . . oh, I can't have been more than three or four. My grandfather took me by the hand and led me up from where we lived into the Family compound. We went into this dark hall, and he had to light a lantern and carry it as we went. It was the Family's portrait gallery. Paintings of all the lords and not a few of the ladies, going right back to the Four Wars. He held up the lantern and there was this high noble face above me in the circle of light. 'That's Harrik Diamondcut, first of the Family,' said my grandfather, and proceeded to tell me all about how Lord Harrik escaped the ambush that did for his father and lived to found his own great house, and amassed a mighty army. Lord Harrik went after the man who'd given the order for the ambush, though it was twenty years after and the man was living rich and quiet in Ansilatra. Lord Harrik hunted him down and burned his house, and . . . did other things. 'That's vengeance for you,' my grandfather said.

"He led me down the gallery, stopping in front of each of them. I thought they were the gods. He told me all their stories. Lord Sarprit, who won the Battle of Conen Feii. Lord Rask, who killed his own brother over an insult to his lady wife. Lady Jarethna, who married a lord of the Quickfires, and when she learned her husband was plotting to implicate her father in treason against the Duke, she killed him and her three children by him too, and went home to her father's house. Lord Karthen, who burned the granaries at Troon and all the harvest fields for fifty leagues around.

" 'There's greatness, there's power, there's honor for you,' said my grandfather. 'And one of *your* ancestors, boy, was always there at hand. One of *us* found Lord Harrik's enemy for him. One of *us* set fire to the enemy's tents at Conen Feii. One of *us* managed the poison for Lord Rask, and then killed himself after, because Lord Rask's brother was a Diamondcut after all, and that was *right*, you see. One of *us* arranged to get Lady Jarethna out of her husband's family's compound and safe home. One of *us* took the torch from Lord Karthen and did his will with it. You've got proud history in your blood and bones, boy,' he told me.

"I remember all their faces. They haunted my dreams for years afterward. When I was eight I was taken to the Family's chapel and sworn into their service. I was scared and proud and . . . you don't understand, do you? I can see it in your face."

"No, I don't understand," said Eliss. "They sound like horrible people, all of them."

"And, do you know, I agree with you?" Krelan closed his eyes. "Gods, I'm tired. I need to sleep. . . . You learn history as your grandfather tells it to you, and on some level that's always going to be the true history that stays in your heart and makes you do things . . . but then when you get older you read books, and you get out in the world and hear other versions of the stories, and you learn how the rest of the world sees your noble family. You learn the things Grandfather didn't tell you. And you begin to wonder . . . and you begin to feel a little bit like a traitor inside. And some of the glory goes away, and never quite comes back for you."

"Stop talking about them. Just sleep," said Eliss, drawing her blanket over him. He smiled at her. He said nothing more and in a few minutes she could tell from his breathing that he was asleep.

She sat on Pentra's bed with her knees drawn up, staring at him. *There are worse lives than mine,* she thought. *How could anyone live like that?*

PENTRA OBLIGINGLY SPENT THE NIGHT in a tent on deck, saying that Eliss couldn't possibly sleep on the floor. Next day Salpin and the other musicians rigged up a sort of hammock-bunk for Krelan between two bulkhead panels where the sacks of beans were kept. He slept well there by night and dozed peacefully by day, except when Wolkin and the other children came down and stared at him and asked him whether it was really true he had killed four demons and an assassin from Mount Flame all by himself. Eliss found herself getting up in the night and going out to check on him.

At the end of a week his wound had closed over, and with his side bound up tight Krelan was able to resume some of his galley duties. Captain Glass called him up to the aft deck and spoke to him for an hour or so, too quietly for Eliss up on the mast platform to hear what was said. Krelan was rather pale afterward and did not bring up the matter over dinner. Eliss didn't ask, either.

She had a dream one night that she was back in the earliest place she could remember living with Falena, some seaside town without a name, but there had been wide crumbling stone steps with pink flowers growing in the cracks, and lizards sunning themselves. Off one landing of the steps a trail had led to a little stone house with a weedy yard and one tree. Fishing nets were sometimes spread out there to dry. Someone had made an outdoor table by stacking stone blocks and laying an old hatch cover over them.

In the dream, Falena was sitting at the table with her. There was a pitcher of something on the table, and three cups. Falena was balancing a cup on her head and making funny faces to make Eliss laugh. Someone else was sitting at the table too. He was laughing with Eliss.

IN ALL THE EXCITEMENT and its aftermath they had almost forgotten about the bank box, stashed away safely in a locker under Eliss's bunk. When Krelan felt well enough she fetched it out for him. They ate their dinner together in the bows, on a hot still evening when mackerel-shoal pink clouds glowed and lingered long after sunset, radiating light on the quiet face of the river. When they had set their bowls aside, Krelan reached into his pouch and drew out the key.

"That poor bank officer," he said, peering down at the key as he turned it in his fingers. "The last thing he did in his life was present me with this key. He did it with a little ceremonial flourish, you know. Everything correct and just so. A minute later he was lying dead on his polished floor and Shellback was pulling off his chain."

"There's a picture like that in Salesh," said Eliss. "A big mosaic wall. 'Fortune's Dance,' or something like that. Rich people and beggars going round and round, changing places, and Death sitting there playing a concertina."

"Shouldn't it be Fortune playing the concertina? If it's Fortune's dance?"

Eliss shrugged. "Same thing, isn't it? Everybody dies."

"How very bleak, my dear." With a certain reluctance, Krelan put the key in the lock and turned it. "Here goes . . ."

The lock clicked. Krelan lifted the iron lid of the box.

"Jewelry," observed Eliss.

"But . . ." Krelan leaned forward to stare. "But these were *his*."

"Well, whose else's would they be?"

"I mean, this is his Family gold," explained Krelan, still unwilling to reach into the box and touch any of it. Eliss looked closely. There was a gold chain with its links worked in the serpent pattern of the Diamondcuts, as well as a heavy gold signet ring with the same device. There was another ring set with a heavy amethyst, and the coiled serpent was also carved into its top facet. Finally, there was a little serpent armlet, like a miniature of the one that had been on Encilian's body when it was found. Tied to it with a silk thread was a little signet ring, a miniature of the other one in the box.

"That was his baby gold," whispered Krelan, pointing at them. "Those were given to him when he was born. There's his name, engraved inside. Once he grew into them he wore them every day of his life, until he outgrew them, and the old lord had new ones made. That's the signet ring of the set." He touched the larger ring. "What are these doing *here*?"

"Maybe he wanted to keep them safe," said Eliss. "He knew he was going to Karkateen, after all."

"I suppose. But the baby gold was kept in Lady Cirellise's coffers."

Krelan stroked his chin, puzzled. "That's his mother. It would have stayed there until he married, if he ever had, and then it would have been given to his wife for their heirs. Why did he fetch it out and bring it with him here?"

"What would have happened if he'd never married?"

"It would have been kept until after the lady had died. Then it would have been melted down and re-cast for some other child of the Family. Something of a punishment, you see, for not marrying and furthering the greater glory of the Family with more offspring."

"That's why, then," said Eliss. "He knew he probably wasn't going to marry anybody, and he didn't like the thought of his baby gold being melted down and given to somebody else, so he stole it."

"It's certainly the sort of thing Encilian would have done," Krelan admitted. Gingerly he picked out the amethyst ring and held it up. In the crimson light from the clouds it seemed to fluoresce with sullen livid fire. "Mind you, he'd have been married sooner or later, whether he wanted to or not. The old lord had been fairly plain about that. 'The way you spend money, my boy, we'll have no choice but to find you an heiress,' he said. I remember that conversation. They had a huge quarrel."

"When was that?" Eliss watched the light play in the carving of the coiled snake. It flashed with the illusion of movement. She put her hand to her own necklace, tracing its pendant's swirl pattern with her fingertips.

"Now that I think of it, it was three months before Encilian vanished." Krelan gave Eliss a shrewd look. "You're thinking he sailed off so as to avoid getting forcibly married?"

"Isn't that the sort of thing he would have done too?"

"It's exactly the sort of thing he would have done." Krelan put the ring back in the box, sighing. "Poor idiot. That's why he took his personal things with him. I wouldn't have put it past him to have decided to live incognito in Karkateen for a while. Maybe until the old lord was dead. And *that* was why he hid them here, or rather there in Krolerett. They'd stay safe in a bank vault until he was ready to reclaim them. And of course he never realized he was giving his servant a perfect opportunity to rob and murder him and get away with it."

"Funny that he didn't put his grown-up armlet in the box too," said Eliss.

"Wouldn't have fit," said Krelan, closing the box to demonstrate. "See?"

"Oh."

"Poor fool," Krelan repeated, locking the box once more. "May I put this back under your bed? It will have to go to the Family, of course."

"How are you going to get it to them? Won't your brother try to kill you if you come back?"

Krelan grimaced. "Yes, but one isn't supposed to let mere considerations of personal safety get in the way of duty. If I kill Waxcast, retrieve Encilian's head, return triumphant to kneel before the old lord and lay his son's missing bit *and* personal effects at his feet—and then find a knife blade in my back the first time my brother manages to be alone with me—well, Grandfather will welcome me into the Garden of Fire with pride. And I'll probably get a little engraved brass plaque somewhere, commemorating my faithful service to the Family. It's my duty," said Krelan, holding up one hand as Eliss made outraged noises. "All I have is my duty. If I fail at this, what use am I?"

Eliss shook her head. She gathered up the bank box and got to her feet. "You're crazy, you know," she told him.

"I'm not," said Krelan sadly. "But the world is. If you know of a better one, let's go live there instead."

"I wish," said Eliss. Something was wrong, some point had been missed, but she couldn't think what it was. She walked away through the pink twilight, going over their conversation in her mind. The quiet evening water pulsed with color like a bed of coals, where fish came up to feed at the surface.

DROWSILY HALF-CONSCIOUS IN HER BUNK that night, Eliss thought about the dreams she'd had lately. She was jolted wide awake by another memory surfacing, an ancient one, a fragment of lost time at the little stone house above the steps.

She had had a tiny boat of her own, with hand-carved oars, and she had sat in it proudly rowing as she had seen fishermen do. She wasn't getting anywhere, because the boat sat among the weeds and pink flowers of the yard, but she was happy. Someone was shaking his head as he watched her, while he mixed up something in a can. And Falena had come out of the house, drying her hands on her apron.

"Poor little thing," the other person had said. "Look at her, sailing nowhere. You should have let me make her a cart instead."

"What, when we live at the top of all these steps?" Falena had shaken her head briskly. "She'd roll right down the steps and split her head open at the bottom." Her face was the face Eliss remembered, and yet it wasn't. The Falena who had died on the river had had a face that seemed to have broken and been mended, a sad foolish face. She looked nothing like this practical and cautious girl, whose clear eyes focused sharply. But Falena had been this person once, hadn't she? *She looked like me,* Eliss realized, feeling a slow shock. *Mama was like me.*

What had happened next? Falena saying something about ". . . a sailor like her daddy."

"Of course she will," the someone had said, leaning down to Eliss, and she had put up her arms and he had swung her up, so high! "All my family were mariners." *Dear gods, was that Daddy? I do remember Daddy, then!* He had a close beard, his skin was burnt by the sun, he was handsome. He had slung her on his hip and turned to the can on the table. He had dipped a brush in it and daubed something on the wall beside the door of the little house, a green ripple pattern in a circular swirl.

"What's that?" Falena had asked, coming and putting an arm around them both. She had kissed Eliss's cheek.

"It's for protection," Daddy had said. "So you'll be all right while I'm gone."

Falena had gone tense, then, but her voice had been neutral as she'd said: "I wish you wouldn't go. I've been having the worst dreams."

"But we need the money, Falena. One last voyage and then I'll stay closer to home. Buy a share in the fish stall. Make a steady income, then, like you wanted."

"I love you more than a steady income," Falena had said. Frowning, she had considered the ripple pattern. "Which god's sign is that? Looks almost like something Yendri."

"My mother used to embroider it on my clothes, for good luck," Daddy had said. He had looked slyly at Falena. "She always swore my father was a river god, you know."

"You look like a god," Falena had said. She had kissed Daddy fervently, desperately, as though she was afraid of losing him. As, of course, she had. . . .

Eliss buried her face in her blanket, feeling the hot tears start. *She did love him. Mama loved him and she lost him and never loved anybody like that again. And she can't have been much older than I am now. What would I do, if life had been that cruel to me? Would I break the way she did? I'm strong . . . but she was strong once too. Beautiful Falena.*

"KARKATEEN," SAID KRELAN, pointing. He had climbed the rigging for the first time since he had been wounded, and once aloft sat rather quietly beside Eliss as she studied the face of the river. She looked up now and saw a distant smoke on the mountains ahead of them, and the late afternoon light gleaming on far high windows.

"I thought we must be getting close," she said. "There's a lot of floating trash coming downriver."

"It's a big city."

"What are you going to do when we get there?"

"Well, I *don't* think I'm going to go to the runner's house to pick up any messages my brother might have sent me. He's probably got someone there watching who'll go after me if I do."

"It would be sort of a dead giveaway, yes."

"I suppose I'll just find out what I can and do the job, if it can be done there. If Waxcast is there."

"You'll have time to look for him," said Eliss. "Mr. Riveter says we put in for a week at Karkateen."

She didn't want to ask, *Will you leave the* Bird *then? Will you go back to the Family by a quicker route? Will I ever see you again, alive or dead?*

JUST BEFORE NOON THE FOLLOWING DAY, they reached the lake of Karkateen.

The great city climbed the flanks of the mountains all around the lake. On one ridge, squalid shacks perched above ravines filled with trash; on the next ridge mansions rose on terraces, magnificent as the palaces of the gods. Down at the lakeshore a busy populace hummed and bustled, in shops dug back into the cliff faces, in sloppily built brick buildings, in tents and open-air markets along the docks. To the west the river flowed from the lake; to the north a canal took its way from the lake through a mountain pass, going down to the sea some miles away at great expense to the Lords of Karkateen. The lake was a dirty green color, choked by the industry of its city and the cloudy streams that came down from the emerald mines. Only at its heart was it clean, where the pure upwelling of the spring that fed it created a swirling center of clear water.

Here was a shrine to the god of the river, built into a moored buoy. It bobbed and swayed on its little platform, and its green jade god raised a hand to bless the city that barely spared it a glance.

"WHY HAVE WE MOORED HERE?" Krelan asked. Eliss shrugged. The *Bird of the River* had dropped anchor in the middle of the lake, just in the edge of the zone of clear water.

"Captain's got to make an offering," explained Mr. Riveter in hushed tones. Eliss glanced down the companionway. When Captain Glass had locked the *Bird's* tiller and gone below, she had assumed he was simply following his usual routine on arriving at a town. But now he came up the companionway again, wearing nothing but a loincloth. She averted her eyes. Mr. Riveter's skin bore so many tattoos, and he was so lean and leathery from the sun besides, that his perpetual near-nudity embarrassed nobody; but Captain Glass was scarily pallid and huge in a state of undress.

Still, he had the dignity of a mountain as he walked to the *Bird's* rail. Salpin and Drogin stood there with a basket that had been covered in cloth and tarred inside and out, like a little coracle. They bowed to him.

"The offerings, Captain, sir," said Salpin.

"Set it down," said the captain. They leaned over and set it carefully on the surface of the water, making it fast with a line tied to one handle. Looking into it, Eliss saw a vial of something golden and a smaller vial of something colorless, as well as something folded in a white napkin. There were also empty vessels, two cups, and a bowl made of what she took to be a particularly thick and cloudy glass.

"What is that?" she murmured to Salpin, but Wolkin answered eagerly.

"They're *sugar*," he said. "Molded into offering stuff. Because they have to be able to dissolve. Because you can't be throwing all kinds of junk into the river. And the yellow stuff is really, really expensive brandy, so the god can have a nice drink. And the white stuff is perfume, so he can smell good. And the berries in the napkin, except they go in the bowl not the napkin because the napkin wouldn't dissolve, see, are so he can have a nice snack."

The captain looked down at him and snorted. "What makes you think the god is a man?"

"Well, there's his statue." Wolkin pointed at the floating shrine. "He has hands and a face and everything, doesn't he? And legs and feet. Only you can't see them because they're under his robe," he added, peering across at the statue. Captain Glass chuckled.

"How do you know what's under his robe?" he said. He stepped over the rail and lowered himself into the crystalline water. The basket bobbed gently on its tether. The captain leaned back in the water with a sigh, spreading out his arms a moment before untying the line from the rail. Taking the end between his teeth, he swam out toward the shrine.

The musicians struck up a hymn, one of the droning river-songs Eliss had heard nearly every day since she had come aboard. She watched the captain's progress across the water. As clear as the water was, it was full of strange distortions from the spring's turbulence, and the captain's body seemed to lengthen and ripple fantastically. The noonday sun struck down and lit the water's depths, unimaginably far down into the spring's heart where it surged from some black chasm in the rock below.

Eliss wondered if she ought to pray. She reached into the neck of her tunic and found the little crystal pendant the captain had given her, and clasped it tightly. *Father of the Green Waters,* she improvised, *this is Eliss, who reads your course. Please keep my friend safe, if you can. He has something dangerous he has to do in this city. Maybe you don't care if the Smith's children kill each other, I'd understand that, but Krelan matters. He doesn't think he does, but he matters.*

Captain Glass reached the shrine. He set up the vessels at the statue's feet and poured out liquor, perfume, and fruit. Then he coiled up the rope and laid it in the basket, sending the basket floating back toward the *Bird of the River* with a push. Shoving away from the edge of the shrine, he leaped like a fish and dove down, down through the transparent water, so far down that his image distorted into nothing human. Eliss and Krelan stepped to the rail involuntarily, peering down.

"That looks dangerous," said Krelan in an undertone.

"He never drowns," Wolkin whispered loudly, in reply. And now indeed the gigantic shape was rising back through the sunlit water, fast and faster, shooting to the surface at last in a fountain of glassy water drops, a white roiling shower, and the captain shook himself, half out of the water as he gasped for air. He laughed as he sank back and struck out with his immense arms, swimming forward, to where they waited for him on the deck of the *Bird*.

AFTER THAT THEY RAISED ANCHOR and sailed off for the lakeshore, where there was a special dock for the *Bird of the River*.

"You're not going ashore, in case someone tries to murder you again," Mr. Riveter said to Krelan, as the *Bird*'s cablemen threw out fenders and moored her at the dock. "Got better sense than that, I hope."

"I hope I have good sense, sir," said Krelan meekly.

"Good. Because we can't have you getting—" Mr. Riveter was distracted by several men who had been waiting on the dock, advancing up the gangplank the moment it was laid down.

"First Mate Riveter?" The foremost of the men saluted. "Karkateen Municipal Navigation Maintenance presents its compliments. What does the *Bird* require?"

"Oh, good—I've got a list—" Mr. Riveter slapped himself absently as though feeling for pockets, but as he was only wearing his customary loincloth, no list was found. "It's in the logbook. I'll fetch it out. And, er, we've got a slow leak in the aft starboard hull—couple of planks need replacing, and likely a new weld on the coppering— and—er—"

People were lining up to go ashore. This was the halfway mark for the *Bird*'s long journey, and no one would be paid until they were all the way downriver again, at the sea, but it seemed everyone on deck had a way to earn a little money in the meantime. The musicians all had their instruments with them, bound for street corners where they might busk, or for taverns willing to hire short-term entertainment. Salpin winked at Eliss as he shuffled forward in line, his concertina under his arm. Mrs. Ironlatch and several others among the women carried great stacks of baskets they'd woven from peeled and split snag-roots, or boxes inlaid with bits of mussel shell, or useful odd-ments like spindles or knitting needles, carved from bone or horn.

"Here," said Krelan in an undertone, nodding his head at Mrs. Turnbolt, who was staggering under a high swaying stack of peeled-bark boxes. He approached her, with Eliss following close.

"Madam, may I just assist you with those? Help you to carry them ashore?"

"Very kind of you, dear," said Mrs. Turnbolt with a gasp, relin-quishing half the boxes to Krelan. One fell to the deck; Eliss grabbed it up before it rolled overboard, and they went down the gangplank all three without drawing Mr. Riveter's notice.

"Where are they going?" Krelan inquired.

"Just over to that street corner there," said Mrs. Turnbolt, nod-ding to indicate direction. "My husband's cousin runs that shop. He never minds if I set up in front." By the time they had helped her cross the thronged street, set down her boxes, unfold her little fold-ing chair, and put out her hand-lettered sign, they were well out of sight of the *Bird of the River.*

"Right. Come on," said Krelan, taking Eliss's arm and striding off purposefully.

"Where are we going?"

"The Harbormaster's office." Krelan pointed at a tower on the waterfront, some two blocks away. They pushed toward it, through a dense crowd. There were men hawking trays of what looked like dingy pebbles, that they swore, perhaps truthfully, were uncut emer-alds; there were other men hawking trays of bright bits of green glass, skillfully cut, and they too swore their wares were emeralds. Yendri grocers had set up barrows full of farm produce, and silently took coin for grapes or radishes. There were artists offering to paint anyone's likeness in a ten-minute sitting. An itinerant fiddler was playing *The Ballad of Falena* while his lady friend sang the lyrics and held an alms basket. There were street corner sharpers offering games of Find the Lady on overturned barrels. Prostitutes of both genders leaned in doorways, sizing up the crowds and idly fanning themselves with placards that advertised their rates. There were hot food vendors with their carts offering freshwater prawns or fried bread or beer or smoked fish. Every available square of pavement had been co-opted as an impromptu market stall, and so it took Krelan and Eliss some time to reach their goal.

Even so, Krelan paused on the doorstep.

"Do something for me?"

"What?"

"Will you go in? All you need to ask is whether the *Fire-Swift* docked here. Get them to show you the ledger entry, if you can. Just in case my brother thought to have this place watched as well."

"Now that occurs to you," Eliss grumbled, but she gave his hand a squeeze and, pulling up her shawl, climbed the stairs to the office.

Within the office it was anything but crowded, or bustling either for that matter. All was silent but for the steady *plink-plink-plink* of the water clock. A young man in uniform was seated on a high stool at the counter, slumped forward on his elbows and staring out the window at the lake. He cast a lackluster glance Eliss's way when she came in, and abruptly sat straight.

"Yes, miss!" Hurriedly he closed up a tablet. It looked as though he had been writing poetry. "May I be of assistance, miss?"

"Do you have the log of boats that have put in over the last six months?" asked Eliss, in her Pentra voice.

"Of course, miss!" The clerk slid a bound codex across the counter to her, and almost pulled it back when it occurred to him to ask, "Er—why?"

"I'd just like to see if my brother's boat put in here," said Eliss, taking hold of the ledger to prevent its removal, and thumbing back hurriedly to the month or two following the spring equinox.

"I can undoubtedly find it for you," said the clerk, making a halfhearted effort to take possession of the ledger once more.

"Quite all right, sir." Eliss tightened her grip on the ledger with one hand while running her finger down the column of entries. The *Sweet Duchess*, the *Handalak*, the *River Mist* . . .

"What's your brother's boat's name?"

"Well, that's the problem," Eliss improvised. "He has two. I'm not sure which one he took out, on that particular sail." The *Fire Goddess*, the *Indomitable*, the *Sprite* . . .

And then it was there, just under the *Sprite*: the *Fire-Swift*, captained by Encilian Diamondcut, accompanied by one manservant. There was her docking entry and there was her date of departure, one week later. The destination given was Silver Trout Landing.

"Here it is!" exclaimed Eliss, releasing her clutch on the ledger. "He took the *Sprite*. Thank you, sir. I'm so relieved!"

"Was there a problem?"

Eliss mimicked a gesture she'd seen Krelan use, the import of which was that this was a private matter and better not discussed. "A family concern only, kind sir. Thank you."

"I mean, if I could be of any further assistance," stammered the clerk, "I'm only on duty another two hours. If you require anyone to escort you anywhere—or we could go somewhere for dinner—"

"Oh." Eliss looked at his flushed face in surprise. "Oh, no. Thank you, but I—I have a friend with me." Now she was blushing too. Hurriedly she drew her shawl around her head and went out, and ran down the stairs.

"Why would someone ask me out to dinner when he doesn't even know me?" she said to Krelan.

"Because you're probably the loveliest girl he's ever seen," said Krelan morosely. "When are you going to figure that out?"

"I'm *ordinary*!"

"You are the least ordinary girl I've ever known," said Krelan. "And you can act as though you're plain as long as you like, but sooner or later you'll have to learn to deal with men acting like fools around you. You're beautiful."

Eliss stared at him, too surprised to be angry. *Men always tell women they're beautiful*, she told herself hastily. *Doesn't mean it's true. They just do it to get their way.*

"Were you able to learn anything?" Krelan asked in a more normal voice.

Eliss told him about the ledger entry. He sighed and shook his head.

"So we know they got this far, and we know they *both* left. And we know Encilian never made it back as far as Silver Trout Landing. Which would mean he was killed somewhere in between there and Latacari. Probably near where the *Fire-Swift* sank, because she couldn't have traveled far with that hole in her hull. And I'm sure Encilian was dead before she was scuttled."

"And Waxcast might have gone anywhere after that," said Eliss.

"That's right." Krelan sagged into a sitting position on the steps. "Ye gods. I've got to go over the whole route again, looking for him. And somehow keep from getting killed before I can find him."

He looked so tired and hopeless Eliss sat down too and put her arms around him.

"We'll find him! Look how much you know now, that you didn't know setting out. You know his *name*. It'll be all right."

"Very kind of you to say so." Krelan patted her hand absentmindedly. Eliss summoned her courage.

"Look," she said. "We could go somewhere for dinner."

"I suppose we could."

"And we could buy you a hat! It'll make you harder to see. If people are here looking for you, they're looking for a man in a hood, aren't they? They won't expect a hat. Come on!"

"All right."

She pulled him to his feet and they threaded their way among the tight-packed shops along the waterfront, dodging between barrows and braziers until they found a stall where hats were stacked in leaning columns, felt blanks with wide ragged brims. It took some arguing to convince the hatter that Krelan didn't want his hat trimmed, shaped, or decked with any particular band or cockade. When they were finally able to leave the stall, Eliss looked at Krelan in his new hat and thought: *Holy gods, he looks like a mushroom. But it makes his face harder to see.*

"Well, this will come in handy when the rains begin," Krelan said with a wry smile, tilting the brim back to peer at her. She smiled back, aware of a painful twinge.

I'm in love with him. I'm in love with this funny little man who's in all the trouble in the world. At least now I understand Mama a little better. . . . This is just the sort of thing she would have done, and I always hated it and wondered why she couldn't love somebody ordinary like a shopkeeper. Somebody who wasn't trouble.

But none of those men were Krelan. . . .

He slipped her arm through his and they wandered together through the crowd, looking for a place with tables where they might eat.

"There's the fish market up ahead," said Krelan, pointing. "That's a good bet. They buy fish straight off the boats. Shall we go there?"

"Why not?"

The eating-houses were all built up on stilts above the stalls, and their rear balconies hung out over the edge of the wharf, so that diners above could crumble bread into the water for the ducks and the occasional far-ranging seagull. Eliss watched a squabbling crowd of waterfowl scattering in all directions as a fishing boat came in to dock behind one of the restaurants.

The boat drew her eye for some reason, even after the birds had fled. It was a small boat, trailing its empty nets. No one stood on her aft deck making offerings to Brimo by throwing unwanted catch to the birds. No one stood aft at all. There were only three men visible in the bows. Two busied themselves with throwing out fenders and tying up. The third man waited until the mooring was secure and then stepped from the bow onto the wharf, in one easy bound. Without so much as a word or glance at his companions, he walked ashore. He wasn't dressed like a fisherman. . . .

"That's Shellback." Eliss gripped Krelan's arm. There was no mistaking the thief; he wore the striped tunic they had last seen him wearing in the Bank of Krolerett. Eliss had seen the same hard hand-some face several times since, in nightmares.

"What?" Krelan followed her gaze. She felt an electric thrill run through him as he spotted Shellback, who crossed in front of the fish market and began to make his way along the pavement, not quickly but purposefully. "Oh. Oh, thank you, gods."

He started to disengage Eliss's arm from his own.

"What are you doing?"

"I have to follow him," said Krelan in a low voice, straining to keep sight of the striped tunic through the crowd. "He knows Wax-cast. Maybe Waxcast is here. Maybe he knows where he is."

"But that was just an idea!"

"It's a good idea and the only one we've got. Go back to the *Bird*," Krelan called over his shoulder, starting away from her. Eliss ran after him.

"Are you crazy?" she cried. Krelan paid no attention, ducking and weaving through the throng, vanishing but for his immense wide-brimmed hat. Eliss followed him doggedly, silent now as she kept Shellback in sight. Shellback moved steadily forward along the wharf, looking neither to right nor left, ignoring the cries of the hawkers who offered him fried food or cheap jewelry. *He knows where he's going*, she thought.

Abruptly Shellback was crossing the street that paralleled the wharf, dodging between the moving pushcarts and people carrying baskets. Krelan's hat dodged after him, and Eliss shoved her way through the moving mass to keep both of them in sight.

There: Shellback had passed a vendor's stall where wooden chests of all sizes were set out. Suddenly he turned, doubled back, and inspected the chests briefly. He took a smallish ironbound one, slung it under one arm, and tossed a coin to the vendor. By the time he started on his way again, Krelan was no more than five paces be-hind him, and Eliss had nearly caught up with them both.

On along the wharf, out of the market district now, and the crowds were thinner. Only expensive boats lay docked at the wharf here, and all the shops were across the street. There were ships' chandlers and a few restaurants of the hushed and expensive kind. Between the blocks long streets struck straight up the hill, where stone houses sat, one above another on terraces overlooking the lake. Eliss craned her neck back to see the mists rolling down from the mountains, bruise-colored with all the water they bore, obscuring the tops of the trees and the highest houses.

When she lowered her gaze, she saw Shellback making his way up the nearest street, walking flat-footed to accommodate the steep incline. Krelan had halted at the corner and was peering up after him. Eliss caught up with Krelan at last. He turned and started when he saw her. "I *said* go back to the *Bird!*"

"No! That's a murderer! He wouldn't think twice about killing you," said Eliss, but Krelan had already turned his attention on Shellback again, watching as the thief climbed steadily. Krelan's face was pale and set, unsmiling.

"All right," he said in a neutral voice. "But you're not going to like me much after today. Assuming we both survive."

He grabbed a paling out of a garden fence and crouched over it, as though he were an old man leaning on a walking stick. "Take my arm and lead me up there," he ordered. "Pretend I'm your aged father or something. And don't take your eyes off him."

Eliss obeyed, clutching Krelan's arm. They crept up the street. Shellback was high above them now, climbing steadily, never looking back. *He isn't wary in the least,* thought Eliss, *he doesn't think anyone would follow him here. But what's the box for?*

They had risen into an area of fine houses, with palanquins set under open stalls in each garden. *Of course they don't walk here, they're too rich. They have servants carry them up and down these hills. . . . What's the box for?*

Eliss worried at the question, perhaps to keep her mounting terror at bay. A loose end, Shellback's little ironbound box. Like the bank box was a loose end. Lord Encilian's baby gold in there, all his personal jewelry. Except for his serpent armlet. Because the serpent armlet would not fit. So he was still wearing it when Waxcast had cut off his head and thrown his body in the river.

Why didn't he cut off the arm too and take the armlet? But he hadn't. There hadn't been a mark on the body, other than the nibbling of crabs. No dagger wounds.

How do you get someone to kneel down and have their head cut off? Maybe by a ruse? *What's that down in the water? Look, my lord, can you see it? Perhaps you had better bend down to look.* Or maybe Waxcast had drugged his lordship? That would be easy. *A cup of wine, my lord? Is my lord drowsy with the heat? Will my lord lie down?*

But the armlet was heavy gold, costly. *Why not remove it, before Encilian's body was rolled into the water?*

How high they had climbed. The noise of the lakeside market had been left behind. Up here it was deathly quiet, with only the sighing of the wind bringing the mist across the housetops. Wealthy places were always so quiet. Eliss nearly glanced over her shoulder to see how high they had climbed, but resisted the urge. Shellback must be going to stop soon. The grand houses were fewer up here, the gardens green and dripping with mist. It was almost like a Yendri place. She wondered where Alder was right now. If something bad were to happen, would he ever hear about it?

Nothing bad will happen, she told herself. *We'll see where Shellback goes and then we'll go back to the Bird. Or I'll go back, and let Krelan do whatever he's going to do. And pray to the holy gods he survives. That's all I can do, really, isn't it? I spent my whole childhood afraid of Mount Flame bullies and the things they do. How stupid would I be, to get mixed up in their business again? And Mama would always wipe her eyes and tell me I didn't understand.*

I won't make her mistakes. I won't be stupid. I'll leave Krelan here and go right back down this hill.

Shellback turned in off the street, where steps led up a terrace to the very last and highest house, a modest mansion built of white limestone blocks. Black and green moss furred the walls on its north face, hid the red roof-tiles under a splotched pattern of green. He climbed the steps past the namepost. It was a new post, carved with the name WHITEGOLD.

"There it is," Eliss murmured. Krelan raised his head and peered from under the brim of his hat.

"*Whitegold?* Not Waxcast?"

"No," said Eliss, feeling sick with relief. "Somebody else. Look, let's go back down and find the city guard. We can tell them Shellback's here. Maybe there'll even be a reward." She turned and looked down at last. There was the wide expanse of the lake, with its clear center and the floating shrine almost too tiny to make out. And there, right over there, she spotted the *Bird of the River* at its dock. It looked small as a scrap of plank, too far below to make out anyone on its deck. But Mr. and Mrs. Riveter were down there, and Wolkin and Tulu, and Pentra, and tonight there would be a fish dinner and Mr. Turnbolt would light the deck lamps and everything would be safe and normal.

"That's a brand-new namepost," said Krelan slowly. "In front of an old house."

"What if it is?"

"Wouldn't you think Waxcast would take a new name?" said Krelan. "An alias? After all he'd done and gotten away with? I certainly would, were I Mr. Waxcast."

"You think that's his house?" Eliss found herself whispering, though Shellback had already knocked on the door and been admitted.

"He'd have the money to buy himself a mansion, wouldn't he? After robbing my lord. A mansion in an out-of-the-way place where he'd have a good view of anyone approaching him," said Krelan harshly, but she knew the tone in his voice was not for her.

"But what can we do?"

"I'm going to do my duty," said Krelan, watching the house. "You're going to go back down the hill to the *Bird*. That's all. If you don't see me by tomorrow morning, I'm not coming back. Eliss, you're beautiful and smart and you're the sort of girl I could never get, a little shrimp like me. But I loved you. Just know that. I really did love you."

He strode away from her, heading for the house. Eliss stood there with her mouth open, watching him go. *Time to walk away. Time to walk away, even if he loved me.*

"Are you insane?" she hissed, running after him. Krelan made no reply, but waved behind himself with one arm, making impatient shooing gestures. He did not climb the steps of the house but kept on walking past it, continuing up the hill to where the street crested at the top.

There was a high green hedge there at street level, masking the view into a terrace garden behind the house. The street continued around past it and down in a service alley on the other side. Beyond the top of the hill was nothing but blowing mist and a sheer plunge into a forested valley below.

Eliss assumed Krelan was making for the service alley, perhaps to find a rear entry to the house. She hurried to catch up with him. As they passed the hedge, however, they heard a door opening and a deferential voice say, "The person to see you, master."

"Thank you," said another voice from the terrace garden. Krelan halted abruptly.

"Hello there," said a voice Eliss recognized as Shellback's.

"Good to see you again! Paver, you may go."

"At once, master."

Krelan sank to his knees beside the hedge. With infinite care, in perfect silence, he began bending the twigs to one side and another, clearing a tiny space through which to peer at what was going on in the garden on the other side. Eliss sat down beside him, trying to catch his eye, but all Krelan's attention was fixed on what he could see beyond the hedge.

They heard the servant depart and what sounded like a set of terrace doors closing. Krelan leaned forward. His face became rigid, like a mask, his eyes staring.

"I'd been hoping you'd call on me soon," said the voice that wasn't Shellback's. "Is that my gold?"

"That's right," said Shellback, in the same amiable voice in which he'd thanked the dead bank officer. "Here you go. Open it and have a look."

They heard the scrape of the ironbound box being—slid across a table? Eliss saw Krelan start forward so violently she thought he'd fall through the hedge. She put out a hand to grab his shoulder.

"What in seven hells is this?"

"That's the gold I *haven't* got." All the smiles had gone out of Shellback's voice. "I lost four good men in Krolerett, and I got nothing out of the job but one gold chain, and you know why? Because you sold me useless intelligence. You said the place had no militia. Well, surprise! They had. So I'll thank you to fill that box with my refund. You can start with those rings you're wearing. I'll walk around behind you now, slow and easy. You call your man. Have him bring your cash box here. Fuck with me and I'll drive this into the back of your neck."

"Look, Tinplate—"

"Call me Shellback!"

"*Shellback.* Am I to understand you didn't get my deposit box?"

"Hell no. The guard chased after us and found where we'd dumped the loot. They got everything back. If you want your fucking deposit box you can go get it yourself, now. After you've paid me. And you *will* pay me. Call your man."

"Shellback, friend, you need to consider whether this is altogether wise. Haven't I made you a lot of money this summer? Are you really going to end a profitable relationship over one bungled job?"

"Money doesn't matter a damn once it's spent. Anyway I've paid through the nose for every one of your little files. And *anyway*, you've outlived your value."

"Gods below, why would you say that? I've only just started my career."

"Ha! Krolerett's on their guard now; we'll never get back in there. Silver Trout's building a wall around itself. Nobody's going to take Synpelene again for another generation. The good loot's all gone. You've run out of files."

"I beg to differ. Wouldn't you like a way into Prayna-of-the-Agatines?"

They heard Shellback catching his breath. "You said you wouldn't sell Prayna."

"That was then. I've cut my ties. It's yours to sack, if you can pay the price. And I'm expanding my influence! There are easier ways to get rich than plundering dirty little towns, Shellback. Think of all the mansions on these hills. What if you knew exactly where the doors and windows were on each one, how many servants were in the house, where the household treasure's kept, when the master comes and goes?

"All my neighbors got stinking rich on emeralds. I've invested in a few mines and expect to get stinking rich myself, soon. I'll be moving in their society. Invited to their dinner parties. Gathering all those little details you'd need. Hell of a lot easier to take a house than a city, Shellback, especially when it's one of *these* houses. And why stop with loot? I can tell you where their nurseries are. There's money to be made in taking kiddies for ransom, you know. And why stop with Karkateen? What's to keep you out of Mount Flame, or Salesh?"

There was a silence, and then a soft whistle of awe from Shellback. "I always thought the rich hung together. You don't give a damn about your own, do you?"

"What kind of businessman would I be if I did?"

"Fair enough. I've still got a problem, Encilian."

The last loose end knotted itself, with a yank that shook Eliss. *Of course.* The point of leaving the serpent armlet on the body had been so people would identify the dead man as Encilian Diamondcut. *Of course.* The point of cutting off the head had been so people wouldn't realize the dead man was really Stryon Waxcast, a poor servant who looked enough like Encilian to be taken for his brother. . . . She cast a cautious glance at Krelan, but his face was hidden by leaves at his improvised peephole.

"Not Encilian! Mr. Whitegold, if you please."

"Heh. All right, *Mr. Whitegold*. This impresses me, but my men will want something more. What about a cash payment? Just the refund for the Krolerett file. That's what any good businessman would do."

"You're right. It is. Well, let me see . . . cash is in short supply just now. I think I mentioned I've been investing, didn't I? But I'll tell you what I can do for you. I've got a few buckets of raw emeralds in my study. Samples from my mines. Lot of big lovely green stuff, probably worth twice what you paid for Krolerett if you get the best stones cut. What do you say I fill this box with emeralds?"

"I'd call that fair dealing." Shellback sounded enthusiastic.

"Why don't you just step to one side here, then—"

There was a muffled crash. "You *fucker*—"

Krelan was gone suddenly, diving through the hedge. Eliss scrambled to the place opened by his passage. There stood Encilian Diamondcut, gripping the wrists of Shellback. They had been struggling together, but not now; Encilian was grinning as he held Shellback up for Krelan, who had knifed Shellback several times and sprung away, watching cold-faced as Shellback died. Shellback groaned and sagged. Encilian opened his hands and let him fall. Shellback toppled to the garden flagstones and lay there with his eyes rolled back in his head.

Wheezing, Encilian pulled up a wrought-iron chair and sat down. He spat on Shellback's body. He was fatter, sleeker than he had been when his portrait was painted. Krelan remained perfectly still.

"Must find myself a better class of client," said Encilian. He looked up. "Gods below, it's little Krelan. I like the hat! Suits you. You *are* a survivor. I always suspected your brother was wrong about you. How did you manage to get past his hirelings?"

"*You* knew about them?" Krelan blurted.

Encilian, having caught his breath at last, smiled. "'You knew about them, *my lord?*' I'll grant you the one slip, after your usefulness just now, but don't push it. Yes, I know all your brother's plans. Just as he knows all mine. He devoutly hoped you'd get yourself killed on the river. Certainly never dreamed you'd get as far as you have. And neither of us imagined you'd actually find *me!* You're not only lucky, you're smart. I like that."

"My lord is too kind," said Krelan stiffly.

"That's better. I'm a bit relieved, to be honest. Having you killed seemed such a waste. Your brother's a little too preoccupied with his own business to be a really effective shadow. Or all that loyal a retainer . . ." Encilian rubbed his index finger across his chin. "To hell with him. I'll send word to your brother you died. You're my man, Krelan. You'll work for me here. I need someone I can trust to run Enterprise Encilian."

"What exactly would that be, my lord?"

"Striking out on my own," said Encilian, flashing a smile. "Just like old Lord Harrik, eh? Founding my own Family. Why be a second-rate Diamondcut when I could be the first of the White-golds? I suppose you found out about Stryon."

Krelan nodded. His face was still impassive, but Eliss saw the building fury in his eyes. "He was one of the Family, wasn't he?"

Encilian made a dismissive gesture. "One of Father's bastards. Your brother found him for me, as a matter of fact. Perfect match, wasn't he? *Nobody guessed!*" He edged forward to the front of his chair, face alight. "What was it like when the body was brought home? Did they weep for me? Did they hire a Cursing Priest? Your brother writes the most unimaginative letters. You must have been there. What was the funeral like? Tell me!"

"Appropriate for a Diamondcut, my lord. Was my lord aware he'd fathered a bastard of his own?"

"What? I never."

"In Krolerett, my lord. A tavern girl."

"Oh, *that.* Gods, what do you take me for? She was some silly cow

Stryon was infatuated with. I let him pose as me to court her. Seemed a good idea to muddy the trail and I wanted to see whether his clothes fit me. So the dirty deed had consequences? I did him a favor, then. She can't come whining after him where *he's* gone!" Encilian laughed and smacked the garden table. "All that and he gets my niche in the family vault too. Which is a nice one. No, he really can't complain."

"He was an innocent man and a Diamondcut, and you murdered him."

"What? He was nothing!"

"He wasn't a broker for thieves. He never betrayed his own people to demons," said Krelan, gasping as though it took more air than was in his body to get the accusations out. "He never dishonored his family. I saw the bodies lying in the streets at Synpelene. You're a disgrace, Encilian." His hand was trembling as he gripped his knife. Encilian's smile faded.

"You little piece of shit. You *disapprove?* You? And here I thought you were the brains of your family. Well, it's a shame, Krelan, but I can get along without you. *Kill yourself.*"

Krelan's arm swung up, as though by reflex, and halted. Eliss caught her breath.

"No," said Krelan. "Your father gave me a job. He wanted your head brought home."

Encilian gaped at him a moment. He leaned back, chuckling as if in disbelief. "You took a vow, remem—" and then without warning kicked the garden table straight at Krelan. The table caught Krelan full in the chest and carried him backward, down a flight of three little steps to the lower terrace, where he lay sprawling. Encilian, with remarkable speed for a man of his bulk, grabbed up the iron-bound box and hurled it straight at Krelan's head. Eliss saw Krelan jerk as the box hit him. Encilian drew a knife from inside his robe and started down the steps, muttering "Fucking disloyal little—"

Eliss wanted, more than anything, to slink away down the hill, and knew it was what she ought to do, and that it was what Krelan wanted her to do. But as in a dream she found herself diving through the hedge onto Encilian's back, knocking him down the stairs too. She hoped he'd fall on his knife, but he didn't. She pounded his head into the flagstones, once and then again, but he got hold of her arms and wrenched her off to the side, and a second later he had rolled over on her and was holding her down, glaring at her. Blinking, catching his breath, he began to grin.

"Hello," he said. "Who the hell are you, Gorgeous?"

He'll kill me. He'll rape me and kill me and Krelan and I will be thrown in a ditch together and I did it for love, I stupidly, stupidly did it for love. Rage gave her strength to heave upward with her whole body. She nearly threw him off. He hit his elbow on the flagstones falling back down, and grunted in pain. Furious, he struck her across the face and got his hand on her throat. Pushing against her windpipe, he raised himself to his knees. The silver chain and crystal charm she wore cut into the skin of her neck. He picked up his knife.

"How did a shriveled little maggot like Krelan get a beauty like you?" said Encilian, panting. "You want to die with him? You'll die with him, bitch. But I get you first."

Through her pain and desperation, Eliss heard Uncle Steelplate roaring at Falena, saw Falena knocked to the floor, and all she could do was huddle under the bed with Alder and pray—

I will NOT be that frightened little girl—

Eliss sat up and punched Encilian in the crotch, as hard as she could. He dropped his knife and doubled up. She dragged herself backward and away from him, struggling to her feet. She hesitated a moment too long before deciding to reach for his knife. He snatched her wrist and jerked her down to her knees beside him. She grabbed the knife with her other hand. He grabbed it too. There was a long moment of silence punctuated only by Encilian's harsh breathing as they strained together. Sweat was running down his face. His teeth were bared. Eliss felt her wrist bending, knew the bones were going to snap soon. *Holy gods, please—*

The wind was blowing loudly. The soft moan coming over the hilltop had taken on an odd bass note.

Eliss felt the flagstones under her knees beginning to vibrate. Hazily she wondered whether an earthquake had chosen that moment to happen. Suddenly the light was gone, as though the day had jumped hours forward into twilight. She looked up involuntarily, and Encilian looked too, and they saw the black cloud mass descending on the house. There came a pattering sound like rain. Eliss thought it *was* rain, until she saw the green bits leaping into the air and realized the moss from between the flagstones was shooting upward in little jets of mud and water. They spattered against Encilian's face, into his eyes, into his nose and mouth. He let go of her wrists and clawed at his face. Eliss crawled away on her knees and elbows. She averted her face from the flying muck, but it whirled around her like flies, avoiding contact.

There was a deep shattering sound. The house was rattling. Eliss could hear Encilian's servants screaming and running out the front door. Flagstones flipped aside as water fountained from the earth, scattering pieces of broken terra-cotta that bounced and clattered away. The sewer pipes under the house had broken, under the strain of a massive surge of dirty water fighting its way skyward from the depths of the lake. The water seemed to be aiming itself at Encilian, striking him from every direction, but instead of splashing off him it wrapped itself around him and clung, as though it became viscous on contact. It turned him round and round, like a floating ball in a fountain. His mouth was open and Eliss thought she could hear him screaming, under the thunder of the broken pipes and the growling wind.

And what was that new noise? A sizzling, a hissing: the very mold and moss was tearing itself from the limestone blocks of the house and flying through the air like leaves, dancing in the slipstream around the spinning cocoon of filthy green water until they too were pulled into it. Encilian was only briefly visible now in the rotating column. Eliss, staring, followed it up with her eyes and saw the moving shape in the boiling black cloud, the form like a dragon or some other sinuous green thing, and yet—no—here was a glimpse of massive shoulder, an indistinct profile, gigantic and dark and blurred. A lashing beard the color of waterweed, that broke the roof-tiles on the house. An immense thick hand reaching down, a glimpse of a vast raging countenance . . .

Eliss averted her eyes. She looked straight into Krelan's blood-covered face. He had been pulling himself across the mud toward her. She reached out to him and they gripped each other, shutting their eyes tight, as the noise grew deafening and, yes, Encilian still screamed. Even under the elemental tumult they could hear him screaming.

AT SOME POINT IT ALL STOPPED. The world had narrowed to the smell of river mud, the rank fragrance of low tide. It was all around, overpowering. Gradually hearing came back: the sound of dirty water dripping from every leaf in the hedge, streaming and hissing down the walls. Cautiously Eliss opened her eyes, just in time to see Encilian's body come hurtling down out of the clouds and smack into the mud by Shellback's corpse a few feet away, boneless as a dead mackerel.

Krelan was trying to get to his feet. She helped him stand. The deluge had washed some of the blood from his face but it still trick-led from a gash on his scalp. Eliss pressed two fingers to it, to try to stop the bleeding. Krelan winced absently, staring at Encilian's body. She didn't want to look, but turned and looked anyway.

Encilian's clothes had been sucked away by the storm water. Fat and pale, blotched with green and black mold, he looked as though he'd lain in the bottom of the river for months.

SHE HELPED KRELAN to the wrought-iron chair. He sat, press-ing his sleeve to the gash but unable to take his eyes off Encilian, as she looked for his hat. *What do you do,* she thought numbly, *what do you do when the gods actually answer your prayers? If it was the gods. I don't know what it was, do I?* Finding Krelan's hat, she shook out the mud and water and brought it back. Krelan cut a few inches off his sleeve and wadded it up for a compress, and with the hat jammed on his head to hold it in place the bleeding finally stopped.

"We need to go," said Eliss, startled at how loud her voice sounded. "Those servants will be coming back."

Krelan got to his feet unsteadily. He staggered over to Shellback's body and, after a moment's searching, found a long knife concealed under his clothing.

"Where's that box?" Krelan said, turning away from the dead man. "Encilian still owes his head."

THEY FILLED UP THE BOX with salt when they got back to the *Bird of the River,* and hid it away in the cargo deck under the bows. So many of the crew had gone ashore that no one saw them hiding it. Then it was time to go present themselves to Mr. Riveter, who clutched his own head when he saw the gash on Krelan's scalp.

"What did I tell you! Didn't I tell you to stay on board? Didn't I *tell* you?"

"I didn't do *anything,*" Wolkin protested from where he was seated on one of the forward capstans, fishing. Then he realized the tirade was not directed at him, and ran close with ears wide to listen.

"I deeply apologize, Mr. Riveter," said Krelan. "This time I can assure you it will never happen again. I swear by all the gods."

"Look at that! Look at that, you're going to need stitches! What'll your lord father say, assuming you ever get back to him alive?" Mr. Riveter swept his gaze around the deck and saw only Wolkin. "Wolkin! Fetch Daddy his medicine kit."

"Aye, sir!" Wolkin took off like a shot.

So Krelan had to sit on a barrel and endure having his gash sewn shut by Mr. Riveter, being scolded all the while. Eliss wandered across the deck and stood looking down the companionway. The smell of river mud was overpowering. The walls were damp. Water trickled from under the great cabin's door. Eliss contemplated knocking. She decided against it.

BECAUSE THE WINDMILL TOWER WAS VACANT that night, with all the musicians ashore, they slept together there, quite chastely. Krelan got a bunk to himself and Eliss slept on a thick pile of borrowed blankets on the floor. But for long hours before sleep would come they lay side by side in the bunk, staring into the darkness and listening to the occasional gentle thump as the wind vanes caught an errant gust and turned.

"At least it's over now," said Eliss, watching the shadowy outline of Krelan's profile. He sighed and nodded.

"It's done. But so am I. I broke my vow."

"But *you* didn't kill him. That was the—"

"Don't," said Krelan, shivering. "Don't let's talk about that. One of my tutors used to say, 'Pray to the holy gods, but never loud enough for them to actually hear you.'"

"You had tutors?"

"Of course I had. Any shadow of the Family must be well-educated. Polished. Schooled in subtlety. I was poured into a certain mold to become a certain man. And now . . . it's all gone for nothing. My entire life. Everything I was raised for, centuries of tradition, everything I'd planned to be."

"Life is like that sometimes," said Eliss. "One day everything is going along the way it always has, and you think it will never change, and then—you lose everything you ever knew. I never thought my mother would die."

Krelan was silent a moment. "That's true," he said. "Childish of me, to imagine I'm the only one in the world with my sorrows. That's something, anyway; your mother's death is avenged."

"It doesn't bring her back, though."

"I know. But I wish I'd had the honor of killing Encilian, for your mother's sake. Ye gods, what blasphemy I talk! If he hadn't hit me with that table I'd have driven my knife into his heart for bringing dishonor on the Family. And then . . . a *good* Family retainer would use the blade on himself next. I would have been dead anyway, as soon as I got home. What a brood of monsters we must seem like, to you."

"They do," said Eliss. "You don't. I finally saw one of the great big Diamondcuts and he was nothing special. I knew men like that my whole life growing up. Nothing like a god! Just a bully with a knife. *You* knew that was all he was too. You know it's all lies and made-up glory, really. Why should you go back and die for those people?"

"But what else is there to do with my life?"

"You could stay on the *Bird*," said Eliss quietly. Krelan groped in the darkness and found her hand.

"You know, I think I'd like that," he said.

ELISS SHIFTED THE BOX from one hip to the other, trying not to think about what was inside. It was an ordinary-looking crate, perhaps twice the size of the ironbound box she and Krelan had brought back down the hill with them.

"Is that too heavy for you, *Mama?*" asked Wolkin with a broad wink. "You want me to carry it, Mama?"

"No, dear, but thank you all the same," she told him, in Pentra's most silver-plated accents.

"I can carry it anytime, you know, Mama." Wolkin did his best to clip his words the same way. Another person moved into the Runners' parcel depot, and everyone else moved a step farther along in the queue. "Oh, good! It's almost us next."

Eliss merely nodded. One of the objects inside the crate was a letter she had written, dictated by Krelan. She ran over its text in her mind, hoping it was convincing.

Dear my lord,

I am fulfilling a vow sending you this. I am a poor man and it is better you do not know my name but I swear I was not mixed up in this. Me and a friend were camping on the creek trying to find some emeralds and this boy came walking along the trail with a box in his arms and when he tripped and fell we saw somebody had knifed him. So we took him into our camp and bandaged up his wounds but he been in a bad fight and we could tell he was not going to live long. He could tell it too. He made us swear by all the gods to help him or a curse would get us. We were supposed to take all his things he carried and the box too with the thing that is in it and post them to you with a letter explaining what happened. After he died I mean.

He said to tell you he did his duty and you will know it by what is in the box. There is gold too but we did not touch any of it for fear of the curse and we also put in his things, we did not keep them after he died, his knives and that picture. That should show you we did what we were supposed to. We do not want any trouble from anybody and would not ever be disrespectful my lord.

And he said to tell you to go to Krolerett where there is this girl working at a place called Golden Hospitality House and she is going to have a baby and it will be your grandson or granddaughter which you will want to know.

And he said also that he saluted you with his dying breath and done his duty. And a little while after that he died. We carried his body into town and had it burnt proper. Now we are going to post this and find someone to take it to the Runners for us.

Post Script, all this happened at Karkateen.

"Look! It's our turn!" cried Wolkin, and added, "Mama."

"So it is," said Eliss. They went inside and set the box on the counter. The clerk inspected the box and paused, sniffing the air suspiciously.

"Would there be . . . something dead in this box?"

Eliss shrugged and pointed to the destination label. The clerk read it.

"Oh, *Mount Flame*. Say no more. You'll want this expedited, I expect."

"Yes, please."

"Just a moment." The clerk set the package on the scales. "Do you want a reply?"

"No, thank you. Just delivery."

"Five gold crowns, then. For the hazard."

Below the counter level, Wolkin clutched at his heart and rolled his eyes. Eliss paid without comment.

"Mama, I have to talk to you!"

"In a minute, Praxas, dear."

Wolkin clutched her hand as they walked out together, and the minute they were clear of the door he yelled, *"Five gold crowns!* Do you know what you could buy with five whole crowns? *Gold* ones?"

"A life without trouble," said Eliss serenely, swinging his hand as they walked back toward the *Bird of the River*.

"Well, do we still have enough for my bribe?"

"Of course."

They stopped at a sweets stall where Wolkin selected a bag of rock-candy emeralds, and after some grudging deliberation added a little box of flower creams for Tulu.

"Except I don't see why she has to be bribed too," he said. *"I'm* the one keeping a deadly secret which I'll never tell even if I'm tortured. What was in the box, anyway?"

"Just some things."

"Maybe instead of a bribe it could just be a present for Tulu."

"Why not?"

"That would be better. Are you going to marry Krelan?" Wolkin inquired, somewhat indistinctly around a lump of candy.

Eliss looked down at him in surprise. "Maybe. Someday. Probably. Why?"

"Because you shouldn't rush into anything. That's what Daddy says. And he turned out not to be an assassin after all, and it was pretty dumb to trip in the street and bust his head open like that, and he's so weasely-looking. You could get someone a lot more handsome." Wolkin threw her a slightly anxious glance.

"Why would I want to marry an assassin?"

"Well, it would . . . it would just have been better. And if his daddy has disowned him now and he won't even be rich and all . . . don't you want to marry someone rich?"

"I don't know. At least a spitboy can cook."

"He *can* cook," Wolkin admitted. They came level with the *Bird of the River*'s dock and spotted Krelan on the aft deck, dumping out a bucket of cooking grease. He looked up and gave them a wry smile. Eliss met his eyes and nodded, just once. Wolkin wrinkled his nose. "But, see? He's just . . . with his head all bandaged and all . . . and . . ."

Across the street the same fiddler from a week ago struck up *The Ballad of Falena*, as his vocalist passed the hat. Wolkin turned and flung out his arm to point at them. "Because there! You're Beautiful Falena's daughter, and you could marry anybody in the world, because you're even *more* beautiful, so you should marry a prince or something."

"Princes come in all sizes," said Eliss. "Even spitboy size."

And it's all right to be Beautiful Falena's daughter, she thought, *as long as I don't make her mistakes. And only Alder and I will even remember what they were, and when we forget she'll still be a beautiful song.*

Mr. Riveter was running to and fro on deck shouting orders, as the crew prepared to warp the *Bird of the River* out of the docking area. His eye ranged across the wharf and he spotted Wolkin.

"What are you doing ashore?" he said. "You're supposed to be grounded!"

"I'm sorry, sir," said Eliss, taking Wolkin's hand and starting down the gangplank. "I asked him to go ashore as my escort."

"And you have to go with a lady when she asks you for help. You said," said Wolkin smugly, and took off like a shot the moment his feet touched the deck. "Tulu! I found some real emeralds! Want to see?"

Eliss walked over to Krelan, who was scraping the last of the grease into the slush barrel, and kissed his cheek. "Isn't this romantic?" he said.

"I'm swooooooning," she replied. They heard a heavy tread coming up the companionway, and turned. Captain Glass stepped on deck. He fixed them in his dull gaze a moment. Eliss thought she saw something flash in his eyes, brief as a fish leaping.

"Cast off, Mr. Riveter! Time to get aloft, Vigilance," he said.

"Yes, Captain, sir." Eliss turned and scrambled into the rigging. As she climbed she saw the musicians assembling on the aft deck, handing around a pipe of pinkweed amongst themselves with all the solemnity of priests. Salpin, however, grinned and held it out to her, with an inquiring lift of his eyebrow. Laughing, she shook her head and kept climbing.

Eliss found her high place and settled in there, watching as the *Bird of the River* backed out and made her gigantic turn for the journey downriver. Slowly the world rotated around the *Bird*'s mast. A gust of wind filled the sail, and they were away.

EpiLogue
Four Years Later, at Moonport

THEY WALKED ASHORE WITH PENTRA. Krelan carried one big market basket and Eliss carried the other.

"I wonder if I can get nuts at a good price," mused Krelan. "It would be nice to dress up the porridge a little, don't you think?"

"You see, that's just one of the reasons people like it better when you cook instead of Mr. Pitspike," said Eliss. "You have ideas."

"How very kind," drawled Krelan, peering at his shopping list. He had let his beard grow, and it had the same sickly penciled-in look as his mustache, but the combination made him look a little less ridiculous than with the mustache alone. He glanced up from the list and added, "There's your brother. I'll just go price melons, shall I?"

"Oh, you know he doesn't hate you anymore."

"Of course. Still . . ." Krelan took both baskets and sidled off to a market stall.

"Caiwyr! Denuseth!" cried Pentra, running forward. Three Yendri walked toward them along the riverbank. Two wore white robes. Pentra embraced them each in turn, and then drew a little apart with her lover and son. They chatted together happily.

Eliss followed more slowly, gazing at Alder in amazement. "You've grown again," she said.

"You always say that," he replied. They embraced a little awkwardly, for he had to lean down to put his arms around her.

"It's always true. How are you?"

"Very well." Alder looked warily across the market at Krelan. "Have you married him yet?"

"No! We both agreed to wait until we're twenty. He says he wants to be sure nobody's going to show up to kill him first."

Alder sighed and shook his head. "And are you well?"

"Yes. And Salpin's girlfriend wanted you to know the ointment cured the baby's rash. Are you coming aboard for the party tonight?"

"Of course!"

"Good! She can thank you herself." Eliss stepped back and looked Alder up and down. "Wolkin will be jealous. He's as tall as I am now, and thought he was all grown-up. Wait until he sees you."

For the first time Alder grinned. "I can go show him my disciple moves."

"What, meditation? He could use some tranquility. The boys have started noticing Tulu. He's becoming overprotective," said Eliss, somewhat pointedly. Alder looked down, sheepish. He had been holding a small package under his arm, and now he held it out to her.

"I got you something."

"Oh! Thank you."

"The Lady says—you know, she worries about your people. Our people. She says it would be awful if you all killed one another off. She's having us collect a library of your books, to copy and study, so we understand you better. I mean, of course *I* understand you, but the others—"

"I know." Eliss fumbled with the package's string. "Go on."

"Anyway, Caiwyr and I, that's our mission. Going to cities and buying books for her library. And I found this. And I remembered you always talking about it, and I asked the Lady and she said you could have it, because you needed to know how it ended."

Eliss unwrapped the cloth slowly and saw the title, faded but still legible, on the book's spine: *The Silvergilts of Delairia*.

"Oh." Tears stung her eyes.

"Is that it? Is it the right one?"

"Yes." She threw her arms around him and hugged him hard. "Thank you! After all these years—"

"I found something else too," Alder said, a little hesitantly. "After all these years."

"What?" Eliss drew back. She touched the book's cover gently, as though it might vanish.

"My father." He watched her face to see her reaction, and when she smiled and took his hand he looked relieved. "His name is Alder too. He's a good man. He has an orchard and he makes brandy. He remembers you and he says he's sorry about Mama. He never knew about me. But he didn't mind me finding him, Eliss! It was the most wonderful day of my life!"

"Does he look like you?"

Alder nodded, his eyes alight with happiness. "I wish Mama could see."

"Maybe she sees. I hope so." Eliss rewrapped *The Silvergilts of Delairia* and tucked it under her arm. "Come on now and say hello to Krelan. And be nice."

Alder rolled his eyes and looked stubborn, and the expression was so like little Alder's on his long adolescent face that Eliss laughed. They walked away together, into the throng of people buying and selling, as the *Bird of the River* sat quiet at her mooring and the long summer day drew to a close.